BUILD
UNIVERSES

Matt Carbutt

Dreamland

© 2021 **Europe Books** | London
www.europebooks.co.uk – info@europebooks.co.uk

ISBN 979-12-201-0963-5
First edition: June 2021

Distribution for the United Kingdom: **Vine House Distribution ltd**

Printed for Italy by Rotomail Italia
Finito di stampare nel mese di giugno 2021
presso Rotomail Italia S.p.A. - Vignate (MI)

Dreamland

I dedicate this novel to my beautiful wife and daughter for their understanding and encouragement.

PROLOGUE

UMHLANGA ROCKS HOTEL, UMHLANGA ROCKS, DURBAN, SOUTH AFRICA, THREE YEARS AGO

The tawny long-legged redhead strolled casually into the up-market hotel bar; seemingly oblivious to the male and female heads that turned to look at her as she strutted past, the scent of her perfume following her, a fresh, sensual, and alluring tease. Seeing an empty barstool on one side of the bar she headed for the lonely barstool and sat down, settling her tight derrière, clad in a short tight black mini skirt, onto the leather barstool and crossing her long, tanned legs one over the other, her short mini skirt riding up a little higher on her enviously well-shaped thighs.

The bartender was immediately there to attend to her, "Good evening, ma'am what can I get you to drink?" he asked her professionally while staring helplessly into her large green eyes. "A white wine spritzer, please," she replied in a bright sexy voice, her green eyes twinkling at him while her full glossy lips broke out into a large smile showing her perfect white teeth. "Certainly, ma'am," the bartender replied returning the smile and turned away to attend to her request.

'Hmm, this is a nice establishment,' she thought casually to herself taking a minute to look around, taking in a couple of possible well-dressed male targets who were trying hard not to pay her too much attention. 'Who says a girl can't make some money on the side?' she carried on thinking to herself as she held the gaze of a handsome good-looking middle-aged man dressed in a well-cut business suit on the other side of the bar. 'I can't sit around in my stuffy little flat all day just waiting for the phone to ring,' she reasoned to herself. 'I need some fun, and if I can make some money on the side at the same time so much the better!'

The hotel was a Five Star luxury hotel, popular with business travellers and the well-to-do. With an international conference in the city, the hotel was a beehive of activity. "Here we go, ma'am," the bartender said to her pleasantly returning with her white wine spritzer. First setting down a small white round paper napkin on the shiny walnut bar counter in front of her, he placed the drink precisely in the centre of the white paper napkin and then asked her politely, "Can I charge it to your room, ma'am?" "Thank you, but no, I'll pay cash," the beautiful redhead replied, and was about to reach into her small purse for some money when a deep male voice beside her spoke out. "Put it on my tab and get me a refill, please, my good man." Turning to her right she saw it was the man who had held her gaze a little too long. "Why thank you...?" she said to him in her bright sexy voice, showing him one of her winning dazzling smiles while batting her large deep green eyes at him. "Gary, Gary Lange," the man replied with a large smile of his own on his open face. "And your name is...? he asked his eyes looking around as if searching for a name.

"Samantha," she replied, giggling at his expression.

After talking and drinking for a while Samantha asked him, "Do want to fuck me, Gary?" Without blushing at the forwardness of her proposition, he nodded his head and asked her, "How much?" Casually taking a sip of her latest wine spritzer she replied, "A grand for a fuck and five for me to stay the night." Pretending to think about it for a couple of seconds he replied, "Okay, a fuck it is," and using smartphone technology he transferred one thousand Rand into Samantha's bank account while standing at the bar with her.

A couple of minutes later, grinning like a naughty schoolboy he finished the electronic transaction, he looked up and said, "Done, well then what are we waiting for?" and standing up, first paid the drinks bill, and together they started walking towards the door hand in hand. Walking out of the bar into the main double volume atrium of the hotel, rather than heading towards the guest lifts Gary led her towards the main doors of the hotel. "I thought you were a guest in the hotel," Samantha asked him a little concerned. This wasn't going according to her plan. "Naw," Gary replied now with a nasty smile on his handsome face, "undercover. You're under arrest for prostitution." "Oh, fuck!" Samantha cried out in alarm, realizing immediately that she was in a pile of trouble, not only with the law but with Sable, her boss, as well! Heading outside, the heavy tropical humid air of the Natal coast enveloped them like a warm wet blanket as the officer led her towards an unmarked police car parked around the corner from the hotel.

"First catch of the night," he cheerfully told the plainclothes detective sitting in the unmarked police car as they approached. Getting out of the car the plain-clothed detective asked with a smile on his face, "Well, well, what do we have here?" as he handed a set of handcuffs to his partner. Roughly Gary, the handsome undercover policeman, secured her slender arms behind her back shackling her hands together with the stainless-steel handcuffs, and opened the rear door of the car for her. Once Samantha was inside and the door shut, he turned to his partner and said, "Okay, she's all yours, I'm off to the next hotel on the list, see you later."

Getting back into the driver's seat, the plain-clothed detective turned around in his seat saying, "Prostitution hey! The judge doesn't like you ladies of the night, you're going to sit in jail," and he laughed out loud at the thought., and then told her, "But if you help me out I'll help you out, and I'm not looking to fuck you!" he told her harshly. "I want money from you, lots of it." "But, but... I don't have any money," Samantha cried out frightened at the prospect of what was happening. 'Fuck it,' she thought silently to herself as she started to cry, 'it wasn't supposed to turn out this way, I was just looking for some fun and extra money.'

"Your tears won't change a thing," the detective told her sharply. Rubbing it in some more, he told her, running his eyes over the contour of her body illuminated by the outside street lighting, "Well, you're definitely going to sit in jail but from the look of your body you won't have a bad time in prison, as long as you're into eating pussy!" Laughing loudly at the thought, he turned around and starting the unmarked police car, put it into gear, and drove out onto the road heading in the general direction of the police station. "Fuck it, Sable's going to fucking kill me for this," Samantha cried out silently to herself, her mind furiously working overtime looking for a way out.

"Officer, I've got a deal for you," she then said to him nervously a couple of traffic lights later. "Go ahead, I'm listening," he replied rather impatiently looking at her in the rear-view mirror. "There's a deal going down later in the week, down on the Wild Coast," she started to say. "I'm not interested in the fucking Wild Coast and deals bitch! I either want money or your tight ass is going to jail! There are a thousand other prostitutes just like you! Don't give me your fucking bullshit bitch!" he shouted at her, looking at her through the rear-view mirror. "It's worth around a 100 million Rand!" she shouted back at him. Stamping on the vehicle's brakes, he brought the unmarked police car to a skidding halt. Turning right round in his seat looking directly at her he growled, "What the fuck did you just say?" "I… I'm supposed to be the honeypot and distract this man, the target, while someone else breaks into the room and steals the briefcase. I overheard them saying it will contain around a 100 million Rand in diamonds." "Motherfucker," whistled the detective. "Down on the Wild Coast you say?" he asked questioning her. She nodded her head sniffing and replied, "Yes, at the Wild Coast Sun, he's a high roller who will be staying at the resort for the night. While I distract him someone else is going to break in and steal the briefcase," she explained.

"Who's your accomplice?" he then asked her excitedly, his mind trying to grasp the concept of a 100 million Rand. She shook her head, and sniffing replied, "I don't know, I will only meet him on the night a couple of hours before it goes down, but it shouldn't be too hard for you to apprehend him once he's broken into the room." "Turn around," he instructed her hoarsely and removing a key from his top shirt pocket he unlocked the handcuffs, releasing her slender arms from behind her back. "And now?" Samantha asked perplexed as well as frightened, rubbing her wrists where the stainless-steel handcuffs had gouged into her soft smooth skin. "If we're going to be business partners you don't need to be locked up," he told her excitedly. "What do I call you?" she then asked him nervously as well as relieved. "You can call me Brant," he told her. "What are your people going to say to you when the diamonds are taken from your target?" Brant asked her curiously. "I know nothing," she replied, "I was just doing my part of the job and fucking the target."

PART 1

CHAPTER 1

THE ROYALE GRACE HOTEL, SEAPOINT, CAPE TOWN, 00H30, SUNDAY

In the soft low lighting of the master suite, the two bodies of the entwined couple were perfectly illuminated on top of the king-size bed. The female was on her hands and knees, her blond head buried deep in the soft luxuriously silken white pillows, her loud moans muffled by the soft feathers while her long tapered manicured fingers gripped the silken white bedsheets in ecstasy. At the same time, she pushed her perfectly sculptured bottom backwards meeting the measured thrusts of her male partner with loud slapping sounds of flesh on flesh. "Ahhhhhh, Ahhhhhh, Ahhhhhh, I'm coming, don't stop, don't stop, please don't stop," she moaned out loudly as she started to lose control as her lover pushed her over the edge of orgasm.

Through the open balcony doors of the 10th-floor apartment, a welcoming Atlantic sea breeze rustled the silken white drapes against the double volume windows. Standing in the shadows by the open balcony doors, the killer watched the couple for another couple of minutes becoming aroused as he stood there. "Oh yes, baby, oh yes, ooohhhh, yes!" she groaned out louder into the silky white pillows as her partner repositioned his pulsing member slick with her juices at the entrance to her most secret of passageways, teasing her. Hearing the blonde moan out, still louder in building ecstasy as slowly the pressure built, the killer could stand it no more.

Striding quickly across the room, the soft deep pile carpet deadening his footsteps, the killer silently pulled a katana from a sheath hidden on his back and in one violent movement jumped up onto the bed behind the man, who was oblivious to his impending doom. Stepping behind him, the assassin drew the exquisitely razor-sharp blade across the man's throat, cutting through his flesh like a hot knife cutting through butter. The razor honed blade cut effortlessly through the sinew, muscle, and bone of the man's neck. "Uurgghh!" he gurgled in surprise as he died where he knelt on the bed, his engorged member still buried deep in his lover's tight back passageway. "What the fuck!" the blonde shouted out in surprise, her pleasure abruptly cut short as she felt a warm wetness spray over her naked skin, dyeing the silky white bedsheets around her a crimson red.

Moving forward, she detached herself from her lover's rapidly deflating penis. Her lover slumped over dead on the bed, his head hanging at an almost comical angle, partly detached from his torso, his red life-giving blood spurting out of his severed neck, painting the balance of the white silk sheets a wet crimson red. Turning around and looking up she spat out, "You didn't have to kill him, I told you I would keep him occupied for you." "You know I'm impatient and extremely jealous," the killer replied with an evil looking smile on his oriental face, wiping his blade on the once-white silk duvet, leaving a long straight trail of scarlet blood that was slowly taken over by the river of blood draining from the dead man's torso.

Grinning, the blonde stood up off the bed, covered in her currently deceased lover's glistening red blood. She slowly rubbed her ruby-red stiff nipples with the long, tapered fingers of her left hand while at the same time running the sculptured fingers of her right hand through her trim blonde bush at the junction of her thighs and down into the sticky wetness of her womanhood and up again to her perfect lips. Tasting herself, she said, "Mmmmh, and you're also horny, from the look of it," as she noticed the large bulge in his trousers.

SOUTHERN SUBURBS, SAP BATCHELOR'S QUARTERS, 03H45, SUNDAY

He was trapped, the room was dark, and he was unarmed. He knew that the killer was in the building, he could feel him, an icy like coldness that crept up his spine, prickling at his senses making the hairs on his arms and the back of his neck stand up. In the background, through the inky blackness, he could hear his sister's voice calling him, "Help me Arnie, help me, help me, oh god, no, he's going to kill me Heeelp! Help me, agghhhhhhh!" that faded to a whimper and then silence. Stumbling around in the pitch-black darkness of the room he eventually felt the familiar cool metallic feel of a door handle and, pulling the door open, he frantically rushed through it. The room next door was bathed in a bright white light in comparison, and it took his eyes a couple of seconds to adjust to the brightness. Then he saw her, Samantha, his younger sister, lying naked and dead on the bed in a pool of blood, her head almost neatly detached from her torso. "Noooo!" he shouted out in heart-wrenching anguish, feeling the pain of having a loved one suddenly and violently taken away from you.

Then, through the mists of his torment, he could hear a phone ringing. 'The killer's got a phone call,' he thought savagely to himself. It kept on ringing. "Answer it goddamnit, answer it!" he shouted out in his sleep. "Let's find out who you are!" It kept on ringing, an irritating old-fashioned ringtone cutting through the darkness of his sleep. Struggling through the blackness of the dream back to reality, realising that it was his telephone, he woke up and fumbled around looking for his cellphone that kept on with its insistent ringing. "Detective Joint," he croaked out, finally finding, and answering the phone, the familiar headache from drinking too much Three Ships whisky taking the place of the regular nightmare.

"Detective, it's Brant here, there's been a double murder in Seapoint, the captain wants you here. I've sent a van to pick you up, it'll be there in about half an hour," and ended the telephone call. Detective Brant was his latest partner and a real pain in the ass. "Fuck it," Detective Joint muttered to himself switching on his bedside light, immediately squinting from the bright light, as he looked around his dismal one-bedroomed apartment that he occupied in the unmarried quarters of the South African Police residence in Wynberg.

Throwing his legs over the side of the bed, he sat up and immediately felt sick, a harsh concoction of neat whisky and bile rising in the back of his throat. Just making it to his almost unhygienic toilet he threw up, depositing his cheap takeaway supper and half a bottle of whisky into the toilet bowl. After waking up most of the unmarried quarters with his loud retching sounds of talking on the great white telephone, Detective Joint stood up and washed his ageing face in the cracked off-white basin with cold water. "Ahhh, that feels better," he said to himself a couple of minutes later as the cold water startled his senses back into some sort of action. Looking at his face in the cracked mirror he saw a grey-haired, past middle-aged man whose face told the story of too much cheap fatty food and far too much whisky.

Getting into the passenger side of the police van that stopped outside the block of flats exactly 30 minutes later the first comment from the driver a Constable was, "Begging your pardon sir, but I would suggest that we stop off and buy you some peppermints along the way, you smell like a piece of shit that's been dragged through a whisky distillery." Nodding his head, Detective Joint grunted, "Good idea," as the driver pulled off.

THE ROYALE GRACE HOTEL, SEAPOINT, CAPE TOWN, 04H15, SUNDAY

The Royale Grace Hotel was a 5 Star 140 room apartment hotel that catered for the whims and desires of the more substantially well-off. Situated on Somerset Road in Seapoint, it was an iconic ten-storey building of Italian architecture, where no expense had been spared. Somerset Road, the normally busy road outside the front of the hotel, was cordoned off with emergency vehicles, the blue and red revolving lights of the emergency vehicles garishly illuminating the gargoyles on the front façade of the hotel along with the facades of the neighbouring buildings.

As they approached closer, Detective Joint could make out several police vans with blue lights flashing, a couple of ambulances with red lights flashing, along with several fire engines, also with red lights flashing away. Not to be outdone, the local Traffic Police, along with the local metro by law enforcement officers, had also staked their claim at the murder scene. Parked to one side up a side street were two Forensic Pathology vans. "Must have been important people who were murdered, most murders in this town don't warrant such an entourage," Detective Joint commented sarcastically as the Constable wound the police van past the throng of growing onlookers and was directed to a parking bay by a serious-looking traffic officer a short distance away from the hotel entrance.

"Sir, Detective Brant said he will meet you at the main entrance to the hotel," the Constable reported as he stopped the van in the designated parking bay. "Thank you, constable," Detective Joint answered and jumped out. Pushing his bulk through the growing crowd of onlookers, Detective Joint pulled out his police ID badge as he waded over the yellow police line. Walking up to the large double volume entrance doors whose door handles were made out of intricately moulded iron mongery, where normally one would find the Concierge in a top hat and black suit along with a bell boy waiting, this morning they had been replaced with two stern-looking policemen in combat gear. "Morning, Brant," Detective Joint said greeting his partner who was standing waiting for him with two cups of steaming coffee in his hands.

"Here, I thought you might need this," Detective Brant replied handing him a cup of coffee, before turning back to the two policemen guarding the front door and continuing his conversation. "No one gets in and no one gets out. Also, make sure that your men are posted at the vehicle entrances. Everyone in the building is a suspect at present." The police officer in charge nodded his head in confirmation. "Thanks," Detective Joint said gratefully taking a sip of the hot liquid. "You still having trouble sleeping?" Brant asked worriedly turning back to look at his partner. "Ja," replied Detective Joint as they walked inside through the double volume doors. "Wow, so this is how the rich live," Detective Joint commented, taken back by the sheer decadent luxury of the reception foyer.

With the entrance doors closing behind them, they found themselves in a foyer bedecked in shining black and white imported Italian marble with a sweeping white staircase in front of them, that led down into a large rectangular double volume foyer ringed with Roman-like pillars of white marble, spaced out supporting the structure above. In between the columns on the left were several highly polished reception desks styled on the French renaissance period for individual personalised check in and check out. On the right were alcoves of soft comfortable looking leather chairs and lounge suites grouped together around 18th century styled coffee tables for private intimate conversations. The lighting was soft and intimate.

The walls were covered in amazingly textured wallpaper made of brilliant crimsons, greys, and purples. On the walls highlighted by their own individual downlighters were hung original prints depicting the designs of many famous buildings found in Europe particularly in Italy and France, some of them designed by Leonardo da Vinci himself. "So, who exactly was killed?" Detective Joint asked his partner as they walked through the imposing reception area to the lift lobby at the rear.

"You ever heard of Mark Bings?" his partner inquired as they entered one of the lifts. Pushing the 9th floor button and the lift doors started to close. "I've heard that name before, doesn't he have something to do with computer programming or something?" Detective Joint answered offhandedly. "Man, you are behind the times you fossil, Mark Bings is the father of Virtual Reality as we know it today," Detective Brant replied, irritated by his new partner's old ways. "What the fuck is Virtual Reality, and why the hell have I been called to a case that I know fuck all about?" Detective Joint retorted angrily.

CHAPTER 2

THE ROYALE GRACE HOTEL, 9ᵗʰ FLOOR, PENTHOUSE 1, 04H55, SUNDAY

If the entrance lobby to the hotel was a precursor to the wealth and extravagance beyond, then walking into the Penthouse apartment was another eye-opener. A large set of wooden entrance doors gave access to the penthouse apartment that led into an airy double volume atrium bedecked in shiny white Italian marble. A glass winding staircase infused with LED lighting on the right hand side led up to the bedrooms. In the centre of the foyer was a white shining sculpture by Michaelangelo, illuminated by hidden lighting in the bulkheads surrounding the atrium. "That's apparently an original," Detective Brant stated offhandedly pointing to the sculpture. The apartments' ninth and tenth floors spanned almost the entire length of the hotel, with a well-tended garden balcony complete with plunge pool looking out towards Greenpoint Stadium and the Atlantic Ocean beyond taking up the foremost part of the floor.

Detective Brant nodded to the police officer guarding the doorway and led the way up the winding glass staircase to the tenth-floor level. Turning left and crossing a bridge suspended over the double volume atrium below, Detective Brant led the way down a short passage and into the main bedroom suite. "What does a pad like this cost these days?" Detective Joint asked curiously. "I heard that the one across the way went for around R 200 million a couple of months ago," came the reply. Detective Joint whistled in surprise. "That's more than all of us would make in a thousand lifetimes," he exclaimed amazed that someone could spend that much on an apartment.

Walking into the main bedroom, the downlighters had been switched on to their maximum brightness, and the crime scene was brightly illuminated. "My god," Detective Joint muttered as he entered the bedroom pulling on a pair of surgical gloves issued to him by a technician at the door. The once white silk duvet was now a dark red turning black, with a trail of blood that had dripped down and congealed into a pool on the soft white double pile carpet. The balcony doors at the end of the room facing out to sea were open.

"So, this was Mark Bings," Detective Joint commented looking at the almost headless naked torso lying on the bed and then froze. Images of his dead sister's almost headless torso flashed through his mind. "Fuck it," he muttered, his hands starting to shake. Taking a deep breath to steady his hands wishing he could smoke a cigarette, then remembering that he'd stopped a couple of years ago asked, "So, what do we know about the victim?"

One of the fellow junior detectives spoke up. "Sir, it seems that the victim was killed somewhere between 00H00 and 02H30 this morning. "Who found the body?" Detective Joint asked out loud to no one in particular. "Now that's the strange thing, sir," one of the SAPS personnel replied, it was phoned in." "By whom?" Detective Joint asked. "No one knows," his partner interjected, "it was an anonymous phone call from what looks like a burner phone." "Shit," Detective Joint replied, "but was it recorded, tell me we do have a copy of the voice?"

There was a noise behind him as someone else entered the main bedroom. "Ah, Arnold, sorry to call you in, but I thought you needed to see this," the voice of his boss, Captain Williamson, said behind him. Slowly Detective Joint turned around to greet his boss. "Morning, Captain," Detective Joint mumbled. Turning to his partner Captain Williamson asked, "He hasn't seen the other body yet?" "No sir, I'm going to take him there now." Looking quizzically at his partner Detective Joint asked, "Second body?"

"Follow me," Detective Brant told him walking out of the main bedroom. Retracing their steps, Detective Joint followed his partner back down the short passageway and entered a slightly smaller bedroom on the left, not as grand as the main bedroom suite. Again, the bedroom lighting was turned up full, and entering the bedroom Detective Joint felt as though the wind had been knocked out of him. Lying on the bed was a naked female torso. Like the body in the main bedroom and like his sister before them, her head was almost detached from her torso, cut off in one straight continuous neat slice.

The once snow-white duvet was now scarlet red with her blood. She was lying on her stomach, her head to the left at almost right angles to her torso. "Fuck it, Brant, the murder scene looks exactly like that of Samantha's," he blurted out feeling sick again, remembering the crime scene photographs of his sister's murder. Brant looked at the murder scene and nodded his head. "So that's why the captain wants us on this, it could be the same killer, Your sister's killer was never caught," Brant stated rather than asked. Detective Joint turned around and stared closely at Brant for a second before correcting him, "No they haven't been caught, yet."

Pulling himself together and changing the direction of the conversation slightly he then asked, "So, what do we have, do we know who this victim is?" One of the lab technicians who was examining the body replied, "No, sir, we haven't found any identification as such, but we believe that it is the first victim's girlfriend. They were engaged in sexual intercourse, as I have found traces of sexual activity in her vagina as well as her anus, along with traces of semen," the technician reported. "So why wasn't she killed with her lover in the main suite?" Detective Joint asked. "No idea at present," replied the technician shrugging his shoulders. "But what I can tell you is that preliminary evidence suggests that this victim was killed a good hour after the first victim was killed," the technician confidently informed the detectives.

"Are there any bruises on her indicating a struggle?" Detective Brant asked. "No sir, we haven't found anything to indicate a struggle, actually to the contrary, I'm of the belief she was killed while engaged in sexual intercourse," the technician ventured. "Why do you say that?" Detective Joint asked, intrigued. The technician pointed to the victim's hands. "See how her fingers are intertwined in the duvet? It's as if she was in ecstasy when she died." Both detectives looked at the long-tapered fingers clutched forever around the white satin duvet. "You're right," declared Detective Joint, and carrying on he surmised "so, either there was a third person in the room who she was fucking at the time of her lover's death or she knew the killer. Make sure you get photos of her fingers gripping the bedsheets."

A couple of minutes later the technician turned the corpse over, Detective Joint saw something on the body and called out "Stop, wait, what's that, high up on her upper inner thigh?" Stooping down closer to the body he saw what it was. A bright red and green rose had been tattooed just to the side of the outer lips of her vagina. "I've seen that tattoo before, not too sure where though," Brant exclaimed excitedly. "Yes," Detective Joint replied hoarsely, his mouth all of a sudden dry and his blood rushing to his head, "Samantha, my sister, had a similar tattoo in the same spot." In his mind, he had a vision of his sister lying naked and decapitated, the red and green rose tattoo shining crudely on her deathly pale skin.

"Sir, you'd better come down to the study," came the welcome call a couple of minutes later. Making their way back downstairs to the ninth floor they made their way to the study. A door leading off the brightly lit marbled atrium led into the large study. 'Hell, the study is bigger than my entire flat,' Detective Joint thought to himself as he walked into the large double volume room clad in dark wooden timbers. The room smelt of cigars and expensive male cologne, a wealthy man's study or mancave. One end of the room was dedicated to a bespoke wooden bookcase made out of dark mahogany wood, stretching from floor to ceiling and the width of the room, full of books, the majority of them having a read look about them. To reach the upper shelves of the bookcase one used a set of wooden ladders attached to runners that ran along the side of the wooden bookcase.

In front of the bespoke dark wooden bookcase were a couple of well-worn, comfortable looking, high back leather chairs, in which the detective could imagine the male victim settling down in and indulging in the vast amount of literature within the bookcase. A large Louis the 18th desk stood off to one side, behind a double volume floor to ceiling plate glass window. In the lightening dawn outside, the detective could start to see the outline of Table Mountain. The third wall was taken up with a bank of large 55," video monitors. The antique desk faced towards the monitor wall.

On the ancient desk, in stark contrast to its antiquity, stood a state-of-the-art LCD monitor. A technician sat at the desk dusting the monitor and desk for fingerprints, the accompanying technologically advanced PC lying discarded on its side on the floor beside the antique desk, now useless, the hard disk drives having been ripped out. On one corner were several gilt-edged frames with photographs in them. "Well, the dead female upstairs is definitely not his wife," Detective Joint pointed out, picking up one of the photographs showing a picture of the male victim; with his head fully attached to his body, along with a beautiful looking younger wife and two teenage children, a boy and a girl.

Built into the one wall was a safe, the thick engineered steel door of the safe standing wide open. "Do we have any idea what was taken?" Detective Joint asked walking across the study to the wall safe. Looking inside he was surprised to see a wad of bank notes and some rather expensive looking jewellery still lying pretty and untouched in the safe. "No, sir," replied another technician dusting the safe for fingerprints.

THE ROYALE GRACE HOTEL, 05H30, SUNDAY

"So, give me a quick rundown of what you know about our recently deceased Mark Bings," Detective Joint instructed his partner as they walked through the set of imposing double wooden entrance doors of the penthouse apartment, heading for the guest lifts and ultimately the security room on the ground floor, leaving the crime scene technicians to do their job. Clearing his throat, Detective Brant replied, "I only know what I've read and heard from my kids," adding ruefully, "they keep me pretty much up to date with technology these days, it's progressing in leaps and bounds." Detective Joint smiled thinking, 'Lucky you, and all the problems that come with having a family.' Stepping into the lift, Detective Brant explained as best he could, "Mark Bings is to Virtual Reality what Bill Gates was to Windows and the PC operating systems that revolutionised computing as the world has known it for the last forty years or so." Carrying on as the lift descended he explained to his partner, "Mark Bings was one of the leading pioneers in developing the world of Virtual Reality, where a computer user no longer has to sit at a PC and work or surf the Internet. Along with designing and writing the code for the world of Virtual Reality, he also developed the wireless Virtual Reality glasses, and the stainless-steel wristband that is a wireless nanocomputer that links you to the VR glasses and the world of Virtual Reality." Stopping and taking a deep breath he continued to explain, "Now, you can sit at your desk and enter the world of VR and work, have meetings, meet friends, watch a movie, buy clothes, go on holiday to an exotic place, do your monthly shopping, browse through shops, the scope is endless. He apparently made an absolute fortune out of his designs. Whatever you do in the real world you can basically do in the Virtual World. All clothes and whatever tangible items you buy in the Virtual world are delivered to you by couriers in the real world." Looking at Detective Joint he saw that he was listening intently, so he carried on. "No more sitting at your computer and looking at a website and adding the items with your mouse to your shopping cart. Now you can try on the clothes in VR or play the game you want to buy in VR and see if you really want it, or even check out a holiday!" Detective Brant finished explaining excitedly as the lift reached the ground floor. "Wow," Detective Joint replied with a small nervous laugh, "I had no idea that technology was so far advanced." Dropping his voice, a couple of octaves Detective Brant said, "You can even get laid in Virtual Reality, I'm told it's quite a mind fuck," and he laughed at his own joke.

The lift reached the ground floor, the lift doors opened, and they walked out into the brilliant black and white Italian marble-clad lift lobby which reminded Detective Joint of a large chess board. With Detective Brant taking the lead they walked out of the lift lobby and turning right walked down a short passageway towards the room which was designated as the Security Control room. The room occupied an extremely small rectangular space of around 1.5 m wide by 2 m with a bank of six LCD CCTV monitors hung from the wall with a short desk beneath the monitors, running the length of the wall.

With the security operator, along with the SAP technician tasked with reviewing the video footage and the two detectives standing shoulder to shoulder there wasn't much space and the room soon became stuffy, the smell of Detective Joint's whisky breath starting to overpower the peppermints. "What do we have?" Detective Brant asked, standing the closest to the SAPS technician. "Nothing, sir," the technician replied, then qualifying his statement saying, "so far we've found video footage of the female victim entering the hotel lobby and then the lift. We see her exiting the lift on the 9th floor and then we see her walking down the passageway towards the penthouse suite and entering the suite, but nothing or anyone else entering the suite after that, and nobody coming out." "What!" exclaimed Detective Joint amazed at the lack of video footage. "How many cameras in the hotel?" he asked the security controller directly looking at the screens and all the video images. "Um, sir, we have around eighty cameras installed in the hotel, however at present, there are a couple that are not working," the security controller explained nervously. "Shit, so there's the likelihood that we've missed the suspect or suspects," Detective Brant interjected. "Sir, we're still going through the footage, but so far there's nothing that sticks out," the SAPS technician explained as patiently as he could. "Okay, call us if you find anything, but we want all the computers and hard drives for further forensic analysis," Detective Joint instructed the technician. Walking back out of the small claustrophobic room, he said to his partner, "Let's go and have a chat with the Hotel Manager and see what he has to say."

They were told that the General Manager was in his office on the mezzanine level. Stepping off the lift on the mezzanine level they found the management offices adjacent to a luxury Spa where the rich and well-to.do along with residents and guests of the hotel could come and be pampered, for a price. Entering the management offices, they heard the haunting sounds of Dire Straits' 'Brothers in Arms' echoing eerily through the empty offices. Heading towards the source of the music, they found the General Manager sitting in his office. The General Manager was a middle-aged, very overweight individual dressed in a suit complete with a waistcoat. Turning down the music with the remote control, he explained: "Good morning detectives. My apologies, the music helps me think." Once they had introduced themselves the General Manager started speaking. "It's a tragedy what has occurred. Nothing like this has ever occurred in my hotel before!"

Clearing his throat Detective Joint said, "Tell me about Mr Bings." "He was the best owner the hotel has had so far, and I've been here for around ten years," the General Manager explained. "What, he owned the hotel?" Detective Brant exclaimed in amazement. "Yes," replied the GM unperplexed by the outburst. "But I thought he was the pioneer of Virtual Reality. Have I got my names mixed up?" Detective Brant then asked, sounding a bit confused. Shaking his head with a small sad smile on his face the GM replied, "No, Detective, Mr Bings is who you say he is, one of the founders of Virtual Reality, but he also owned the hotel." "Uh-huh," Detective Joint muttered and then said, "so he was well off?" The General Manager sat back in his black leather executive chair and laughed before replying, "Detective, Mark Bings is... was one very wealthy individual, listed in Forbes as one of the world's wealthiest individuals." "Wow, okay, I didn't know that," Detective Joint admitted. "Do you know where Mr Bings' wife is?" Detective Brant then asked the General Manager, changing the subject. "Yes," he replied. "His wife, I spoke to her a little while ago and she and the kids are on the way back." "From where?" asked Detective Joint. "They took the family jet to Mauritius a couple of weeks ago for a holiday," the General Manager casually replied.

After a couple more hours of searching through the hotel as the pre-dawn turned into another glorious morning in Cape Town, they came away empty-handed. No one in the hotel had heard or seen anything. Another couple of detectives and policemen had gone from apartment to apartment in the ten storey 144 roomed hotel getting statements from all the occupants.

"Who are you, what were you doing between 00H00 and 02H30 this morning?" was the general line of questioning which they were asking. Everyone accounted for seemed to have an alibi, and so far, the camera footage supported their claims that they were in their rooms at the time. "Okay guys let's wrap it up here," a frustrated Detective Joint told the team a little later. "We'll have to wait and see what the forensic evidence comes back with and what good old-fashioned detective work turns up."

CAPE TOWN CENTRAL POLICE STATION, EARLY AFTERNOON, SUNDAY

As Detective Joint had quite rightly pointed out earlier that morning, when the rich get murdered, the police jump and throw all their resources into solving the crime. When a normal run of the mill citizen gets murdered, one, maybe two detectives get assigned to the case and it gets added to their already overburdened case load. South Africa was a very violent country. "Okay guys and girls, orders from upstairs, high upstairs, drop all your current cases and concentrate on the Mark Bings killings," Captain Williamson, Captain of the Cape Town Detective Branch instructed his team of detectives.

Carrying on, he said, looking directly at Detective Joint, "Arnold, I want you and Brant to be the lead detectives on this." There was a lot of mumbling at that. "I know, I know," he said holding up his hands to ward off the objections from Detective Joint among others, "it's asking a lot from you and it'll open up old wounds, but come on, the killings look strikingly similar to that of your sister's, and I know as does the whole department that you're still actively looking for her killer. It could be your chance to kill two birds with one stone." Detective Joint sat there for a few moments and stared hard and long at his Captain and then replied slowly, "Okay, you're right, but we do it my way. No interference from on high, you run all political and media interference for me, let me concentrate on catching the killer or killers." "Deal," replied the captain, "you have the floor." Everyone missed the look that crossed Detective Brant's face.

Standing Detective Joint looked around at his colleagues. "Okay, the longer we wait the further away the killer or killers are getting. This is how I propose that we tackle this case. Juliet, as the division's Intelligence liaison officer, I want you to act as the central data conduit through which all information will run. Set up the Crime Board and add and collate all the information as it comes in." Juliet looked at Detective Joint and nodded her head. "Got it." Turning to the next two detectives he said "Pieter and Jannie, I want you two to concentrate on the crime scene and liaise with the Crime Scene Technicians. Sit on their backs until you have back all the forensic data. Also, I'm not convinced that the CCTV Cameras didn't record anything. There are over eighty cameras installed in the building. Whatever information you get, channel the information directly to Juliet to update the board and the case file." Both detectives nodded their heads in unison.

Turning to the last two detectives, he said "I want you two to look into the dead girl. Who is she? There was no identification found at the crime scene. I don't know if it's worth anything, but my sister also had a rose tattoo on her upper inner thigh."

Detective Lindiwe and her partner Detective Ross nodded their collective heads. Detective Lindiwe asked, "Do we have access to all your records relating to your sister's death?" Detective Joint gestured affirmatively and said, "I'll hand all the information I have over to Juliet."

Carrying on he told the group of detectives sitting around the table, "Myself and Detective Brant will focus on Mark Bings." His parting words to his fellow detectives were: "We'll have a meeting here every morning at 08H15 to bring the rest of the team up to date and plan going forward." As the detectives stood up and started to clear the room, Detective Joint said, "Captain, sorry but can I have a word in private with you?" "Sure," replied the captain. Waiting until the room was empty, Detective Joint asked "Sir, it's not every day that we're instructed to clear our desks and concentrate on one case. Can you tell me who ordered it?" "Sure," the captain replied with a grim smile on his face, "the Commissioner himself."

CHAPTER 3

MID SOUTH ATLANTIC OCEAN, EXEC DECISION 1, *SEA TRIALS NEARING ST HELENA, 16H00, SUNDAY*

"Yeehaaa," came the wild shout of excitement from the stern of the 60-foot foiling racing yachts' cockpit as the Windex showing the wind speed on the forward centre bulkhead of the cockpit between the two companionways leading down below, hovered at 50 knots on the large LCD screen. The 50-knot wind pushed hard against the mainsail currently with one reef in it and the smaller J2 Genoa on the bow attached to the 100-foot black carbon fibre rotating wing mast. In order to support the massive 100-foot wing mast, two outriggers were attached to the foot of the mast poking out at a 45-degree angle on both the port and starboard side of the yacht, the thick stainless-steel rod rigging linking the outriggers to the mast. The sails were made of exotic space age materials with Mylar and Kevlar interlaced in between.

The 50-knot wind captured by the space age sails generated massive forces down through the black carbon fibre mast, down into the specially designed carbon fibre hull to which the state-of-the-art designed carbon fibre foils were attached to the hull on both the port and starboard side of the hull. The forces spurred the 60-foot-long hull along, the leeward foil fully extended and digging hard into the cold Atlantic Ocean generating lift, lifting the 7-ton hull partly up and out of the water, thus presenting a smaller damp area to produce less drag. Less drag meant more speed. Only sections of the leeward part of the hull and the bright luminous yellow hydraulic ram operated canting keel, currently fully chanted to windward were still in the water, along with the equally yellow and luminous leeward rudder. "Bloody hell, 20 knots to windward, she's flying along!" the same voice remarked a couple of minutes later as the 60-foot monohulled yacht thundered along to windward lost in a sea of spray as the foil did its job.

The voice belonged to Nick Scott, the skipper and proud new owner of the IMOCA Open 60-foot foiling beast they were currently sailing mid Atlantic putting it through its sea trials. "So, do you think it's worth the US $ 100 million you've sunk into her so far?" the voice belonging to his long-time friend and sailing companion, Pete Gossling. Pete was standing in the cockpit along the centreline of the yacht, gripping the centre pedestal winch handles, similar to bicycle pedals, with his hands and started to furiously wind them, trimming the large J2 genoa as the wind picked up a further notch, the yacht revelling in the howling forces of nature, ploughing its way to windward through the growing swells of the approaching mid-South Atlantic low pressure system.

Nick gripped his left hand tighter on the central tiller of the twin rudder system while at same time adjusting his balance to the heeling deck of the flying yacht, dodging the constant spray of water that was flowing over the coach house roof; the bright luminous yellow windward rudder currently in the up position and out of the water, the trajectory of the flying yacht relying solely on the leeward rudder, and corrected their wild flying course through the gathering swells and laughed out loud, the rich deep laugh of a person who was at peace and content with life. He could have extended the tiller extension and sat down in the specially designed seat under the enclosed cockpit covered by the coach house roof and steered the yacht protected from the elements, but right then Nick was revelling in the raw elements of nature.

As the founder and owner of Executive Decisions, an international security company, the retired ex-Major, British Royal Marine Commando, made his vast fortune in Africa by being in the right place at the right time, along with some shrewd investments with the proceeds. With a personal fortune of over a billion US dollars, even he had to admit that it was a small fortune what he'd sunk into the yacht *Exec Decision 1*, but fuck it, it was worth it. It was to undertake a personal adventure, a solo undertaking pitting himself and the yacht against the untempered elements of nature, the Southern Ocean. It was an adventure that would require him to dig down deep into his inner core to pull through.

The yacht race was known as the *Vendee Globe Challenge* and was a single-handed nonstop yacht race around the world without any outside assistance. The race was run every four years, and Nick was aiming for the next race in two years' time. From a start line just off of Les Sables-d'Olonne a small fishing village on the west coast of France, solo yachtsmen set off down the Atlantic Ocean passing the Cape of Good Hope to port, then sail clockwise around Antarctica keeping Cape Leeuwin (the southernmost tip of Australia) and then Cape Horn (the southernmost point of South America) to port, then back up into the Atlantic Ocean and back to finish at Les Sables-d'Olonne. Competitors may stop at anchor but may not come alongside any quay or other vessel and may receive no outside assistance for the duration of the race.

Running between November and February it was a 3-month race to dash around the world as quickly as possible. The most challenging part; apart from being on one's own for around 72 to 82 days was the Southern Ocean where they would spend around five weeks sailing in sub-zero temperatures around the bottom of the world with 50 and sometimes 60 knot winds coupled with swells of up to 50 feet high. Sailing down in those low latitudes thousands of kilometres away from both land and help it was just you and your yacht. If you hit an iceberg or an object in the water and sank, it was then just you and (hopefully) your life raft, and you hoped like hell that there was a competitor nearby who could come to your rescue and that your survival skills were up to the task to survive in the sub-zero conditions until they arrive. Because that's all the help there is, thousands of nautical miles away from civilisation!

Over the cacophony of the sound of the wind and the waves was the sound of a phone ringing from down below. "I've got it,"

Pete gestured towards Nick and slipped down through the currently open starboard side companionway being the windward one and headed over to the communication and navigation station module, a futuristic-looking white carbon fibre module with a fighter jet-like seat placed along the centreline of the yacht. The whole navigation module could rotate left to right to offer as much comfort and stability as possible while flying along single-handed on autopilot. The navigation station was equipped with all the electronics that Nick would require to navigate safely around the world single-handed from the Chart Plotter, GPS, AIS, SATCOMM Transceiver, weather routing PC, and VHF Radio. There was also a radar and SSB radio on board. All the equipment was doubled up, so, if one system broke, he had another while he went about attempting to repair the first: if possible.

With the sound of the water rushing across the hull being amplified via the carbon fibre hull, Pete donned a headset with microphone before patching the satellite call through to the blue tooth headset. "Hello, Nick's phone," he answered to the sound of a sobbing female voice, "I... I need to speak to Nick, is he available?" Taken aback by the sound of the sobbing female voice, Pete replied standing up from the communication console and immediately taking hold of a grab rail to prevent himself from being flung across the cabin by the wild motion of the hull, "Stand by ma'am, I'll get Nick for you right away," Pete replied hurriedly, unaccustomed to having sobbing women phone the yacht in the middle of the Atlantic Ocean. "Hey, Nick, you better put the yacht on autopilot for a while and take this call, I'll keep an eye out on George," he shouted out up the companionway. George was the name they'd given to autopilot No 1 that had given them problems earlier on in the day.

Wiping a hand over his wet 7-day stubbled face and rubbing the salt water out of his eyes, Nick sat down at the communication console in his yellow Musto & Hyde Deep Ocean oil skins and settling the blue tooth headset and microphone on his head answered "Hi, Nick Scott speaking." "Nick – sniff – Nick, is that you? It's Veronica Bings," a crying distraught voice replied over the clear satellite link. "Hi, Veronica, what's wrong?" Nick asked concerned, as a loud crashing sound reverberated throughout the hull as the bow of the flying yacht still doing around 20 knots crashed into a large swell and carried on. "Mark is dead, he was fucking decapitated while screwing another woman," she shouted out in anguish. "Did you know he was fucking another woman?" she then asked just as hysterically.

All of a sudden Nick felt as if he'd been shocked, one of his friends murdered. "Hey Veronica, calm down, no sorry, look I had no idea Mark was messing around. I haven't seen him in several months. We've both been pretty busy," Nick explained as there was another loud boom that reverberated through the cabin as they ploughed through another large swell. "Where the hell are you, in a large washing machine?" Veronica asked, the microphone of Nick's bluetooth picking up the loud noises. "Something like that, I'm mid Atlantic, nearing St Helena, putting *Exec Decisions 1* through her sea trials," Nick explained to a now calmer Veronica. "Oh god, I'm sorry to disturb you but I don't know who else to turn to right now," she replied and began crying again. "No, don't apologise, damn, sorry, my condolences, what happened, take your time," Nick told her as calmly as possible while his mind raced ahead. 'What the fuck,' he thought to himself, 'Mark, murdered.'

Taking a deep breath, the recently widowed wife of Mark Bings started to explain. "Myself and his kids flew to Mauritius for a holiday. Mark has been under a lot of pressure lately to complete his newest project and we thought it best if we got out of the way for a while," Veronica explained between sobs and sniffles to Nick. "I had no idea he was fucking another woman, I thought I was the only one he was fucking. How could I be so stupid!" she cried out. Sitting in the hull of the high-tech yacht skimming across the Atlantic Ocean swells, Nick replayed the last time he had seen Mark, a developer on the cutting edge of Virtual Reality software development who had helped set up the Executive

Decisions Virtual Reality Suite and application software. Over time they had built up a friendship, and Mark had opened to Nick about his life. Veronica was his second wife; he'd met when he'd moved to South Africa a short while ago.

He was married before in the USA; he'd gotten married at a young age and had two kids with his first wife before she died in a terrible motor vehicle accident. Unable to bear the pain of losing her, everything he looked at reminded him of her, along with the US government's constant hounding of him for his Virtual Reality technology that he was adamant he was not going to sell to the military, he uprooted his life and along with his now teenage children moved to Cape Town. That was where he'd met Veronica and got married after a whirlwind romance.

The last time that Nick had seen Mark he'd been explaining his latest invention to Nick, a device to his Virtual Reality suite that made you invisible to all other users and anti-virus software alike. It was originally designed innocently enough as a tool for software engineers to be able to enter the Virtual World and perform maintenance tasks and the likes without disrupting the VR users' experience. The device was like Harry Potter's invisible cloak! It was to be the Holy Grail of Virtual Reality, making you invisible, unfortunately, something that hackers and governments alike would also want.

"So, I got a telephone call from the hotel manager, informing me that Mark had been killed and what were his orders, as Mark also owns the Grace Royale!" Veronica carried on explaining to Nick. 'Huh,' Nick thought silently, 'I didn't know that.' "I immediately flew back and then I heard the full story, his head had basically been cut off his body along with that of another fucking bitch!" Veronica explained her voice starting to get high-pitched and break again.

After listening to Veronica explain for another couple of minutes Nick said, "Try to calm down, I'll be back in Cape Town as soon as I can. In the meantime, I'm going to contact my team to start looking into Mark's murder." Just as Nick was about to end the conversation Veronica said "It's missing, Nick, the Prototype he was working on, along with all his workings, is missing." "Oh, fuck," replied Nick, a chill going down his spine thinking of the ramifications of the 'invisible cloak' falling into the wrong hands. "I need to speak to you face to face, contact me when you reach dry land, I'm staying at the One&Only in the V&A Waterfront," she blurted out and ended the call.

After ending the call, Nick sat silently in the navigator seat for a while, his mind working furiously over the information he had just received, trying to gather his thoughts. 'Damnit, Mark murdered, almost decapitated,' he thought to himself. "Who the hell was that, a girlfriend who's missing you?" Pete asked good-naturedly, sticking his head down through the companionway, speaking over the roar of the yacht and the wind. Turning in his futuristic navigation seat Nick replied, "Sorry to disappoint you this time pal, that was Veronica Bings, Mark's wife. He's been murdered while shagging another woman," Nick told him. "Oh fuck, I'm sorry mate, you and he were good friends, weren't you?" Pete asked. "Uh-huh," Nick replied nodding his head.

"So, what now?" Pete then asked. "Well, Veronica is hysterical, and the police aren't telling her much and don't seem to have many leads to work with. Also, the latest invention Mark was working on is apparently missing," Nick explained to his friend. "Invention? Sorry, mate, you've lost me there," Pete replied with a shrug of his shoulders, his hands gripping tightly onto the coaming of the companionway as the yacht shuddered as the bow hit a larger than normal swell and tons of water swept across the deck of the yacht, pouring over the coach house roof above Pete's head. Nick quickly explained to Pete what Mark had been working on. "Fuck, mate, that's serious shit," Pete replied.

"We're going to have to cut this pleasure cruise short. We'll head to St Helena and arrange for the yacht to be shipped back to

Cape Town," Nick explained to Pete. Seeing the disappointment on his friend's face, Nick tried to cheer him up, "Don't worry, we're still going to do the Jacques Vabre race at the end of the year, that doesn't change." The Transat Jacques Vabre was a double-handed yacht race from Le Havre France down the Atlantic Ocean to Salvador in Brazil between August and October. This was the first of three races and the only double-handed race in the run up to the Vendee Globe Challenge. The other two races were the single-handed Route de Rhum race to Salvador and the single-handed Transat Race, Portsmouth to New York. All three were warm-up precursor races to the Vendee Globe Challenge in November in two years' time.

CHAPTER 4

CAPE TOWN CENTRAL POLICE STATION, MONDAY, 08H10

The common sounding name 'Veronica Bings' didn't make justice to the outstanding woman of stature and beauty who was seated in the general waiting area of the Cape Town Central police station along with the rest of society waiting to report some form of crime that had occurred to them or they had witnessed. Wearing a simple black loose-fitting dress with flat black sandals on her feet, she could have been wearing a black plastic bag and would still have looked amazing. 'Money buys beauty, but does it buy love?' Detective Joint silently asked himself as he ushered the beautiful widow into an interview room on the ground floor and shut the door behind them.

After settling his ample bulk down into a chair on the opposite side of the table and introducing himself, Detective Joint told her, "I'm sorry for your loss, Mrs Bings. Thank you for coming so promptly down to the station. In the message I left you I mentioned that I was more than happy to come to you at your earliest convenience." Looking at him through wide bright blue but pain-filled eyes, Mrs Bings replied, "Thank you, Detective, this is my earliest convenience. I arrived back in Cape Town last night and want to get this out of the way as quickly as possible, but at the same time, I don't want to advertise to the whole world what's going on. I have my husband's children's privacy to consider," she replied in a strong voice with a slight accent which he couldn't quite place.

"So, the children aren't yours?" he asked amazed. Shaking her head and giving a small laugh she replied "No, Jimmy and Megan are from his first wife. She died in a car accident in the US about three years ago." "Where are the children now?" Detective Joint asked curiously. "When I heard what had happened, I sent them to stay with Mark's parents in Miami. They flew straight from Mauritius to the States. I chartered a jet for them," she explained to him matter-of-factly. "May I ask where you are staying now by the way?" he asked. "The One&Only in the V&A Waterfront," she replied.

"Mrs Bings, do you have any idea who would want to kill your husband?" the detective then asked, getting down to business. "You left out 'and his fucking slut', and no, I have no idea who would want to kill him or her for that matter," Mrs Bings replied angrily. Detective Joint was taken back by the words coming out of the blonde goddess's mouth. "I take it that you didn't know that your husband was having an affair then?" he then asked. "No," came back the curt reply, followed by, "trust me if I'd caught the bastard, I'd have cut his fucking dick off, not his big head!" Detective Joint smiled inwardly at that. Carrying on, he asked, "Can you tell me why you and the children went on holiday to Mauritius and left your husband behind?" "Sure," replied the blonde widow. "When Mark gets engrossed in a project, he shuts everyone and everything out and concentrates fully on what he's doing. It became unbearable and I and the kids decided to get out of his way while he finished his project."

Making some notes in his small pocket-sized notebook Detective Joint then asked, "Do you know what he was working on?" Mrs Bings shook her beautiful blonde head and replied, "No, he never really confided in me what he was working on. All I know is that it had something to do with Virtual Reality." 'Okay," Detective Joint then said, "just a few more questions. Do you know what was taken out of the safe?" "No," came the reply. "Who has the combination to the safe?" Detective Joint then asked her. "Only Mark had the combination to the safe in the study," answered the widow. "So, you then had to ask him for your jewellery pieces stored in the safe if you wanted to wear them then?"

Detective Joint asked as casually as possible staring at her closely.

There was a second of slight confusion that the detective would have missed had he not been staring closely at her when she answered "Yes, yes, I had to ask him to fetch them for me." "Okay Mrs Bings, that will be all for now if we need any more information, I'll contact you," Detective Joint told her standing up.

CAPE TOWN CENTRAL POLICE STATION, MORNING MEETING, 09H15, MONDAY

"Sorry we're a bit late," Detective Joint said to the team as he and Detective Brant rushed into the meeting room. Explaining Detective Joint told the team seated around the large table, "we've just interviewed Mrs Bings, she was waiting for me when I walked in the front door this morning. Well, I interviewed her, and Brant observed." "And?" the captain asked impatiently. "She definitely knows more than she's saying, but she had no idea her husband was being unfaithful, nor did she kill them," Detective Joint informed them confidently as he sat down.

Carrying on, he told them she lied about the jewellery in the safe. "She had no idea that there was jewellery in the safe, and it caught her off guard for a split second. I'm damn sure she knows or has some idea what was stolen out of the safe. She's hiding something." "So, are we saying that the murders were for whatever was in the safe?" the captain asked them. "That what it's looking like at present," Detective Joint replied cautiously to his superior. "Do we have any idea what was in the safe?" the captain then asked his detectives. Detective Joint answered the question, "At present, we have no definite knowledge of what was in the safe, but we are assuming that it had something to do with the deceased's occupation, something to do with Virtual Reality."

Detective Joint explained, "The deceased's wife alluded to a project that he was working on, but she says she has no idea what exactly her husband was working on, only that it had something to do within the realms of Virtual Reality. With the hard disk drives being ripped out of the deceased PC as well, it doesn't leave us with many leads right now." "And backups?" another detective asked. "The widow says she does not know much about what her husband did. To me it looks like she's more of a trophy wife, his first wife died in a car crash in the US just over three years ago," Detective Joint informed them.

"Okay then, moving on, what do we know about the anonymous caller who reported the crime?" asked Captain Williamson. Shaking her head Juliet answered, "Unfortunately nothing. The call came from a pay as you go cellphone with the call line identification blocked." "And the signal from where the call was made, can't the network operator at least trace the signal back to where it came from?" Detective Brant asked. "We're still waiting for the network operator to come back to us," was the reply. "Let's push them a bit harder for the information," Detective Joint instructed her.

"Do we have any more information on the second victim? What's her name for starters?" the captain then asked them. Detective Lindiwe shook her head and explained, "No, unfortunately not yet, we have received a copy of her fingerprints from the coroner which Juliet is busy running through all databases, but nothing yet." Juliet backed her up, "I've also sent the prints to Interpol, but again nothing has come back yet." Detective Joint then asked, "How did she arrive at the hotel? Let's send out her picture to the local taxi companies in Cape Town, maybe we get lucky," "On it," confirmed Detective Lindiwe. Turning to Pieter and Jannie the captain asked, "Any feedback from the crime scene?"

Pieter cleared his throat and replied, "The crime scene technicians have reported finding a boot print in one of the flower beds on the outside balcony. The shoe size doesn't match any of the Bing households. They're waiting for a boom lift to inspect the side of the building, as it would seem as if the killer somehow climbed up the side of the building and gained access to the balcony." "So, we're looking for Spiderman then," Detective Brant suggested. They all had a good laugh at that comment. As the laughter quietened down, Detective Joint told them, "If the most logical answers don't fit, then the illogical answer has to be it." Carrying on he told Pieter and Jannie, "Go and check all other buildings in the vicinity and see if they have any cameras looking at Somerset Road and the side street adjacent to the hotel. Maybe we get lucky and see something we can use." "Good idea," the captain answered. After talking for another couple of minutes the meeting broke up, the detectives each heading out in different directions, all trying to find a positive lead that would point them in the direction of solving the murders.

CAPE TOWN MAIN POLICE STATION, 15H00, MONDAY

Juliet found Detective Joint sitting at his desk along with Detective Brant. It was late afternoon. "Detectives, the first DNA samples are back," she informed him. "It's been confirmed that the female victim had vaginal and anal intercourse with the male victim, and then anal intercourse with someone else. The sperm in her anal passage does not belong to the first victim, nor is there any trace of the other man's sperm on the deceased. We have, however, found traces of the woman's bodily fluids all over the deceased's body," Juliet confirmed to the detectives with a deadpan face. "A *ménage à trois* that went horribly wrong and the prize was whatever was in the safe," suggested Detective Brant. "You know if we had video footage of the two victims plus one entering the penthouse suite, I would say that you weren't far wrong," Detective Joint replied to his partner with a grim smile on his face.

Carrying on Juliet told them, "They can also confirm that the murder weapon used was an extremely sharp blade, however, they cannot confirm that the same blade was used to kill your sister." "Damn," muttered Detective Joint. "A sharp blade is a sharp blade it would seem." Juliet cleared her throat and said, "That's not entirely correct. The coroner said that both victims, as well as

45

your sister, had been cut by an extremely sharp honed blade, like a Japanese Katana blade or something similar. Also, the killer is right-handed, cutting from left to right."

Pointing to a photograph on the large white Crime Scene Board showing a close-up of the male's neck minus his head, Juliet explained, "See how perfect the cut is? It's like a hot knife through butter." Then, pointing to the female victim's neck, the cut was the same. There was a third picture on the board. Detective Joint felt his mouth go dry as he recognised his sister's dead pale body with fiery red hair. Samantha. She looked nothing like him.

Samantha had been a vivacious redhead with a trim toned body, not like his fat ass. In life, she had always had a golden suntan. In death, her tan had faded into insignificance leaving her skin pale and ugly, only the small tuft of fiery red pubic hair at the junction of her thighs and the ink of the bright red and green rose tattoo stood out brightly like traffic beacons.

"Uh, Detective, you still with me?" Juliet asked shaking him out of his thoughts. "Yes, sorry, I was just thinking," stammered Detective Joint his throat suddenly dry. "I was saying that looking closely at the pictures that were taken of your sister's neck, the cuts look very similar, but to be one hundred percent positive we'd need the murder weapon," Juliet explained. Detective Joint nodded his head. "Another angle that we need to look at further are the tattoos," Juliet informed them. The lab has confirmed that the tattoo on the female victim's upper inner thigh is the same as the tattoo on your sister's body, and in the same spot on their bodies as well, to within a millimetre or two."

Detective Joint turned his attention to the picture on the board of the dead girl's tattoo, identical to his sister's, the red rose with green leaves inked onto her most secretive of places. "It's a very intimate tattoo," Detective Brant pointed out to no one in particular. Then he asked, "Is there any way of finding out who inked the tattoos? That's intricate work, it takes skill. Not anybody could do it," then adding with a sly grin, "I'm sure everybody would love to try, though." "I'll instruct the technicians to try to get a sample of the ink off the body and see what we can do," Juliet confirmed, not biting to Detective Brant's crude comments. The rest of the afternoon passed by quickly with theories and suggestions being punted around back and forth about the tattoos.

WYNBERG SAPS BATCHELOR QUARTERS, MONDAY EVENING

Clocking out at 17H00, Detective Joint said goodnight to his fellow detectives and ambled out as quickly as he could out of the building, trying to get away as quickly as possible, hopefully keeping the demons at bay long enough until he could get home. 'I thought I could handle seeing her again,' he thought to himself, remembering the sight of his sister's naked body, lifeless on the bed. Walking outside he found his friend and fellow detective Jannie waiting for him. "I'm going to take the train tonight," he told Jannie, that usually gave him a lift back to the Southern Suburbs. "I want to clear my mind," he added. "Okay, pal. Pick you up in the morning," Jannie replied and sped away only to sit for another hour in rush hour traffic on the way back to the Southern Suburbs.

As Detective Joint headed towards the Cape Town Train Station to catch a train on the southern line to Wynberg, one of the many stops along the southern line between Cape Town and Simonstown, he joined the mass of humanity of similar-minded office workers all heading home. From the Wynberg train station it was a short walk back to the bachelor's quarters. Along the way to the Cape Town Train Station, he stopped off at a bottle store. "Bottle of Three Ships Whisky, please," he told the store owner behind the counter. A couple of minutes later with the bottle of Three Ships encased safely in a brown paper bag and clutched tightly in his left hand he re-joined the multitude of people still streaming towards the train station. Getting off the train a bit later at the Wynberg Station, he picked up a cheap take away dinner and was back in his flat by 18H45. All the way home he was fighting with the demons in his head, trying to push the picture of his sister's dead, naked, decapitated body from his mind.

Sitting down with his cheap takeaway dinner he watched a bit of TV while he ate, the food bland, oily, and tasteless to him, his taste buds refusing to cooperate. All the time while he ate, all he could see in his mind was the picture of his dead sister and the bright green and red tattoo of the rose. Finishing his supper and washing it down with a glass of Coke, he reached down for the bottle of Three Ships Whisky at his feet and poured himself a stiff shot, replacing the Coke in the glass with the amber-gold liquid.

"Ahhhhhh," he grimaced as the first neat shot hit the back of his throat and rushed down unopposed into his stomach, searing a path of warmness as it travelled down, hitting his stomach with a burst of fire, a glowing warmth of heat that spread out quickly throughout his body. Immediately he started to feel better, more relaxed. Pouring himself a second tot, then a third, and then another, the demons started to disappear. Losing track of time, he passed out in front of the television, his head lolling to one side as he began to snore.

The dream started the same way it always did. He was trapped, the room was dark, and he was unarmed. He knew that the killer was in the building, he could feel him, an icy like coldness that crept slowly up his spine, prickling at his senses. In the background through the inky blackness he could hear his sister's voice, but this time it was different. "Ha, ha, ha, ha," he heard Samantha laugh out loud in a deep, sensual, throaty laugh that he had not heard before. 'Oh god, that's nice, don't stop," he heard another voice moan and then some more sensual laughter. But this voice wasn't his sister's. For some reason, he knew what was about to happen next. "No, sis, no! Run, run and take your friend with you, he's going to kill you both!" he shouted out loudly in his dream. "Ha, ha, ha," the tinkle of gay laughter went on ignoring him, then replaced by silence and then a building moan getting heavier and

48

heavier. Through the foggy darkness of the dream, he heard "Oh, fuck yes, fuck me, oh god, fuck me, fuck me, it's so nice! Ahh-hhhh, ahhhhhh, yes!" came crying out through the darkness. His hands frantically clawed their way through the dark, looking for the door handle, all the time he was shouting out, "Get out, Sam, get out, he's going to kill you!"After what seemed like an eternity with the sensual sounds getting heavier and the moaning more frenzied, he found the cool metal door handle and wrenched open the door. He saw his sister lying on her back, her long-toned legs spread wide open with a man he didn't recognise between them, his large, engorged member pounding away at the fiery red furry junction between her legs. Sitting on her face with her eyes closed and her head thrown back in wild ecstasy was the dead blonde from the penthouse, his sister's tongue buried deep within her wet pink slippery folds.

It seemed like only the man pounding away between his sister's thighs saw him enter the room and could hear him, as he turned to face the detective with an evil grin etched on his face, at the same time pulling a sword from a sheath on his back that the detective hadn't yet seen. In one vicious controlled swing, the blade sliced through the blonde's neck as she suddenly sat up, straightening her back and rubbing her throbbing vagina hard onto his sister's face. Her neck was at the perfect angle for the blade. There was a silver flash as the finely honed blade cut through the air and the blonde's neck from left to right with the same efficiency, the head balancing on the torso for a second before falling over to rest on her shoulder, still attached by some sinew. A fountain of red blood spurted up as the carotid artery was severed and the body fell over lifeless.

"Agghhhh, no! Help me! Aaagghhhh!" his sister screamed out in panic as she was covered in the dead girl's blood, pulled brusquely out of her sexual ecstasy. The detective rushed forward shouting, but it was too late. In the flick of an eye, the killer had changed his grip on the katana and ran the finely honed edge of the blade across Samantha's regal neck, severing her head from the rest of her body.

CHAPTER 5

SOMEWHERE OVER THE ATLANTIC, GULFSTREAM V, 40 000 FEET ENROUTE NEW YORK TO DURBAN, SOUTH AFRICA, TUESDAY

"Gregori, darling, I'm glad you called. We have a problem, your man overstepped the mark and killed my girl." The well-dressed lady, in a short white mini skirt and matching blouse with a pair of perfectly sized man-made breasts, straining at the fabric, was speaking into her blue tooth headset in perfect Russian, reclining back slightly in her deep white leather seat in the passenger cabin of her Gulfstream V private jet. As she reclined back listening to the caller's reply, her white mini skirt slipped further up her long well-toned even sun-tanned legs. "He's your man, my dear, but he seems to lose control occasionally. This is the second girl of mine he's killed. You owe me!" The beautiful woman laughed out loud, a deep, husky, sensual laugh, and taking a sip of bubbling champagne from a fine-cut crystal flute champagne glass, replied, "Not my problem, darling, that he's disappeared with what he was sent to steal for you. My girl was supposed to keep the target busy and preoccupied while your man did the job. Your man has caused enough trouble for me. If the police trace Lee Anne back to me, I'll have a police investigation to clear up, that'll cost me dearly in calling in favours," the goddess explained keeping her voice even.

After speaking for another couple of minutes, she ended the conversation. Turning in her comfortable leather chair, she turned to her companion in the cabin, a long raven-haired brunette of perfect proportions, saying, "This is really messed up, he's gone too far this time. He could expose me." Her clients and staff knew her as Sable. She was an enigma, a beautiful siren who, with her just as beautiful string of consorts, seemed to appear overnight in the most affluent cities of the world, London, Washington, New York, and Cape Town, catering for the sexual pleasures and whims, the deepest, darkest sexual desires of both men and women, for those who could afford it. As in most societies, those with the most money to spend on exploring their unlimited sexual appetites and fantasies were normally those with the power to go with it. The distinction between the ones with power and the ones with money always seemed to blur. The women and men who worked for Sable were both beautiful and of above-average-intelligent, able to hold an ongoing intelligent conversation on the pros and cons of an interest rate hike, while the next minute turning on their sexual charms that would leave their partner squirming in pre-sexual ecstasy, shivering with anticipation of what was to come. No one knew her real name, or how old she was, or anything personal about her. That's how she liked it. In her business of information gathering and prostitution, it was better that way, the fewer people knew about her personally the better.

Pressing a button on the inlaid control panel on the right-hand side of her seat that connected her with the cockpit she asked, "Captain, how long until we land in Durban?" "Ma'am, another three hours," the pilot replied with a German accent. "Perfect," she replied smiling, showing perfect white, evenly spaced teeth. "Let me know when we're 30 minutes out, until then don't disturb us." Turning her deep pile leather executive seat around to face her companion she opened her perfectly proportioned legs exposing her expensive panty-clad vagina. "Come, eat me, I need to relax," she commanded. Her raven haired companioned smiled and licking her lips in anticipation slipped out of her executive leather seat onto her knees and placing her hands with intricately manicured fingernails on the inside of her lover's thighs lowered her mouth toward the white pair of panties, feeling her warmth and moistness as she ran the tip of her tongue up and down the gusset of the expensive silk French panties. Then, with the intricately manicured fingers of her right hand, she moved the panties aside, exposing her lover's pink, wet, sweet-smelling vagina, and her tongue dived right in. On the inside of her upper left thigh nestling just below her pouting outer labia was a small tattoo, a red and green rose.

CAPE TOWN MAIN POLICE STATION, MORNING MEETING, 08H30, TUESDAY

Detective Joint rushed into the meeting room and abruptly stated, "We need to relook at my sister's murder. The clues to this case lie with Samantha's murder." His colleagues stared at him as if he was mad and the captain asked him to explain himself. Turning to the captain, Detective Joint reasoned, "How many of exactly the same tattoos like what we've seen on both my sister and the dead female are in exactly the same position and they get killed literally the same way, albeit 3 years apart?" There has to be a connection." "Please sit-down, Detective, sit down. Detective Lindiwe was just about to explain a similar theory to us but from a different angle," the captain instructed him harshly.

Once Detective Joint had taken his seat, Detective Lindiwe stood up and, looking directly at Joint, started to explain. "As I was going through your sister's case file and the police reports something didn't seem right. Everything was too neat, everything was there, all the T's had been crossed and the I's dotted, but it all seemed too clinical to me, too perfect. Then, when I read the name of the investigating officer, a Detective van Rensburg, I remembered overhearing his name being mentioned in a conversation my father was having with someone over the telephone a couple of years ago, something about him being a dirty cop, but no one had so far been able to prove it. My father was a police sergeant at the same police station at the time. The Durban Central police station was where the case was lodged and investigated, so I phoned him and asked him if he remembered the case. He retired soon after the murder happened but was around for about 6 months of the investigation prior to retiring." "What did he tell you?" rasped out Detective Joint impatiently, thinking, 'Why was this information never recorded?' "As I was saying," Detective

Lindiwe told them nonplussed, "my father confirmed that Detective van Rensburg was on the take, a dirty cop. He was smart, it was never proven beyond a reasonable doubt, but my father confirms that it was common knowledge among certain members of the station that he was dirty. My father clearly remembers when the murder occurred, Inspector van Rensburg personally asked for the case, actually demanded that he got it, even though he had an overflowing workload."

"A detective only asks for a case if he has a personal or underlying interest in it," Detective Pieters pointed out excitedly. "Correct," Detective Lindiwe nodded her dreadlock styled hair and carried on explaining. "I have contacted the Durban Central police station and requested all other information which they may still have on the murder, along with all the physical evidence collected at the scene to be sent to us. They promised me that it should all arrive here in the next day or so." "Good work, Lindiwe," Detective Joint told her. "If you need any help let me know." "Will do," she replied. "Where is van Rensburg now?" Detective Brant asked somewhat excitedly. "He's dead," Joint told him. "Apparently he was killed shortly afterwards in a gang land style hit, case is still open, no one's been charged." "Oh," replied Detective Brant, the wind apparently taken out of his sails.

"Ok guys, now here's the juicy bit," Detective Lindiwe said carrying on. "What my father also told me was that the guarding company at the time was a company called Executive Decisions. They had some evidence which Detective van Rensburg didn't even look at, said it wasn't necessary as it couldn't be used in court for some reason or the other. They were wasting his time," Detective Lindiwe explained to them. "Well then what are we waiting for, let's get hold of this material, why is it only coming to light now?" Detective Joint asked excitedly. He missed the look that the captain and Detective Brant exchanged between themselves. "Okay then," the captain said clearing his throat. "Follow up with them and see what they can tell us. Maybe there is something that we don't already know. I've got the top brass breathing down my neck on this case, we've got to make an arrest soon."

"Guys, there's another bit of information that came in late yesterday afternoon from the lab techs," Detective Jannie then told the team. "They found traces of the male victim's blood in the main bedroom shower." "Now that is interesting," Detective Joint muttered staring at Brant. "Your theory of a fucked-up *ménage à trois* is starting to bear fruit." Turning to the rest of the team he said excitedly, "What if it was a setup? What if the blonde was a honeytrap to distract the male victim while her partner breaks in and steals whatever they came to steal?" Stopping to take a deep breath, he continued, "When her associate killed the male victim she would have been covered in his blood. When we found her in the second bedroom, she was clean, so it stands to reason that she was the one who showered." "So, you're saying that she was still horny and went to fuck her associate before he surprised her and killed her as well?" Detective Pieter asked jokingly. "That's what it's starting to look like," Detective Joint replied grimly. "But, Arnie, if what you're proposing is true, and with the evidence linking your sister's murder to this one, your sister was also used by someone as a honeytrap," the captain mentioned as kindly as possible to Detective Joint, the same burning statement that was on the rest of the team's tongues. With a sad look on his face, Detective Joint replied, "Sadly, Captain, yes, that would be correct."

CHAPTER 6

KWAZULU-NATAL, KING SHAKA INTERNATIONAL AIRPORT, 14H30, TUESDAY

The Gulfstream V touched down at 14H30 and taxied straight to the private operator terminal. As soon as the pilot had shut down the engines and opened the main cabin door, Sable stood up and picking up her carry-on bag headed for the exit, her raven-haired companion following close behind her. "Thanks, Captain," Sable purred as she passed the youngish well-built Captain of her aircraft. "I'll be here for a day or so, then we have to be in Cape Town on Friday. Have the jet refuelled and ready, I'll be in touch." As she walked past him to the cabin door, he swore he could smell pussy. Then she was gone, her long well-proportioned legs a sight for sore eyes as she headed for the entrance doors to the Private Operator Terminal with their dedicated Passport Control and Customs desk, just a per functionary task that had to be completed.

A couple of minutes later, Sable and her companion were outside in the hot sultry tropical air of the South Coast, a light sweat starting to form in the valley between her breasts and in the small hollow of her evenly suntanned back. Waiting outside the main entrance was her ice white Panamera Porsche Turbo along with her driver and bodyguard Ian when she was in Durban. A couple of minutes later, they were both strapped into the luxurious rear sports seats with Ian behind the wheel. "Take us home, Ian," Sable instructed him wearily, the 16-hour flight and jet lag starting to kick in. "Yes, ma'am," Ian replied, and putting the Panamera into Drive headed for the airport exit and the N2.

Leaving the airport grounds, Ian turned the sports car South onto the N2, and sticking in the fast lane they passed the turnoff for the North Coast and Umhlanga Rocks a favourite playground for the rich and famous in South Africa. Keeping on the N2 they kept on heading south past the turnoff for Durban CBD itself and drove on for another 150 kilometres, the speedometer never under a 160km/h, the passive speed trap radar detector in the front grille of the vehicle seeking out the sneaky hidden cameras of the traffic police before they registered the low flying sports car. After crossing over the Umkomaas River, one of the navigable tidal rivers on the Natal south coast, just before the small seaside town of Umkomaas itself; named after the river, Ian slowed the sports car down and indicating left turned off the N2 onto a smaller road that ran parallel with the deep blue Indian Ocean, where surfable waves were forming and crashing down onto the golden sandy beach. Driving on a little further the landscape on the left gave way to large palatial properties sitting on acres of lush tropical landscaped gardens with the golden beach and deep blue warm Indian Ocean on their doorstep.

Slowing right down and turning left again, Ian guided the white Porsche into one of the driveways, the front of the property walled off by a large 12-foot white concrete wall with an electric fence and cameras spaced every 20 metres around the property. On both sides of the large white walls was a sign that read DREAMLAND. As they approached the large black wrought iron gates, the security guard on duty recognised the car and its occupants and remotely opened the gate from his secure gatehouse built into the 12-foot-high white wall. Driving through the tall black wrought iron gates onto the property, the driveway on either side was lined with tall tropical palm trees whose green fronds were gently swaying in the light sea breeze that was moving the heavy tropical scented air around. Beyond the palm trees were green immaculately kept landscaped gardens. Scattered around the property, out of view, were several armed guards. At the end of the driveway sat a large white Spanish style villa. Waiting in the shade under the Porte Couche, at the front entrance to the villa, was Sable's business manager, Ricardo Alvarez, a large muscular bald man who took care of all her business operations in South Africa.

The Spanish style villa was built in a large square U shape facing towards the beach and deep blue warm Indian Ocean. In the centre of the U was a large open courtyard with a water fountain as the main feature in the centre, styled on a village square of a small Spanish village. Planted around the courtyard and the fountain were a number of orange trees that provided additional shade as well sweet oranges when in blossom. The centre courtyard was accessible from every room on the ground floor and led onto a large veranda that overlooked a green, immaculately kept, landscaped tropical garden that led down to the golden sandy beach and ultimately the warm, deep blue Indian Ocean. To the left of the garden was a pool deck complete with a separate pool house that contained changing rooms, sauna, and an indoor as well as outdoor jacuzzi. "Ahh it's good to be home again," Sable exclaimed as she walked through the cool double volume entrance hall and out into the centre courtyard. She owned properties all over the world, but DREAMLAND was one of her favourites. "I'm going for a surf," declared Sable's raven-haired companion. "Okay, Debs, I have a lot to discuss with Ricardo, I'll see you later," Sable purred to her lover in acknowledgement. Turning back to her manager Sable told him, "Give me half an hour to freshen up and I'll meet you on the terrace."

NATAL SOUTH COAST, DREAMLAND, 17H00, TUESDAY

True to her words, exactly thirty minutes later, after having a quick shower and now wearing a white loose flowing dress and simple white sandals, Sable walked out onto the covered terrace to the right of the main courtyard, the exotic smell of her perfume wafting around her. Ricardo was waiting for her and stood up as she appeared. "Sit down," she told gesturing to him with a perfectly sculptured hand. Once seated, a maid mysteriously appeared as if out of nowhere, asking, "ma'am can I get you something to drink?" "Yes, please, my dear, do we still have a chilled bottle of Chenin Blanc?" Sable asked her. "Yes, ma'am," the maid immediately replied. "Bring me a chilled glass then," she requested and dismissed the girl. The maid knew better than to offer Ricardo anything to drink. He was also a staff member, and staff didn't drink with Sable unless she invited them to.

"You realise that we have a problem if the police trace Lee Anne back to us?" Sable explained to Ricardo as the maid disappeared back inside. He nodded his smooth-shaven head and replied, "Yes, I heard on the news about the murder, and then, when Lee Anne didn't return, I put two and two together." "Who else knows she was doing a job for us in Cape Town?" Sable then posed the question to Ricardo. Staring out to sea for a couple of seconds, watching his employer's lover carve up the waves on her surfboard, he replied, "Only the three of us: you, me, and Grigori. The rest of the girls had no idea that she was working for us. She flew to Cape Town on a commercial flight using a false name and took a taxi to get to the hotel. There's no connection back to us." Breathing out a deep sigh of relief Sable replied, "Well then, there's no need to act irrationally if she can't be traced back to us, is there?" "Uh, no, I suppose not," he replied and then added, "if need be, we can have the guys in Cape Town sniff around for us." Looking closely at him she asked again, "Are you sure that she had no contact with the girls in Cape Town?" "No," Ricardo replied emphatically. "Okay let's hold back on taking more drastic action, maybe we're lucky, we didn't have to last time when the courier killed our last girl," she replied with a grim look on her face. "Remember last time it happened locally, and we, fortunately, had a detective and his merry men we were able to steer in the direction we wanted them to look." Ricardo reminded her.

With a slight shudder, Sable cast her mind back three years ago to poor Samantha, who was murdered by the Courier undertaking a similar job of distracting the target to allow the Courier to break in and steal the merchandise. Again, it was her client Grigori's plan, his meticulous planning. She was just supplying the honeytrap, supplying the decoy to distract the target while his psychopathic employee did the rest. For that job she'd used Samantha, a girl relatively new to Durban who apparently grew up in Cape Town, a girl so far unknown to the high society circles and scenes in the city. "We never did find out why he killed her," Ricardo pointed out. "No, we didn't, did we?" Sable replied absently.

Sitting on the ground floor veranda, watching her lover surf, she thought about what had happened this time. This time round Grigori had come to her with a similar demand. Get a distraction close enough to his target, Mark Bings, to allow his man he referred to as the Courier to break in and steal a very specific item while the target was distracted. Somehow her client had found the target's weakness, the chink in his armour. Mark Bings liked fucking women other than his wife and having that piece of information made it very easy for her to go ahead and plant Lee Anne a gorgeously stunning blonde of perfect proportions in his sights.

Once the target was hooked, a date had been set up. It had been easy. Too easy for that matter. The idea was that while she was giving the target the screwing of his life, the courier was supposed to have entered the penthouse and stolen the item of interest. "Do we know what the client wanted to obtain?" Ricardo asked her breaking her daydreaming. "Yes, apparently it was a black metallic box, a little larger than a cigarette packet that the target referred to as his prototype," Sable explained. "A prototype for what?" Ricardo asked posing the question that had been in the back of her mind once she'd heard that Lee Anne had been killed. "That is the burning question," Sable answered ruefully.

The maid reappeared on the deck with a glass of chilled Chenin Blanc. "Thank you," Sable said to her with a smile on her face. "Pardon me, ma'am, but Chef has asked if you and Miss Debbie will be eating in tonight," she asked referring to Sable's raven-haired lover. Thinking for a second Sable replied, "Yes. Please, tell Chef we will." "Perfect, ma'am," the maid replied with a small curtsy and then said, "the chef then instructed me to tell you that he has got a freshly caught yellowtail. Would you like that or prefer a dish with red meat?" "Mmmmh," Sable replied sensually, "let's go with the fish. Chef knows how I like it." "Yes, ma'am, certainly," the maid replied and hurried away.

Taking a sip of the chilled semi-sweet white wine, Sable told her manager, "Would you believe it that not only did the courier kill Lee Anne but he's also double-crossed Grigori himself and disappeared with the Prototype?" Grinning, Ricardo replied, "Well, I never, this courier is a real badass guy to have the balls to cross Grigori," "You can say that again," Sable replied, shivering slightly at the thought while taking another sip of her chilled semi-sweet white wine.

Sable sat there for a couple of minutes watching her lover casually and easily carve up the waves of the Indian Ocean as they formed and then crashed down on the beach soon thereafter. The more she watched her lover, the more aroused she could feel herself getting. 'Wow, this wine is loosening me up,' she thought to herself. "She could have gone professional; did you know that?" Sable mentioned absently to Ricardo. "No, I didn't," he replied. Clamping her thighs tightly together and putting the thoughts of Debbie out of her mind she got back to business.

"So, tell me," Sable asked Ricardo getting back to business, "are we all set for Friday and Saturday?" "Yes, ma'am," Ricardo replied almost immediately expecting the questions. "All invitations for Friday evening have been sent out and everyone invited has indicated that they will be attending." "Wonderful!" Sable exclaimed excitedly, reaching for her wine glass. It wasn't often that an invitation to one of Sable's parties was turned down. "And Saturday?" she then asked. Ricardo nodded his head replying, "The meeting has been set up and confirmed. You'll be watching SA take on the Wallabies at Loftus where the client representative will meet with you," Ricardo told her with a smile on his face. "Perfect," Sable purred. Then she instructed, "Give me an update on my business activities in South Africa." Ricardo cleared his throat and began to give his boss an update. It was completely dark by the time that he had finished speaking, her business interests were numerous.

CHAPTER 7

CAPE TOWN, V&A WATERFRONT, THE ONE&ONLY HOTEL, 09H30 - WEDNESDAY

The Bombardier Global 6000 of Executive Decisions arrived back at Cape Town International Airport a little after 09H30 in the morning and taxied straight to the designated parking bay in front of the Private Operator Terminal. "Thanks, guys, sweet landing," Nick told the flight deck crew as he exited the aircraft. Slipping his Ray Ban Aviator style sunglasses onto his very suntanned face now devoid of salt or a couple of days beard growth; he'd used the onboard shower facility of the aircraft to clean up, and swopping the bright yellow Musto & Hyde deep ocean sailing gear for a charcoal grey Pierre Cardin light summer suit he walked down the aircraft steps with his black leather carryon bag slung casually over his left shoulder, his right arm ready for use, a habit he couldn't drop from his old army days.

Reaching the Passport Control point the guard on duty looked up and smiled sadly at Nick, recognising him as a regular traveller saying, "Good morning Mr Scott, welcome back to South Africa," as he accepted Nick's passport and stamped it. "Thank you, Joseph. Sorry for my asking but why do you look so sad today? Normally you're happy," Nick asked concerned. "Ah, sir, my son lost his job, the security company he was working for had to close, the boss was a crook, and now he is out of work." Looking closely at the immigration official, Nick said, "Tell you what, here's my business card," pulling a card from his rawhide wallet and giving it to the guard. "If he's anything like you, he's exactly the kind of stuff I'm looking for. Tell him to phone and ask for my secretary, Julie. What's his name?" "Solomon, sir, Solomon Mhlangu," the guard answered handing Nick'spassport back. "Thank you, Mr

Scott sir," the guard told him humbly. "No problem, I'll always help where I can," Nick replied with a big smile on his face and taking his passport back headed through the small terminal building to the exit where the driver in the Mercedes S350 was waiting for him. "Good morning, Boss," the driver and close protection officer named Pete said, taking his bag and stowing it in the trunk. "Where to this morning, boss?" he asked. "The One&Only please Pete, as quick as you can," Nick replied to the driver.

Sitting with the remains of the morning traffic jam into Cape Town, Nick finally made it to the One&Only Hotel in the V&A Waterfront where Veronica Bings, was waiting for him in the breakfast restaurant on the ground floor. "Hi, Veronica. Again, my condolences. I'm so sorry for your loss," Nick said, kissing her on her proffered cheek before he sat down. "Thanks for dropping everything for me Nick, I didn't know who else to turn to," she gushed out, her voice starting to break. "Shhh, relax, calm down. Let's order breakfast and you can tell me all about it. I'm famished, the last time I ate anything was quite a while ago, and then it was a dehydrated mush that you steam into an edible form," Nick explained to her. Veronica seemed to cheer up slightly at that and picked up a menu. "Okay," she said. "Let's order breakfast, and then I'll pack it all out to you." "Deal," Nick replied with a smile on his rugged suntanned face. After they had ordered breakfast and the smell of rich peculated coffee wafted over the table, after being poured into porcelain white coffee cups by an immaculately dressed waitress, Veronica took a sip of her coffee and started to speak.

"I'm not sure where to start," she began hesitantly. Smiling reassuringly at her, Nick replied, "Just start talking, if you lose me, I'll stop you and we can rewind." Veronica gave a small nervous laugh brightening up slightly and said, "Okay, here goes. Mark and I were having problems, his work was causing immense stress and pressure on him and he was snapping at me and the kids all the time and we were all snapping back aggravating the situation. Both Mark and I agreed that it would be best if I took myself and the kids to Mauritius for a while," she started to explain. "We own a beach house in the Blue Bay reserve," she added. "Nice," Nick commented with a smile on his face, remembering a holiday he'd taken not too long ago in Mauritius. "Anyway, I had no idea he was fucking some slut. I thought he was hard at work finishing his latest project," she said ,carrying on. Just then the waitress arrived with their breakfast. With his stomach rumbling asking if his throat had been cut Nick started to dig into his full English breakfast.

Listening to Veronica ramble on for a while about how the police had no leads and wouldn't tell her who the dead girl was, while he ate the really delicious breakfast, Nick decided that it was time to get to the point. "Okay, Veronica," he said to her after swallowing a mouthful of sautéed mushrooms with a hint of garlic and garden herbs, "how serious is it? This missing prototype, is it this invisible cloak? I remember Mark trying to explain it to me when I last saw him, about his 'Harry Potter Invisible Cloak' as he put it."

Slowly nodding her head Veronica confirmed his suspicions, "Yes Nick, that's it. He really did it. He got it to work, his 'Harry Potter cloak', as he put it. He was able to work on systems and do maintenance work on the Virtual Reality systems themselves without other Virtual Reality users seeing him. His prototype would save Virtual Reality hosting companies millions of Rands, Dollars, Pounds, whatever, by not having to shut down their sites to do maintenance work or redirect users elsewhere while doing maintenance work. It could all be done in the foreground while the site ran as usual," she explained. Nodding his head, understanding what she was saying, Nick interjected, "The problem being that the Prototype can also be used by individuals or dodgy governments for nefarious means without being caught." "Yes, thank god you understand," Veronica replied, relieved. She reached across the table and grabbed hold of his arm saying, "I'm afraid Nick, very afraid. It also had another application whereby security system installers for large CCTV Systems could use it to step into the camera via Virtual Reality and set it up for optimal view." Nick nodded his head understanding what a headache it was to set up large CCTV systems that sometimes could run into two or three hundred cameras, sometimes more, sometimes spread all over the world if the company was a multi-national. At present, you required physical access to a camera to set it up and focus it. If you could do it via Virtual Reality, it would save time and money to companies all across the world. Operators could also use the system to do fault finding before calling out a service technician to fix a simple fault.

Carrying on, Veronica explained further to Nick, "He showed me the software Nick, it wasn't yet loaded into the Prototype and tested with the system as a whole, but Mark ran his code on the Royale Grace's camera system." With a small smile on her immaculately made-up face as she remembered, she explained, "We were seeing exactly what the camera was seeing. We were the camera, and what's more frightening is that on doing play-back of the Hotel's recording system there was no hint of us ever being there, nor did the security guard monitoring the system pick us up." Nick sat back, stunned, and then said, "So one can walk into any IP based camera system and look at whatever you want to without being seen or caught?" The pretty blonde-haired widow just nodded her head. Taking a sip of her now very cold coffee, she told him, "If this prototype is used to do harm, even though Mark is a complete bastard, I don't want his name dragged through the mud and associated with the type of evil and chaos it would create if it fell into the wrong hands. I have his children to protect." "I understand," Nick assured her. "Nick, I want you to find who killed my husband and stole his prototype. When you find the Prototype, I want you to bring it and the designs back to me so that I can personally destroy it all, keeping the world safe from this type of electronic nightmare."

After listening to Veronica speak for another couple of minutes, Nick stopped her and asked, "You said that the hard disk drives and notes of Mark had also been stolen, do you know if he had any backups?" Veronica nodded her beautiful blonde head and added "Yes, he did backup to a cloud-based server, but I'm not too sure of his passwords." Flicking some curly blonde tendrils of hair out of her face, she explained, "He'd become paranoid lately and had started changing all our passwords and user codes in the penthouse." With a slight grin on his handsome suntanned face, Nick replied, "Don't worry about that, I'm sure we can find a way to bypass his security systems."

Executive Decisions was the first security company to invest heavily in cybersecurity and that was one of the services that they offered. With Steven, the head of his IT Department, a protégé of Bill Gates himself, Nick had a uber strong IT Department that was highly respected throughout the Security Industry. "Veronica, I'm going to get a lady called Nicky who works for me and whom I trust with my life to meet up with you here this afternoon. She'll ask you a whole bunch of questions about Mark's back-up protocols that I need you to answer as accurately as possible. This will all be verbally," Nick explained to her. "Oh, and another thing," Nick added. "Please tell your General Manager that when the police release the penthouse to lock it up and call me, I want my team to have a look before housekeeping starts cleaning up." Veronica nodded her head.

After waiting for the immaculately dressed waitress to clear the table and refill the coffee cups, Veronica said to Nick, "One last thing, I wasn't entirely honest with the detectives looking into the murder." "What do you mean?" Nick asked. "I lied when I told them that I didn't know what was stolen," Veronica explained to him. "We don't need the whole world knowing what Mark was working on, it'll create panic." "I understand," Nick replied sympathetically. "We'll cross that bridge when we get to it," he concluded.

EXECUTIVE DECISIONS OFFICES, 13H00, WEDNES-DAY

The Cape Town offices of Executive Decisions was a custom-designed and built building, built on a parcel of vacant land in Airport Industria, an industrial suburb adjacent to the Cape Town International Airport. From his corner office on the third floor, Nick was able to watch aircraft landing and taking off. The building was purpose-designed and built with two basement levels and four stories above ground, ground to third. The basements were not for cars but were for the secure facilities of the company. Basement B-1 housed secure boardrooms, as well as a drive-through cash in transit drop off point for Cash In Transit Vehicles, while Basement 2 housed the vaults, the Server Rooms and the space age control room that monitored alarms and CCTV systems throughout the country, along with an adjoining advanced space age Virtual Reality Suite.

Executive Decisions South Africa was a multi-disciplinary Security Company that not only offered guarding, armed response, and Cash in Transit solutions, they also offered all aspects of electronic security installations from alarm systems to access control, CCTV, and fire detection systems, amongst others. A complete menu of security services. The Cape Town offices also handled all the African Operations where they ran security and cash in transit services. They were also the first multi-disciplinary security company to invest heavily in cybersecurity and Virtual Reality, with the help of Mark Bings.

His team was waiting for him in one of the secure boardrooms on the B-1 Level. For the last couple of days ever since Nick had received the satellite call from a hysterical Veronica and subsequently made a call of his own, his special hand-picked team had been sniffing around in the background. "Thanks for waiting for me," Nick told the team as the heavy oak boardroom door closed behind him and the white noise background sound system was activated. At Nick's insistence all cellphones, laptops, and smart devices were left outside and all the usual secure network switches supplying the Secure Boardroom with Wi-Fi, Data, Voice, and Satellite feeds were cut off.

"Aren't you being a bit extreme?" William, his day to day business manager, who oversaw his massive operations, asked. "Yes," piped up Steven, his IT fundi and his IT Director. "It's a Digital

Fort Knox in these boardrooms." With a grim smile, Nick sat down and looked around the boardroom table at the people he regarded as his family, "Guys, what if I told you that it's not electronically safe anymore?" and began to bring his team up to date. "Fuck me," William blurted out when Nick had finished giving them the run-down. "So, your mate Mark developed this prototype that's like a Harry Potter Invisible cloak that he can roam around in the Virtual World and do what the fuck he wants? Now he's been killed, and the Prototype stolen?" he asked astounded. Nick nodded his head and said, "It gets better. There is apparently a function whereby the Virtual user can get inside an IP Camera network or smart phone network and become a voyeur." "Ah hell fuck no!" Steven added, never one to swear. "Now do you see why I have insisted that we keep this room sterile?" Nick asked his team.

"So boss, whatever electronic move we make, they'll have the ability to monitor us without us even knowing they're there," Nicky, Stevens assistant, and extremely intelligent computer pro-grammer, said. "Correct," Nick replied nodding his head, "but right now he or they for that matter do not know that we know that they've got the Prototype so there should be no reason for them to look in our direction, for now." "Nicky," Nick said car-rying on speaking, "I want you to go and have afternoon tea with the widow, Veronica Bings. She's staying at the One&Only in the V&A Waterfront. She says that her husband did backups to a cloud-based server. You know the drill, get as much information as possible and then we'll hack the cloud."

Turning to his IT Director Nick instructed him, "In the mean-time, until we have a better understanding about what we're deal-ing with, I want you to ensure that all our security systems within the building are isolated from the external networks. We can't, however, switch off any of our client monitoring networks or Vir-tual Servers. That will definitely raise alarm bells." Carrying on Nick said, "As soon as we know more about what we're dealing with we need to find a way to track it down and secure it. That is the instruction from Veronica Bings, she's hired us to find out who killed her husband, retrieve the Prototype and hand it back to her." "Perfect," Steven replied rubbing his hands together in anticipation, always looking forward to a challenge.

"Okay team, what have you found out so far?" Nicky answered his question, "Information is limited at this time, but what we do have is very interesting. We know that a Detective Joint has been appointed to run the case." "Where have I heard that name before?" Nick asked stopping her. Nodding her head with a smile Nicky replied, "Exactly, his sister, Samantha Joint, was murdered three years ago, basically the same way at the Wild Coast Sun." Nick remembered it extremely well.

Executive Decisions had and still did the guarding and cash in transit contract for the Wild Coast Sun, a hotel and casino complex on the Natal South Coast where she had been murdered. "We had some pretty decent video footage of that evening if I remember correctly," Nick stated. "Correct," Steven said confirming Nick's thought, "I believe that it was a Detective van Rensburg or someone who was in charge of the case, he wasn't interested in the footage due to a time discrepancy on two of the cameras." "Was the killer ever found?" Johan asked after having kept quiet up until this point. Steven shook his head. "No," he said. "So, it's possible that the killer struck again," Johan suggested.

After speaking for another couple of minutes, Nick stopped the conversation and said, "Okay going forward for the next 24 hours this is what we're going to do. Looking at Nicky he told her, "Tea with Mrs Bings to find out all we need to know about Mark's cloud back up." "On it, Boss," Nicky confirmed. "Steven, sort out our internal security networks and make sure that they're bullet proof. Also, get together all the information we have on the Samantha Joint murder and sent it to my Inbox." Turning to Johan and Eben he told them, "Take a drive into town and do a recce for me, see what buildings facing the street and the Grande Royale hotel have cameras, maybe we get lucky." "On our way, Boss," both Johan and Eben confirmed in unison.

CHAPTER 8

EXECUTIVE DECISIONS, 10H00, THURSDAY

Julia, Nick's secretary ushered Detective Joint into his office. "Nick, this is Detective Joint," Julia said, introducing the detective to Nick. Standing up and, smoothing the wrinkles out of his black Hugo Boss suit, he walked around to the front of his desk and extended his right fist; these days the shaking of hands was taboo. The detective reciprocated with his right fist. "How times are changing, eh, Detective?" Nick said to the middle-aged, grey-haired, overweight man standing in front of him. "Welcome, I was just about to phone you. Nick Scott, pleased to meet you. Please, come and take a seat," ushering the detective to a black leather lounge suite and matching black leather chairs placed around a glass coffee table in the one corner of the very large and exquisitely furnished office.

In one corner of the office adjacent to the leather lounge suite was a 1/40th scale model of *Exe Decisions 1,* built by the naval architect who had designed her for Nick. There were also several photographs mounted on the one wall leading up to the small executive lounge. The detective stopped and looked at the one; it showed Nick in full combat gear of the British Royal Marines standing in some dusty village. "You were a Major in the Royal Marines," he blurted out impressed. With an embarrassed looking smile, Nick replied, "Yes, a long time ago. Come, please, sit down."

Once they were seated and their coffee orders taken by Julia, Detective Joint started the conversation. "Excuse my curiosity, but what is that yacht for? It looks pretty high tech," he asked pointing to the model yacht. Nick gave the detective a big smile.

"She is high tech, Detective, she's my yacht *Exe Decisions 1* that I plan to race in the next single-handed alone around the world race, the Vendee Globe Challenge," Nick explained to the really interested Detective.

"I've read about that race, it's a pretty challenging race. You got to dig deep down to your core to complete. I remember reading somewhere that less than 100 competitors have ever completed the race," the detective replied, impressed. "Good luck." "Thanks," answered Nick. Then he asked, "You do much sailing?" "Me?" Detective Joint laughed pointing to his ample belly. "And on my police salary, can't afford it. My father used to own a day sailor many years ago when I was a kid and he used to take me and my sister sailing," the detective explained, his face lightening up at the happy memories of sailing with his father and sister.

His face clouded over again coming back to the present. "Getting down to business," Detective Joint said, "thank you for seeing me at such short notice." "No problem," the handsome middle-aged man with grey specks in his crew cut black hair replied. "Why were you going to phone me?" Detective Joint asked. "You first," Nick offered with a big smile on his face. Nodding his head, he began, "I understand that your company was the guarding company at the Wild Coast Sun Hotel and Casino, the night Samantha Joint was murdered," the detective stated. "Yes, Detective," Nick replied, "that is correct. I'm sorry for your loss." "Thank you," Detective Joint replied. Carrying on, the detective explained to him, "As you are most probably aware the case was never solved, and some new evidence has come to light in lieu of the recent murders, which I'm sure you've heard about." Nick nodded his head in confirmation.

Detective Joint said, "I understand that you had some video evidence that the Investigating officer at the time rejected for some or other reason?" "Yes," Nick replied, taking a sip of the coffee that Julia had silently brought into the office and placed on the coffee table next to both of them. "There is video footage spread over six cameras, however, there was a problem with one of the video recorders at the time and the time date stamp was different for two of the cameras as compared to the rest," Nick explained to the detective. "So, he wasn't even interested in the four that had the correct date time stamp?" Detective Joint asked amazed. Nick shook his head and said, "No, apparently not."

"I assume that you still have the video footage?" the detective asked, his heart starting to pound heavily in his chest in excitement. 'Finally, I might get a lead into Samantha's murder,' he thought excitedly to himself. "Naturally," Nick replied. "I'll get my IT department to make a copy for you. Would you like to see a preview now? "If I could, please," the detective replied eagerly. Standing up, Nick headed over to his desk and picking up a remote turned on a large 50," monitor on the wall adjacent to the small lounge. "Standby, here it comes," Nick said slaving his Apple Notebook to the monitor. "We have the video footage in their own self-executable files, so you'll see them one after the other," Nick explained. Detective Joint just sat there his heart beating furiously in his chest, his mouth going very dry. While he was taking a gulp of his coffee, the first video clip started playing. It showed a side view of what the detective assumed were drivers stopping at a vehicle entrance point and being issued a ticket before driving onto the premises. Nick confirmed his assessment when he said, "Covert camera at one of the Entrance Ticket Dispensers capturing driver details on entering the premises, here comes your sister's vehicle now."

It was early evening, Detective Joint deduced from the background view of a darkening sky. He saw the side of a vehicle drive up and stop and then there she was, alive again for a few fleeting seconds. His sister was laughing gaily at something funny the passenger apparently said as she turned to the ticket dispenser and pushed the button for the ticket, reached through the window with a slender hand to grab the ticket, and then drove away. "There's someone else in the car with her," the detective rasped out loudly.

"Correct," replied Nick from his desk as he opened the next clip. "Here's the next clip. Also, from the front entrance, it's a forensic camera facing the vehicles that was focussed to see as much of the inside of vehicles as possible."

Sitting on the comfortable black leather lounge suite, Detective Joint watched in anticipation as he saw a car approaching. As it came into the focal viewpoint of the forensic camera his blood ran ice cold. Sitting there in crystal clear view of the camera was his current partner, Detective Brant, in civilian clothes, sharing a joke and laughing with his sister. The angle of the camera showed that his right hand was placed comfortably high up on her left thigh. "What the fuck, I know that man!" Joint shouted out. "Did Detective van Rensburg see this footage?" he asked. "Yes," Nick replied. "Bastard," growled Joint angrily. By the end of the fifth video clip, Detective Joint was shaking with anger.

It was when Nick played the last video clip that Detective Joint completely lost it. It showed a general overview of the reception lobby of the hotel, looking across the busy area. In the picture, he clearly saw his sister walking across the lobby towards the elevator. In the background, a gentleman reading a newspaper lowered it and watched his sister. The colour drained completely from his face. "You son of a bitch!" Detective Joint shouted out when he saw the face of the gentleman reading the newspaper. It was his current captain, Captain Williamson.

Nick stood up from his desk and walked over to the small wet bar in the far corner of his office and selecting two crystal cut whisky glasses poured a tot of Glenlivet into both. Returning to the small executive lounge, he sat down opposite the detective and offered him the one glass. With shaking hands, the detective gratefully accepted the glass and threw the whisky back down his throat. It burned a delicious warm trail down his throat into his stomach. "Thank you, I needed that," he said putting the empty cut crystal glass back down on the coffee table a bit of colour returning to his face.

"You seem to know a number of people in the video clips, Detective," Nick stated to a visibly still very shaken Joint. "Yes, yes, huh, it seems I do. The man sitting next to my sister is my current partner, Detective Brant, and the man sitting in the lobby reading the newspaper is my current captain, Williamson!" "Bloody hell," Nick muttered under his breath. "So there was a cover-up, and I'll bet you what you want it's still happening," as he stood up and went to refill the cut crystal glasses. Returning Nick sat down and passed another shot of whisky to the detective. The second shot tasted better than the first. Detective Joint looked at Nick and said, "They must both be psychopaths, they can both sit down with me and propose all sorts of scenarios with regards to the death of my sister and what occurred, when all along they know exactly what happened or at least know more than what they're letting on."

"Have you any idea what your sister was doing at the Wild Coast Casino?" Nick asked gently, probing. Slowly, Detective Joint shook his head and replied, "No, there were a number of theories, but none make any sense, except one, and I'm glad that our parents aren't alive today to hear it." The detective paused a moment, took a deep breath, and continued, "She was a high-class prostitute." After saying it, admitting out loud what she was, he somehow felt a whole lot better.

Sitting in the comfortable leather armchair, Nick took a hard-long look at Detective Joint and realised that the detective was near breaking point. "Detective," Nick said speaking gently, "may I speak frankly to you?" and carried on without waiting for a reply. "I see that your sister's murder has really fucked you up, eating you inside. You haven't found closure yet. If you want an ear to listen to and advice, I suggest that you seek professional help, however, if you are also seeking closure as to who killed your sister, why and for what, I believe I can help you there. My friend was murdered the same way your sister was. From what you've just told me, it would seem that there is a conspiracy and or a cover-up with regards your sister's murder within the ranks of the SAP, and right now I'm sure you're wondering whom you can trust. Veronica Bings has commissioned my company to look into the murders, find out who murdered her husband and lover and retrieve the item which was stolen from the safe." "She knows what was stolen from the safe," the detective spat out angrily, not missing a beat. "Then why did she lie?" "To protect you, me, her husband's children, the world," Nick explained calmly. "I don't understand," replied Detective Joint, totally confused. "Detective, I'll tell you what, it's almost lunchtime and I need to eat. Come and have lunch with me and I'll explain the best I can, and show you after lunch," Nick proposed.

Feeling his stomach rumbling on the two shots of whisky he'd had and not much else since the previous evening, the detective nodded his head. "Agreed," he replied. "Great," Nick said, clapping his hands together and reaching across to the telephone on a side table adjacent to his leather armchair. "Julia, the good detective and I will be taking lunch in the Executive Boardroom," Nick confirmed to his secretary. Before ending the call, he said, "Please, make sure that Steven joins us for lunch at 12H30."

"Tell me," Detective Joint asked a little while later while they were waiting for the waiter to bring them lunch, "does anybody else know that you still have a copy of the video footage from my sister's murder?" "No, I don't believe so," Nick told the detective. "If I remember correctly, Detective van Rensburg initially asked for a copy and then later informed us that the footage couldn't be used, and we might as well start using the hard disk drives again." "I see," replied Detective Joint softly his mind working overtime.

"Detective, have you ever experienced the world of Virtual Reality before?" asked a geeky-looking man in glasses and long black unkept hair who had been introduced to the detective before lunch as Steven Bass, the head of the IT Department at Executive Decisions. "Uh, no," replied the detective. Steven looked at Nick and suggested, "Maybe I should take Detective Joint for a short tour of the World of Virtual Reality to put it more into perspective, and then you can explain the situation." "Good idea," Nick replied. "Let's finish lunch and get on with it then."

EXECUTIVE DECISIONS, BASEMENT LEVEL 2, VIR-TUAL REALITY SUITE, 13H00, THURSDAY

Sitting in the comfortable black leather chair in the quiet low ceiling soundproofed room with strategically placed downlighters offering soft illumination, the air kept at a constant 18 degrees, Detective Joint followed Steven's lead and slipped the mirrored glasses onto his ample unshaven face covering his eyes, after slipping a thick stainless steel bracelet over his left wrist. There was a moment of auditory and sensory blackness followed by a second of feeling like one was free-falling when the next second the lights came on and equilibrium was immediately re-established on all axis.

'Where am I?" Detective Joint heard himself ask as he looked around him. He could tell that he was on some kind of underground station, the concrete platform stretched out around him, the lighting not too bright or too dark. There was a damp smell about in the air. A set of round shaped tracks ran from left to right a couple of metres in front of him. "This is called a station module in the Virtual Reality world," he heard a man's voice beside him explain.

Turning to face the voice, the detective saw Steven, his guide. Seeing the concerned look on the detective's face, Steven continued to explain, "One enters and leaves the virtual world by way of a station module, like getting on and off the underground tube. This is our station module or platform where Executive Decision staff enter and exit the Virtual Reality world. If they can afford it a VR user has their own platform which can be customised, alternatively users' group together to share platforms."

As he explained to the bewildered detective how one entered and left the world of Virtual Reality, another couple of human forms materialised on the station platform in front of them. The next second a round cylindrical tube arrived without a sound on the tracks in front of them, and a door silently opened. Without paying the two of them any attention the newcomers entered the tube, the door closed sealing the occupants inside, and then sped away. "What the hell just happened?" spluttered Detective Joint hopelessly confused and getting agitated. "Relax, Detective, and take a deep breath," Steven calmly commanded. After the detective had taken a couple of deep breaths Steven said, "As I was saying, to enter the virtual world one uses what is described as a station module, where you can either summon a tube to take you somewhere specific in the world of Virtual Reality; basically the same as you typing the name of a website you want to look at into your search engine in the real world and viewing it on your PC screen, now you go to it and enter the site in the virtual world, or you use the escalator to enter the virtual world where you are now," Steven explained pointing to a set of escalators that the detective hadn't noticed yet to one side of the platform.

A set of automatic escalators led up and another set back down. Looking up, he saw that there was a gaping blackness at the top of the escalators. Taking a minute or so to look around and take in his surroundings the detective then said, "I take it that is the way back to reality?" pointing to a small door to the side of the escalators that had a sign saying EXIT above it. "Yup," Steven replied. "Also, if you look in the top left-hand corner of your vision, there is a drop-down menu which gives you access to your nano-computer and other functions. There's an exit tab there as well, that'll take you straight out of Virtual Reality," Steven explained. "For now don't worry about it, just follow me," and nodding his head towards the escalators started walking towards them. "Let me show you the world of Virtual Reality," and he stepped onto one of the steel steps and started heading up towards the black yawning rectangle above. Turning around, Steven grinned and shouted down, "Come on!" Hesitantly, Detective Joint took his first step forward; his first step in the world of virtual reality and then another, and then stepped onto the steel escalator steps and was whisked up.

Stepping off the top of the escalator the detective's senses were immediately overloaded with multi psychedelic colours and sounds. "Wow, what the hell," he stammered looking slowly around him, taking it all in. He was standing on an electronic sidewalk next to a wide electronic street, with buildings stretching away to the left and right and in front of him, massive high rises whose floors were lost high up in the night sky. On the streets below there were crowds of people milling around on foot, entering and leaving the buildings. Staring at the crowds, he noticed that not all looked normal, there were different forms and types of caricatures. Mickey Mouse, Minnie Mouse, pirates, body builders, WWE wrestlers, all types of different looking forms of representation. Looking closer, the detective saw that there were illuminated signs on the outside of most of the buildings advertising everything from clothing boutiques, music shops, superstores to bars and houses of pleasure to tattoo parlours to holiday resorts advertising everything from exotic island getaways to adventure rafting to sex holidays, the garishly lit neon signs throwing their psychedelic colours out into the night.There were shops and stores and boutiques of every size advertising and selling every imaginable item. "My god," muttered Detective Joint. Interspersed between the neon signs were other shops and buildings, some big, some small, some looking like citadels. Everywhere there were what looked like armed centurions striding around on the sidewalk in the street and in the air above. Some buildings looked more friendly and inviting than others.

"Every on line server, computer, and smart device that makes up the internet is found somewhere in the Virtual World," the detective heard Steven explaining to him. "It's just a difference of how the computer owner, or sometimes the computer itself decides to represent themselves in the VR world." Remembering the rather short briefing he'd been given before slipping on the Virtual Reality bracelet and glasses Detective Joint exclaimed, "So, rather than sitting in front of a PC surfing the internet, I can now immerse myself in the internet in the world of Virtual Reality." "Correct," Steven answered beside him nodding his head in agreement. "All one needs is a Wi-Fi router with an Internet connection and the Virtual Reality kit. It's as simple as that." "Oh, and a comfortable chair to sit in," he added with a grin.

"Follow me, I want to show you something," Steven then told him and walked a couple of metres down the electronic street. The detective followed Steven into a Travel agency. "Want to feel what a holiday in Mauritius would be like? Put your hand over there," Steven asked him with a grin on his face, pointing to a palm reader on the counter. "Okay," replied the detective intrigued, "I've never been to Mauritius before." He placed his left hand over the palm reader, and then the next second without warning he was standing on a white sandy beach, the soles of his bare feet sinking down into the warm white sand. Without prompting his toes started to curl and squirm their way into the sand. The sun was a large bright hot ball of fire above him in the azure blue tropical sky. The hot humid tropical air was made bearable by the constant steady slow south-easterly trade wind that blew lazily moving the hot humid air around. In front of him was a large turquoise blue lagoon that stretched away out of the periphery of his vision, stretching from left to right. In the distance, he judged about a thousand metres distance he could see the breakers pounding on the rocks of the outer reaches of the lagoon. There were people wading and swimming in the water in front of him. On the white-hot sandy beach surrounding him were permanent beach umbrellas built into the sand, clad with palm fronds around and under which sun loungers lay scattered, occupied by bronze tanning bodies of both males and females alike. "This is one of the beach resorts on the east coast of Mauritius," Steven explained to the detective. "My word," exclaimed Detective Joint, "so this is what I would experience if I took a holiday to Mauritius?" "Yes," confirmed Steven with a definitive nod of his head.

"Come, let's carry on with the tour," Steven then said, "follow me." And exiting the Travel Agent he turned left and walking a short distance across the wide sidewalk he strolled towards the entrance of a high-rise building that said EXECUTIVE DECISIONS over the front entrance. "This is our Virtual Headquarters," he explained walking past a large armed Centurion, who stopped and looked closely at both Steven and the large detective. "Who the hell are these guys?" Detective Joint asked curiously nodding towards the green-looking Centurion. Steven replied seriously, "They're called the Gate Keepers, they are the protectors, the anti-virus software that stops viruses and hackers from accessing our electronic data systems and networks. Throughout the world of Virtual Reality, all anti-virus software and security systems for computers have Gate Keepers that look like this lot." As if on cue just as Steven finished explaining there was a loud siren-like noise from the direction of the busy electronic street and a couple of metres away two of the Gate Keepers suddenly turned red and started shooting what looked like red bolts of energy at a number of quite normal-looking humans and caricatures. Stopping to watch the incident Steven explained what was happening to a very bewildered Detective. "Hackers," he told the detective, as the hackers withered away and disappeared under the onslaught of sustained energy fire from the two Gate Keepers. Once the threat disappeared, the Gate Keepers turned back green and continued to patrol.

"Follow me," Steven commanded and continued walking up the wide set of concrete-like steps to the main entrance doors of the Executive Decisions building. Walking inside they were confronted with a large triple volume foyer with an oversized half-moon shiny black space-age-looking reception desk in the middle of the floor flanked on both sides by waist-high pedestrian turnstiles with biometric access control readers on both sides. Behind this arrangement was a large lift lobby that looked like it was made from highly polished stainless steel. Walking up to the space age reception desk Detective Joint noticed for the first time a beautiful young woman sitting behind the desk working on a computer terminal who looked up as they approached.

"Good evening, Steven, how can I help you?" she greeted him with a wide smile showing her perfect white even teeth, the perfect smile. "Good evening, Bianca," Steven replied. "I require visitor access for Detective Joint linked to my access profile." "Certainly, Steven," Bianca answered still with a wide smile on her flawless face. Turning to Detective Joint, she asked, "Good evening, Detective Joint, how are you this evening?" "Fine, why thank you for asking," he replied. "I think it's the little things in life that count, like a smile and being courteous," she told him pleasantly. "Please, place your preferred hand on the scanner, Detective," Bianca instructed him. Miraculously, a biometric scanner pad appeared to morph out of the surface of the black space-age-looking reception desk. Tentatively the detective placed his right hand onto the shiny surface. It was surprisingly cool to the touch. "Thank you, Detective Joint, access authorised, you may proceed. Enjoy the rest of your evening," Bianca confirmed a couple of seconds later, again with a large smile on her pretty face.

Following Steven's lead, the detective placed his right hand on the biometric scanner on one of the waist-high pedestrian turnstiles. The glass barrier dropped down and he crossed over towards the shiny stainless-steel lift lobby. "Bianca is an AI computer; you were aware of that?" Steven informed him with a grin on his face. "Huh?" Detective Joint grunted looking surprised, "Sorry for my ignorance, but what the hell is AI?" he then asked. Without laughing or mocking him Steven replied, "Artificial Intelligence."

Just then the lift arrived, and Steven said, "Follow me," and he stepped into the waiting lift. "You mean that beautiful lady I saw sitting behind that desk who held a conversation with me is a computer?" Detective Joint stated incredulously. "Yip," Steven confirmed as he entered the floor he wanted on a keypad. Floor 100. With the same feeling that one gets when riding in a high-speed lift, Detective Joint had the same feeling of leaving his ample stomach behind as the lift shot upwards. What seemed like only a couple of seconds, the lift stopped, and the doors opened depositing them out into the lift lobby on the 100th floor.

Without hesitation Steven stepped out of the lift into the lift lobby, the detective feeling as if in a dream followed. "Is this a joke?" Detective Joint asked incredulously looking at the lift lobby sign. "There is no building with a hundred floors anywhere in the country!" With a slight smile Steven replied, "Correct, Detective, but this is Virtual Reality. In the Virtual Reality world if you can conceptualize something you can make it happen. Come, this is what I need to show you," as he placed his one finger onto a biometric scanner on the wall and the lift lobby door automatically opened into the building proper.

Following Steven through the now open-door, Detective Joint found himself on a glass dome-like observation deck. Looking out as far as the eye could see were hundreds of thousands of clusters of lights of different shades, and intensities that depicted similar buildings to the ones on the street below and the one he was currently inside. Some of the lights were flashing, some solid. Some were far apart with large blank spots of darkness between them, others closer together. Looking closer, he saw that all the clusters were connected by what looked like roads of light, with different colours of lights flashing past in the blink of an eye. The view was the same as he walked around the observation deck in total amazement. "All those lights represent servers, computers, and smart devices in the Virtual World that are connected to the Internet. The light streams you see running between them is the information highway and data flowing between them, as well as users interacting." "Wow," was all Detective Joint could say.

Pointing to a rather large cluster of lights on the distant horizon in front of them, Steven said, "Over there, for example, is the country's Energy Supplier, Eskom, and that's their Nuclear Power Plant over there, and the lights over there is another of their power stations." Pointing to another large cluster of lights depicting another large building he said, "And those lights over there are one of the local cellphone operators. Look closely at that cellphone operator, do you see those red flashes?" Steven asked the detective pointing at the tall skyscraper in the near distance. "Yes," replied Detective Joint, enthralled by the view. It reminded him of a picture he'd once seen of New York at night, but on a much larger grander scale. "Care to guess what they are?" Steven then suggested. "Gate Keepers attacking hackers and other non-desirables," ventured the detective. "Well done, Detective," said Steven congratulating him. Carrying on, he said, "If you look closely at most of the big companies, you'll see exactly the same thing, Gate Keepers working overtime to protect systems from hackers and their viruses." Pointing in another direction he said, "Government sites and networks aren't safe from attacks either."

CHAPTER 9

JAPAN, TOKYO, (+7 HOURS) 20H00, THURSDAY

It was night time in Hong Kong and the apartment was in darkness, save for a single low wattage light bulb in a lamp that burned dimly in the corner on a low table. The flat was one among a thousand of similar living quarters in several similar-looking high-rise apartment blocks in Tokyo, Japan. The apartment block had high-speed internet access and that's what the killer was counting on. He'd taken out the lease through a number of front companies a while ago in anticipation for this moment. 'I refuse to be Grigori's bitch anymore, at his call day and night, kill this one, steal that item. No more,' the killer thought silently to himself, the sounds from the busy street below softly reaching up to him in the high-rise apartment.

Being careful; as his ex-employer had spies all over the world, it had taken him a couple of days to get back to his home city, where he felt safe, where he could blend into the local population in order to carry out the next part of his plan. 'Pity I had to leave my katana behind,' he thought, 'hiding it in the roof space of the Royale Grace above the penthouse'. He'd entered South Africa via a private charter flight courtesy of Grigori, and he'd been able to bring his katana in without any problems.

On stepping outside the airport terminal he'd changed his disguise and name like a chameleon. On completion, he was supposed to have headed back to the airport with the Prototype in his possession and a waiting charter flight. Instead, he'd double-crossed Grigori and stolen the Prototype for himself. That was always his plan, once he'd overheard his employer talking about it. "I have it on good authority that the Prototype is busy being designed and built. We have around a 3-month window before it will be ready for testing," he had overheard his employer saying on the phone. From that moment on he started putting a plan together, realising that the Prototype could be his ticket to financial freedom. His only regret was that he had to leave the katana behind. There was no way they would allow it on board a commercial flight as hand luggage and it would definitely raise alarm bells that Grigori and his spies would pick up if he tried to charter a private jet. They would be on him like a pack of dogs seeking revenge.

Shrugging the loss of the katana aside the killer thought, 'I first need to make sure that this device works correctly.' According to his most recent employer, the victim had finished the Prototype, but to play it safe he'd taken the victim's hard disk drives and all the notes that he could find in the study with him. 'Pity about Lee Anne,' he thought to himself sitting in the almost dark apartment, feeling his scrotum contract in his pants at the thought of her. They'd done a few jobs together and he'd always had a desire for her, but he'd managed to keep it professional. 'But seeing her moaning on her hands and knees being fucked in her tight pert little arse was too much for me and I had to have her. And she wanted me too,' he thought smiling as he remembered how she moaned as he had plundered her tight back passage in the adjoining bedroom. 'Pity I had to kill her, but this time round she would definitely have been a loose end,' the killer thought remorsefully.

Standing up, he walked across the small apartment to the only access, the front door, and made sure that his advanced monitoring system and covert CCTV system were working correctly before confirming that the door was locked and bolted. A couple of months ago, in the dead of night, he had secretly mounted a small high-resolution camera head into the frame of his apartment door, looking down the passageway towards the only access onto the floor. The camera was slaved to a i7 PC inside the apartment running CCTV analytical, facial, and behavioural recognition software. Over time, the camera and software had recorded the comings and goings of all the residents on the floor. Once armed should it detect a person it did not recognise or persons acting in an unprecedented manner, it would send a signal to the alarm system which was slaved to his thick stainless-steel wrist band that would warn him in the virtual world.

The thick stainless-steel wrist band was the VR Users nano-computer and link to the World of Virtual Reality, and using one of the spare inputs on the bracelet he was able to trigger an alarm in his subconsciousness should the CCTV system detect anything unusual or heavens forbid the door to be opened. The big problem for the killer was that while he was in Virtual Reality his human body was defenceless from real-world attacks. If his human body was killed or captured there was nothing he could do from the Virtual World. 'If they break in, I'm fucked,' he thought to himself, 'but at least I'll have about 30 seconds warning, it'll have to do for now.' Walking back towards the table and chair at the far end of the apartment the killer kept thinking, 'I really need to find someone to help me, someone I can trust, who can guard me while I'm in Virtual Reality.'

Shrugging his thoughts aside, he said to himself, "Well, let's get down to business and test this prototype." Then he looked at the black metal box a little bit bigger than a box of cigarettes on the table in front of him in the dim light. The box was charged using a standard cellphone charger and slaved via a Bluetooth connection to the standard VR kit. Switching on the black box via a small on-off switch on the side, he clipped the heavy thick-set stainless-steel bracelet over his left wrist and slipped on the wireless VR glasses. There was the usual moment of auditory and sensory blackness followed by a second of feeling like he was free-falling when the lights came on and equilibrium was immediately re-established on all axis. He found himself standing on his private platform, his jump-off point into the world of Virtual Reality.

The platform was one of over a million other like platforms in Virtual Reality routed through so many servers he was literally lost in the ether. Something about him felt different this time. He felt more alive as if charged with energy. Looking at his hands and arms and then his torso, he realised what it was. He was encased in some kind of black body sheath. Then he noticed the drop-down menu in the top left-hand corner of his view. 'Now this is interesting,' he thought and with his left index finger touched the drop-down tab. Immediately, another screen with green print out was superimposed over the view of his platform. 'Wow,' he thought reading the drop-down menu options.

MENU OPTION

– MAINTENANCE CLOAKED

– MAINTENANCE UNCLOAKED

– CAMERA SETUP CLOAKED

– CAMERA SETUP UNCLOAKED

'Let's try Maintenance Cloaked,' he thought with a grin on his face and with his left index finger touched the Maintenance Cloaked option. Immediately there was a subtle change to the sheath and his body disappeared in front of his eye's. "Wow," the killer muttered out loud to himself and headed for the escalators up to the street above that was a busy Virtual Reality street in Tokyo his home city. This VR street was packed with thousands of VR users, data, Gate Keepers, and the likes all heading in different directions all on specific tasks and journeys through the world of the Internet via Virtual Reality.

'Right, let's see how this is going to work,' the killer thought silently as he headed directly towards a large corporate bank a short distance down the electronic street. 'I've no business being at this Tokyo bank.' Outside the bank were the bank's Gate Keepers all showing the colour green. Steeling himself for the pain of being shot at by electronic bolts and having to reset his VR connection, the killer headed straight for a pair of Gate Keepers. As he approached them, he veered away and kept walking straight for the bank entrance. The Gate Keepers stood still, showing their green neutral colour. 'It works!' he thought triumphantly to himself.

Entering the bank, he was able to roam around with no one paying him any attention whatsoever. Spending over an hour walking through the virtual bank no one stopped him or even looked in his general direction. He was able to look over the shoulders of employees working in virtual reality and walk into meeting rooms while virtual meetings were in progress without interrupting the meetings. 'Wow, Mark Bings, recently deceased, you've really outdone yourself with this prototype,' the killer thought triumphantly.

'Being a complete sexual pervert, amongst other things, I have another local test to try,' he then said to himself feeling the familiar tingle in his scrotum as he walked out of the bank. Again, the Gate Keepers paid him no attention as he walked out and passed by right next to them. Turning right he walked down the electronic street, past thousands of other VR users. No one paid him any attention as he walked on by. Soon he came to the business of ill repute that he was looking for. There were no Gate Keepers outside, but the killer knew that in this VR establishment the owner ran some different software that he was keen to try the Prototype on. If he was a pervert then the owner of the VR house of ill repute was a sexual deviant who spied on his girls while they were working and sold the footage on the black market.

'It's amazing,' thought the killer as he walked inside, still in Maintenance Cloaked mode. 'With the advent of all these new killer bugs and flu that spread like wildfire across the world and how social distancing is becoming the norm, the world of Virtual Reality is booming, and a mind fuck these days is quite literally a mind fuck.' Walking inside past the AI bouncer who looked a lot like The Rock from WWE Wrestling the killer walked into the bar, where there were a number of Japanese and Oriental looking ladies of the night sitting at the bar on bar stools in various stages of undress. 'God, they look so real I could fuck them all,' he thought looking carefully around.

Walking past the ladies of the night, unnoticed, he found the small office he was looking for at the back of the bar. 'Ah the CCTV recording system,' he thought silently as he entered the room. Cueing the drop-down tab with his left index finger he thought 'Okay here goes, let's change to Camera set up cloaked.' Instantly his view changed. Now, in front of him, he had thirty-two smaller screens; depicting all the cameras installed in the VR whore house. He found a view to watch and tapped his left index finger on the tile. There was a moment feeling of weightlessness then he was in the room looking at the bed from a side view.

The lighting was low. Lying on the queen size bed draped with red and black bed sheets was a lithe looking, naked Japanese lady. She was lying on her back with her long legs hooked behind her head while a male figure had his head buried between the black furry junction of her thighs eating her out. "Oh, oh, oh, oh," he heard the female form squeaking out loudly as the client worked earnestly between her legs bringing her to a shrieking juddering orgasm. As she orgasmed, she released her legs from behind her neck and wrapped them tightly around the man's neck grinding her wet orgasming vagina into his face, his face starting to glisten wetly from her juices. The killer was enthralled and started to play around with the camera settings.

"Great," he said to himself, "I can zoom in, change the aperture settings, and do basically what I want." All the while he was keeping an eye out for the software security suite of the entrepreneur, that didn't materialise. 'Great the Prototype can fool his software, wonderful,' he thought. After watching and playing around for another couple of minutes he left the room and changed the Prototype back to Maintenance Cloaked and exited the CCTV system. A couple of minutes later he walked out of the VR whore house, the same way he had entered.

Back outside on the sidewalk with all the traffic milling about him and through him, he decided on one more test. However, where he wanted to go, he needed to take a tube so he headed back towards his private platform. A couple of minutes later, just as he was about to step onto a tube, the alarm system in his flat activated, triggered by the CCTV analytical software that was viewing a group of men bursting through the stairwell door and heading down the passage; triggering the spare input on the bracelet, a red warning sign flashing in front of his vision. "Oh fuck," he muttered to himself as he swiped the EXIT tab in the top left of his view for a quick exit, rather than walk through the door marked EXIT.

Coming out of Virtual Reality and regaining consciousness, he was just in time to reach under his chair where a Heckler & Kock 9mm automatic pistol was taped to the underside, as the wooden front door to his apartment was violently kicked in. Chambering a round while at the same time bringing the H&K sights to bear on the first assailant who stormed through the door with his companions right behind, he emptied the 19-round magazine into the door opening, the 9mm copper jacketed slugs ripping through skin and bone of the assailants with indifference. Reaching for a spare magazine he effortlessly reloaded the H&K and stealthily worked his way to the door. Another assailant burst into the room and the killer dispatched him with equal impunity.

Quickly grabbing his bag and VR equipment he rushed out of the flat. 'Gotta get out of here quickly,' he thought as he stepped over the bodies of the dead men as his neighbours started to come out of their apartments to see what all the noise was about. 'Fuck, it is Gregory's men,' he thought as he recognised a couple of the dead assailants. As the killer headed for the stairs he thought 'I definitely need someone to look after my back while I'm in VR.' His solution came to him as he reached the street and got lost in the sea of humanity, 'Nobody will expect me to go back to South Africa. I can run it all from there. I'll coerce that gorgeous bitch

Sable into helping me. I can always blackmail her. It'll be in her interests to help me,' the killer thought lightly to himself. Then smiling, he realised, 'I can collect my katana as well! Life is getting better by the minute.' He blended into the night-time pedestrian traffic that was almost as heavy as during the day.

EXECUTIVE DECISIONS, BASEMENT LEVEL 2, VIRTUAL REALITY SUITE, 17H00, THURSDAY

Gaining consciousness on the comfortable leather chair, Detective Joint was amazed at what he had just experienced. Looking around the room there were a number of Executive Decisions personnel sitting in similar executive chairs spread out around the Virtual Reality suite. "What are they doing?" he asked Steven curiously. Steven pointed to one group of men and women and explained, "That's our Cape Town marketing team, they're sitting in one of the boardrooms of our 100 storey VR office block having a meeting with the sales and marketing teams in Johannesburg and our other centres based throughout South Africa and Africa."

Pointing to another group of operators he went on, "They're part of our cyber warfare team who surf the Virtual World tracking down hackers and viruses." What Steven didn't tell the detective is that they also carried out specific anti-hacking operations vital to the security of corporates and governments alike. "Wow," the detective muttered. Then, getting back to the deal, he said, "I still want to know what was in the safe." Steven nodded his head, his unkept hair falling all over the place, "And so you shall, Nick's waiting for you in one of our secure boardrooms. Come, follow me." With that, Steven stood up and walked to the door of the Virtual Reality Suite.

The detective found Nick in one of the secure boardrooms one level up. Steven followed the detective into the small secure board room, first ensuring that all cellphones and smart devices were left outside. "Coffee all round?" Nick asked casually standing at the small sideboard where freshly brewed coffee was waiting in a coffee pot. A short while later they were all settled down around the boardroom table with a cup of coffee in front of them, the white noise system hissing away softly in the background, Nick started to speak.

"Detective, remember how I said earlier on that Veronica hadn't told you what was in the safe in order to protect you, me, her husband's children, and the world?" Nick asked. "Yes," Joint replied. "And bear in mind what you've just discovered with regards to your sister's untimely death and people within the police force." Taking a sip of coffee Nick carried on, "Mark Bings, a friend of mine was an extremely talented individual who invented a prototype that is like Harry Potter's Invisible Cloak, however, for Virtual Reality engineers and programmers."

The detective nodded his head and replied with a smile on his face, "But come on, gentlemen, what the hell, it's just Virtual Reality, it's not real." Both Nick and Steven nodded their heads and Nick agreed, "Correct, but remember: Virtual Reality is controlled by servers, computers, and software written by humans based in the real world and the virtual world is just another way for all users and computers to interact with each other. Every server, computer, smartphone or device which is linked to the World Wide Web is accessible in the virtual world as well." Steven added, "Virtual Reality is an extension of the Internet giving a user a more personal intense experience."

Steven then explained, "You saw how the Gate Keepers, the anti-virus software attacked hackers trying to gain access and how from the observation deck, for as far as the eye could see there were hacker attacks happening?" he asked. Detective Joint nodded his head slowly. Carrying on Steven told him, "You must remember, it's not just individual hackers and groups of hackers, it's also governments running cybercrime programs, the main culprits being China, North Korea, and Russia. In retaliation western countries, particularly the USA and their European allies, are running counter cyber operations and selective cyber-attacks

91

themselves. Detective, it's a war zone in cyberspace, and Virtual Reality is one aspect of it!"

"Imagine if the Gate Keepers and anti-virus software couldn't see the hackers. Can you imagine what would happen if the hacker could just walk straight past the Gate Keepers and all anti-virus or PC security protocols and gain access to whatever server or information database they wanted to?" Nick asked. The detective's face started to visibly pale when the ramifications started to sink in. "There would be chaos," he finally muttered.

"I rather like the word 'apocalyptic'," Steven added, grim-faced, "No electronic device would be safe, and that would include, satellites, aircraft, power stations, banks, food processing plants, the whole enchilada. Not even nuclear launch sites would be safe." "So, where do we go from here in order to keep the world safe?" Detective Joint asked curiously. Smiling Nick replied to him, "I'm glad you asked Detective, somehow it would seem that the deaths and the robbery are all somehow connected, all with a bit of a twist, your current partner Detective Brant and the captain being the twist."

Taking a sip of coffee, Nick sat back in his executive chair and intertwined his hands behind his head and thought for a while and then said, "Now we know why Detective van Rensburg suppressed the evidence and tried his all to get us to part with the hard disk drives barring issuing us with a court order. I suggest that you drop the bombshell that you've seen us, and we'll be sending you the video footage, we've got to find it first. That'll put the cat amongst the pigeons, and we can see what happens," Nick explained. Taking another sip of coffee, he carried on saying, "At the same time we'll start a private investigation and see where we get." "Perfect," Detective Joint replied with a grim smile on his face.

CHAPTER 10

It was hard not to want to lunge across the meeting room table and beat the living shit out of both the captain and his partner Detective Brant until they confessed all they knew about the murder of his sister, but Joint was old enough and wise enough to know that it only worked like that in Hollywood. No, after seeing the video clips yesterday, he realised that what had happened then and now was bigger than just the murder of his sister and two other persons. For some reason, she had been involved in something dangerous that had killed her.

There was something much bigger at play and he had decided to accept Nick's offer of help. He saw straight away that the resources of Executive Decisions were far wider and ran much deeper than anything the SAP could muster, anyway at present he didn't know who he could trust within the ranks of his SAP comrades, knowing that both Detective Brant and Captain Williamson were dirty. 'I just need to build an airtight case,' he told himself. He couldn't remember where he had once read that "unconventional situations call for unconventional means." 'At the time I didn't understand what that meant, but now I have a pretty good idea.' he thought silently to himself.

"Detective Lindiwe, has the evidence from Durban Central arrived yet?" the captain asked starting the meeting. Detective Lindiwe had a frustrated look on her face as she answered the question, "Negative, Captain, they tell me that they're still looking for it, they seem to have misplaced it." "Oh dear," the captain replied, not sounding upset at all. If Detective Joint hadn't been

93

intently studying the captain's face, he would have missed it, but a look of relief passed quickly across the man's face when he heard those words.

Turning towards him the captain then asked, "Detective Joint, did you find out anything from Executive Decisions that we don't already know about your sister's murder?" he asked as casually as possible. "No, sir, we seem to know what they know, not very much at all," he replied bitterly. Then, brightening up, he said, "but they did say they might still have copies of the CCTV footage that they sent to Detective van Rensburg on one of their archive servers." "What!" Detective Brant cried out over-excitedly, almost pushing his chair over, at the same time the captain's face fell. Inwardly, Detective Joint smiled, and he thought, 'On the way to catching you, you bastards!' "Yes," he replied brightly, "they say they'll make it a matter of urgency and get back to us asap. Juliet, I gave them your email address, they'll send whatever material they have straight to you." She nodded her head in acknowledgement. "Oh, yes," Detective Joint said carrying on enthusiastically, "I was also informed by Executive Decisions management that Veronica Bings has appointed them to run an independent investigation to find her husband's killer or killers."

The captain stood up without warning saying, "Carry on people, I've got another meeting to get to," and rushed for the door. Glancing at his partner across the table, Detective Joint saw Brant nervously toying with his pen while at the same time watching the captain leave the meeting room. 'Yes, you bastards start getting worried, because I'm going to find out the truth,' Detective Joint thought angrily to himself. With the captain gone, Detective Joint took over the morning meeting. "Okay, let's put my sister's murder on the back burner for now and wait until we have the information from Executive Decisions. I want us to concentrate on the current two murders." Looking at Juliet, he asked, "Any further feedback from the cellphone operator?" "Sorry, Arnold," Juliet told him. "The signal was bounced off of so many cellphone towers and between three different cellphone operators at the end of the day, all three of the operators asked me if I was pulling a joke on them and testing some new equipment when I asked them about it." "Damnit," muttered Detective Joint. Then he spoke up saying, "Well, one thing we have learnt about whoever phoned the call in, they're tech savvy to be able to pull off a move like that." "Add that to the killer profile: technologically advanced," Detective Joint instructed Juliet.

"What other new information do we have?" he then asked the team looking at the detectives one by one. Detective Pieter cleared his throat. and said, "Unfortunately not much. The tech guys looking at the side of the building came up empty handed. They report finding a couple of scuff marks, but that's all. The killer must have worn gloves and climbed up the side of the building like a monkey, or Spiderman." Carrying on, he told the rest of the team, "We're getting the CCTV servers from the lab a bit later to look through ourselves, but they've found nothing other than what we've already seen." Speaking on for a couple more minutes, Detective Joint said, "All right, then let's leave it there and carry on with following the threads we have at present. Remember all new information; pass it straight onto Juliet." Taking his time to pack up his notes, he saw Detective Brant literally run out of the meeting room.

Waiting until he was alone, he pulled out his cellphone and dialled a number he had pre-programmed yesterday afternoon. "It's done," was all Detective Joint said when the call was answered by an automatic call answering system. Then he hung up and walked back towards his office.

EXECUTIVE DECISIONS, B-1 SECURE BOARDROOM, 08H30, FRIDAY

"Morning all," Nick said greeting his team as he walked into the B-1 Secure Boardroom shortly after 08H10 the next morning. Sitting down at the boardroom table, once everyone had a fresh cup of coffee at hand, the door to the boardroom was shut and the white noise system activated, Nick got down to business. "As I'm sure you all heard and some of you were introduced to him, we had a visit from Detective Joint yesterday. They have linked the murder of Mark Bings and his girlfriend to that of Samantha Joint his sister who was murdered a couple of years ago."

"She was murdered at one of our client's sites, the Wild Coast Casino if I remember correctly," Johan added. "Correct," Nick told him. "Now here's the kicker, I showed him the video clips we got of his sister and the passenger in her car, remember up till now we never did identify who was in the car with her. He identified the passenger in a flash as his current partner, Detective Brant." "What!" all the occupants around the boardroom table shouted out and all starting to speak at the same time. "I knew it! Remember I told you something didn't feel right, especially when that detective said he couldn't use the video footage as evidence," Eben said excitedly to Johan.

Holding up his left-hand to quieten them down, Nick told them, "Wait. I haven't got to the best part yet." When silence was restored, he continued. "The detective also identified the gentleman in the one video clip sitting down reading the newspaper as that of his current captain, Captain Williamson." "What the fuck!" Nicky blurted out, not one prone to swearing. "Yup, it pretty much pushed him over the edge when he saw his current partner with his sister in her car and then his captain in the video footage. As we've always believed and said, there was a cover-up. Something went down that evening in the complex which we weren't aware of until housekeeping found Samantha Joint and her companion dead in the hotel room the following morning."

"With the revelation that both Brant and Captain Williamson could be crooked and on the take, I've offered him our resources to help him get to the bottom of his sister's murder," Nick explained to a rapt audience. Carrying on he explained further, "At the same time we're going to run a parallel operation and find the Prototype and killer of Mark Bings and his companion, as per

Veronica Bings' request." "Wow, pretty tall order," William muttered. "It is, but as always we'll make it happen," Nick said with total conviction looking at his small close-knit team. Turning to Johan, Nick said to him, "I want a surveillance team put onto our Detective Brant for a while and see what it reveals." Johan made a mental note and nodded his head.

Then, looking towards Nicky, he was about to ask if she got the information when he noticed that both herself and her boss Steven were still wearing the same clothes when last he'd seen them yesterday. "I take it that afternoon tea with Veronica Bings was successful?" he asked the two of them, his face brightening for the first time that morning. Steven looked at Nicky who gestured to him to take the floor, he cleared his throat and replied, "To some degree, yes, it was. It seems that Mrs Bings knows quite a bit about what her husband did and was able to point us in the right direction to his back up cloud server." "I sense a but coming in here somewhere," Nick butted in. "Uh-huh," Nicky answered, "there's over a terabyte of data, some of it heavily encrypted, some of it not, so it's going to take a bit of time to go through it all and see what we have." 'Okay, understood," Nick replied. "Drop everything else you were doing or were going to do and get the information we need, it's critical."

Turning to Johan and Eben, he asked, "Any luck with any neighbouring cameras around the hotel?" "Sorry, boss, there were two cameras that might have viewed something, but we were too late, the police had already done the rounds, they apparently viewed the footage and took the HDD's as evidence," Johan explained. "So, the cameras definitely picked up something," Nick mused. A thought flashed through Nick's mind and he said, "Give the names of the businesses to Steven and let's see if any of them did any offsite backups. Maybe we get lucky. There was a soft knock on the door to the secure boardroom and Julia, Nick's secretary entered. Heading directly over to Nick she bent down and whispered into his ear. Nick nodded his head and said, "Thanks, Julia."

Once Julia had left and the board room door closed again, Nick told them with a grin on his face, "The trap's been set. Detective Joint has mentioned to his team of detectives that we still have video footage of the night of Samantha Joint's murder and will be sending it over to them later, also that we have been commissioned by the widow to investigate the murder and retrieve what was in the safe." Turning to face Steven he said, "Please, arrange for copies of the video clips to be sent to this email address," and he slid a piece of paper across the highly polished boardroom table towards Steven. "Will do," Steven confirmed noting the address and sticking it into his top pocket. "I don't need to tell you, but you need to hide the original copies of the CCTV footage deep, we can't be sure who's going to come looking for them," Nick mentioned gravely to Steven who nodded his head. Turning to William, he said, "I asked Detective Joint if there was any indication in the original police report as to who his sister worked for, as we've all deduced that she was a high-class call girl. He told me that it was never established. Get one of our investigation teams in Durban to sniff around and see what they can dig up." As an afterthought, he said, "Better get a team to pass her picture around in Cape Town as well."

14H00

The call came through to Nick at around 14H00. "Hi Nick, it's Veronica here, the police have just released the penthouse back to me," she informed him. "Perfect," replied Nick. "Please, tell the General Manager to lock the door and let no one in. I'm sending a team over there now." Nick couldn't go along with the team as William grabbed him for another meeting. While Nick was sitting in the Executive Boardroom on the third floor listening to the Marketing Director pitch a new marketing campaign, his iPhone vibrated indicating a call. Glancing at the Caller ID he saw that it was from Johan who was heading up the intelligence-gathering team at the murder scene. Excusing himself from the meeting, he stepped outside. "Boss, are you aware of anyone who would want to spy on Mark?" Johan asked him excitedly. "That's a good question. Why?" Nick asked. "It was quite by chance that we did a spectrum scan and found a number of UHF frequencies in the penthouse that shouldn't be there. So far, we've identified three wireless miniature cameras. Really high-tech stuff, very impressive," Johan informed him. "Local?" Nick asked. "Na, definitely not from around here. The frequencies are in the UHF range according to the spectrum analyser, military and above," Johan explained further. Carrying on he asked, "What do you want us to do with them?" Thinking for a couple of seconds Nick replied, "Leave them in place and let's put someone to monitor the penthouse."

CHAPTER 11

CAPE TOWN, BISHOPSCOURT, 21H30, FRIDAY EVENING

The large, sprawling mansion, hidden amongst two-hundred-year-old oak trees, was situated in the rich leafy residential suburb of Bishopscourt, in Cape Town. The property was a couple of erfs down from the British Ambassador's Residence, set well back behind a large white wall and foreboding wooden oak entrance gates that gave no hint of the opulence which lay behind them. From the back garden, for one lucky enough to be invited onto the property, one had an unlimited view across the Constantia Valley all the way to Muizenburg and the Indian Ocean beyond in the south.

Entering the mansion through the large, imposing wooden doors led into an amazing, triple volume entrance hall with winding marble staircases on both sides leading up to the first floor. The entrance hall was bedecked in imported Italian marble and granite. Past the entrance hall, a number of passageways led off to various entertainment rooms and lounges. Along with a large bar came an entertainment area that led out onto a spectacular outdoor deck, with sunken lounges, gazebos, and a large sparkling blue swimming pool.

The ground floor also sported a kitchen that would not have been out of place in a 5-star Michelin restaurant. The wine cellar built beneath the bar would have brought tears to the eyes of most sommeliers. The cellar even boasted a couple of cases 1989 Grand Vin from Chateau Margaux. The first floor of the mansion consisted of a master suite and eight slightly smaller suites, all with their own en suite marble bathrooms with gold plated taps amongst other amenities that included a Jacuzzi.

There was another room on the first floor, smaller than the others, attached to the master suite. This room had a 48U modem rack full of DELL rack-mounted servers and DAS units linked to the large array of covert and hidden cameras, along with microphones that had been built into the mansion, a number of 40," LCD monitors had been mounted to create a video wall. Underneath the video wall was a control and mixing desk.

Vehicles started to arrive at the foreboding gates promptly at 21H30. There were a number of Porsches, Maseratis, and Ferraris in the mix along with a couple of Mercedes and BMW's that arrived at the gate. As each car pulled up to the gate, the cellphone of the driver was presented to the security guard showing a unique 3-dimensional emblem, and entry was granted onto the property. This wasn't the kind of party where chauffeurs waited outside. The couples exiting the multi-million-rand vehicles were all dressed to kill.

The dress code was formal, with the men wearing tuxedos, the women dressed in a blinding display of haute couture and elegance. Sable's guests were a mixed lot. There were a couple of industrialists, leaders in their particular field, there was a judge along with his girlfriend (his wife was on holiday with the kids). A playboy and a playgirl or two, whose bottomless trust funds paid for their life of sex, drugs, and fun, not always in that order, were thrown into the mix. There was also a couple of advertising executives and fund managers.

A butler in black coattails was waiting at the large double entrance doors. "Good evening, sir, good evening, madame. Welcome to Villa Horizon. May I have your coats and cellphones please?" the butler asked each set of guests politely as they entered. Without asking why the guests gladly shed their outer coats and handed over their cellphones. "Thank you. This way, please," the butler said after stowing both coats and phones and showed the guests to another door to the left off the entrance hall.

"Good evening," Sable said in a low sensual voice, dripping with warm sexuality to the latest of guests who arrived. Kissing some on the cheeks, others on the lips, she welcomed everyone personally, one after the other. There were fifteen couples in total, however, the evening was only about one person: the daughter of a German steel industrialist who was on holiday with her older lover in South Africa. Her father thought he was invincible in business and could do what he wanted.

Unfortunately, he had upset some people who needed leverage against him. His Achilles' heel was his beautiful, blond-haired daughter. Her Achilles' heel were several: sex, drugs, and party-ing, again, not always in that order. The other guests had no idea. To Sable, they were rich sexual deviates who she could use to her benefit and sometimes, when it suited her, for her enjoyment. To them, she was a conduit through which their cravings of sexual exploration and pleasures could be channelled with no bounda-ries, strings, or legal attachments.

Sable was encased in a tight-fitting, very low-cut white dress that showed off her perfect valley of cleavage, the white material wrapping around her enviously well-toned trim body, and stopping just after the juncture of her thighs, exposing her long, shapely, perfectly suntanned, toned legs, only leaving her most private of parts to one's imagination. Debbie, her lover, was standing beside her, dressed in a tight black leather top and low skirt, cut low on her cleavage, showing the deep suntanned valley of her breasts.

As the guests entered, Debbie handed each guest a small red leather 'goodie' bag. Turning to Debbie beside her a couple of minutes later, Sable purred, "I think all our guests are here now." Winking at her, Debbie grinned naughtily and replied, "Let the games begin." Sable gestured the butler over saying, "Thank you, Devon. You may close the doors and leave us now." "Yes, ma'am," Devon replied, straight-faced, waiting until his employer was inside the room and closing the white double doors that led into the main bar and entertainment room.

The guests had congregated in small groups, all with a drink of some sorts in their hands, served by several beautiful ladies dressed in frilly black and white French maids' uniforms. Picking up a long flute glass of bubbling champagne, Sable turned to her guests in the sunken entertainment area below and tapped her glass with the long-tapered fingernails of her left hand. Getting everyone's attention, she told them, "Thank you for coming! Sorry, my apologies, you haven't come yet," to a tinkling of laughter.

Carrying on with a sensual grin on her face, she continued. "Friends, thank you for joining us this evening. I hope you all make acquaintances before this night ends. You have all been given a little gift pack. Don't be shy to indulge in your wildest deepest fantasies and desires. To fun," and with that she raised her champagne glass and took a long sip of the golden bubbly liquid.

Taking hold of her lover's hand, she stepped down a couple of steps and started to mingle with the guests. The patio doors leading out onto the pool deck were open, and already a couple were indulging in the contents of their goodie bags, the sweet smells of high-grade marijuana wafting inside, while in one secluded corner of the main entertainment area another couple at a table were snorting thin white lines up their noses off of one of the shiny tabletops.

CAPE TOWN CITY CENTRE, 22H30, FRIDAY EVENING

"Have you seen this girl before?" Eben asked the bouncer standing outside the Titty Bar Strip Club at the start of Long Street, showing him a picture of Samantha Joint. "No," the bouncer replied. "What about this one?" Eben then asked him, showing him a picture of the dead blonde's head, cutting off the part where the neck ended in a bloody line. "Nope," the bouncer replied, disinterested, as he turned his attention to a group of young men walking into the club. "Sorry, gents," the bouncer told them, "I need to search you for weapons."

Eben turned to Johan standing beside him saying, "Let's carry on." "It's still early in the evening," Johan mentioned to his pal. "Let's find somewhere to have a bite to eat and drink and carry on a bit later. I believe I saw a steak house a bit further back." "Roger that!" Eben replied enthusiastically. Both Johan and Eben were bachelors and had decided to take it on themselves to trawl the bars and strip clubs of Cape Town in an attempt to find out more about the murder of Samantha Joint and the dead blonde in the penthouse. Finding the steak house, they were soon seated, both ordering a decent size steak and a light draught beer.

It was an hour or so later that they exited the steak house restaurant back onto Long Street. Long Street is one of the epicentres of nightlife in the Cape Town CBD, the entire 2.5 km of road consisting of bars, night clubs, backpacker lodges, guest houses, small restaurants, more bars, strip clubs, whore houses, and more. Long Street was busy when they had entered the steak house, now, exiting, it was completely different. It was packed with humanity. Men, women, lovers, couples, and friends all heading from one bar to the next, from one strip club to the next, drinking and partying their collective way through Friday evening into the early hours of Saturday morning, and sometimes beyond.

Drivers of motor vehicles had to slow right down to a crawl on the street as the nightlife surged around them. The noise was deafening, music from one establishment competing with the music from its neighbour. Further up Long Street the different bars were competing against each other as well, as competing against a tricked-out Beemer that was stopped outside in the street, literally vibrating its way across the road from the bass from the massive speakers and amplifiers kitted throughout the car. For the next hour, they wandered up Long Street from one bar to another, from strip club to strip club, showing the bouncers, barmen, and women alike the pictures of the two women. Each time they received a definitive no!

"Next club on the list," Eben noted to Johan as they came up to the next strip club along the rocking and rolling street. The club was almost at the end of Long Street. The sign outside read The Pussy Cat Club, a club for discerning gentlemen. With a grin, Eben stood aside at the door saying, "After you, my friend. It's tough but I suppose we have to take one for the team, from time to time," and opened the door for Johan. Grinning and shaking his head, muttering, "Imbecile," under his breath, Johan took the lead and walked inside.

The set up was the same as nearly all the other clubs they had visited. In the centre of the club was the round stage with the stainless-steel pole upon which the dancer or dancers did their acts. There was a small runway leading from a curtained off area at the back of the club out of which they entered and left the stage. Surrounding the round stage there were about two dozen tables and chairs, currently, nearly all occupied with members of the male species staring transfixed at the stage where a brunette with a stunning figure was busy with her routine around the pole, her skimpy white g-string leaving little to the imagination, where the group of businessmen sitting right in front of the stage had a bird's eye view. From where they stood, both Johan and Eben could see that their tongues were literally hanging out every time the brunette squatted down in front of them, her legs wide apart, the skimpy white g string hiding nothing at all, just soaking up the moisture of her arousal at dancing in front of a bunch of horny men who were throwing money at her.

Eben followed Johan through a small crowd of discerning gentlemen gawking at the brunette on stage towards the bar. Finding space at the bar they staked their space. "Two Castles please," Johan shouted to the barman over the booming noise of the music as the brunette continued to strut her stuff on stage. While they were waiting for their beers to arrive the brunette's act finished and she left the stage. As an unbelievably beautiful redhead strutted along the catwalk towards the stage, the barman returned with two cold Castles. "Fifty Rand," the barman shouted out as the music started up.

Handing over a pink Fifty Rand note, Johan also pulled out the two photographs and placed them down on the bar counter. "You ever see these girls before?" he asked the barman. The barman glanced at the two photographs before looking strangely at Johan and saying, "No, never seen them before, man." Then he turned around and walked away down the bar counter to attend to another customer. Johan was turning around with his beer to take in the new act, when out of the corner of his eye he caught the barman speaking hurriedly to a man sitting at the far end of the bar, with a couple of well-built men in suits sitting behind him, pretending to watch the girls but actually watching the patrons. 'Oh, shit,' Johan thought as the man looked up and stared hard directly in his direction. 'Troubles on the way, we're getting warmer in our search.'

Eben nudged him in the ribs. The redhead had just slid down the stainless-steel pole and spread open her long supple legs in their direction revealing her most intimate of secrets. There, on her left inner thigh, nestling right next to the side of her g-string and her outer labia, was a red and green tattoo of a rose, shining bright and looking exactly like the tattoos on the two dead girls. "We've hit a nerve. Incoming, eleven o'clock," Johan said speaking urgently into Eben's ear as he tracked the two suited heavies walking towards them with grim expressions on their hardened faces.

Standing at the bar in their jeans, t-shirts with black leather jackets, and Hitech boots on their feet, both Johan and Eben looked tame enough. That, however, was a mistake that the two suited gorillas would never make again. Both Johan and Eben were ex-South African Reconnaissance Force who were trained experts in hand to hand combat, along with various forms of martial arts and the Israeli Krav Maga method of fighting; that emphasises the use of any technique that will end the fight quickly.

The patrons standing around Johan and Eben had no idea of the violence about to be unleashed. Eben glanced in the direction that Johan was looking to and nodded, saying "You take your left, I'll take the righthand gorilla. God, they're built they brick shit houses; do we get danger pay for this?!"

"Why are you asking questions about girls you have no business with?" the one suited gorilla asked with an accent that Johan couldn't quite place, shouting at Johan above the music as his suited partner eyed Eben out. "Why do you ask? Have you got some information for me?" Johan replied with a large open smile on his face. "Wise guy," the gorilla spat out and threw a powerhouse of a punch with his left arm where Johan's face had been a split second ago. Pivoting lightly to his left away from Eben, Johan grabbed the gorilla's left arm as it whizzed past his face, and pulled it towards him, using the gorilla's momentum to his advantage.

Not expecting it, the gorilla stumbled forward right into Johan's straightened and extended forearm that felled him across the throat, completely fucking up his Adam's apple. As he dropped like a ton of bricks to the floor, the gorilla's downward-moving face connected with Johan's upward moving knee. There was a loud crack over a sudden silence in the music as the suited gorillas' jaw broke. Eben's adversary fared no better as he found himself heading headfirst out of control into the side of the bar, in a crash that knocked him out and concussed him. The discerning gentlemen standing around Johan and Eben looked on in horror. The music carried on playing as the redhead continued to dance.

Turning back to the bar, Johan picked up his beer and took a long deep pull of the cold golden liquid, quenching his thirst. "Come," he growled towards Eben who was also in the process of finishing his beer. "Let's go and speak to the boss of this place." "With you," Eben replied finishing his drink and walking over the two fallen and unconscious gorillas, following behind Johan towards the corner of the bar. The sea of discerning gentlemen moved out of their way like the Red Sea parting for Moses. As they approached where the man had been sitting, they found the seat empty, instead, a whole bunch of suited gorillas were waiting for them, the club's patrons moving aside sensing that more violence was in the air.

It was a very uneven fight. The suited gorillas were bullies rather than fighters and were no match for Johan and Eben who were trained soldiers. Restraining themselves as much as possible, three and half minutes later five more suited gorillas were lying writhing on the floor in agony, some with broken limbs and bones, one with internal bleeding. "Let's get out of here before the cops arrive," Johan suggested lightly to Eben as they made their way to the front door of the gentlemen's club, the patrons who saw what happened staring on in amazement, all thoughts of pussy wiped clean from their brains for a couple of seconds.

Walking out of The Pussy Cat Club back onto Long Street, the night-time air fresh and invigorating, they heard a woman's voice behind them. "Excuse me guys, excuse me." Turning around, Eben recognised the pretty woman hurrying towards them as one of the waitresses that had been serving drinks in The Pussy Cat Club. Reaching them, she told them, "I know the girls you are looking for, but I can't talk here. Meet me at Tiger's Milk in twenty minutes."

CHAPTER 12

CAPE TOWN, TIGERS MILK BAR, 00H15, SATURDAY

"I know the girls you are looking for," the pretty young woman told them. The three of them had found a vacant table at the back of the bar called Tiger's Milk, a bar about 500 meters back down Long Street. It was a strange name for a bar, and tiger milk was the last thing that they sold, so, rather than alcohol, they all settled for strong cappuccinos. She introduced herself to them as Lilly. "I saw you show the barman a picture of my old roommate Samantha and a friend of hers. I believe that her name is Lee Anne, Lee Anne Strydom," Lilly started off explaining.

Just then a waitress delivered the cappuccinos, waiting until she had left, Johan asked, "How did you meet Samantha?" "She danced with me at the club for a couple of months, The Pussy Cat Club," Lilly explained, unabashed. "And Lee Anne?" Eben asked her, speaking for the first time. "One evening Samantha arrived at the club with Lee-Anne saying that she was in town for a couple of days and was staying with us and brought her along for some fun," Lilly replied, taking a sip of her cappuccino.

"And...?" Johan prompted her. Putting down her cappuccino cup she continued, "Well they both ended up dancing on the stage and making out with each other. It was a wild night," Lilly explained blushing slightly. "And then what happened?" Johan asked, again prompting her lightly. Taking another sip of the delicious cappuccino, she licked the froth off her lips with the tip of her tongue and continued. "I was working tables that night. We're not allowed to dance when we're having our period. Anyway, while they were dancing, this woman called Sable came in and couldn't take her eyes off them. After the act, she called them over to her table and they spent the rest of the evening sitting at her table and drinking with her. They left with her when the club closed. I never did see them again." Eben and Johan glanced at each other, paydirt was the expression on both of their faces. "Sorry," Lilly blurted out "I forgot; I did see her once after that. She was all dressed up looking like a million dollars. We spoke for a while. She couldn't stop talking about how she was flying with Sable all over the world in her private jet."

"Okay," Johan said collecting his thoughts. "How do you know this woman called Sable?" "I was introduced to her once as the owner of the club," Lilly told him. Carrying on, she explained a bit further, "I've worked at the club for about three years now; it's really a great place to work, the pays really good if you've got a good-looking body and enjoy fun," she explained with a sexy smile, batting her blue eyes at Eben. Carrying on Lilly explained, "As I was saying, I've worked there for around three years now and only seen her a couple of times." "What does she look like?" Eben asked her curiously. "Tall, long-legged, suntanned, green eyes with long dark brown shiny hair," Lilly told them without hesitation.

Changing the subject slightly Lilly then asked them, "So, tell me, how is Lee Anne? I know that Samantha was murdered, poor girl, I blame Sable for that." Eben looked at Johan with the look 'I've got this'. Johan nodded his head. Clearing his throat, Eben looked at Lilly and said "She's also dead, unfortunately, she was the girl found dead at the Grace Royale Hotel a week ago." "Oh my god, no!" she cried out, burying her face in her hands and starting to sob. "Excuse me, I'm going to the bathroom," Lilly sobbed and standing up headed off towards the toilets. Lilly never came back to the table.

CAPE TOWN, BISHOPSCOURT, 10H00, SATURDAY MORNING

The mansion was quiet again, the last of the guests taking their leave at around 4 am. Waking up in the master bedroom on the 1st floor with Debbie still fast asleep beside her, Sable carefully untangled her lover's entwined arms and legs off from around her and stood up. Glancing at the bedside clock she saw that it was just after 10 am. Her mouth was dry, she had a pounding headache and her pussy and anus were throbbing from the affections of her lover's strap-on dildo and the cocks that had fucked her. She was bisexual, after all. 'Fuck it, all in a night's work,' she thought ruefully to herself as she walked naked across the bedroom into the marble encased ensuite bathroom.

After relieving herself and wincing slightly as the acidity in her urine washed past her tender vagina, she brushed her teeth and slipped on her silk dressing gown that was hanging behind the bathroom door. In all her houses all over the world, she had a master bedroom stocked with her clothes and cosmetics. This enabled her to travel light and always have her style of clothes and cosmetics ready and available wherever she may find herself. Her house staff had instructions to keep all her cosmetics and the likes up to date.

Walking back across the cream deep pile carpet, she headed for a door hidden behind a Japanese silkscreen, picking up her cellphone and slipping it into the pocket of her dressing gown as she passed the bed. On the wall next to the door, behind the intricate Japanese screen, was a small covert camera built into the doorframe and linked to facial recognition access control software. Standing still for about a second in front of the doorframe directly in front of the covert camera, there was a soft beeping sound and the door released with a click. Walking inside, a light sensor sensed her and switched on the lights. Closing the door behind her she headed for the control desk.

"Right let's see what we recorded from last night," she said to herself as she sat down in front of the control desk. Switching on the monitors, she started to review the CCTV footage which her numerous covert cameras had recorded from the evening's encounters. After watching for about 30 minutes she muttered, "Perfect," to herself as she viewed the long blonde-haired girl in her birthday suit performing all sorts of sexual acts with men and women, partaking in numerous lines of cocaine as she fucked, sucked, and snorted her way through the evening. Copying the video footage that she wanted into a separate folder, she then pasted a copy of the folder to a backup cloud server and sent a copy to her client. She received a reply 10 minutes later as she watched some more of the evening's sexual encounters. "Job well done; I have transferred your payment as per usual. "Perfect," she purred again to herself. "Another 10 million US for a night's work."

'We still have three hours until our flight,' Sable thought to herself, considering going back to bed and her lover, feeling the familiar glow between her legs after watching the video footage. Her cellphone began to vibrate in her pocket. 'Damn it, who can this be?' Looking angrily at the caller ID, she saw that it was Ricardo. "This better be good, it's Saturday morning," Sable snapped, irritated at being disturbed. "Sorry, Sable, but we've got a major problem. I received a call last night and I tried to get hold of you. Apparently, two guys walked into the Pussy Cat Club in Cape Town with pictures of Samantha and Lee Anne wanting to know if anybody knew them," Ricardo told her. "So, didn't the boys take care of them?" Sable asked impatiently. "That's the problem, the two of them beat the living shit out of the eight bouncers putting five of them in hospital," Ricardo explained to her getting tense. "Fuck it," Sable fumed. "What do we know about them? How many of my girls are dancing there at present?" Sable asked, her mind working overtime. "Only Lillian and Dianne came the reply," "Okay, send them to the house in Durban for a while," she instructed Ricardo. I'll phone you back later. With that Sable stormed into the master suite, all thoughts of another round of sexual acrobatics with her lover forgotten, "Come on honey, time to get up."

EXECUTIVE DECISIONS, B-1 SECURE BOARDROOM, 09H00, SATURDAY

After receiving the call from Johan at around 3 am, Nick immediately sent a message out on their encrypted Messenger group, giving William, Steven, Nicky, Johan, and Eben the heads up that there was movement on the case and they needed to meet up in the morning. With a fresh pot of coffee sent down from the Catering Department on the Ground Floor, it was a 24-hour operation albeit scaled down slightly over weekends.

"Thanks for coming in, guys," Nick told them gratefully, even though he knew that they'd go to the ends of the earth for him if required. "Johan and Eben took one for the team last night and trawled the strip clubs," he informed them to chuckles of laughter around the boardroom table. Carrying on when the chuckles had died down, he added, "And they got lucky." Everyone looked at Johan and Eben. "Better tell them what you guys found out," Nick suggested looking at Johan.

Grinning like a Cheshire cat, Johan cleared his throat and began, "After trawling through most of Long Street, we got lucky at a strip club called The Pussy Cat Club, a club for *discerning gentlemen*." There was another round of laughter at that. Johan carried on talking. "I showed the barman the girls' picture, but the barman denied knowing them. Then, a couple of minutes later, I caught him talking to a bad looking guy sitting at the corner of the bar. He had a couple of suited gorillas sitting behind him guarding him. Well, they came over and asked us why we were asking questions. I asked if they had some information for us, and then they tried to get nasty with us and we had to take evasive action, using minimum force," he told his audience as casually as possible, with a grin on his face.

Taking a sip of his coffee, he continued. "Well, Eben and myself then decided to go and talk face to face with the boss man, but by the time we got around the bar he had vanished," Johan explained to a rapt audience. Eben took up the story. "The boss man had been replaced with six really big ugly looking gorillas in suits. We used minimal force," he explained as innocently as possible.

"Well, minimum force is subjective to the time and place, they must have been fucking big," William replied. "I'm looking at last night's crime stats for the Cape Town CBD and I see that it was reported that there was a fight at the same club you mentioned, eight casualties, all needing some form of medical attention." Executive Decisions had guarding contracts in the Cape Town CBD so were part of the crime intelligence service, receiving daily reports listing crimes and disturbances over the last 24 hours in the Central CBD and surrounds.

'As I said, we used minimal force, they were big motherfuckers," Johan explained putting an end to it. "So," Nick said, "it seems that you struck a nerve." "And how," Steven said, getting into the conversations. "Guys, I haven't finished yet," Johan told them. "It gets much better." "Carry on, o slayer of big motherfuckers," Nicky muttered under her breath. "As we were walking away, one of the strippers came up to us outside saying that she knew the girls," Johan informed the team. "It turns out that Samantha used to work at the strip club and the dead blonde turns out to be a friend of hers, named Lee Anne Strydom."

Talking for another half an hour, Johan and Eben took the rest of the team over what they had found out. "Well," Nick said after Johan had finished talking, "we've learnt a number of things from old fashioned detective work." All around the table nodded in confirmation. "Okay, this is what I want," Nick said thinking quickly ahead turning to Johan. "Put an undercover team onto the strip club and see what we can find out." Next, turning to Nicky, he said, "Put one of your helpers onto searching for everything to do with the Pussy Cat Club." Nodding her head Nicky confirmed, "On it boss." "Also," he said, carrying on, "we need to track down this woman called Sable. Anyone got any ideas?" On a hunch that came to him, Nick said, "Nicky, also get your team to run a search on all stories to do with high-class prostitution." Looking at Eben Nick said, "Eben take a drive to the airport and go and have a word with the ground crew that looks after our aircraft. See if they have seen a woman matching Sable's description using the Private Operator Terminal recently."

CHAPTER 13

CAPE TOWN, V&A WATERFRONT, THE ONE & ONLY HOTEL, SATURDAY 10H00

"Thank you for keeping me updated,Nick," Veronica Bings said gratefully over the telephone. For the last ten minutes, Nick had been updating her on their progress to date. "We have a lead," he had told her with an upbeat tone in his voice when she answered the phone. "What, you've found the killer and the Prototype?" she gushed out, excitedly thinking that all her problems were over.

"I wish it were that simple," he replied. "No, it turns out that your husband and his lover were not the first victims to be killed the same way. It may be a complete coincidence but there was another murder a couple of years ago where the same modus operandi was used. Also, it could also be a coincidence, but both the female killed three years ago, and your husband's lover were known by the same person." Carrying on, he added, "And I don't believe in coincidences." He didn't tell her that they got the information from a stripper. "No, I don't either believe in coincidences," she said almost to herself. "Okay, thanks for the update, hopefully, we can get this resolved quickly," she added.

Then Veronica told him, "The police informed me that the coroner will be releasing Mark's body in the next couple of days. As soon as it's been released, I'll be flying back with the body to the States, Mark's parents want to bury him next to his wife." Clearing his throat Nick replied, "I was going to ask you about his funeral, I would like to attend." "No problem," Veronica replied light-heartedly. "I'll SMS you the details later." Speaking for another couple of minutes, Veronica ended the telephone call.

For some reason, she felt better after speaking to him. She didn't know Nick all that well, he was one of Mark's friends and she had only met him a couple of times. But the couple of times that she had met him, he had always come across as the perfect gentleman, always ready to help the next person, always ready with a smile and a word of encouragement. On hearing the news of her husband's death and that the safe had been opened she had at first panicked. 'No fuck it, this is all I need now,' she ranted to herself, mentally kicking herself for leaving Mark at such a critical point in the operation. 'What was I to do?' she silently asked herself. 'He insisted that I take the kids and get away for a while so that he could finish the Prototype in peace! If I had said no and made up an excuse to stay, he would have become suspicious. I saw nothing out of the ordinary on the covert cameras which I installed. What the fuck happened and why the hell didn't Centre pick up that he was a target?!' she ranted silently to herself. Remembering what Mark had told her about Nick, "He's a good man to have on your side," she decided to put him to the test and phoned him.

"Damn it!" Veronica then swore in Russian, her mother tongue, feeling her emotions starting to get the better of her. 'This was to have been the assignment that catapulted my career into the upper echelons of the SVR and become a hero for Mother Russia. Steal the ultimate weapon for Mother Russia so that my country could finally surpass the West in covert VR weapons technology,' she thought silently to herself. She remembered her commanding officer explaining the importance of the operation to her. "Battlefields of future wars will not only be fought the conventional way, but also in cyberspace. Virtual Reality is cyberspace, cyberspace is virtual reality. Once an opposing force is inside your network and has corrupted your data, the war is lost. Imagine if we can attack our enemies without our enemies even knowing we are there!? We need this VR Prototype before the West takes advantage of it!" her commanding officer had explained excitedly to her.

Veronica Bings had been born Sashenka Petrovich and she was an only child of parents who were Russian diplomats. She had led a privileged life, getting to live all over the world and experience all types of different cultures. With an extremely high IQ, she had mastered eight different languages with absolute ease, and with her parents' position in the Diplomatic Corps, she had had doors open for her that was not possible for ordinary Russian citizens. She was also a staunch patriot who believed in her country, Mother Russia, and would lay down her life for it, if necessary. She was also beautiful. She was the perfect material for a spy. Entering the Russian Military, she passed her basic training with ease and she soon found herself in a training camp for the Foreign Intelligence Service; largely due to her speaking eight languages. The FSI, also known as the SVR RF, was the external intelligence agency for the Russian Federation, tasked with intelligence gathering and espionage activities outside of the Russian Federation. She passed their selection and training course with flying colours.

Thinking back, she could still remember the day she had been summoned to her commander's office at SVR Headquarters in Moscow. There was another man sitting in the only spare chair in the office. "Comrade Petrovich, may I introduce Comrade Colonel Andreyev Petroski?" Glancing at the colonel, she noticed an older grey-haired man in an immaculately pressed SVR uniform sitting ramrod straight in his seat. "The colonel will explain your mission to you," her commanding officer had explained her.

"Comrade Petrovich, I have a mission for you. It will take you away from your homeland for a number of years, but, if you succeed you will return home a hero," Colonel Andreyev Petroski had explained to her in a strong authoritarian voice. Carrying on, he told her, "Some information has come across our desk, that Mark Bings, the founder of Virtual Reality, is developing a new system which he calls the Prototype that makes you invisible in Virtual Reality. He is moving to South Africa from California. His wife died in a horrific car accident a couple of months back. He wants a new start." As he said that he had a lopsided grin stretched across the thin lips of his face. "You want me to become indispensable to him and eventually steal the Prototype," she had replied with a just as large a smile forming across her beautiful face. "Correct, Comrade Petrovich, that is exactly what we want you to do," he replied, his face breaking out into a large cruel grin.

Her phone rang again breaking her thoughts. Looking at the caller ID she saw that it was a blocked number. She knew exactly who it was. "Yes, sir," she said answering the call. "How far are you in tracking down the Prototype?" Colonel Andreyev Petroski asked her getting straight to the point. Walking back inside the hotel suite and closing the balcony door so that no one could overhear her, Veronica replied, "Sir, the Executive Decisions team is working on it." Before she could utter another word, the colonel cut in, "That's what you told me a couple of days ago Comrade!" he growled over the cellular connection. Hurriedly she continued, "Sir, I have just got off the phone with Nick Scott and they have a lead that they are currently following up."

Listening to her explain he told her, "You need to find the Prototype, and quickly. The operation has piqued the interest of some very powerful people within the Russian Military and we cannot disappoint them, otherwise, I fear we shall spend the rest of our days in a labour camp somewhere in depths of Siberia or Outer Mongolia!" Veronica shuddered at the thought. "I will mobilise additional help for you." With that, the colonel sitting in Moscow ended the conversation.

'Damn it,' Sashenka thought to herself putting down her smartphone. "You do your job well and all they want is more." In a stroke of luck, a month or so before Mark was murdered, she had been able to gain access to his computer and copy part of the program before his computer mysteriously shut down. "The Centre was over the moon with what I sent them, now they want it all and it's a total fuckup," she said to herself furiously.

Colonel Andreyev Petroski sat back in his squeaky office chair after slamming the telephone receiver back down and swore. He was currently sitting in his office on the 4th Floor of the SVR Headquarters building. Even though it was a Saturday morning, the building was a hive of activity. The SVR never slept. The building was in the Yasenevo District of Moscow, one of the many sprawling districts of Moscow. His rank and position entitled him to a modest size office in the building. On the one wall was the regulation picture of the President of the Russian Federation staring down at him with eagle eyes, while on the opposite wall was a picture of Stalin scowling back at him. Under the picture of Stalin along the wall was an old sofa that the colonel occasionally slept on when working late. "Damnit," he swore to himself in Russian, pounding his table with his one fist after replacing the telephone receiver. 'Operation Viewpoint is going to shit. It's taken me three years to get it this far and just when the end is in sight the Prototype is stolen! From right in front of our fucking eyes!"

Colonel Andreyev Petroski was a product of the older generation KGB, back when rubber hose pipes and the pulling out of fingernails was the norm to get information out of a suspect. However, even with the morphing of the KGB into the 21st century and changing the name to the SVR, things didn't really change. A leopard can never change its spots or characteristics and neither did the men and woman of the SVR and affiliated services. 'Comrade Petrovich is going to need help in finding the Prototype, I don't care how much faith she has in Executive Decisions,' he reasoned and picking up his telephone handset, dialled an internal number to another office on the same floor in the building.

After speaking to the subordinate on the other end of the line for a while, he ended saying, "Make sure the six of them are on the next flight to Cape Town, South Africa." Replacing the telephone receiver, he breathed a sigh of relief, 'The more help the better,' he thought smugly to himself. The six he was referring to were a trained team with multiple skills. Lighting a cigarette and taking a long deep pull, feeling the smoke filling his lungs, the nicotine starting to course through his bloodstream, he sat in his office pondering his next move.

'We have to obtain the Prototype!' he lectured himself. 'The section of the Prototype program that Sashenka sent us is incredible, it will put us years ahead of the West in cyberspace technology. To be able to roam around an enemy's network without them even knowing you are there. Now that's priceless!' he mused to himself. "There is no room for failure," he then growled as he stubbed out his cigarette into an almost overflowing ashtray and picked up the telephone handset dialling another internal number.

"Ah, Comrade Popov, it's Colonel Petroski here," he said when the call was answered. Captain Popov was one of the leading figures in the SVR's Cyberwarfare Department and was working closely with the colonel on Operation Viewpoint.

Getting straight to the point, he said, "We have a problem, Captain; the Prototype has been stolen." "Shit!" exclaimed the captain in Russian. "What can I do to help?" "I am sending a multi-skilled team to Cape Town to help track down the Prototype, and think it would be prudent if we include one of your VR interrogations teams, hopefully of the same calibre of the example that you previously showed me." "I can assure you, Colonel, that Lieutenant Yuri and his team are the best in the game," was the answer. Gone were the days of brutal physical torture in the dark dank cells of the Lubyanka Prison interrogating prisoners to extract a sliver of information.

The prisoner was a terrorist, a Ukrainian Loyalist who was an enemy of the state. The colonel recalled how through a Virtual Reality interrogation chamber the VR Interrogation Team had broken the man in 30 minutes, all by playing in the prisoners' mind, while the prisoner lay strapped to an operating like table in a cell in the Lubyanka Prison. Electronic probes were attached to his temples that were in turn connected to a Virtual Reality Interface module. 'Remarkable," the colonel had told the captain, clearly impressed after the demonstration, "not a mark on his body and he told you all you wanted to know. Your technique will revolutionise interrogation techniques." he told Captain Popov excitedly.

Putting down the phone, he shouted out to his adjutant in the outer office, "Dimitry, office, now!" Less than fifteen seconds later the colonel's adjutant, Lieutenant Dimitry Kirkov was standing ramrod straight at attention in front of the colonel's desk. "At ease, Lieutenant," the colonel commanded. Then said, "Alert our Cape Town safe house operator to expect around ten to eleven guests within the next twenty-four hours. Comrade Petrovich needs help in finding the Prototype." "Yes, Sir Colonel Sir," the Lieutenant confirmed smartly, taking a small notebook out of his top pocket, and making a note in it. Putting the notebook away, he came to attention, saluted, and turning smartly around marched out of the colonel's office. "Right," Colonel Petroski thought to himself as he watched his adjutant leave the office, 'I have a team with mixed skills along with a VR Interrogation team to assist Sashenka. We cannot fail, failure is not an option.'

CHAPTER 14

EXECUTIVE DECISIONS, BOMBARDIER GLOBAL 60000, 45 0000 FEET ENROUTE TO JOHANNESBURG, SATURDAY AFTERNOON, 14H30

Detective Joint was awestruck. Just over two hours ago he'd gotten a telephone call from the number he'd been given a couple of days ago, now he was sitting onboard the Executive Decisions' private jet heading towards Johannesburg. Hesitantly he'd answered the call earlier on. Since his meeting with Executive Decisions, things had gone quiet for a couple of days. When his phone rang, he'd been downstairs in the dilapidated courtyard of the bachelor's quarters, having a BBQ with the rest of the guys who found themselves hanging in limbo on a Saturday afternoon. There was a rugby match in the late afternoon, South Africa versus Australia at Loftus in Pretoria which they were all planning to watch. First burn some meat while having a couple of beers followed by several brandy and cokes and then sit down and watch the rugby match drinking horrendous amounts of brandy and coke while supporting the Springboks.

"Detective, it's Nick, we've got a break in your sister's murder, I'll pick you up in 30 minutes down at the train station, we don't need to let any of your neighbours know what we're doing," Nick told him before he had a chance to say a word, and then ended the call. Turning to his mates, the other five bachelors standing around the fire talking excitedly about the upcoming rugby match he said in a surprised voice, "Sorry guys, gotta head out, somethings come up." As he reached his one-bedroom apartment his cellphone rang again. "Forgot to mention we're taking a trip, so pack a bag and, if you've got a passport, I suggest you pack that as well. You might need it," Nick said. Quickly packing an overnight bag, the detective headed out of his bachelor flat and walked the short distance down to the station.

Thirty minutes later, an ice white Porsche 911 Turbo pulled up into an empty parking bay adjacent the train station. Seeing Nick behind the wheel, Detective Joint ambled over towards the sports car, admiring the sleek lines of the vehicle. "Jump in," Nick said through the open passenger window, the sports car's engine idly burbling away, waiting patiently. Opening the passenger door, the smell of new leather wafted out of the open door. "Throw your bag in the back, we've got a plane to catch," Nick told him with a big grin on his Ray Ban clad face.

Selecting Drive on the PDK Doppelkupplung automatic transmission, Nick floored the throttle and the 3.8 litre twin turbocharged engine roared into action flinging both occupants roughly back into the leather seats as the vehicle catapulted forward. An alarm started to chime from the dashboard and Nick said, not taking his eyes off the road, "You'd better put on your seatbelt; he doesn't like it when you don't wear it."

Driving as quickly as possible through the side streets up onto the M3 Nick quickly brought the detective up to speed. "You mean to tell me what the SAPS couldn't find out in 3 years your guys uncovered in a couple of days?" Detective Joint asked flabbergasted a couple of minutes later. "Sad but true," Nick replied as he looked across the detective into the left hand side mirror to confirm if it was clear; there were a couple of slower cars ahead in the fast lane. 'View clear, blind spot indicator off,' Nick subconsciously thought to himself as he switched on his left-hand turn signal and goosed the throttle a bit more, moving over into the left-hand lane flying past the slower-moving cars.

Flying past the University of Cape Town, affectionally known as UCT, built on the bottom slopes of the rear of Table Mountain on the way towards the N2 and ultimately the airport, Detective Joint, as he saw the speedo hovering at 170km per hour, asked worriedly, "Aren't you worried about speed traps?" Turning his head slightly towards the detective as he braked hard for the up-coming left hand hairpin bend leading onto the N2, Nick replied with a large grin on his face, "Nope," and he pointed with his left hand towards the centre console LCD display. "Don't tell a soul, but Porsche have as an optional extra, a built-in radar detector," Nick said. Detective Joint laughed out loud, the black cloud of his personal demons seeming to lift somewhat in the easy-going company of Nick.

Carrying on, Nick finished bringing the detective up to speed, "The stripper mentioned that Samantha couldn't stop talking about flying around in this woman's private jet. We asked a couple of questions at the aircraft hangers of the Private Operator Terminal at Cape Town International; all private jets have to go through these guy's hands, and we hit pay dirt. A lady, matching the description we were given, regularly flies in and out of the Cape Town Private Operator Terminal and as luck has it her aircraft took off one hour ago enroute to Lanseria Airport. One of the ground crew overheard the pilot mention that they were going to watch the rugby match at Loftus. We have a team standing by on the ground at Lanseria to follow the passengers of the aircraft."

As Nick was talking, they reached the entrance lanes for the Cape Town International Airport, and instead of heading for the parking terminal and ultimately the Airport building, Nick put on the right-hand turn indicator and turned right. "I thought you said we were flying to Johannesburg?" Detective Joint asked a little confused. "We are," Nick replied with a grin. "We fly private," and headed for the Private Operator terminal and hangers a short distance away. Pulling into an empty parking bay they both exited the sports car and removed their single bags from the rear bucket seats.

Locking the car Nick headed towards the terminal building with the detective one step behind him, struggling to keep up. "What about my 9mill?" the detective asked, referring to his police issue 9mm holstered on his waist. "Relax, it's a private flight, you can bring on board what you want," Nick explained to him, lifting his jacket to reveal a Glock17 9mm parabellum strapped to his left hip. After walking through the airconditioned comfort of the terminal building, only being stopped before they walked outside onto the aircraft parking ramps to check for identification, the detective followed Nick outside.

There were a number of private jets parked facing the terminal building and Nick headed for the last aircraft in the row, a shiny white Bombardier Global 6000 that sparkled in the afternoon sunlight. "Nice," the detective muttered under his breath. "Thanks," Nick replied matter of factly. "We use it to transport cash, valuables and VIP's all over the world." Milling around outside the aircraft were a few people who the detective hadn't yet met. Quickly Nick introduced the detective to Johan, Eben, and Hannah, the aircraft stewardess, security operator sometimes co-pilot, and aircraft purser. Nothing came on board the aircraft without Hannah knowing about it. Boarding the aircraft, the detective was taken aback by the luxury. He'd never flown in a private jet before. "Good afternoon, Detective, may I take your jacket?" Hannah asked with a large pretty smile on her face. Now he was sitting in an executive leather multifunctional seat on board flying at 45 0000 feet towards Johannesburg. "Detective, a cup of coffee for you?" Hannah asked him with a big smile on her face. "Yes, please," he answered.

Sitting across the aisle in a similar seat but facing back towards him Nick told him, "Don't let that cute smile fool you, Detective. Hannah is an ex-Israeli special forces member." Carrying on he explained, "Hannah handles the security and operation of the plane for us. She's also a qualified co-pilot." Just then there was the sound of a telephone ringing, and Nick reached down to a console built into the side of the seat the detective hadn't yet noticed and removed a wireless phone. Listening for a couple of seconds he said, "Keep us informed." "Well, guys," Nick said replacing the wireless phone in its cradle, "they've landed, and it looks like they are enroute to Loftus." Twenty minutes later another call came through. Ending the call Nick informed all in the passenger cabin, "Sable and her entourage are settled into a suite at Loftus about to watch South Africa versus Australia."

LOFTUS VERSFELD, 17H00, SATURDAY

Landing at Lanseria International Airport, Nick had the pilot's taxi as quickly as possible to the Private Operator Terminal gate. As the engines were spooling down, the main cabin door was opened and they all rushed as quickly as possible down the steps and across the apron to the Private Operator Terminal gate, with Eben and Johan bringing up the rear after removing some baggage from the luggage bay of the aircraft. In a flash, they were through the building. Outside two black Porsche Cayennes were waiting, their engines burbling away waiting patiently. Detective Joint followed Nick to the first black SUV. Nick jumped into the passenger seat beside the driver and the detective into the rear behind Nick. Johan jumped into the other rear seat. "Drive," Nick commanded. As the driver pulled off Nick turned in his seat and explained, "These are the bulletproof beasts that we use to transport VIP's around in. It's a jungle out there and we gotta keep our clients safe."

Loftus Versfeld was a rugby stadium situated in the Pretoria suburb of Arcadia. Pulling up outside the stadium to a screeching halt thirty minutes later they all piled out. "Detective, stick close to me," Nick instructed as they headed for the main entrance, the roar of the excited crowd reverberating around from within the stadium. "Heading for my suite," Nick explained to the guard showing him some documentation. A minute later they were being whisked up in one of the elevators to the top floor of the stadium. The top two floors were made up of suites. "We keep a suite here on the upper level," Nick informed the detective. "There are a couple of our Johannesburg clients there at present, but they won't be a problem, they're here to watch the rugby," Nick explained to him. Detective Joint just nodded his head in amazement.

The entertainment suite was luxurious. Walking inside there was a large wooden bar built along the back wall of the suite, seemingly stocked with every imaginable alcoholic drink known to man. Past the bar was a small entertainment area with raised small round tables with accompanying leather wrapped barstools that led up to a set of sliding doors. On one side of the suite was a sideboard buckling under the weight of an array of hot and cold finger snacks. Along the opposite wall was a comfortable looking lounge suite. The walls were decorated with all types of rugby memorabilia. Outside on the balcony the seating area consisted of three rows of concrete tiered seats, the width of the private box. Below and in front of them was the brilliant green rugby pitch where South Africa and Australia were currently engaged in battle.

Standing in the suite behind the glass sliding door looking across the green expanse of the field far below to the opposite side of the stadium was a man with a large set of binoculars mounted on a tripod. Nick introduced the man to Detective Joint as Ian. "Where are they, Ian?" Nick asked. "Sir, the target and her entourage entered suite No.5 that's to the right of the FNB sign on the other side of the field." From where they were standing in the suite it was directly in front of them to the left on the opposite side of the field. Carrying on Ian explained, "The target and her companions are presently all sitting outside. The well-dressed African gentleman to her left joined them around fifteen minutes ago."

Standing aside, first Nick had a look through the high-powered binoculars at the entertainment suite on the opposite side of the field. "Here, Detective, take a look, there's your quarry, there's the woman everyone refers to as Sable." Looking through the binoculars he thought to himself, 'There she is, the woman who can shed some light on the three murders.' The binoculars' optics brought her close up, close enough that it felt as if he could touch her. She was currently holding an animated conversation with the well-dressed African gentleman on her left.

'God, she's beautiful,' he thought silently, staring at the long dark brown-haired beauty sitting in front of him. Her hair shone brightly in the late afternoon sun. She wore what looked like a pair of very expensive sunglasses on her perfectly proportioned face, her lips pursed in grim determination as she watched the action on the field below. He noted that she was wearing tight stonewashed jeans and a t-shirt that was stretched over a set of perfectly formed breasts. Suddenly she laughed at something her dark-haired companion beside her said, throwing her head back gaily and showing off a set of perfectly even white teeth.

"Okay, Eben," the detective heard Nick say, "I want mug shots of everyone in the suite. As soon as you have them email them immediately to Nicky in Cape Town. She's standing by for them." Removing his eyes from the binoculars, the detective turned to see Eben standing next to him with a camera complete with a long telephoto lens mounted on another tripod. There was a sudden roar from the South African supporters as the rugby ball popped out of the scrum and was quickly fed down the Springbok back-line to the left wing who caught the oval-shaped ball on the run and headed arrow-straight down the field towards the Australian tri line, the thundering roar of the crowds spurring him on.

Placing his eyes back to the rubber stoppers of the binoculars, he was in time to see his quarry jump up, jumping in excitement as the South African wing headed for the Australian tri line. 'Fuck me, she's beautiful, every man's wet dream,' he thought to himself again as he savoured the sensual contours of her breasts, down to her flat stomach to her perfectly sized hips and her long legs encased in the tight stonewashed jeans. Feeling himself getting aroused watching her, he pulled his eyes away in disgust. The game passed by in a blur for Detective Joint between catching glimpses of the game to taking a quick look at the woman referred to as Sable. Just before the game ended; with South Africa winning 13 – 9, Ian alerted them all. "Heads up guys the target and her entourage are on the move." Bending down and taking one last look in the binoculars, Detective Joint was in time to see the rear of his quarry walk up the couple of concrete steps and enter the entertainment box, then she was gone.

Speaking into a concealed microphone linked to an encrypted 2-way communication system Ian instructed his team that was standing by outside the stadium. "Heads up, Bravo Team, target on the move." "Bravo One, Bravo Two, confirmed. Bravo One Bravo Three confirmed. Bravo One Bravo four confirmed," the surveillance teams reported in one after the other. The last call sign then called in, "Bravo One, Oversight standing by. Out." "Who's Oversight?" Detective Joint asked curiously, listening in on a spare headset that Nick had given him. "That's our counter surveillance operator. We're not taking any chance here," Nick explained grimly, as Ian packed up his binoculars and hurried out of the suite. "We're not going to follow?" Detective Joint asked hurriedly wanting to follow Ian. Johan shook his head. "No, it's best if we don't interfere, Ian and his teams will tell us where they go. We don't want to spook her, just yet."

CHAPTER 15

JOHANNESBURG, SATURDAY, 13H00

Shedding and changing his identity like a chameleon changes colour, confident that he had lost whatever tail Grigori had put on him, the killer changed from one identity to the next. Stepping off of the Cathay Pacific Flight direct from Tokyo to Johannesburg, Mr Senji Yakamoto presented his passport at the OR Tambo International Passport Control and a few minutes later was walking through the International Arrivals with his carry-on bag, with the Prototype and his VR gear safely inside the laptop bag. Making it past the Customs officers without a hitch he walked outside into the early afternoon sunlight.

'That was simple enough,' he thought silently to himself with a smile as he sat down in the rear of the taxi. 'No one stopped me, asked me any questions or searched my bags!' he thought happily. "The Michael Angelo Hotel," he had instructed the driver. 'Middle of Sandton is a good place to start looking,' he had reasoned. He had done some research while on the flight over. The Michael Angelo Hotel offered all the amenities he required.

"Are you here to watch the rugby match this afternoon?" the taxi driver had asked him trying to strike up a conversation. "No," the killer cut him short. The driver left it at that. An hour later the killer had checked himself into the Michael Angelo Hotel and was shown to his suite on the eighteenth floor. Exhausted from the flight, he made sure his suite door was double locked, and after taking a long hot shower fell asleep on the bed.

When he awoke it was night outside and the suite was in darkness. Turning on a bedside light, he first perused the room service menu and ordered something to eat and then went about setting up his VR Connection using the hotel's high speed internet as his access point. There was a knock on the door a short while later and, confirming that it was room service, the killer opened the door. "Thank you," he said politely to the young room service girl. "I'll take the tray from you." He didn't want her in his room. Signing the bill and adding a tip for the girl he headed back inside, double locking the suite door behind him.

Loading the IP addresses of the servers he was looking for into the bracelet via his smartphone, he thought to himself, 'Right, let's get down to business. Let's find out where you are,' as he sat down in the comfortable lounge seater and slipped on the stainless-steel bracelet and mirror-like glasses, the Prototype on the coffee table in front of him, charged and slaved wirelessly to the bracelet. Before feeling the usual feeling of falling his progress was stopped and a message from the Prototype appeared WARNING YOU ARE ENTERING A PUBLIC ACCESS PLATFORM DO YOU WISH TO ACTIVATE SYSTEM? 'Of course, I do,' he thought. Pressing the YES tab on the menu screen, he felt his body charged with energy as it was encased in the black sheath.

Accessing the Maintenance Cloaked option, he immediately went invisible. A second later landing on the hotel's VR platform he was cloaked and invisible. Seeing a tube arrive that was going near where he wanted to go, he got an idea and followed the occupants on board. The tube occupants had no idea he was there. 'Now here's a way to use the tubes and stay invisible, just hijack one without the occupant even knowing I'm here,' he thought to himself with an evil grin on his face as the tube stopped and he followed the occupants out on to the platform.

Taking the escalator up, he found himself in a busy electronic street. Consulting his onboard computer, he turned left and headed down the electronic sidewalk. Soon he found the IP address he was looking for. Passing the Gate Keepers without even breaking a sweat the killer entered the building. Looking up at his drop-down menu he confirmed that he was at the correct IP Address, one of the Johannesburg houses belonging to Sable.

He entered via a PC that controlled the home integration system linked to the buildings' network and ultimately the internet. Searching around he soon found what he was looking for and accessing the drop-down menu changed the Prototype to Camera Setup Cloaked. The next second he was inside the IP based CCTV system, with 32 cameras laid out before him. It was a two-storey building, the ground floor almost one big room with a bar on one side and loungers strewn around. Siting and lying around in the loungers were beautiful women, all scantily clad in lingerie, all in various stages of undress. The ground floor was monitored from a number of different cameras.

The first-floor cameras were more interesting. The camera titles mentioned that they were covert cameras and the killer could understand why. All the cameras had microphones. Accessing the first room camera on the first floor came the sounds of, "Oh yes baby suck me suck me oh yes, just like that!" The camera showed a brunette laying on her back with her john straddling her, his hard cock deep in her mouth. The next camera showed a redhead lying on her back with her client pounding away enthusiastically between her legs.

Looking through all the images he couldn't find what he was looking for. Then, "Ah, what's this?" he asked himself softly as he found a link to a backup server. Following the link, he soon found what he was looking for. "Sable, you are a complete slut," he chided her silently as he found video footage of her and her companions indulging in highly erotic sexual acts. Making copies of what he found, the killer moved on. "Not in Cape Town, either from the look of it," he said to himself as he scrolled through the cameras. Following the same procedure by hitching a ride, unbeknownst to the tube's passengers, he soon found where he wanted to be. The server's name was titled DREAMLAND. 'So that's where you are,' he thought silently to himself with a big smile on his oriental face.

JOHANNESBURG, SANDTON SUN HOTEL, 20H00

Hanging back in the suite until most of the stadium crowd had left, they had headed back to the waiting vehicles. Over the encrypted comms circuit, they were kept updated as to the progress of the surveillance team. "Bravo Team, Bravo Two, target heading out on N1 towards Johannesburg," was the first indication as to where they were going. The next message was, "Bravo Team, Bravo Three, target heading into Sandton," and then, "Targets entering the parking garage at Sandton City."

"Let's hang around for the next 24 hours or so and see what the surveillance team digs up," Nick suggested. "Perfect," Johan replied with a grin looking at Eben, "we can continue our quest and see if Samantha and Lee Anne were known in Johannesburg." "You might as well also ask about Sable, get a decent picture of her printed out from this afternoon and show it around," Nick instructed them, "rattle the cage a bit." Carrying on he said, "The detective and myself will hang back and see what transpires." "Bravo team, Overwatch, your tail is clear at present."

Detective Joint closed the hotel room door behind him, double locked the door, and looked around. Once it was established that Sable would be partying for a while, Nick had decided to check them into a hotel for the night. The Sandton Sun and Towers was Nick's favourite when in town, so that's where they ended up checking in. Across the road, about 200m away was the Michael Angelo Hotel. Nick and himself had had a late dinner in the hotel restaurant while waiting for feedback from Bravo Team. The last message they got was, "Target has entered the Thunderdome night club." "Boy, this woman has got lots of energy. Where does she get it from?" Nick commented to the detective. Realising that not much would happen, Nick decided to call it a night. "Let's hear in the morning what the team finds out and take it from there," he suggested. Detective Joint had to agree, he was starting to feel

133

tired.

The hotel room was luxuriously appointed. There was a large queen size double bed in the centre of the room against the wall with a white duvet on top and a mountain of what looked like white fluffy comfortable pillows. The opposite wall was taken up with a long wooden sideboard with drawers, complete with a fridge and a well-stocked bar. Attached to the wall above the wooden sideboard was a large 49," LCD flat-screen TV. But what really intrigued the detective was the VR bracelet and glasses that were resting on the sideboard. There was a note attached to the glasses. 'Dear Guest, the VR Bracelet and Glasses are for your use and enjoyment. Regards, Management.' 'Hmmm,' thought the detective. After throwing back a couple of tots of whisky, compliments of the small minibar, Detective Joint sat down in the comfortable chair in his room and slipped on the VR bracelet and glasses.

Expecting the couple of seconds of auditory and sensory blackness, he was surprised when it didn't occur. Instead, a drop-down menu appeared in front of his eyes. Realising that he needed to use his index finger, he scrolled through the menu. 'Wow, I can change my appearance,' he thought reading the options, and as a joke settled on the appearance of a muscle-bound jock. Pushing the accept button he found himself travelling through a moment of auditory and sensory blackness. Then, he was awake and standing on a platform. The walls of the platform were adorned with ads for the hotel group and specials they were running. 'This platform is different to the one I last was on' he thought to himself and looking around found the customary escalators and headed up.

Exiting onto the electronic sidewalk above, the vivid colours and sounds along with the different looking caricatures and human forms again amazed him. Turning right he started to walk down the sidewalk, past tall sky scrapers standing right next door to one and two storey buildings constructed right next to and on top of each other, the lights from their neon lit signs garishly illuminating the walkway in front of him with their bright reds, yellows, greens, and blues. There were bars next door to banks, next door to whore houses, next door to hospitals next door to travel agents and so the electronic sidewalk went on and on.

Outside most of the buildings green Gate Keepers stood duty, every once in a while, turning red and sending a bolt of debilitating electrical energy towards some nearby form that looked as normal as could be; however, the Gate Keepers always seemed to sniff out the hacker or virus. The traffic was almost constant, with human and sometimes other looking forms surging around him. In his subconsciousness, he felt the urge to have a drink, longing for the relaxing feeling alcohol gave him. Looking ahead he saw a neon sign advertise 'Whisky and Girls.' "Now that's where I'm first going to visit, a virtual reality bar!" he said to himself excitedly.

Pushing the saloon-style bar doors open he walked inside. The detective found himself inside an old western cowboy style saloon. The entire bar was made of what looked like cheap pine wood. A long bar stretched the length of the room. Looking around the detective saw that there were more women than men in the bar, the majority sitting on bar stools along the one wall, a couple of them glanced in his direction as he walked in, looking him up and down. Walking up to the bar, he sat down on an empty bar stool. "What will it be, partner?" the barman asked walking up to him dressed as a barman from the Wild West. "Shot of whisky, please," Detective Joint answered.

To his amazement, a bottle of whisky materialised in the barman's hand and a glass appeared on the bar counter in front of him. The barman opened the bottle and poured a tot of the amber liquid into the glass. "Enjoy, partner," the barman said and stood back. Tentatively he reached out and touched the tot glass. 'Wow it feels real,' he thought, 'it feels like real glass.' Slowly he picked up the tot glass and brought it to his lips. There was a golden liquid inside and it smelt exactly like whisky. Bringing it to his lips he drank it, feeling the familiar burn as it ran down his throat and into his stomach. "Is this your first experience in Virtual Reality?" the barman asked watching the detective. "Yes," replied Detective Joint, feeling the familiar sensation of the whisky seeping through his body. Without asking the barman poured him another tot and walked away to serve another virtual customer.

"Howdy stranger, I haven't seen you here before," a strange female voice beside him spoke up. Looking to his left he saw a beautiful blonde with long blond hair in a short mini and crop top sitting next to him, her breast pointing perkily at him. "N-n-no," he stammered not used to having a beautiful woman striking up a conversation with him. "My name's Stacey, what's yours?" she asked him in a bright voice. "Arnold, but my friends call me Arnie," he replied with more confidence. Stacey reached over and placed her hand onto his leg. It felt warm and comforting to him and started to arouse him. All of a sudden, she asked him "Would you like fuck me?" the pink tip of her tongue running seductively across her gloss cherry red lips as she stared right at him. "Yes, yes, I would," he replied feeling a stirring in his loins. "Come," Stacey told him getting off her barstool and taking his hand firmly in hers. Walking through a door he hadn't noticed yet they walked up a set of stairs to the first floor.

Walking down a dimly lit passageway with doors on both sides, the detective heard screams of intense passion and moans of pleasure intermingling with each other. Opening one of the doors on the right, Stacey led him by the hand into an empty room. "Where do you want to fuck me?" Stacey asked seductively. "In a hotel room, on the beach, in a plane, your parents' bed, in public?" "Huh," the detective stammered at first not understanding the question, then it dawned on him."A hotel bedroom," he replied. "Okay," Stacey replied non fazed and the next second the room transformed into a Holiday Inn bedroom with a Deluxe King size bed. Stacey walked over to the detective and started to undress him. "You can touch me," Stacey told him, and he raised his hands and placed them hesitantly onto her perky breasts. "They're so firm and real," he said amazed, feeling the warm firm feeling of her breasts. Stacey smiled and removing his shirt started to run her tongue down his muscular rippled chest.

'Motherfucker, will you look at my washboard stomach,' he thought to himself in amazement. Stacey squatted down and unbuckled his pants, pulling them down, his aroused cock springing free. "Mmmm, I like a man who goes around combat style," she moaned as she held him with her left hand, opened her mouth, and encompassed the head of his cock in her mouth. "Ooohhhh, fuck, your mouth is so wet and warm," he moaned out as she started to suck him off, her right hand playing with his scrotum, gently tickling, and squeezing.

The intense wet sucking sensation ceased, and he heard Stacey say, "I want this big hard cock inside me," and she pushed him back onto the bed behind him. Straddling him, her dress rucked up around her waist, he saw that she was also combat style, her pantyless hairless vagina just inches from his face. He could smell her arousal. "Grrrrrr! Come here, I want to eat you," he snarled and placing his hands around the tight globes of her buttocks pulled her up onto his face and started to eat his way through her wet pink slippery folds. "You taste so real," he said out loud as he came up for air before Stacey ground her aroused womanhood back onto his face again. It was then that he saw it, the green and red rose tattoo high up on her left inner thigh.

CHAPTER 16

SANDTON SUN, SUNDAY MORNING, 07H45

There was knocking on the door followed by a male voice asking, "Detective are you awake?" cutting through his unconsciousness as he lay sleeping a dreamless sleep on the bed. Getting the shock of his life after spotting the bright red and green rose tattoo on the prostitute's upper inner thigh, he had run out of the room, retracing his steps through the electronic world. Getting lost back on the virtual sidewalk he had run around frantically until for some reason he had looked up and noticed in the top left hand of his vision a flashing sign saying EXIT.

'Fuck what's happening to me,' he silently asked himself as he came around sitting in the comfortable lounger in the hotel room. His heart was racing, and he was covered in sweat. "A green and red rose tattoo," he muttered to himself as he ripped off the nano bracelet computer and mirror glasses. "Another fucking rose tattoo, what the hell's going on?" he asked himself again as he stood up and stumbled over to the mini bar, and proceeded to interrogate the bar fridge.

There was another knock on the door, a bit louder this time followed by, "Detective, are you still alive in there?" "Uurgghh," he groaned opening his eyes through the fog of the alcohol, the light still tame on his eyes due to the heavy material of the closed curtains keeping the sun's rays at bay. "Hey, Detective!" the voice said a little louder. Recognising the voice as Johan's, the detective groaned out, "Alive and kicking," immediately wishing that he hadn't spoken so loud as a pain shot through his skull. "We're all meeting downstairs for breakfast in fifteen," Johan confirmed to him through the closed door. "I'll see you guys soon," he groaned out again, not so loudly this time.

Walking into the hotel breakfast room twenty minutes later looking a little bit worse for wear, Detective Joint found Nick and his team starting to dig into the breakfast buffet. Nodding a morning to all, Detective Joint headed to the coffee percolator and poured himself a large mug of black filter coffee.

Sitting around the table eating a decent English breakfast, Nick brought them up to speed. "Bravo Team reports that Sable and her companions partied at the Thunderdome Night club in Sandton until the early hours of this morning and then headed back to the airport to her waiting jet." "Ahh, the life of the rich and shameless," Eben commented sarcastically. Ignoring the comment Nick continued. "They landed in Durban and the Durban team was able to pick them up and follow them to just over the Umkomaas River where they turned left off of the N2 onto a beach road that runs past millionaires' mile, just before the town of Umkomaas, and then they lost them."

"Damn it," muttered Johan, "how the hell did they lose them?" "Not too sure, but at least we have an idea of to where to start looking," Nick told him. "They are currently watching the road from an observation point and will hopefully pick them up again when they move." "Okay, how did it go last night?" Nick then asked Johan. "We hit a number of bars and night clubs and showed the pictures around, no one's saying a word, but we did get a couple of dirty looks, and one guy looked as though he wanted to say something, but then didn't," Johan reported back. "Okay," Nick said swallowing the last bite of his breakfast and consulting his watch. "Nicky will have some news for us in about thirty minutes, she apparently spent all night at her desk and is just waiting for something or the other. Let's meet in my room at 09H30, listen to what she has to tell us, and plan our next step," he said brightly.

SANDTON SUN, 09H30, SUNDAY

All of them were gathered up in Nick's suite, with his laptop open on the coffee table in front of them. Using a secure encrypted link, they were holding a video call with Nicky who was sitting at her desk in Cape Town, and William who was sitting in his study at home in Camps Bay. "I hope you guys enjoyed the rugby while I sat at my desk," Nicky grumbled. She was an ardent supporter of the Springboks. "Who was playing rugby? We were working," Eben replied with a smile on his face. "What do you have for us?" Nick asked her bringing her back on course.

"Okay, boss, got some good news for you that is most probably going to raise more questions than answers," Nicky said with a grim smile over the data link. "Shoot," Nick instructed her. "The good news is that I've been able to get into Mark's emails," Nicky told them. "But…" Nick said. "But this is where it gets interesting," Nicky told her rapt audience. "It seems that a couple of hours before he was murdered, he was busy drafting you an email boss," she explained. "Me?" Nick asked her amazed. "Yes, your email address is nick@execdecisions.com, correct?" Nicky confirmed with him. "Uh-huh," Nick nodded his head. "You might as well read the email out to us, Nicky."

Clearing her throat Nicky began reading. "Hi, Nick. Sorry to bother you, I know that at present you are somewhere in that big cold washing machine called the Atlantic Ocean. I don't know what you see in it… Anyway, my friend, sorry to trouble you, I need your help, and I wouldn't ask you if I had another option (knowing what you're currently undertaking), you're the only one I can trust." Nicky stopped to catch her breath, then carried on reading. "I am being watched, people are trying to steal my work. It looks like even Veronica is a spy." Nicky stopped there. "That's all there is, he didn't get to finish it," she explained to Nick. "Wow, that's quite explosive," Johan commented.

Turning to Detective Joint, Nick asked, "Detective, your comments?" Smiling, he replied, "In my official capacity as a police detective, I have no idea what you're talking about as the evidence you are referring to has not been collected or submitted to me as evidence through official channels. However, in my personal capacity, sitting here in this room off duty, I would say that Veronica Bings would become the number one suspect with a statement like that." "Correct, Detective," Nicky replied nodding her head. "However, she has an alibi. She was out of the country at the time." "So maybe she was an accomplice, set the whole thing up," Eben suggested. "But what is her motive?" Detective Joint asked. "We looked at his life insurance policies, it was one of the first things we looked at, she had no reason to kill him, she got more when he was alive than dead. It all goes into a trust fund for his kids. She only gets a couple of million."

Grinning like a Cheshire cat Nicky said, "Now that's what I was also thinking, and I did a bit of digging around. I can't find any mention of Veronica Bings prior to her marriage to Mark." "What do you mean?" Nick asked. "I found their marriage certif-icate; her maiden name is Terblanche, but I can't find any social media records of her anywhere until a couple of months prior to her marriage to Mark." "That's strange," Detective Joint said. "I'll pass the name onto our Intelligence Liaison Officer. Let's see what she can find out," he offered. "Good idea," everyone agreed. They were about to end the conversation when Nicky said, "Oh wait, one last thing, the pictures that you sent me of the suspect and her friends, I'm sure I've seen her before, I just can't remem-ber where. As soon as I remember I'll let you know."

After ending the video call with Nicky, William connected a bit longer and they discussed what they'd discovered so far. Nick brought the discussion to a close, "Right, this is what I propose we do until we have more information to work with. William, please arrange to have a couple of investigators from our Joburg office sniff around the nightlife some more showing the pictures of the three around." William nodded his head and made a note on his desk pad. Eben climbed in saying, "Based on the size of the suited gorillas who came for us in Cape Town, they need to be able to handle themselves." William nodded his head again and confirmed, "Noted they need to be big buggers."

Carrying on Nick turned to the detective. "Detective, I'm sure you'll agree that right now the best way forward for you is to go back to work tomorrow and continue your official investigation and see what unfolds." Detective Joint nodded his head in agreement and replied, "Correct, I agree. I'll get our Intelligence Liaison Officer to run the pictures of Sable and her entourage and see what I can find from my side. I'll also add the name Veronica Terblanche to the mix and see what comes back." "What about us, boss?" Eben asked. Turning to Eben and Johan he said with a grin, "We're going to the South Coast for a bit of R&R."

UMKOMAAS SOUTH COAST, DREAMLAND, SUNDAY, 14H00

Sable sat outside on her private deck on the first floor of her Spanish style villa looking out to sea, where on the horizon shipping was passing back and forth in the shipping lanes, absently listening to her lover prattle on about how much fun she had yesterday. 'Almost time for her to go,' Sable thought to herself, as she turned and gave Debbie a big smile.

After the rugby match, they had driven into Sandton for dinner and then hit the Thunderdome, one of the trendy night clubs in Sandton that Sable owned. At four o'clock in the morning, they had headed back to the airport and flown back to Durban. Her iPhone started to vibrate in her silk dressing gown pocket. Answering the call, it was Ricardo. "Ma'am, Ricardo here, we need to talk," he told her urgently, "but not over the phone." "Okay," Sable sighed looking at her gold Cartier watch on the slender left arm, "be here at four," and she ended the call.

16H00

Precisely at four o'clock, Ricardo was welcomed by the guard at the gate and a couple of minutes later he was sitting with Sable outside on the terrace again. "So, what is so important?" Sable asked curiously. "We have a problem. Two nights in a row, men have been asking questions about Samantha and Lee Anne in Sandton as well as in Cape Town." "What!" she exclaimed almost choking on the mouthful of Chenin Blanc wine she had just swallowed. "As I told you yesterday morning, two men were asking for the girls at The Pussy Cat Club in Long Street Cape Town and subsequently beat up all 8 of our bouncers." Ricardo patiently explained to her "Yes, I remember," Sable told him irritably.

Carrying on Ricardo explained to her, "Last night two men were asking around clubs and bars in the Sandton area about them." And then he dropped the bombshell. "And they were also asking for you by name, passing your picture around." Ricardo stretched across the table passing his smartphone across to her showing a picture of Sable and her entourage sitting in the box at the rugby match yesterday afternoon. "How the fuck did this happen?!" Sable asked out loudly, dropping her wine glass in shock. It fell onto the terra cotta tiles with the glass shattering, spilling the contents and sharp glass shards across the terrace. "They were watching us yesterday," she snarled angrily now. "How did they find me?" "We're not sure, but we've got video footage of the men asking questions at the clubs," he mentioned to Sable. "Show it to me, I want to see it now," she demanded furiously.

Leaving the maid to clean up the mess on the terrace, Sable led the way into one of the smaller lounges on the ground floor, and Ricardo placed a laptop on the coffee table in front of her. "This is the footage from the Pussy Cat Club in Cape Town," he explained to her pushing the play button. 'My god,' Sable thought silently to herself as she watched the video footage of both Johan and Eben, two regular looking guys, taking on and obliterating eight of her bouncers. guys who all spent a good couple of hours a day in the gym pumping iron. "Who are they? It looks like they have military training," Sable said, getting aroused by the violence. "That was also my impression," Ricardo confirmed to her. "Show me the Joburg clips from last night," she instructed him impatiently.

"It's the same two guys," Sable exclaimed hoarsely a couple of minutes later. Ricardo nodded his head in agreement. "Are you sure that they didn't ask for me by name on Friday night," Sable then asked questioning him closely. "No, ma'am, but I'll check again," Ricardo replied, wondering where this was going. "If they didn't ask for me by name on Friday night. but did on Saturday night, they must have learnt something on Friday night. Find out all you can about these two gentlemen. Use all our resources but find out about them quickly," Sable instructed him and then dismissed him.

As he was walking away, he turned around and said to her, "There was also a very strange occurrence last night in our Sandton VR House." "What?" asked Sable rather rudely her mind spinning with the information she just been given. "A john walked into the house and started getting it on with one of the girls when he got frightened for some reason and exited before the end of the transaction." "Why? Was there a glitch in the programming?" she asked amused at what she was hearing. "No," Ricardo replied. "The girl said he mumbled something about the same rose tattoo."

'Shit. The rose tattoo that myself and my top girls got a long time ago is coming back to haunt me' Sable thought worriedly to herself, remembering the younger, wilder days. "Is there any way we can trace the transaction?" she asked hopefully. "Yes," Ricardo nodded his bald head. "The VR set used was a complimentary set in a hotel room, The Sandton Sun and Towers to be precise," he told her with a smile on his face. "Get on it, I want all the information they have," Sable instructed him, a cold shiver of trepidation running down her spine. Picking up her iPhone she consulted her Contact List and dialled a South African number. When the call was answered she spoke four words, "We have a problem," and ended the call. Ten minutes later her iPhone rang, from an unlisted number.

CAPE TOWN, PICKWICK TAVERN, SUNDAY, 20H30

"I'd love to get my hands on this sick mother fucker who's chopping off heads again, he's just opened up the Samantha Joint murder, something I thought that we had been able to bury, forget about and move on," Detective Brant growled to his long-time friend and associate in crime, Captain Williamson. Carrying on he whined, "I'm not sure how much longer I can last being Joint's partner. It's as if he knows something." "I know, that's why I arranged that he got the case, hoping that he would show us his hand, but instead new fucking information is coming to light. I could kill that fucking Lindiwe," Captain Williamson growled back. They were sitting in a dark dingy bar in a part of Cape Town not frequented by many tourists. They were sitting at the corner of the bar, comfortable in their surroundings.

Both looked up as the doors burst open and a couple of noisy bikers in riding leathers entered the watering hole and headed for the opposite corner of the bar. With natural cops' instinct, they both looked the bikers up and down. Nothing unusual about the two of them, they both decided. The two new comers looked like real bikers, faded worn leathers, like the rest of the patrons in the bar, not the flashy new riding leathers that high paid doctors and lawyers wore on a Sunday riding around on their hogs feeling bad ass.

Not paying the two bikers any more attention they got back to nursing their drinks and talking. The one biker placed his crash helmet on the bar counter, the silver mirrored visor facing towards the two men huddled in the corner of the bar. "So, could I, so could I," Detective Brant replied ruefully thinking back. What neither himself nor the captain could see was the hi-tech video camera and microphone that had been built into the helmet, recording every word they spoke.

The plan had been fool proof. They both worked at the Umhlanga Rocks Police Station and together with Detective van Rensburg from the Durban Central Police Station whom they had previous nefarious dealings with, they quickly put a plan together once they heard of the diamonds.

Their plan had at first gone smoothly. Staking out the hotel room and exit points they had waited. After Samantha and the target had entered the suite, no one else had entered and no one came out. Only around three hours later did they realise something was horribly wrong when there was no movement from inside the room. Even the insistent ringing of the telephone went unanswered. It was only much later, when housekeeping went into the room the following morning and found Samantha decapitated on the bed along with her 'lover', that it was confirmed that there was a big cluster fuck. Her lover the target turned out to be a well-known jewel thief in the crime world. To hide their identity, it had been imperative that van Rensburg got handed the case, which to their relief he had.

Somehow Samantha's boss had found out what had happened and in an about twist to save their own skins they had thrown Detective van Rensburg under the bus and made him out to be the one trying to steal the diamonds. Sable had had him killed and the captain and Detective Brant had unintentionally become another set of bitches in Sable's stable to do her bidding whenever it fancied her. "Relax, Brant. I've got it under control," Captain Williamson told his subordinate. "I've deleted the two video clips of us from the email, but we're going to have to get the copies from Executive Decisions," he told him. "How the fuck we going to do that?" Brant asked astounded. "If Sable finds out that we lied to her I'd rather take my chances in jail than with her." "I'm working on a plan; we are the law, after all," the captain said with a grin. Catching the bartender's attention he shouted out, "Another round and a couple of chasers for us!"

"She contacted me earlier on," the captain told Brant after the next round of drinks had arrived. Taking a sip of his fresh drink the captain continued speaking. "Somehow Joint has found her and together with Executive Decisions is asking questions about her. She's going to get her guys to pick up Joint and interrogate him and make an example of him," the captain explained with the same emotion in his voice he had just used to order the next

146

round of drinks. "Great idea, once he's out of the way and you've found a way to silence Executive Decisions things should quieten down and come back to normal," Brant said with a relieved sigh. "She wants you there in case an official representative is required, in case something goes wrong," Captain Williamson said with a sly grin. "When is it going down?" Brant asked. 'Tomorrow evening," Captain Williamson replied. "Cheers to that," grunted Detective Brant picking up his chaser. Soon after that they finished their drinks and left, one after the other, they didn't notice the bikers move to a rear booth and the one biker slip on a set of headphones. Neither did they pay any attention to the couple of bikers who left after them.

"Evening, Boss, it's Pete here, the detective is in trouble, they plan to pick him up, interrogate him and then kill him tomorrow evening," the one biker who happened to be a surveillance specialist said informing Nick. Carrying on he quickly explained for a couple of minutes and then said, "I'll upload the audio file to you in a couple of minutes. Karl and the boys are busy following Detective Brant." "Thanks, Pete, good work. Make sure that your team keeps a close eye on the situation," Nick told him. He was currently checking into a Bed and Breakfast on the Natal South Coast, after spending the afternoon trawling Umkomaas and the surrounding countryside.

"Are you going to inform Detective Joint of his impending kidnapping and torture?" Pete then asked. Nick thought about it for a couple of seconds and then answered "Yes, I'll contact him now and explain. You better make sure that you and your team are on the top of your game and that no harm comes to the detective. If you need additional resources let me know." "Aye, aye, sir," Pete replied and ended the call.

CHAPTER 17

CAPE TOWN POLICE STATION, MONDAY, 08H15

Detective Joint arrived back in Cape Town late Sunday afternoon, the only passenger on board the Executive Decisions Bombardier Global 6000. The jet had first flown to Durban and offloaded Nick, Johan, and Eben, and then with only the detective still on board had flown back to Cape Town. En route to Cape Town the phone in the detective's seat rang. Figuring how to open the walnut cover and remove the wireless handset, he answered the call. "Detective, Nick here, we've got to talk. Some new information has just come to light, and there's an audio recording I need you to listen to," Nick said, starting to explain to the detective.

A couple of minutes later, after listening to the recorded conversation, the detective was shaking with anger. "The bastards," he growled down the phone to Nick. "Let them bring it on and we can catch them in the act!" he said carrying on talking. "I was rather hoping that would be your answer," Nick replied. Speaking for another couple of minutes, Nick ended the conversation saying, "Good luck, Detective, remember to act natural, we'll have a team watching your every move from the minute you step off the aircraft when you land this afternoon."

An hour later the Bombardier landed at Cape Town International Airport and taxied to the Private Operator terminal. "Nice to have met you, Detective, just walk straight through that set of open doors," Hannah explained to the detective pointing with a big smile on her face to the set of open double doors leading into the Private Operator Terminal. Inside the building, no one stopped him, and he walked straight through. A driver was waiting outside to take him back to Wynberg and dropped him off around the corner from his bachelor quarters. Walking back into the batchelor quarters he didn't see any of his buddies as he headed up the stairs to his one-bedroom apartment.

Walking into the Cape Town Police Station on Monday morning, the detective felt invigorated, excited even, as if the dark cold blanket of his sister's murder was finally starting to lift. 'For the first night in a long time I haven't woken up in a cold sweat dreaming about Samantha's murder,' he thought pleasantly to himself. 'And it's taken a billionaire with a private security operation to help me,' he further thought ruefully, his thoughts on the rich starting to change slightly, 'not all rich people are stuck up arseholes it would seem.' Also, the fact that he knew he was going to be accosted at some point during the day seemed to spur him on. Entering the detective's office, he found Juliet at her desk. "Wow, you look refreshed this morning. Did you have a good weekend?" she asked him surprised.

Normally he looked like shit on a Monday morning from the constant drinking over the weekend. "Yes, thanks," he said brightly and left it at that. Before he could say another word, Juliet said excitedly, "The video clips arrived in an email late on Friday afternoon just as I was leaving the office for the weekend, I'm just about to look at them." A couple of seconds later she looked at Detective Joint in horror and said "Huh, Detective, we have a slight problem here, I could have sworn there were six attachments. Now there's only four! Someone's been tampering with my computer." "Shhh, keep it down," Detective Joint said excitedly to her "I've was expecting this, we've got them rattled." Looking at him as if he was mad Juliet asked, "Sorry Detective, but what the hell are you talking about?"

Quickly looking around to make sure that they were alone, Detective Joint asked her "How long have you known me, Juliet?" "Long enough to know that you don't normally act this way," she replied. Nodding his head in agreement he told her, "Some startling new information has come to light about my sister's murder that seems to have a direct bearing on the latest murders, and for some reason implicating certain members in this department," he told her softly. "My word," Juliet gasped astounded, "do you know who?" Grimly Detective Joint nodded his head and replied, "Yes, the missing two video clips revealed them, but right now it's safer that you don't know, I'm still trying to put all the pieces of the puzzle together." Explaining a bit further he told her, "I saw all six video clips while at Executive Decisions the other day." "So, whoever it is accessed my PC over the weekend and deleted the two incriminating video clips," she surmised. "Correct," Detective Joint replied.

Handing her a brown envelope that contained the pictures of Sable and her entourage from the rugby match on Saturday he explained to her, "Some new information has come up. Could you please run these pictures through all your databases and see what pops up? Please bring the information directly to me and tell no one else about it, for now." "Yes, sir," Juliet confirmed ominously accepting the envelope. "May I ask where you got them from?" Shaking his head, he answered, "Sorry, again for now it's better if you don't know."

Sitting down at their morning meeting twenty minutes later, Detective Lindiwe kicked the meeting off, "Sorry," she told him frustratingly, "the Durban Central police station can't find the evidence we are looking for. Now it turns out that there was a theft from the evidence locker." "I expected nothing less," Detective Joint replied rather ominously looking around the table at his fellow Detectives. Juliet then spoke up excitedly; as pre-arranged with Detective Joint, "We've received the video clips from Executive Decisions." "Well, let's play them then, what are we waiting for?" Detective Brant said eagerly, exchanging a quick glance with the captain. "There, I told you nothing new," the captain exclaimed ten minutes later after watching the four video clips. "Now," he snarled, "get back to solving the latest murders!"

UMKOMAAS SOUTH COAST, 13H00, MONDAY

"Boss, you're not going to believe what we've just found," Nicky gushed out over the satellite link. "Tell me I'm all ears," Nick replied eagerly. The three of them were sitting in a local restaurant in the small seaside holiday town of Umkomaas on the KwaZulu-Natal South Coast having lunch. They had spent the morning driving around getting a feel for the area and seeing if they could spot Sable or the white Porsche, she was last seen driving in. "We were able to break through another layer of Mark's encryption and we've found his AI Server," she told him excitedly. "Say that again, a bit slower," Nick instructed her. "He has a high spec server loaded with Artificial Intelligence mapped around his thoughts and personality." "What?!" Nick asked astounded. "He has a high spec server loaded with Artificial Intelligence mapped around his thoughts and it is asking for you. Boss, please get your ass back to Cape Town, I can't explain it over the telephone. I have briefed William and he's sending the jet for you now," Nicky explained hurriedly to him. Realising that something big was up Nick agreed.

Turning to Johan and Eben he said to them with a grin, "Been called back to Cape Town, think you two can do a bit of surveillance without getting into any trouble?" "Boss that's not fair," Eben whined back with a smile on his boyish looking face. Setting him up with a fishing rod and bait, they left Eben on an outcrop of rocks to catch supper while Johan drove Nick back to the airport just over a hundred and fifty kilometres to the north. From the rocks using a set of high-powered binoculars he had a perfect view of the millionaire homes scattered along the stretch of beach front a kilometre or so up the coast.

CAPE TOWN POLICE STATION, 17H15, MONDAY

"Goodnight, Detective," the last of the detectives and his colleagues said to him as they left for the evening. He was planning on working a bit late to clear up the mounting paperwork on his desk and take the last train on the southern line back to Wynberg. Walking out of the Cape Town Central Police Station just after 18H00, he turned left and followed his usual route down to the Cape Town Train Station. He failed to notice the two burly men across the road from the police station looking in a shop window and start to follow him as he stepped outside.

Reaching Adderley Street with the Cape Town train station just across the road he stopped for the red pedestrian signal. "Ouch," he cried out in pain, feeling a pin prick like a bee sting on his neck. A second later the ground seemed to open and swallow him whole as the fast-acting toxin went to work. As his knees started to buckle, in one practised move two sets of strong hands gripped him under both of his armpits, while at the same time in a chor-egraphed move a nondescript panel van screeched to a halt in front of them, the sliding door opened and Detective Joint was un-ceremoniously dumped inside, his two assailants following close behind. The door slammed closed and the nondescript panel van drove off. It had taken less than 10 seconds.

CAPE TOWN, EXECUTIVE DECISIONS, 17H30, MON-DAY

Landing back in Cape Town just after 17H30, Nick collected his white 911 Turbo from the Private Operator Terminal parking lot and drove to his office, a 5-minute drive away from the airport. Nicky, Steven, and William were waiting for him in the secure B-1 Boardroom. "Right guys what's up?" he asked them curi-ously sitting down. Taking a deep breath Nicky began to explain, "We were able to break through another level of Mark's security and have found an AI Server that has been imaged around your friend Mark. There were a few interesting puzzles to solve to get to the AI Server, but we managed to get in. He's asking to speak to you."

"Well then, let's go," Nick told them standing up. Rushing out of the B-1 Boardroom they all headed for the VR Suite on the lower basement level. "Just Nicky and I go, the rest of you wait here," Nick instructed them. Reclining in one of the comfortable leather executive chairs of the VR Suite, Nick strapped on his stainless-steel bracelet and placed the mirrored glasses over his eyes. There was the usual moment of auditory and sensory blackness followed by a second of feeling like he was free-falling when without warning the lights came on and equilibrium was immediately re-established on all axis. "Okay, Boss, we've got to take a tube," he heard Nicky say.

The tube travel seemed like hours but was in fact just a couple of seconds when the tube stopped at a platform. Following Nicky out of the tube on to the platform, Nick looked around him. It was an unused public platform, looking very unkept, dark, and dingy. "Any idea where we are?" he asked Nicky. Turning to him she smiled and shook her head saying "No, not really. It's a public platform in a subnet VR world, it's definitely not within the borders of South Africa." Walking up the steel escalators; as they were not working, they entered out onto a dark electronic street, with not much traffic around, as compared to the mainstream Virtual Reality.

Here and there Nick saw movement, traffic moving from one deep shadow to the next created by the dim neon signs on the outside of a couple of buildings in the street while the majority of the electronic street was in darkness. "So, this is what a subnet world looks like?" Nick quipped to Nicky as he followed her down the dark street. In order to hide their identity, both Nick and Nicky were wearing long flowing capes with large deep hoods, looking somewhat like Jedi Knights from Star Wars. "Here we are, I think this is it," Nicky said a couple of minutes later as they reached a non-descript small rise building with no neon sign or Gate Keepers standing guard outside. "No gate keepers?" Nick asked. "Gate Keepers are frowned on in these subnet worlds," Nicky explained patiently to her boss.

The inside of the building was nothing like the outside. Inside

153

it was a sterile white bright lit computer room with a single door at the far end of the room. As Nick was about to walk across the white square tiled computer room floor, Nicky grabbed his arm and pulling him back said, "Wait." Entering a 6-digit code into a keypad on the wall that he hadn't seen the lights changed colour to ultraviolet light and a path was magically demarcated across the white computer room floor tiles in luminous colours. "Whew, thanks," Nick said. "I assume walking off the demarcated path could have ruined my day in Virtual Reality." "Something like that," Nicky answered him grimly. The path across the computer room wasn't a straight one from one side of the room to the other and seemed to take forever to walk across, all the time Nick heeded Nicky's words, "Keep to the path." Reaching the door on the opposite side it silently slid open automatically as they approached and they walked through.

Walking into the white sterile room on the other side of the door, smaller than the one they had just walked through, Nick stopped dead in his tracks. Sitting on a raised bar like stool was his friend Mark. Turning around as if sensing he was there the image of Mark turned fully around. "Good afternoon, Nick," the image said using facial recognition software. "Thank you for coming so quickly. I can see and sense your apprehension. I am Mark's AI. My creator named me Arthur. The reason why you are here is that my designer and father has been killed. In order to proceed, I need to ask you some questions." Nick silently nodded his head.

Without warning a square steel wall shot up around Nick trapping him inside with the AI image, Nicky on the outside. "Sorry," the image said with a slight smile, "I need to ensure that we are not overheard by whoever has the Prototype." "You know about the theft of the Prototype?" Nick asked amazed. "All in good time," the AI image called Arthur replied. "I have been preprogramed to first ask you some questions to confirm your identity. Once you have answered them correctly, I will allow Miss Nicky to join us. May I proceed?" Arthur asked politely.

A couple of minutes later after answering all the questions correctly, the steel wall moved to encompass Nicky and a table and chairs appeared. "Please, take a seat," Arthur told him gesturing to the seats. "Are you okay?" Nicky asked her boss worriedly sitting down in the proffered chair. Grinning Nick replied, "Me and old Arthur are getting on just fine."

"Ah, good day, Miss Nicky. You are a fine adversary. I was monitoring your progress, and if you don't mind me saying you have great analytical skills to be able to crack the code that my creator put in place," Arthur told her with sincerity. Blushing slightly at the compliment Nicky replied, Thank you, but I sensed that there was some help." "Caught", Arthur replied. Carrying on, he said, "You were always supposed to gain access to me. I just needed to see how good you are for the task ahead, a little test if you want to call it that," he explained with a small laugh.

"Before I start, Mr Scott, my master had asked me to monitor you and your yacht's performance. For your information, I calculate that you have a 56% chance of winning the Vendee Globe Challenge based on the data made available to me," Arthur told him with a smile on his electronic face. "Why thank you, Arthur," Nick replied. "I'll bear that in mind when I'm down in the South Atlantic."

His face getting serious again Arthur began talking. "As I said earlier, the reason that you are here is that my creator and friend has been killed; I have access to all news feeds," he said by way of mentioning. "My creator put into place protocols should he mysteriously die, and these protocols have now been activated." "What are these steel walls for?" Nicky asked. "It is to shield us from the Prototype," was the answer. A screen then appeared on the one steel wall and a video began to play.

The video showed Mark Bings, the creator of Virtual Reality, sitting behind his desk in what Nick assumed was his study. "Hi, Nick," Mark began speaking. "If you're seeing this video being played by Arthur, it means that I'm dead," he told them bluntly. Continuing he said, "Congratulations, by the way, on following the trail to my AI. I was always worried that you wouldn't find the trail, but then I remembered the calibre of the staff you have and then began to worry if I made it too easy," he told them with a small laugh.

"Anyway, back to the topic at hand, it's a morbid subject really but the fact is I'm dead, and I didn't die of natural causes. I am assuming that I was killed for the Prototype which I completed a couple of days ago. If the Prototype isn't sitting in my wall safe in the study, then that means it has been stolen. Nick, the Prototype must be found. I am scared that it could have fallen into the wrong hands. I was wrong in thinking that it would only be used by like-minded individuals such as myself for the betterment of the world of Virtual Reality and the users' experience. Since word got out of what I was developing, I sensed I was under surveillance, and it's not just by one person. I know you must think I'm going crazy, but my wife is also spying on me. She's a spy," Mark said to the camera with utter conviction.

Holding up his hand and saying, "Before you ask how I know; I caught her planting cameras in my study. And I thought it was love and she loved me, my dick, and my money, and not always in that order. How wrong I was!" he said with another short laugh. "I didn't tell her but when I moved into the penthouse, I found that the previous owner had installed a couple of covert cameras, and as a joke, I decided to leave them installed. Imagine my surprise when reviewing the footage one day I viewed her installing hi-spec wireless cameras into my study."

He stopped speaking for a couple of seconds and then continued. "Anyway, I never told her that I knew. It was then that I realized what was going on and started putting the pieces of the puzzle together. I never did find out who she was working for." With tears in his eyes, he carried on, "I am now also convinced that Sally's car accident and subsequent death was no accident either, it was planned, it was somehow part of the larger plan to get me away from the United States and to a country easier for foreign security services to move around in."

"Nick you have to find the Prototype, secure it and hand it over to the US military, to a General Dwayne Perrington, based at the US Cyberspace Command Centre. Arthur will give you all the details." Holding up his hands again, Mark said "I know, I know, I said my work would never be used for military use, but at heart, I'm also a patriot and I now realise that what the General was trying to prevent happening has just happened." Leaning forward in his chair, Mark stared intently into the camera of his monitor and said, "Nick, you have to find the Prototype, the future of the world as we know it rests in your hands."

Mark sat back in his seat looking exhausted and drained, "I've setup an account with my bankers in Switzerland for you to draw whatever funds you need to track down the Prototype. When you have found the Prototype, do whatever you like with the balance. After spending a couple more minutes confirming the bank account and contact details in Switzerland, Mark sat back in his chair and told them, "Good luck." The video went blank and the screen disappeared. Nick sat silent for a few moments collecting his thoughts. Nicky and the AI said nothing. Then, turning to the AI image, Nick said grimly "Okay, tell us all you know about this Prototype and how we're going to get it back."

CHAPTER 18

EPPING INDUSTRIAL AREA ABANDONED WARE-HOUSE, MONDAY, 20H00

Slowly Detective Joint opened his eyes. His head was pounding, and his throat was dry as if he had been drinking, but with a metallic aftertaste in his mouth. "What the fuck, where am I?" he moaned out as he struggled to sit up but realised that something was holding him down. "What the fuck," he cried out a bit louder when he realised that his hands were also stuck. "Ahh, Detective, I see you are awake now. Sorry for the inconvenience, it's no use struggling," a voice with a foreign accent said to him, speaking through the blackness of the detective's sub consciousness.

Coming fully awake, he opened his eyes. 'I'm in some sort of abandoned warehouse,' he thought silently to himself seeing the steel structure of the roof high above him. A face that he didn't recognise came into his view. "You know that I'm a detective in the South African Police force," he shouted out, hoping that it would shock them into releasing him, all a bad joke and all that. All that it brought was laughter. He started to get worried, very worried. 'Fuck, I hope Nick's men are here,' he thought worriedly.

"Detective, you have apparently upset some very powerful people with your nosing around. They want me to ask you nicely what you have found out about them so far," the foreign voice said to him ominously. A vision of his sister lying dead and cold came into his head and a cold anger rose from the pit of his stomach. "Go fuck yourself!" the detective snarled back at them. Out of view from behind his head, a strong pair of hands roughly placed a dirty foul smelling towel tightly over his face covering his mouth and nose, pushing his head firmly against the wooden table while another set of hands started to pour water slowly out of a 2 litre Coke bottle onto the towel, the clear precious life-giving liquid cascading over the towel inundating it with water, now becoming a weapon of torture. He felt like he was drowning, the wet towel making it impossible to breath.

He held his breath for as long as possible and then the natural human instinct for survival kicked in. His lungs screaming for air he opened his mouth and water gushed down his throat and into his lungs. He started to drown. "Stop, don't kill him, we still need information from him," he heard the foreign voice snap out through his barely conscious consciousness. The wet foul-smelling towel was pulled away from his face. Coughing and spluttering up a large amount of water along with the contents of his stomach, panting he took a couple of lungsful of air.

"I'll ask you again. What have you found out about your dead sister?" the voice asked again even toned. "Fuck you, nothing," spat back the detective. "I don't believe you, partner," a new voice spoke up from behind him. It was the voice of Detective Brant who walked into Detective Joint's view. "Why you piece of shit!" Detective Joint roared out loudly, all the pent-up frustrations releasing, struggling to break free from his bonds. "You can struggle all you like, but we can do this all night," his now ex-partner Detective Brant told him harshly. "Now what have you learnt from Executive Decisions?" Brant then asked. "Go fuck yourself, Brant!" Detective Joint hissed back.

The leader nodded his head and the wet dirty cloth was shoved back over his face and the torture continued. Without warning through the torment of being water boarded came the unmistakable sounds of gunfire and the continuous stream of life-giving water miraculously stopped. The foul-smelling rag was pulled off his face and a voice he hadn't heard before asked, "Are you okay, Detective?" as another set of hands started to cut him free.

"Thanks, guys, just in the nick of time, they were starting to get serious," Detective Joint said shakily as his bonds were cut loose and he was helped up off of the wooden table. Standing up he looked around, surveying the dead and wounded captors on the floor. "He's not here, Brant's not here. He got away," Detective Joint shouted out in frustration. "Spread out, guys, find the now ex-detective Brant," the leader, who introduced himself as Pete, rapidly instructed his team. "Sorry, Detective, he got away," Pete said apologetically to Detective Joint a couple of minutes later after the team searched the derelict warehouse and came up empty-handed.

"Hey, this one's still alive," one of Pete's team shouted out. "Great," Pete replied rubbing his hands together. "Let's ask him some questions, then, shall we?" Pulling on a set of plastic surgical gloves Pete strolled over to the assailant now laying on the dirty floor bleeding out. Squatting down beside the dying man Pete asked him, "Who sent you, who do you work for?" "Go fuck yourself," the man gasped back at Pete. Pretending not to have heard, Pete looked at the injured man examining his wounds and then stuck his plastic index finger into one of the bullets wound in his chest. "AAAAAAAH!" the man screamed out in agony and slipped into unconsciousness.

The detective picked up one of the bottles of water they were planning to drown him with and with no emotion whatsoever emptied the contents over the man's face and said angrily, "It isn't constitutional but what the fuck, right now I don't give a shit!". Moaning the assailant came around. "I'll ask you again," Pete said calmly waving his blood-covered hand in the man's face, "who sent you? Who do you work for?" Nothing. The man started to scream out louder in extreme pain "AAAAAAAH!" as Pete plunged his finger into the wound again, this time a bit deeper. "Sable, we all work for Sable!" the man screamed out loudly in agony, unable to take the pain. Detective Joint squatted down next to the dying man and asked, "How did you find me?" "Whisky and Girls," the man groaned softly, barely audible. Before leaving, Detective Joint took pictures of the scene on his smartphone, including the bodies, the table as well as the plastic bottles and the water lying around the table.

CAPE TOWN, EXECUTIVE DECISIONS, MONDAY, 21H45

"And what did you find out?" William asked them anxiously as they came back around in the VR suite. "Tell you all back in the secure boardroom," Nick told him. Without warning, he felt his stomach starting to grumble. Looking at his Rolex he noted that it was almost ten in the evening. "Bloody hell, we were gone for three hours, no wonder I'm starving," Nick said out loud. "Now that you mention it, Boss, my stomach is also asking questions," Nicky told him with a grin across her pretty face.

Twenty minutes later armed with toasted sandwiches from the 24-hour staff canteen on the ground floor they all headed back down to the secure boardroom on the B-1 level. As William was about to put his internal phone into the cellphone holder outside the boardroom door, it rang. "Yes," he said answering the call, "tell the boys to bring the detective down to the B-1 conference room."

"And?" Nick asked when Detective Joint walked into the boardroom looking like a drowned rat covered in what looked like grease and dirt. "Brant was there, but he got away, the bastard," Detective Joint exclaimed angrily. Then continued, "But we've got confirmation that Sable's involved up to her pretty eyeballs, as well as some other powerful individuals, if you can go on the questions that they asked me before being dispatched."

A couple of minutes later once Detective Joint had finished talking Nick replied with a small smile on his face "So, we're starting to rattle their cages." "What about the dead bodies, you just left them there?" Steven asked. "Yes," Detective Joint said grimly, "I phoned it in anonymously, I want to see what crawls out of the woodwork." "Good idea," Nick agreed. "I feel sorry for Brant's family though," Detective Joint said sadly to no one in particular. Pete, who had joined them in the board room, gave a laugh and replied "Family? What family detective? He lives alone in a flat in Woodstock."

Clearing his throat Nick spoke up, bringing the detective up to speed, "We've also been able to gain access to Mark's backups," Nick then informed the detective. "Take a seat and I'll bring you all up to date on the investigation." "What!" Detective Joint loudly exclaimed a couple of minutes later. "His wife is a spy!" "Yes," Nicky replied to him. "We saw the video footage of her planting the cameras." "Bloody hell, do we know who she's working for?" Both of them shook their heads. "Shit," the detective grunted settling back into his chair. "So do we have any idea how to track this prototype and get to the bottom of this?" "Yes," Nicky replied brightly answering the detective.

"The AI has given me all the information I need to write a software program to create a Mark II Prototype that will be able to sniff out the Prototype in real time, as well as have all the features of the original Prototype," she explained excitedly. "All we do is load the software into the bracelets and off we go a hunting." "But…," William said, starting her next sentence. "The new Prototypes will only work with the AI," Nicky concluded dropping the bomb shell. "What?" explained William. "Yes," Nicky said carrying on, "think of the AI like the brains and the bracelets the dumb terminals." "So, you mean that if the AI goes offline for any reason, we lose the advantage of surprise," Detective Joint surmised. Nicky nodded her head. "Correct Detective." They all turned to look at Nick. Shrugging his shoulders, he told them "It's an operational hazard we're going to have to work with."

Moving on William then asked Nicky, "How long until the program is ready?" "I need a couple of days to sort out the coding," she replied looking at Steven. "Okay. In the meantime, I want protection officers watching you at all times until we solve this," Nick instructed her sternly. "But hang on the Prototype could be anywhere in the world right now," William protested. "Correct," Nick answered.

Carrying on Nick explained further, "According to Arthur, Mark's AI, he is able to track where it's been, but can't track it in real time at the moment until Nicky completes the code. He got a hit on the Prototype from a VR network in Hong Kong."

CHAPTER 19

UMKOMAAS SOUTH COAST, DREAMLAND, TUESDAY 03H15

In her subconsciousness, she thought she was having a nightmare. A man dressed all in black was standing over her while she was sleeping and held a sharp blade against her throat. "Sable, wake up, Sable wake up," she heard in her dream. Opening her eyes, she realized that it wasn't a dream and she opened her mouth to scream. The sharp blade against her throat was replaced with a leather clad hand over her mouth. "Keep it quiet, we don't want to wake up your lover, just yet. Remember, if I wanted to kill you, I wouldn't be talking to you right now," the black clothed intruder told her. 'Can't argue with that logic,' Sable thought rationally to herself as she confidently got out of bed naked. With the killer watching her every move she walked shamelessly across the bedroom to the bathroom to collect her dressing gown.

Ten minutes later they were sitting in her private lounge on the first floor of the villa. "I have a proposition for you," the killer told her, the sounds of the Indian Ocean pounding down on the golden beach a hundred or so meters away. "And why should I trust you? You've already killed two of my girls," Sable spat out. "Samantha was planning on stealing the diamonds for herself and Lee Anne was a security agent," he told her lying, then adding, "a very beautiful one at that. Anyway, as I said if I wanted you dead, I would already have killed you."

Sable sat there stunned for a couple of seconds, thinking. 'I found out that Samantha was planning on stealing the diamonds, and in the process, I inherit a couple of dirty cops for that caper, but I didn't see Lee Anne as a security agent.' "Prove it," she snapped back. "The proof is sitting on Gregory's server," he lied to her with a straight face. "And how am I supposed to get it?" Sable replied sarcastically. "That's my cue to put my proposition to you," the killer told her grinning and standing up walked over to a sideboard laden with a variety of alcoholic beverages. "Drink?" he asked her. "Scotch on the rocks and make it a double," she snapped.

Once he had poured them each a drink and sat down again, he started to speak. "The Prototype is an amazing device with which untold riches can be reaped. The Achilles' heel is that one's physical body is not protected while in the VR world and consequently I could be killed," he explained to her in an even toned voice. "So, you want to use me for protection and probably my VR servers. What do I get, what stops me from slitting your throat while you're in VR?" Sable asked mildly.

Swirling the 30-year-old scotch around in the crystal cut glass the killer smiled and replied with a cruel smile on his face, "This is where unfortunately you stop being Grigori's bitch and become mine for a while." Pulling a USB stick out of his one pocket he stood up and walked across to the flat screen TV and turning on the screen inserted the USB stick. Almost choking on a sip of scotch Sable cried out, "You are a fucking bastard! How the fuck did you get all this?" The screen depicted scene after scene after scene of couples in all positions of sexual ecstasy fucking each other. Other video clips showed well known people shoving long white lines of Bolivian marching powder up their nostrils as well as eating it off male and female body parts. Several scenes showed herself being impaled by cocks and dildos alike. It was all video footage that Sable had recorded from her various house parties and in VR worlds.

Sable sat back, ashen faced. "If this gets out it will ruin me," she rasped. "Relax, I have no intentions of releasing this footage to the world unless you fuck me over while I'm in VR," the killer told her mildly taking another sip of the nicely matured scotch.

"You and I are alike, you know?" he told her. "So, what do I get out of helping you apart from maybe getting my pussy and arsehole flashed all over YouTube?" she asked him sarcastically. Grinning at her crudeness he replied, "Name your price." "A hundred million US deposited into an account number that I will give you," Sable replied without a second pause. "Done," the killer replied.

"There is one other thing though, and it all stems from your last killing spree," she said. "I need you to take care of a small problem for me called Executive Decisions. They are sniffing around asking far too many pertinent questions," "Consider it done," the killer said with a large smile on his face. "You better go and release your guards, they're all knocked out and tied up," he added.

CAPE TOWN CENTRAL POLICE STATION, 08H45, TUESDAY

Purposely being late, Detective Joint walked into the Cape Town Central Police Station feeling even happier than he had yesterday morning. 'Now the case is really moving along,' he thought merrily to himself. 'The players are starting to reveal themselves. Brant will have a big nerve if he shows up here this morning.' Self-consciously he took his right hand and felt across to where his police issue 9mm parabellum was sitting in its holster on his hip; just checking. After speaking to Nick and his small team, Detective Joint had gotten a lift back to just around the corner from the SAPS Batchelor Quarters in Wynberg.

In his hand, he held a cup of takeaway coffee from the coffee vendor on the street corner, the other was firmly back in his left-hand pocket, his fingers playing with the USB stick that he had been given yesterday evening. "All the information you need is on the USB to sink the captain and Detective Brant, wherever he is now," Nick had told him handing him the flash drive. 'The fact that I was abducted and almost killed twelve hours ago is beside the point,' he carried on thinking as he took the stairs two at a time to the first floor. 'I can feel I'm getting closer to solving Saman-tha's murder, and the Mark Bings' killings.' His thoughts were interrupted by a very scared-looking Juliet.

"Thank goodness you're here! Where the hell have you been?" she cried out in a panic. "What's happened? "he asked Juliet in-nocently thinking that it was about Detective Brant "Those photos that you asked me to try to put names to have stirred up a hornet's nest. When I arrived at work this morning, there were a couple of agents from NIA sitting at my desk going through my desk and computer. They want to know where I got the pictures from and why my computer log shows that I have recently deleted infor-mation from my computer without following proper channels," Juliet informed him. Then she said, "The Station Commissioner is waiting for us in his office.

'Great,' Detective Joint thought to himself, 'the actors are re-ally starting to feel nervous and reveal themselves.' As they were walking up the stairs to the second floor, he asked "Were you able to confirm any names before the suits descended on your PC?" She shook her head and answered, "Sorry, nothing." "No prob-lem," he replied happily. Juliet stared at him as if he was mad.

Waiting in the Commissioner's office was Captain Williamson looking very pissed off and two men that Detective Joint hadn't met before. For some reason the captain wasn't at all surprised to see him. "Morning all, sorry I'm late" Detective Joint told them with a smile on his face. The captain just eyed him curiously. The Commissioner introduced the two men in suits saying, "They're from the NIA, Captain Hans Kruger and Major Sam Katemba," and got straight to the point. "Joint, what the fuck are you up to?" Commissioner Ngoma ranted. Acting innocently Detective Joint answered, "I'm not too sure that I understand, sir," looking towards the two dark suited gentlemen.

The one well-dressed African man introduced as Major Sam Katemba cleared his throat and looked at the Commissioner saying, "Commissioner, if I may." He then turned to look directly at Detective Joint and asked, "Detective, where did you get these photographs from?" In his hand were the pictures of Sable and her entourage from the rugby match on Saturday. "It's part of an ongoing investigation into the murder of my sister and the two recent murders of Mark Bings and his lover that are all somehow linked. I'm not sure how yet, but this woman who goes by the name of Sable is somehow involved," Detective Joint explained to them. "Why don't I know about this?" Captain Williamson spluttered out loudly. "Captain, it is a lead that I'm still following up on and would have told you about it once I had all my facts correct," Detective Joint explained rationally to all and sundry in the room, adding "I know that you're a very busy man and I didn't want to waste your time."

What he wanted to say was, 'Because you are part of the fucking problem!' Juliet backed him up saying, "Yes, Detective Joint only handed the photograph to me yesterday morning." "Who took the pictures?" the captain then asked, struggling to contain his anger. "I'm not at liberty right now to divulge that information," the detective replied.

The second NIA agent, Captain Hans Kruger then turned to Juliet and asked, "So, Miss du Pont, why did you delete evidence on your PC without following proper protocols? You know that it is a criminal offence?" Looking helplessly at Detective Joint, Juliet cried out, "I didn't. The emails came into my Inbox late on Friday afternoon just as I was about to shut down and leave for the weekend, so I decided to leave them and deal with them on Monday morning," she explained. Taking a deep breath, she continued, "When I arrived at work yesterday morning and opened the email, there were only four attachments. Ask Detective Joint," she cried out pointing to the detective. "He was present when I opened the email and made the discovery."

Shifting his gaze to the captain, Detective Joint saw that he was intently watching Juliet as if trying to prompt her what to say. "So, who did delete the emails?" the NIA agent then asked. Shrugging her shoulders, she replied, "I don't know." "Don't lie to us, Miss Du Pont," the African NIA agent shouted out harshly. Deciding that it was time to play his hand, Detective Joint cleared his throat saying, "I might be able to shed some light on what's happened." All heads in the room swung immediately towards Detective Joint.

Standing up he headed over to the LCD screen on the Commissioners' wall and begun to talk. "It all started three years ago." "I thought I told you to forget about your sister's murder and concentrate on the current murders, Joint!" Captain Williamson snapped out, getting angry. The commissioner starting to get irritated said. "Shut up, Captain Williamson, let's hear what Detective Joint has to say." Sullenly the captain sat back down in his seat.

Detective Joint started talking again, "Unfortunately, my sister was a high-class prostitute who I have confirmed worked for this woman called Sable, as photographed on Saturday afternoon at the rugby match at Loftus. Somehow, I'm not exactly sure how yet, Samantha was the honeypot to attract the target. While the target was distracted, someone else breaks in and steals the merchandise. Somehow both Detective Brant and Captain Williamson found out about a deal going down in Durban."

"Tread carefully here, Detective," Captain Williamson growled out loudly. Ignoring the captain, he carried on. "Somehow something went wrong, and my sister and her target ended up dead. The video proof which was deleted was the following," he further explained and pressed the play button on the TV remote control and the video footage of Samantha driving up to the ticket dispenser started to play.

"My god," spluttered the Commissioner amazed. "That's Detective Brant sitting beside that girl in the car." Captain Williamson just sat there, his face starting to lose colour, getting paler and paler, as the blood drained from his face. The next video clip showed the captain sitting in the reception area of the hotel. The captain didn't say a word. No one saw him under the table slowly slip his 9mm Parabellum police issue Beretta out of its holster on his waist. It was the last clip that got a reaction out of the captain. A violent reaction.

The video footage showed both the captain and Brant sitting in the bar on Sunday evening talking. The audio was crystal clear. Knowing that the footage had sealed his fate, as the captain said "She's going to get her guys to pick up Joint and interrogate him and then make him an example," the captain suddenly stood up shouting, "I've had enough of this shit!" his police issue 9mm Parabellum in his right hand. Detective Joint stood there frozen, thinking, 'Fuck me, I wasn't expecting such a violent reaction!' Then, as if in slow motion, he saw the 9mm spit a bright orange flame out of the front of the large round black barrel and buck backwards in the captain's right hand as the following nano second it felt as if a massive pantechnicon truck had run into him, smashing him full force in the chest, the momentum of the 9mm copper jacketed parabellum round violently pushing him back into the wall behind him.

He didn't see or hear the second shot go off, but the next second there was an exquisite pain in his left shoulder as his entire arm and shoulder went numb. As he slid down the wall, he heard another two shots go off one after the other in quick succession, and he saw Captain Williamson's head explode, blood and grey brain matter spraying the closed window and wall behind. "Thank god for bulletproof vests," he thought to himself as he lost consciousness, eyeing a smoking gun in Captain Kruger's left hand.

PART 2

CHAPTER 1

GULFSTREAM V, 45 000 FEET, TUESDAY, 04H59

The sun was starting to climb on the eastern horizon, a bright orange ball of flame rising magnificently into the sky chasing away the darkness, as the unlit ground 45 000 feet below the Gulfstream V started to take on definition and reveal itself again.

"Good morning Johannesburg Control, Gulfstream 759 with you at 45 000 feet en route to OR Tambo, over," the co-pilot on board the private jet said with a Russian accent speaking over the VHF radio frequency as the aircraft passed over into South African airspace. "Gulfstream 759 Joburg Control good morning, squawk 3128 over," the controller replied. The co-pilot sitting in the right-hand seat reached across with his left hand and changed the TCAS on the centre console and set the setting to 3128. A couple of minutes later the controller in Johannesburg had positively identified the Gulfstream, radio callsign Flight 759 on his radar screen. "Okay, Gulfstream 759Joburg Control, I have you at 45 000 feet, 125 Nm north west of the Louis Trichardt beacon. Proceed on course. Out," the controller confirmed.

A couple of minutes later the radio channel activated again. "Gulfstream 759, Joburg ATC turn left onto new heading 085 degrees over," the controller instructed. "Joburg ATC 759 turn left onto 085 out," the co-pilot replied repeating the instruction as the pilot leant forward and adjusted the heading selector on the autopilot. The port wing of the Gulfstream dropped slightly with the starboard wing rising, the nose of the aircraft coming around onto a more easterly heading, the rising sun reflecting off the shiny white aluminium fuselage of the aircraft.

"How long till we land!?" the rich Russian voice belonging to Grigori boomed out with a yawn from the passenger cabin. The pilot quickly consulted his flight display and replied in Russian over his shoulder, "Just over an hour and a half, sir, there seems to be a backlog of traffic coming into OR Tambo and air traffic control are routing all arriving flights to the east." Flight 759 was a Gulfstream V that had originated in St Petersburg, Russia, and had Grigori with ten of his employees on board, all ex Russian Special Forces, all with one mission in mind; to find the killer, dispose of him and retrieve the VR Prototype.

In the passenger cabin, the occupants started to wake up, roused by Grigori's voice. The next second the flat screen 19," monitors installed at all the passenger seats and the main 40," monitor used for video conferencing attached to one of the main bulkheads automatically switched on. "Good morning, guys, you looking for me?" the killer asked them, his eyes black and cold seemingly to stare at each occupant of the cabin individually. "How the fuck...!" Grigori shouted out in alarm at seeing the killer stare at him. It felt as if he was in the passenger cabin with them. "Now, now, Grigori, I just came to tell you personally that I quit, no hard feelings, and... oh, yes, you're all about to die!" the killer explained to them, his voice emotionless.

As he said that the nose of the Gulfstream dropped down in a gut swooping dive towards the ever-lightening ground while at the same time a cacophony of alarms started to sound from the flight deck. "What the hell?!" the pilot shouted out in alarm as he lunged forward and gripped the control column trying to pull the nose of the aircraft up, out of its dive. "It won't move, help!" he shouted frantically to the co-pilot. Their combine strength couldn't overcome the force pushing the control columns down. "Fuck, fuck, fuck!" the pilot shouted out as the OVERSPEED, OVERSPEED, OVERSPEED warble siren calmly starting to add to the cacophony of the noise on the flight deck.

As the Gulfstream V plummeted towards the ground now 35

000 feet away, the speed and g forces continued to build up, putting more and more pressure onto the occupants of the aircraft, pushing them back further and further into their comfortable leather executive seats. The sound of the air noise rushing passed the aircraft skin started to add to the noise. "Mayday, Mayday, Mayday this is Flight 759 we are descending through 30 500 feet we have no control," the pilot shouted out frantically into his radio, as he glanced at his PFD and saw the altitude ribbon unwinding downwards at an unbelievable rate. Over all the noise of the alarms and the wind noise he distinctly heard the voice in his earphones saying "it's no use, I've switched off all your radios."

"Fuck we're all going to die!" one of the occupants shouted out, unable to contain himself. "Yes, you motherfuckers that's exactly what's going to happen," the killer replied calmly as he watched the death throes of the occupants of the aircraft through the video conferencing camera. The Gulfstream V nose-dived into a small hill of the Limpopo River Valley slamming into the hard-rich fertile soil at just over 900 km/h. The devastation was immense. The ground shook and the booming explosion echoed across the Limpopo River Valley frightening both humans and livestock alike.

The impact caused a massive crater in the fertile soil. There were no survivors, the largest part of the wreckage that was found in the crater could be put into a shoebox. On the termination of the satellite communication data link to the Gulfstream the killer's VR world reset and he found himself standing back on the VR Platform that he was currently using. Five minutes later., Air Traffic Control at OR Tambo reported that a private flight had dropped off their radar screens and gone missing, presumably crashed.

'Right, first part of the exercise completed,' the killer thought gleefully to himself. 'No more problems coming from Grigori and company.'

NATAL SOUTH COAST, UMKOMAAS, DREAMLAND, TUESDAY, 07H00

'What the fuck have I gotten myself into?' Sable asked herself as she watched the killer now asking to be called Senzo, lying in a state of semi-consciousness, plugged into the VR world in her private VR suite in the villa. Her server for her private suite was hidden behind a wall of proxy servers and routers, and it would take a genius to unravel her connection. For the last two hours, the killer had been submerged in Virtual Reality.

Before entering the VR world, he had given her a small transmitter that looked a lot like a key fob transmitter saying, "If there's a problem push the button once. It's slaved to one of the auxiliary inputs on my bracelet and will alert me." Then, with a large smile on his oriental face, he told her, "Remember, you fuck me over while I'm in VR all those naughty pictures of you and your friends get posted all over the net, along with a record of all your dodgy dealings." Then with a laugh he had slipped his VR glasses over his oriental eyes and entered the world of Virtual Reality. On his instructions, she had directed Ricardo to double the guards patrolling the perimeter of her property.

There was a knock on the door of the VR suite disturbing Sables thoughts. "Yes?" she asked irritably. Ricardo entered the VR suite. "Ma'am, I thought you should know, it's on all the news channels, they are reporting that a private jet crashed in the Limpopo valley a short while ago" Ricardo told her. "And what does it have to do with me?" Sable asked him sarcastically. "Replying he said, "It looks like it was Grigori's plane." Sable sat there stunned. 'Shit, it's true, it really does work, he wasn't bullshitting,' she thought to herself staring at the killer lying on the reclining chair. "I'm trying to get hold of his office to confirm if he was on the flight," she heard Ricardo telling her. At that second, Debbie her lover walked into the suite, "Honey, I want to do some shopping, can I take the car?" she asked brightly. "Yes, yes of course," Sable replied with a wave of her left hand, her mind elsewhere at present. "Ian can take you," she told Debbie. "No, I'd rather take myself if you don't mind," Debbie replied. "Okay, have fun," Sable replied absentmindedly and turned her attention back to Ricardo.

Leaving Senzo in the VR suite, Sable headed for one of her informal lounges and a TV set with Ricardo following close behind her. Switching on the set, she caught a rerun of the headline news. The TV presenter was saying, "And with breaking news this morning it has been confirmed that a private jet en route to OR Tambo International Airport has crashed into the side of a hill in the Limpopo Valley. Initial reports indicate that the jet was registered to a Russian listed aviation company. First responders to the crash say that there are no survivors." 'Fucking hell, he really did it,' she thought silently to herself, 'the Prototype actually does work.'

Turning to Ricardo standing there transfixed watching the news report she said, "You asked me earlier what the Prototype does." Pointing to the TV screen she said, "That's an example of what it can do!" Just then his cellphone rang. "Answer it," Sable instructed him. Putting down the phone a couple of seconds later he nodded his head and told her, "Grigori was on the plane." "Wonderful," Sable replied and rubbed her hands together. "This calls for a celebration." "I agree," Senzo said walking into the informal lounge with a large smile on his oriental face.

UMKOMAAS, TUESDAY, 09H30

"Okay, Boss, good news we've got eyes on the white Porsche," Johan reported to Nick over the cellphone connection. For the last 48 hours, they had trawled through the small holiday village of Umkomaas and the surrounds hoping to catch sight of the white Panamera and its occupants. For the time being, they decided not to show her picture around. Both himself and Eben had recreated themselves and were playing the part of friends on holiday and were hitting the beach and surfing during the day and the bars and clubs at night hoping to catch sight of them. "Who's in the car?" Nick asked. "It's just the brunette who we saw sitting next to Sable on Saturday at the rugby match," Johan told him. "We're sitting out on the sidewalk of a coffee shop and she just casually drove past and parked a couple of meters away from us. It looks like she's going shopping," Johan explained. "Follow her and keep a close eye on her every move," Nick instructed.

Johan looked at Eben across the table who nodded his sun-glassed close shaved head, took a final sip of his coffee and stood up, and started to walk, slowly moving in the direction of the brunette who had exited the white sports car a couple of minutes ago. As he walked past the rear of the Porsche he stopped and bent down as if to tie his shoelace. Surreptitiously his left hand shot out and placed a small magnetic GPS tracker onto the chassis of the vehicle. Standing up he continued walking. It had taken less than two seconds. Speaking into a miniature collar microphone that was slaved to a blue tooth encrypted radio transmitter and an earpiece in his ear he said, "Bug's been planted." Still sitting at the outside table on the pavement Johan picked up his smartphone and clicked on the Tracking App designed by Steven, their IT Di-rector. The active bug showed up pulsing dark green overlaid on a map of the area. Johan replied, "Copy that, the bug's in play."

Following the trim healthy-looking brunette in front of him, Eben hung right back and observed her as she casually walked slowly down the main street from shop to shop, sometimes peer-ing into the window looking at the display, otherwise entering a shop here and there. Then, crossing the road, she entered a large shopping mall that bordered the beach and the main road. Waiting until he saw her walking through the main doors of the mall, he quickly crossed the road after her.

Eben entered the mall in time to see her wander into the local Woolworths clothing store. After wandering around the store for a while she brought a couple of items and paying for them with cash wandered back out into the main mall. Hanging back, he ducked into a tobacconist shop as the target doubled back to look in a shop window. 'What the hell is she up to, is she checking for tails?' Eben asked himself curiously.

A couple of minutes later, just as he was about to exit the shop and follow his earpiece activated. "We've got a problem. I've picked up at least four other persons interested in our target, they've got her in a box formation," Johan said as he was running counter-surveillance, walking past the shop which Eben was standing inside without acknowledging him or even looking in his direction.

Scanning the mall passage, he soon picked up the four-man team. "Copy that, I've picked them up. The man in the black t-shirt, the African girl with the blue tank top, and the two Rasta-looking gents at the rear, sloppy field craft," Eben confirmed softly. "Confirmed, you got them, target has entered the Mugg and Bean," Johan then reported back to Eben who had exited the tobacconist and was slowly following the procession through the mall. "I'll go inside and see what's happening, you walk on by and keep an eye on the box," Johan instructed Eben.

TWO HOURS LATER

"What you got for me?" Nick asked Johan when his phone rang two hours later. "Boss, we've got good news and bad news," Johan informed him. "Good news first," Nick said. "Okay, we were able to plant a tracker and we've found Sable's lair, it's a mansion called Dreamland along millionaires' mile," Johan told him. "And the bad news..." Nick asked with trepidation. "The brunette seems to be an undercover agent. She met with what we assume is her handler after running a counter-surveillance op that involved four other persons before the meet," Johan explained.

"My, my," Nick muttered under his breath. "Exactly what have we stumbled onto? Any idea who this other surveillance team is?" he then asked. "Negative," replied Johan, "but I'm sending you a couple of pictures which I was able to take." "Great," Nick replied. "Going forward I want the two of you to recon her property. If we need to see Sable without an invitation, we need a way in," Nick explained to Johan. "On to it, Boss," Johan replied. "What did she do after the meet?" "She shopped a bit more and then headed back to Dreamland," Johan informed him.

UMKOMAAS SOUTH COAST, DREAMLAND, TUESDAY 16H00

"We're in luck, tides in and there's a decent swell running," Eben mentioned excitedly to Johan pointing towards the surf line. It was late in the afternoon, with the sun well into the western half of the African sky. They were sitting in the cab of the Toyota Prado 4x4 that they'd been issued as part of their disguise, surf boards strapped to the roof, mountain bikes on the rear and a whole plethora of camping equipment in the rear. They were parked as far off the road as they could get with an expanse of rocks stretched out in front of them leading out into the Indian Ocean.

To the left of the rocks, the golden sandy beach stretched away up coast towards the mouth of the Umkomaas River a couple of kilometres away. Starting about 800m away on their left bordering the golden sands and the Indian Ocean was the start of Millionaires Mile, with DREAMLAND snuggled right in the centre. Not only did the owners of the mansions have unparalleled sea views and golden sands at the of bottom of their properties, but there was also a really decent surfable wave that formed along this particular section of the beach, pounding with tempestuous fury onto the golden sands. "You're right," Johan said as he placed a set of high-powered binoculars to his eyes and scanned the coastline and the properties along the beach, "there is a surfable wave." Both Eben and Johan had grown up along the coast and were avid surfers whenever the chance came around.

"Right, well let's go surf then!" Eben cried out enthusiastically and opened the door to the Prado and climbed out. Quickly changing into baggies with half vest wetsuit tops, they unstrapped their surfboards from the roof of the Prado. Before locking the 4x4 and heading across the rocks to the beach Eben opened a large stainless-steel case in the rear of the Prado and removed a standard off the shelf four-engine battery-operated drone. The drone had been handed over to Steven and his team, and that was where the 'standard off the shelf' ended.

The drone could operate at altitudes of up to 2000 feet, its re-designed engines making very little noise, and circling lazily overhead at low speeds had a flight time of over three hours. The drone was also equipped with a high definition camera complete with an electronic 12mm – 85mm lens with IR capabilities and when linked to a i7 laptop, all footage viewed by the camera was recorded onto the HDD. There were also various ways to control the drone, this afternoon would be via a waterproof smartphone using a specially designed app, also written by Steven. Setting the drone to fly at 100 feet and follow them, both Eben and Johan started out over the rocks towards the beach and ultimately the pounding surf line.

Jumping off the rocks they both landed firmly on the still warm golden sand and with surfboards tucked under their arms, they started walking towards the water's edge. "Don't lose the smartphone," Eben egged Johan on as the drone hovered above their heads slowly following them, homed in on the waterproof smartphone in a pouch on Johan's waist. Reaching waist-high water, they both climbed onto their surfboards and lying flat on their stomachs started to paddle out towards the thundering surf line 400 meters out. Diving under the resultant oncoming rushing wall of white tumbling water of a just broken wave as it came rushing towards them; by pushing down hard on the front section of their surfboards, they dove under the white wall of water at the same time being pulled back slightly by the current generated by the water. Popping back up again like corks they continued paddling out, the drone silently following above them.

A couple of minutes later after having to repeat the same diving exercise they found themselves just beyond the surf line sitting on their boards with their legs dangling over the sides in the water. "Right, let's earn our keep, shall we?" Johan said with a large smile on his face as he removed the waterproof smartphone. "Nothing better than being able to mix business and pleasure hey," Eben shouted to Johan as he spotted a decent size swell approaching and lay back down on his stomach and started paddling hard in the direction of the beach. After paddling hard for a couple of seconds, the swell caught up with him and started to pull him along with the gathering wall of water.

As the swell started to form into a wave, Eben was positioned on the lip of the forming wall of water, being pushed along. Jumping onto his haunches, he started to surf down the face of the wave. Picking up speed, he stood up fully and, by altering his balance and weight displacement by pushing down with his feet on either the left or right rail of his surfboard, he changed the direction of the surfboard and started to surf across the front of the now fully developed wave. Surging along the face of the wave, he changed direction again and once at the top, moving his body around with his feet planted firmly on the board, he started to surf back down the face of the wave. As he surged along on the wall of water, cutting up to the top and back again, Johan followed him with the drone. However, the high-resolution camera was not pointed or focused on Eben, it was focused on the beach and the properties, in particular the property that had been identified as DREAMLAND.

"Yeehaaa," Eben shouted out loudly as the wave dumped him, burying him under tons of tumbling water as the sea washed over him. After being tumbled around underwater in the waves' motion as if in a large salty washing machine, he surfaced again. Pulling his surfboard back towards him via the tether cord attached to his left ankle, he slipped back onto the surfboard. After paddling out and catching another wave in Eben looked towards the shore. He saw that he was now directly parallel to DREAMLAND and had a good view of the whitewashed Spanish style villa and the green immaculately kept lawns leading down to the beach. Standing in the waist deep water, reeling his surfboard back towards him again, he noted to himself, 'She definitely likes her privacy, those are at least 10-foot walls on both sides of her neighbours.' All the while the drone was following him, controlled by Johan sitting on his surfboard behind the surf line.

"You think you got enough footage?" Eben asked Johan when he met up with him again a couple of minutes later past the last line of breakers. "Here," Johan said passing Eben the smartphone in the pouch. "You drive the drone for a bit, I'm going to catch a couple of waves." Sitting on his surfboard flying the drone from the smartphone he didn't see the surfer paddling up to him. "Hi there, what're you doing?" he heard a female voice call out. Startled he almost dropped the waterproof smartphone into the water. "Oh, hi there," he said to the brunette on her surfboard. 'Fuck, it's her,' he thought silently to himself. 'The woman from this morning. She also surfs!' Thinking quickly, he replied, "Myself and my buddy are doing a YouTube series on surf spots in South Africa and we're using a drone to capture surfing video footage of ourselves." "Cool," the brunette replied. His mind churning over scenarios he asked, "Do you mind if we take some footage of you surfing?" "No, not at all, just edit the parts where I wipe out," she replied with a large smile on her pretty face.

CHAPTER 2

CAPE TOWN HARBOUR, 07H30, WEDNESDAY

Standing on the quayside at Berth 2 of the Duncan Dock, Cape Town Harbour, Nick watched the Maersk freighter *Purple Beach* slowly move towards the dock being shepherded fore and aft by two of the Cape Town harbour tugs, as he mulled over the happenings of the last 24 hours. "She's a fast-looking yacht, do you know how to sail her?" a male voice with a British upper-class accent spoke up beside him, startling him out of his reverie; of concentrating on the sight of *Exec Decision 1* which was standing high and proud on the cargo deck of the freighter.

Luckily for Nick and his team, the Maersk freighter *Purple Beach* had stopped at St Helena 24 hours after Nick had left, on her usual run between the European port of Hamburg and Cape Town South Africa. Having cargo space on the main deck, Pete and the team had been able to prepare the yacht for transport in record time, and using one of the freighter's cargo cranes, the yacht had easily been shipped aboard. Another bonus for all concerned was that they were able to keep the mast up and didn't have to remove it for transportation. Turning around Nick grinned, "Andrew you old devil," and gave his old friend from the Regiment, Lieutenant Andrew Peterson Intelligence Liaison Officer, a big bear hug.

"My god, it's been what? Ten years since I last saw you," Nick exclaimed, surprised to see Andrew standing on the quayside. "Are you working for one of the other teams to spy on my progress?' he asked good naturedly, referring to his *Exec Decision 1* Vendee Globe Challenge. Laughing Andrew replied, "I wish it was something as easy as that." Getting serious Andrew told him,

"I'm working for big brother now, and some information came across our desk of a very serious nature." Nick knew that he was referring to MI6 as big brother.

"Congratulations, you always said that's where you wanted to end up," Nick told Andrew. "What information?" he then asked. Nick remembered that Andrew always said that he wanted to end up being a spook. "Thanks. Look, we know that Veronica Bings has employed you to run a parallel investigation into the murder of her husband and to retrieve the Prototype for her," he explained to Nick. Carrying on he said, "I've been ordered by Her Majesty's government to impart this information on you, bearing in mind that you were an officer in Her Majesty's forces and still are a citizen of Great Britain." He stopped there and looked hard at Nick. Nick nodded his head in agreement. "Okay. Veronica Bings, her real name is Sashenka Petrovich, and she works for the SVR, the later day KGB. Her orders were to get close to Mark Bings and eventually steal the Prototype, however, someone beat her to it," Andrew informed Nick as casually as possible standing on the quayside.

Continuing he said, "We can't have you handing the Prototype over to Veronica or the Americans." "Why not the Americans?" Nick asked curiously, looking up at the vertical steel side of the freighter looming closer and closer as she was pushed sideways onto the quayside, with stevedores on the quay standing by to pick up the mooring lines of the vessel. With a grim smile on his boyish-looking face, Andrew replied cryptically, "Let's just say that the Americans aren't as secure as they think they are, and the Prototype would end up back at the Kremlin." "Understand," Nick answered grimly, thinking of the implications.

As crew members stationed in the bow and stern on board the freighter *Purple Beach* threw down the mooring lines to the stevedores on the quayside, Nick asked Andrew, "So what's the end game on this one?" "We were rather hoping that you work with us on this one old chap and hand the Prototype over to Her Majesty's Government for safekeeping when you locate it. In return, we'll supply you with all the intel you need, as well as open doors where we can. It would also stand you in good stead for future projects," Andrew explained again as casually as possible.

Thinking it over quickly in his head, Nick said "Mark Bings' last words to me via a video recording were that his wife was a spy, but he wasn't sure for who. He asked me to find the Prototype and hand it over to a General." "That would be General Dwayne Perrington," Andrew replied immediately finishing the sentence for Nick. Nick took a step back. "You know this General Perrington?" he asked astounded as the mooring lines were finally fastened, securing the freighter to the quayside.

Taking a step towards Nick, Andrew lowered his voice in a conspiring manner and explained, "It's a very sensitive subject, General Perrington and his department. We can't let on to the Americans that we have certain information without alerting them to the fact that we have an asset in place. Trust me, if a member of General Perrington's department gets hold of the Prototype, then the Russians will have a copy of it twenty-four hours later." "Okay, I understand," Nick confirmed nodding his head. Andrew breathed a sigh of relief. Handing Nick, a card he said, "Here's my number, call me directly." With that, he turned around and walked away.

The next second there was the sound of running feet behind Nick and then, "Hi Nick, fuck sorry we're late!" It was the voice of his Project Director for his Vendee Globe Challenge attempt, Mike Harrington. Turning around Nick saw Mike and the other team members arriving to take care of his pride and joy. "Hi, guys. You're late," Nick said good naturedly. "Who was that guy, a spy from one of the other teams?" Mike asked. Laughing Nick replied, "something like that."

A short while later the same way that *Exec Decision 1* was shipped aboard, it was shipped off of the cargo deck again using one of the vessels' cargo cranes to lower the yacht into the waters of Cape Town Harbour. Standing off 100 metres away from the cargo vessel lowering the IMOCA 60-foot yacht into the water was a semi-rigid inflatable with a Yamaha 80HP outboard on the stern. Mike and his team were onboard waiting to take *Exec Decision 1* in tow and move her to her temporary mooring at the Royal Cape Yacht Club.

Once he saw that Mike and his team had her safely undertow and heading back to the Royal Cape Yacht Club on the far side of the harbour, he waited for Pete to disembark and clear immigrations and customs. "Hey, pal you looking good," Nick joked to his pal a short while later as Pete completed all the formalities and walked over towards him. A week in the sun on the deck of the freighter had tanned his skin dark brown. "Thanks, pal," Pete replied.

Once in Nick's car, driving over to the Royal Cape Yacht Club to have a quick go over of the yacht along with his team, Pete informed him, "I found the fault with the autopilot, substandard fucking wiring. I had to pull it all out. Luckily, we still had spare cabling on board, and I was able to rewire it. We won't have that problem again, that I can guarantee you." "Thanks, mate," Nick said slowing down as they reached the entrance gates to the Royal Cape Yacht Club. Seeing the RCYC member sticker in the windscreen of the 911, the guard opened the vehicle barrier and let them through.

EXECUTIVE DECISIONS, 13H30, WEDNESDAY

"Okay guys, it's been confirmed by another source that Veronica Bings is not who she says she is. Her real name is Sashenka Petrovich and she works for the Russian SVR," Nick told his small team less Nicky, who said she would be joining them shortly. "Fuck!" Steven exploded, that's all we need now, fucking Russian KGB agents running around!" "SVR not KGB," Willian corrected him. "Bullshit," Steven retorted. "You can call them what

186

you like, but a leopard can't change its spots!" Nodding his head Nick had to agree with Steven. "Guys, Steven's right, they're just as dangerous, we've got to be careful," Nick told them.

'So, I assume we won't be handing the Prototype back to Veronica Bings, if and when we find it?" William then stated. Nick nodded his head again and added, "Neither will be handing it to the Americans." "What!?" William asked amazed. "Apparently they're also compromised." "Bloody hell," William muttered shaking his head. "Remember Andrew from the Regiment?" Nick asked William. Nodding his head, William replied, "Okay understand, say no more."

"How is Detective Joint doing?" Steven then asked concerned. "He was in surgery last night having the bullet removed, I'm off to see him in a couple of hours' time," Nick explained to him. "Thank god we suggested that he wears a vest," Steven said, referring to the bulletproof vest, that stopped the one 9mm round. "Pity Captain Williamson was such a crap shot and nailed him in the shoulder rather than the vest," Nick grumbled about the second round that had hit the detective in the shoulder.

Just then the electronic lock on the board room door released with an audible click and Nicky rushed in. "Sorry I'm late guys, I've been speaking to Arthur. Mark's AI, the Prototype, has been used!" Nicky gushed out. "Where?" Nick demanded. "Here in South Africa, the plane crash earlier this week." "What?!" Nick asked her stunned at first. Then, remembering what the Prototype was capable of, replied "How did you find it?" "I didn't, Mark's AI did," Nicky told the stunned table. "It started a search on its own after following the news report about the crash over the internet." Stopping to catch her breath, she carried on, "Arthur found a trace of the Prototype in the aircraft satellite data network feed. The Prototype was able to get into the aircraft systems and crashed the plane intentionally, Boss! We're dealing with a mad man here." "Or one who's also highly intelligent," Nick replied his mind furiously churning over scenarios. "Why a small aircraft, why not a large passenger jet if you wanted to make a statement?"

Waiting a couple of seconds, Nicky then dropped the bombshell. "Arthur has been able to track the Prototype. He says that it was working from some network somewhere along the South Coast, but that's all he was able to get." "What!" William exclaimed surprised. "It's operating from somewhere along the KwaZulu-Natal South Coast?" Grinning Nicky nodded her head and replied, "Correct, that's what I said." Stunned at what he heard, having visions of the Prototype being somewhere on the other side of the world, he sat in silence for a couple of seconds thinking furiously and then turning towards William said, "Where there's smoke there's usually fire, Dreamland's on the South Coast. Give Eben and Johan the heads up. Let's observe for a while and see what happens."

Turning towards Nicky, Nick said, "Please, try to confirm who was flying in the Gulfstream, that might also give us indication of what we're dealing with." As an afterthought, he asked her, "What would have happened if the pilots had switched off their satellite data link?" "They would have cut him off, and they should have been able to regain control of the aircraft," she replied. "I take it that there's been no posts on social media platforms bragging about what has happened," Nick then asked. "No, Boss," she replied. "We've set up search engines and tripwires scanning both the net and VR world, but nothing stands out. Yet," she added.

"And how far are you with writing the code to track the Prototype?" Nick then asked Nicky, changing the subject slightly. "Boss, honestly I need another day to finish writing the code, and then we need to do a couple of tests," she told him. "Okay," Nick said. "As soon as you're ready, let me know." "By the way, how many bracelets can the software theoretically support?" William asked her. "As many bracelets as you have bodies for. Remember they're like dumb terminals talking back to the AI," Nicky replied standing up and heading for the door and ultimately her office on the lower basement. Spending another hour or so going over the video footage that Johan and Eben had obtained from the surfing expedition, a plan was slowly starting to form in Nick's mind.

They soon had an answer as to who was on the aircraft when Nicky came rushing back into the secure boardroom. "Okay, guys," Nicky said breathlessly from running ."Apart from the pilot and co-pilot there were ten passengers on board, all from a specialist security company based in Russia along with the owner named Grigori Kaminski." "Thanks Nicky," Nick replied as she turned around and headed back to her computer lab on the B2 level.

Once back in his office, Nick picked up his iPhone and dialed a mobile phone number he had only learnt earlier on in the day. When the call was answered, he said, "Grigori Kaminski, I need to know all there is about him." "We thought you might, I assume that you have intel linking him to the article in question, and his untimely death a couple of days ago?" Andrew asked curiously. "Correct," Nick confirmed. "I'll send you a link to a secure server where you'll find all the unsavoury information on the subject," Andrew replied and terminated the connection.

CHAPTER 3

UMKOMAAS SOUTH COAST, DREAMLAND, WEDNES-DAY

"Do you know why I've survived so long?" Senzo asked Sable. They were sitting in the main lounge on the ground floor of the villa. "Let me see. Because you're careful and you have a habit of killing off all your witnesses," Sable replied to him sarcastically. "Touché," he replied with a grin. Then said, "No, because I'm careful." "Oh, I see, that's your secret, is it?" Sable answered, her voice dripping with sarcasm. "But you, you're not careful," Senzo stated carrying on ignoring her sarcasm, "and now you have a problem." "What problem is that?" she answered wearily. "The one where one of my girls was killed a couple of weeks ago by a psychopathic killer and the spotlight is starting to expose me?" Secretly she was already making plans to leave the country. 'It will be sad,' she thought to herself, she really loved DREAM-LAND but her intuition and the intelligence that her informants were giving her had led her to the decision that it was soon time to leave the country for a while.'

"No," replied Senzo coldly staring at her with his cold hard dark eyes. "A Captain Hans Kruger from the National Intelligence Agency." "What the fuck!" Sable exploded rising to her feet. "Sit down," he snapped harshly at her. "I followed your lover by interrogating the Porsche's GPS to see where she went the other day. You see, I don't trust anybody," Senzo stated. "You," he said pointing at her "I have under control, but Debbie is another story. How well do you know her?" "So how did you deduce this, Mr Sherlock Holmes?" Sable asked sarcastically. "Simple, by looking at the CCTV footage of cameras at your local strip mall," he replied with an evil-looking smile on his face. "Remember, I have the Prototype that gets me into every single data system. It's simply amazing what you find when you go looking," he told her cryptically. Taking a nano drive stick he plugged it into the side of the nearest LCD monitor and said, "Watch."

The video footage showed the local Mugg & Bean coffee shop in the Umkomaas Mall. Her heart pounding in her chest, she soon spotted Debbie entering and sitting down at a table near the back of the coffee shop. A waiter came over and took her order. A couple of minutes later, a middle-aged European male joined her. They seemed to speak in a subdued manner for about 10 minutes and then the male stood up and left. Debbie finished her coffee, paid the bill, and left five minutes later.

"So, what does that prove?" Sable laughed out loud. "She's a gorgeous fuckable woman, any blue-blooded male in his right mind would want to make moves on her," she said laughing some more. "I agree, but I did a bit of digging. I do have access to whatever database I want, remember?" Senzo replied slyly. "And what did you find?" Sable snapped out getting weary of the game. "The male suitor who spoke to your lesbian lover is a Captain Hans Kruger of the NIA," he explained to her with an evil glint in his coal dark eyes. Then with a small smile on his face, he asked her, "Would you like to know Debbie's real name? I also found those records. Without waiting for Sable to reply, he told her. "Tanya Delport." Sable sat there, stunned, speechless, not knowing what to say. 'I was so careful,' she cried out silently to herself as her personal world started to come crashing down and unravel around her.

1 Hour later

"Where, where am I?" the scared voice of Debbie cried out. "What do you want with me?" "Answers," Senzo answered nonchalantly looking down at the woman called Debbie lying flat and strapped to the operating type table. The operating table stood in the middle of a square room entirely made up of dirty white tiles.

In some places the tiles were missing, and in others cracked. The single light bulb cast a dull yellow glow across the stark room, hiding the corners of the room in shadows.

"You know the beauty of VR Interrogation?" the killer had asked Sable shortly before entering his VR Interrogation chamber; courtesy of and unbeknown to the Russian SVR. Sable shook her head, still rattled that she had let a spy come so close to her. "You can reset their interrogation time and time again, over and over and they have no recollection of the previous interrogation experiences; to a point," he had told her with a laugh.

"Who are you?" Debbie asked in a scared voice. She was lying on the operating type table wearing only her 2-piece swimsuit, her standard clothing selection when at DREAMLAND. Without reason, it started to get cold in the room, bitterly cold. She started to shiver uncontrollably, her nipples starting to stiffen against her will pushing out stiffly against the fabric of her swim top. "Sable stop this! Stop this at once!" Debbie shouted out loudly, starting to panic. Then the coldness stopped. "Who do you work for?" Senzo asked her: even though he knew the answer. "I don't work for anyone," she replied. The coldness was replaced with a furnace-like heat that started to burn at her from the soles of her feet upwards. "Agghhhh," she screamed, shrieking out loudly as she watched her toes starting to catch alight, the flames lapping around her feet. "Aaagghhhh!" she started to scream out again. The pain was intense and unbearable. Then the smell of burnt flesh started to seep through the chamber. A fire extinguisher materialized in Senzo's hands and he put out the fire, the cold CO_2 extinguishing the fire. The CO_2 was at first cooling, soothing the pain, then starting a pain of its own, an excruciatingly freezingly cold pain. "I'll ask you again. Who do you work for?" Senzo asked the quivering human form writhing in shackled pain on the operating table. "I don't work for anyone," she groaned through the pain of her burnt feet. The fire started up again. "Aaaaagggh-hhhhh," Debbie shrieked out in a frenzy of complete brain splitting absolute agony as the flames started to consume her flesh, the sickly-sweet smell of burnt flesh intensely strong in the small room. As the killer directed the flames up her shapely legs Debbie groaned out "NIA, I work for NIA," and she passed out from the pain. The killer reset the scenario.

"Where am I?" Debbie groaned out the shackles holding her down. "I know you work for the NIA and I know your real name is Tanya Delport." Debbie lay there stunned. "That's not my name," she started to say when a massive electric shock wrenched her body tight against her bonds. "Ahhhhhh," she screamed out in agony as the electrical voltage coursed through her muscles, making her lose control of her bodily functions, her bladder letting loose. "What was your mission?" he asked her.

The killer toyed with her for a couple of hours like a cat plays with its prey, wringing every last bit of information out of her pain-filled body. Every time she passed out; the killer reset the scenario again. At the end of it, he exited the VR world to find Sable sitting there in the VR Suite ashen face. "I still don't believe it," she muttered looking at the heaving sweating body of her now ex-lover; still wearing her swimsuit, strapped to one of her executive chairs in her VR suite. Sable was devastated that she had come so close to being betrayed by her lover. "What do you want to do with her?" the killer asked her casually, pointing to the obviously mentally stressed, mentally in pain, and still unconscious Debbie. "Get rid of her, I never want to see the traitorous bitch again," Sable snapped out. "Okay," the killer answered and pulled a revolver from the small of his back that he had liberated from one of the guards. The noise was deafeningly loud in the small acoustically secure room. Debbie's body jerked once and then again as the .38mm copper jacketed rounds ploughed into her defenceless body, ripping through her chest, killing her where she sat.

CAPE TOWN HARBOUR, 16H45, WEDNESDAY

Turning left out of the Executive Decisions parking lot, Nick headed towards the N2 with the intention of first going back to RCYC and *Exec Decision 1* and then when visiting hours came around at the hospital, go and visit Detective Joint. He had Julia, his secretary, go and buy the detective a couple of newspapers and magazines, not too sure what he liked to read. Hitting the Airport approach road heading away from the airport, he gave the 911 Turbo its head as he entered the long winding right then left-hand S bend that fed one onto the N2 highway heading towards Cape Town.

The 3.8 litre twin turbo charged engine howled in delight as Nick held it down in the gears, the G Forces pushing him firmly back into the leather sports seat, as the German engineered machine surged forward. Making light work of the traffic on the highway, Nick was in his element, behind the wheel of the fast sports car driving fast. As he looked in his left-hand mirror checking to see that the inside lane was clear to overtake a slower moving vehicle in front of him he caught sight of what looked like a silver Mercedes doing the same as he was, weaving in and out of the traffic and didn't pay it too much attention. All the way into Cape Town, the silver Mercedes stayed two and sometimes three cars behind Nick.

Once through the per functionary security checkpoint on entering Cape Town Harbour, Nick put on the right hand indicator and making sure that there was no oncoming traffic turned right onto Duncan Road, the main harbour service road that ran on the outside of the restricted area from one side of the harbour to the other. The road ran from the Paarden Eiland harbour entrance right around the harbour ending up at the Victoria & Alfred Waterfront.

As he turned right, he caught a glimpse of the same silver Mercedes that he'd seen earlier on the N2 in his rear-view mirror stopping at the security checkpoint. "Shit," he muttered to himself. "You don't believe in coincidences, Nick," he said as he punched the throttle hard to the floor. The 3.8 litre twin turbo German engineered engine responded immediately catapulting the

Porsche along the harbour service road, the engine howling with glee. Controlling the trajectory of the sports car with his right hand, while with his left he felt behind his seat for his day bag that contained his Glock 9mm and spare magazines, just in case.

Taking a quick glance in the rear-view mirror, he saw that the silver Mercedes was still following him, now coming up hard on his rear. "Okay guys, let's see what you've got," he muttered to himself as he manually downshifted the PDK automatic gearbox. The engine took on a new liberated howl as the twin turbos pushed out 397 kw which was transferred to the rear Pirelli shod wheels, pushing the rear of the 911 down, the air spoiler automatically extending, throwing the car forward.

Flying past the Royal Cape Yacht Club on the left-hand side, Nick looked to his right and saw that the roads outside of the dockyard were blocked with traffic. 'Shit, rush hour. I'm stuck in here for a while' he quickly thought. 'Need to keep the potential body count as low as possible.' Seeing a road coming up quickly on the left-hand side he took his foot off the accelerator and wanted to turn left, but realized he was going way too fast. Looking ahead he remembered that there was another turning to the left coming up in a couple of hundred metres.

He stamped his foot back down on the accelerator. A second later, coming up quickly upon the second left-hand turn, he took his foot off the accelerator, tapped the gear box down twice, the rev counter red lining with the engine howling like a banshee as he pulled up the handbrake and spinning the steering wheel to the left at the same time he broadsided the multi-million Rand high-performance sports car into changing its trajectory heading now towards the left-hand turn.

Once the nose of the vehicle was pointing in the direction that he wanted to go, he floored the accelerator again, the automatic gearbox and engine working together in flawless German engineered synergy, the Porsche surging forward. The road was little more than a track that he went flying over, the construction sheds of Cape Town Marine looming up large on his right-hand side. Looking quickly in the rear-view mirror he saw the silver Mercedes sliding into the left-hand turn, 'Yep, the Mercs still there,' Nick thought to himself as it loomed larger in the rear-view mirror.

Nick flew into the shipbuilding dockyard with a massive dry dock on the left; currently occupied by two large ocean-going vessels, one behind the other and large triple storey sheds on the right in which smaller vessels and marine parts were manufac-tured. The last shed was where *Exec Decision 1* was built, and that was where Nick was heading, a plan forming in his head. "Shit!" he shouted out as he saw vehicles still parked in front of the construction sheds. His mind was made up for him when the rear window of the 911 disintegrated, shattering from a gunshot round that expended of energy gouged into the headrest of the passenger seat beside him and stopped. "Fuck, they're armed and mean business," Nick muttered to himself under his breath.

"Siri, phone Control Room," he snapped into the onboard blue tooth microphone. "I'm sorry, network unavailable at present," Siri replied almost immediately. "Fuck," he muttered again and swung the car down a small side road between two large sheds and stamped on the brake pedal bring the car to a sliding stop. Grabbing his Glock out of his day bag, he chambered a round and shoved it into the waistband of his trousers. Throwing his iPhone into the day bag he sprang out of the car. Running across the nar-row road he made it through a side door into the adjacent building just as the silver Mercedes skidded around the corner and headed directly towards the parked Porsche. Slipping his day bag over his back, he removed the Glock from his waistband with his right hand, slipping his trigger finger around the trigger.

Adjusting his eyes to the gloomy interior, Nick realised that he was in one of the marine metal fabrication workshops. Lying on large steel tables suspended on hundreds of stainless-steel balls were what looked like large untreated 10 and 15mm thick steel plates that were in the process of being cut into prefabricated sections by cutting lasers. The stainless-steel balls secured in the table made it possible to move the heavy steel plates around on the table with ease, before securing the plate down and cutting it. The laser cutters were presently still and silent. From where he stood Nick saw that in another part of the workshop the prefabricated cut sections were welded together, at present the massive steel sections were lying unfinished and mostly unidentifiable as ship parts.

Luckily it was after 5 in the afternoon and the majority of the workers had already left for the day, apart for one or two workers that he could see on the far side of the workshop, the unmistakable sound of metal hitting against metal reverberating through the now almost silent workshop. Moving quickly, Nick walked deeper into the workshop and found a position from where he could monitor the door that he had just entered through. Settling down behind what looked like a 10mm thick steel plate, he took aim with his Glock at the door and waited, sighting down the fixed polymer combat sights, waiting for a target.

Inhaling steadily and deeply, slowing down his breathing, Nick waited, crouched down behind what was a robust shield, his Glock extended double handed. He didn't have to wait long. He was however surprised at their next move. 'Mother fucker flash bangs,' his mind screamed out as he saw the door open slightly, a shaft of sunlight cutting into the gloom of the workshop. A cylindrical object came sailing through the air. Hunkering down behind the steel plate, hands over his ears he was spared the brunt of the concussion wave.

Immediately after the flash and concussive blast, he popped up around the side of the steel plate and fired double tap shots at the figure entering through the doorway. The Glock bucked pleasantly in his firm double grip, barking out loudly in the now quiet workshop. Aiming for the body mass of the target, the centre of the target's chest, Nick was surprised when the target staggered backwards and disappeared around the corner of the door. 'Fuck! Bulletproof vest,' his mind screamed out as he emptied the clip at head level through the side of the old prefabricated wall of the building. The slide of the Glock locked back with a resounding click and Nick quickly ejected the empty magazine and replaced it with a fresh one from his day bag.

Looking across the workshop he spotted a fire exit door on the far side and realizing the minute that his assailants figured it out, he'd be fucked having to defend himself on two fronts. Laying down a couple more rounds of rapid fire towards the door that the assailants had just tried to enter through, he made a beeline for the newly spotted door, crouching low and running as fast as he could across the workshop floor. Luckily the employees who were still at work when he had entered the workshop had dropped their tools and ran at the first sound of the concussion grenade exploding.

As he crashed through the fire exit door, the wall around him erupted in stone chips and brick dust as the assailants shot back. 'Damn, they've got fucking silencers as well,' Nick registered when he didn't hear the accompanying gunfire, ducking as a round whizzed past close to his right ear. Exiting the workshop, he almost ran headfirst into one of the assailants who was running around the side of the building, attempting to outflank him. Nick's only saving grace was that he was running with his Glock up and close to his chest. The assailants' silenced automatic was not. As he ran into the very surprised attacker Nick double tapped him almost at point blank range in the face. The back of the assailant's skull exploded, and he crumpled to the ground dead.

Spotting a couple of large steel skips filled with scrap metal standing between the building and the dry dock with the two large ships, Nick made a beeline for the cover of the steel skips, glad to be able to put some steel between him and the incoming subsonic rounds. He managed to make it to the safety of the corner of the steel skip, diving to the black oil grimed concrete ground as the grimy concrete around him was chewed up by silent subsonic rounds, a number of rounds hitting the steel skip with loud metallic chewing noises. "Too fucking close," he muttered to himself as he waited for the fusillade of rounds to cease before peering around the corner of the steel skip.

The area was clear of targets, and he was just in time to see the back of an individual disappear around the corner of the workshop. Standing up with his firearm extended double handed out in front of him he quickly checked his quarters and looked towards where the dead assailant had been lying less than forty-five seconds ago. The black oil grimed concrete surface had an additional pool of red blood to add to the multitude of stains and colours, however, the body was missing. "Damn it," he muttered to himself.

The next second, from the other side of the workshop there was the sound of an engine starting up, revving loudly and then roaring off. Turning around, Nick sprinted as fast as he could back across the grimy concrete dock and around the corner of the workshop in the direction of the noise. "Damn it!" he shouted out loudly as he rounded the corner of the workshop just in time to see the rear of the silver Mercedes disappear. 'We'll see about this,' he thought as he sprinted towards his car aiming to give chase.

"Fuck it!" he shouted out in frustration as he neared what was once his new white immaculately presentable Porsche Carrera 911 Turbo. Now it looked like it had been used for target practice. The tyres had been shot, not once but a number of times, the windows all shot out and as Nick approached, he could see that they had even shot up the engine, the vehicle's mechanical fluids leaking out onto the ground. The ground around the 911 was littered with brass shell casings. "Bastards," Nick muttered angrily as he knelt down and looked at one of the shiny brass shell casings. "Standard 9mm issue, nothing special about the rounds," he said to himself.

By this time the sounds of the gunfire had alerted a concerned citizen who had phoned the police, and in the distance, Nick heard approaching police sirens. Just before the police arrived, Nick was able to make a couple of phone calls alerting his team to what had just occurred.

MOSCOW, YASENEVO DISTRICT, SVR HEADQUARTERS, 17H45 (One Hour ahead), WEDNESDAY

Colonel Andreyev Petroski swore furiously in Russian. "What do you mean that Boris is dead and Ivanovich injured? It was supposed to be a simple grab operation you moron not a fucking killing field," he ranted loudly. The colonel was getting impatient and had decided to up the ante and go right to the source of the supposed information. They had ways and means of getting people to cooperate with them.

"Sir, we were not given all the information. The target definitely has military training," the agent complained to the colonel. "So why did Mother Russia spend all her roubles training you, when it definitely hasn't paid off? One man. One man!" the colonel ranted, spittle flying from his mouth all over the telephone mouthpiece. "One man against six of you and he fucked you up!"

Shrugging aside the colonel's sarcasm the agent said to him, "My apologies, Colonel, now we know the calibre of the man we are up against we will not fail you a second time," "You better not or there won't be another chance," the colonel hissed back menacingly. "We need to know where the Prototype is and who has it. I am told that he has a close team of operators whom he uses. I am sending you the particulars of a few of his team members who we now have intel on," Colonel Andreyev growled down the telephone. Dossiers on Nick, Nicky, Steven, and Johan had been hurriedly put together, thanks to Veronica's input and that of other assets.

Slamming down the phone, the colonel swore again. "Damnation, this is the second bit of bad news in twenty-four hours," he ranted out loudly to himself. "It was supposed to have been a simple snatch and grab operation and hand Nick Scott over to the interrogation team. Dimitry!" he called out, calling his Adjutant into his office. "Dimitry, send Jurgen the latest information we have on Nick Scott and his team," he instructed.

The first bit of bad news was when the head of the Command Council had personally phoned him to ask for an update as to the progress of obtaining the Prototype. The fact that it was the Chairman himself who phoned! That was fucking scary; if he failed who knew what fate was waiting for him?'

Picking up his smartphone and accessing his one to one voice encryption software he dialled Veronica's number. "Tell me," he asked when she answered doing away with formalities, "does Nick Scott know who you are?" Without hesitation, she replied "No! The only way is if there was a leak on your end somewhere." Carrying on he asked her hopefully, even though he knew the answer, "Do you have any new information from Mr Scott and company as to how far they are with tracking down the Prototype?" "Nothing promising at present," she reported. "He informed me earlier that they were busy following up a couple of leads but nothing definite as yet," she further explained to him, much to his rising ire.

CHAPTER 4

CAPE TOWN, EXECUTIVE DECISIONS OFFICES, THURSDAY, 08H30

"Boss, we're just glad that you're still alive. If you hadn't been vigilant you could have been killed!" Nicky stated shaken after Nick explained to the team what had occurred. He had spent most of the previous evening at the local police station trying to explain to the detective who had been assigned the case that he had no idea what occurred, maybe a botched hijacking?

"Officer, I was on my way to the Royal Cape Yacht Club and I noticed a silver Mercedes following me. The next second the rear window of my Porsche exploded, and I realised that there was a problem and that my life was in danger so I took evasive action," Nick had explained rationally to the detective. Grudgingly the detective had to let Nick go. At that point, Nick thought it prudent not to mention Detective Joint's name.

"Any idea who they were?" Johan asked next. Shaking his head Nick replied "No, but they definitely had military training, throwing a flash bang into the workshop before entering." "Guesses?" William suggested. Thinking for a couple of seconds Nick replied, "It's either some of Sable's ex-military misfits trying to make a point or else some other organisation interested in the Prototype, maybe the Russians?" Nodding his head William replied, "Those were my thoughts as well." "Maybe we should start making the list smaller and pay Sable a visit, now that we know where she is," Johan suggested. Looking at Johan, Nick grinned and replied, "I like it, set it up."

16H00

It took a while but by late afternoon on Thursday, a very tired-sounding Steven phoned Nick from his computer lab on the secure B2 Level. "It's done," is all he said. "I'll be right there," Nick replied excitedly jumping to his feet. He was currently sitting in his office looking at the damage report from Porsche.

'The assailants obviously have a beef with Porsche,' Nick had been thinking ruefully to himself. From the photographs attached to the report, his Porsche now had the looks of a Swiss cheese. He hadn't heard the shots due to the silencers the attackers were using, but they made sure that he wasn't about to follow them. The report stated that they found 35 bullet holes that destroyed the engine, body work: inside and out and wheels. "Sorry, Mark, my old friend, but some of the funds you left for the hunt need to go to replacing my Porsche," Nick said to himself as he headed for the lifts and the secure lower basement level.

"Right, what do we have?" Nick asked a couple of minutes later as he walked into the Secure IT Lab on the B2 level. He found Steven and Nicky along with one of their assistants Kelly standing around a lab bench on which a number of computers stood along with a couple of stainless-steel bracelet nanocomputers with the associated wireless coupled mirror glasses. William joined them a minute later.

"Well, what are we waiting for?" William asked impatiently. "Hang on, before we get started is there anything, we should be aware of?" Nick asked his IT team. "Yes," replied Nicky nodding her head, "these bracelets have a link back to Arthur and he will be able to help the users wherever he can in the VR world. "I assume that the original prototype doesn't have this feature?" William asked. Grinning Steven replied, "no, it's an upgrade feature only available to the latest range." That brought a smile to Nick'sface. He had the feeling that they would be needing all available resources. "Another feature is that we will be able to communicate with each other without being overheard," Nicky informed them.

After listening to a brief overview from Steven as to the operation of the device they all headed for the adjoining VR Suite.

Settling into one of the executive leather seats in the VR suite Nick placed the mirrored glasses over his eyes and tapped the stainless-steel bracelet on his wrist, instantly activating the system. Steven had setup a private platform for the three of them to land on. Feeling the usual couple of seconds of auditory and sensory blackness as he entered the VR world, he was surprised when he landed on the platform. 'Something feels different, I feel alive as if charged with electricity,' he thought to himself, and glancing at his torso and arms he realized what it was. 'I'm encased in some form of white body armour.'

Looking at his two companions, William, and Nicky he saw that they were also encased in the same white sheath like armour. "This is a snug fit, but it's easy to move in," William commented. Nick had to agree with him, even though the sheath felt tight and restrictive they were actually very easy to move around in. "Okay, guys, if you look in the top left-hand corner of your view you will see a drop-down menu tab," Nicky explained to them over the open communications circuit.

MENU OPTION

– NORMAL MODE - SHEATH ONLY

– MAINTENANCE - CLOAKED

– MAINTENANCE - UNCLOAKED

– CAMERA SETUP - CLOAKED

– CAMERA SETUP - UNCLOAKED

– COMMS LINK -

– TARGET ACQUISITION & TRACK

"Boss, you stay in Normal Mode," Nicky suggested. "We'll change to Maintenance Mode cloaked." "My word," Nick commented a couple of seconds later as both William and Nicky vanished in front of his eyes. The Comms Link command started to flash and once Nick pressed it; he heard Nicky's voice asking, "You with us boss?" "Bloody hell, you disappeared right in front of my eyes," Nick told them in a surprised voice. "You want to try and track us?" Nicky then asked him, happy that it seemed to be working. "Yea, hang on, I'll find you now," Nick replied activating the Target Acquisition and Track function on the drop-down menu. A second later the ghosting outlines of both William and Nicky appeared in front of him. "Wow, so you reckon that we'll be able to track down the Prototype with these puppies?" Nick asked, intrigued with what he was seeing. "You will with my help," the voice of Arthur, Mark's AI spoke up over the comms channel.

CHAPTER 5

DURBAN SOUTH COAST, 10NM OFFSHORE FROM UMKOMAAS, 23H30, FRIDAY

"It's nice and dark, just the way we like it," Eben commented joining the rest of the team on the bridge deck of the motor launch *Scuttlebutt*. "I suppose it's a sign of good luck," Johan commented, as they closed in from the ocean on the small cluster of lights that demarcated the coastline of Umkomaas. Both Eben and Johan had met the rest of the team in Durban earlier in the day, changing positions with two surveillance specialists who would keep DREAMLAND under surveillance. The surveillance team had the radio callsign Oversight. No one in the team could contradict Eben, the night sky was pitch black, with the stars covered by a scattering of high-level cloud. "Ja, just what we're looking for," Jimmy commented overhearing the conversation.

According to the Nautical Almanac and *Scuttlebutt's* GPS, the moon would only be rising over the eastern horizon at 04H33, and by that time they expected to be long gone. Anyway, sunrise was at 04H55 just over fifteen minutes later. Looking at his Rolex Nick saw that the time was 23H30. Around an hour ago all standard shipboard lights on board *Scuttlebutt* had been doused and the red LED night lights switched on, illuminating the bridge in an eerie deep red glow. The red light spectrum not only preserved one's night sight but also made it possible to make one's way around the vessel. The GPS and chart plotter LCD displays had also been turned down low to preserve everyone's night sight. They were also currently motoring without any navigation lights, the customary red port and green starboard navigation lights along with the white stern running light purposefully switched off. The electronics on the bridge being the AIS and Radar had also been turned to standby. To all intents and purposes, they were invisible, apart from the deep growl of the twin Pentow Diesel marine engines coming from the stern of the vessel pushing them along comfortably at 15 knots.

"Okay Nick, we're 30 minutes away from the drop off point," the captain, a good friend of Nick, told him a couple of minutes later after consulting with the GPS. "Thanks, Captain," Nick answered patting the older man on his left shoulder. Turning around he looked at his small team who were dressed just like him in skin-tight black neoprene wetsuits. On their chests they wore black body armour, with side arms consisting of Glock 9mm's strapped to their waists. Spare magazines were carried in special magazine pouches. They all carried black balaclavas which they would slip over their heads before they hit the beach.

Slung around their necks were high powered taser rifles; the objective wasn't to kill anyone. They were in constant communications with each other via an encrypted high frequency comms set consisting of an earpiece wired to a small TX RX unit strapped on to their utility belts which was wirelessly linked to a throat microphone. A couple of minutes later the comms circuit activated in the team's ears, "Alpha 1, Oversight over." "Oversight Alpha 1 send over," Nick replied. "Reporting in, target quiet and all clear. Out."

"Okay guys gather round, just under 30 minutes to drop off, let's have one last review of what we're going to do," Nick instructed his team. The five of them sat around the table in the main cabin, the hull of *Scuttlebutt* rolling gently on the light ocean swell which was currently running as they motored towards Umkomaas and Dreamland. "All right guys as you know we've been able to track Sable to a villa called DREAMLAND, which is right on the beach along a stretch of coastline called Millionaires Mile which is our current destination. There is also the possibility that the Prototype is there or in the vicinity," Nick said bringing all up to speed. Stopping to pause and catch his breath, he looked at each one of his men, staring at him intently, waiting for his orders. 'Fuck,' Nick thought silently to himself, 'they'll follow me to the gates of hell, no questions asked.' Clearing his throat, he carried on, "According to the captain, we're just under 30 minutes out. Our eyes on the Target is Oversight 1 and they report all quiet in the villa, all settling down for the night," Nick informed them.

At the head of the table was an open and running laptop showing a video feed. It was the video uplink from the UAV currently circling lazily just over 500m offshore from the beach showing an IR picture of the ocean side of the mansion. The 'standard off the shelf', drone which Glen and Johan had used earlier had been replaced with an Orbiter 3, a combat-proven Small Tactical Unmanned Aerial System developed by Aeronautics, an Israeli defence company. With sensors and a camera package mounted in the nose turret of the small unmanned aircraft it was equipped for both day and night operations. Coupled with a 4.4m wingspan the electric motor could keep the UAV airborne for up to seven hours. This ability along with a datalink with a range of up to 150 kilometres, when the Orbiter 3 was deployed in an intelligence-gathering role was a force to be reckoned with, an ace that Nick and his men had previously put to good use.

"Nice property," Jimmy quipped looking at the live feed. Part of the architect's design called for low spotlights to light up the gardens and the centre courtyard of the mansion, so with ease the drone was able to monitor the property sending back usable video feed. Quite clearly, they could all see the guards patrolling the beach front section of the property.

Looking at Johan, Nick motioned for him to continue, "The captain will drop us approximately 1000m offshore from the villa and we will launch the RIB and head for the beach, landing approximately 40m from the start of the property called Dreamland," Johan recited from memory. Clearing his throat Glen continued, "Once we hit the beach, I go left and straight up the side and Jimmy goes right and straight up the side to clear up any hostiles," Holding up his hand Nick said "remember no live rounds and no killing, use the tasers to subdue the guards. Only use live ammunition as a last resort." Nick had arranged a shipment of tasers used by US officials. The tasers could shoot projectiles up to 50 meters incapacitating the target. "Once the guards are down tie them up using the cable ties as issued to you and gag them. We don't want them advertising that we are on our way," Nick then instructed.

Silently they nodded their collective heads in agreement. Carrying on Nick said, "While you two take care of the guards and guard our rear, myself and Johan will work out way up the centre of the property to the house and enter the house. Remember stealth is the key here. We want to be in the house without being seen or heard. We snatch Sable and the Prototype, if it is in her possession, and head back to the beach and rendezvous back at sea with *Scuttlebutt*. Any questions?"

UMKOMAAS SOUTH COAST, 1000M OFFSHORE FROM DREAMLAND, 00H30, SATURDAY

So far, the operation had gone according to plan. Launching the black RIB with a 40HP Yamaha on the transom, the five of them had disembarked from *Scuttlebutt* into the rubber inflatable and crouching down low with Johan at the helm they had motored off towards the distant shoreline. At this time of night, not many lights were on in the houses along the shoreline and Johan relied on the Garmin handheld GPS unit to guide them in. All five were wearing head mounted night vision glasses, the night taking on an eerie green glow.

They were halfway to the beach when the call came over the encrypted radio circuit "Alpha 1, Oversight we have movement in the house, stand by." Nick double-clicked his PTT in reply. Looking over at Johan, Nick motioned for him to cut the throttle. Closing the throttle, the RIB came down off the plane to a bobbing drift in the water. "Oversight, Alpha 1 confirm current status over?" Nick transmitted. The reply came back immediately, "Alpha 1, lights have come on, on the upper floor of the villa. Your orders?" Thinking quickly Nick replied, "Oversight, Alpha 1 keep observing and keep us posted. We're proceeding as planned. Out."

Signalling Johan, he opened the throttle again and they surged forward, the inflatable quickly getting back onto the plane again with only the rear section of the inflatable along with the propeller of the outboard motor in the water. Glen and Jimmy were crouched down in the bow, keeping the bow of the RIB down as much as possible to prevent it from lifting and flipping over backwards and depositing them in the darkened waters. Looking towards land, they all could see the lights on the shoreline, shining a bright green in the night vision glasses, a beacon to guide them in amongst the dark gloom of the surrounding mansions.

After crashing over the swells for another couple of minutes, all the time the lights on the shore were getting larger and taking on definition. "Alpha 1, Oversight, standby to receive an aerial view of the property, it looks like they're leaving Over." "Oversight Alpha 1 standing by," Nick snapped into his throat microphone while signalling to Johan to cut the 40HP outboard again. A couple of seconds later the sound of the outboard faded away to be replaced with the sounds of the pounding surf a short distance away.

Pulling out his iPhone Nick accessed the video app, and very soon the IR picture of the mansion from 500 feet up in the air could be seen. "There," Johan pointed excitedly, "they're definitely leaving." Johan was right, the operator zoomed the UAV camera in and they clearly saw the Porsche Panamera leaving the property followed by another couple of vehicles. "She must have the Prototype with her, it looks like all her guards are leaving with her to protect her," Nick commented, watching the small convoy of vehicles leaving the property. They all saw the last vehicle stop and the guard at the gate climb into the rear, the wrought iron gates closing behind them.

Pushing his PTT Nick instructed "Oversight, Alpha 1 follow the convoy and keep us updated. Out," Looking at his small team he said softly "let's go and have a look but be careful they might have left a house sitter or two behind. As they negotiated the surf line, a 20 second gut dropping ride as they started to surf down the face of a forming wave before Johan maxed the throttle and they shot ahead of the forming wall of water, then again on another wave before hitting the beach a short while later. A couple of seconds before grounding Johan leant back and released the tilt pin on the outboard, so that as the tip of the outboard fin hit the sandy bottom the outboard lifted with the rise in the seabed saving both motor and transom of the inflatable from damage. As they hit the beach the one burning question that was going through Nick's mind was 'Who tipped them off?'

UMKOMAAS SOUTH COAST, DREAMLAND, SATURDAY, 00H15

'Fuck, fuck, fuck,' Sable ranted to herself while sitting at her dressing table starting to take off her makeup and prepare for bed. 'She had me fooled, the fucking bitch.' The thought kept on going around and around in her mind. Casting her eyes around the room her pussy involuntary twitched and started to get wet when she saw Debbie's strap on dildo lying casually on her bed side table. Thinking back to the last time they had used it, the morning before learning about her traitorous streak. She started getting aroused thinking of how she had been lying on her back, her long smooth suntanned legs splayed wide apart while Debbie had knelt between them powering the large strap on dildo to the hilt into her sopping wet pussy.

"Mmmm," Sable moaned softly to herself thinking about that last sexual tryst, wetting her lips with the tip of her pink tongue, her right hand trailing its way down to her right breast, toying with her nipple feeling it harden under her tender ministrations.

As she started to become more aroused, all thoughts of her dead lover now gone from her mind, replaced with the sole objective of self-pleasure. With her right fingers now sharing some of the pleasure with her left nipple, her left hand casually trailed down her tight stomach to the junction of her thighs. Sitting on her makeup chair she spread her long tanned legs, about to run her hand through the small tuft of light brown pubic hair at the juncture of her thighs and plunge her fingers into the centre of her burning moisture when the irritating ring of her smartphone abruptly broke her sexual fantasy.

"Fuck! Now who the hell could this be!" she asked herself reaching for the phone. There was no caller ID. "Hello," Sable snapped answering the call. "You don't know me, but I know you. You need to get out of DREAMLAND now. You are about to be captured," a male voice quickly explained to her. Her heart began to race, beating loudly in her chest. She didn't recognize the voice. "Do I know you?" she asked. "No. but if you want Nick Scott and his team to catch you stay where you are." 'Fuck, that fucking name again,' she thought quickly to herself. "Why are you helping me, what do you want?" she asked the mysterious caller. The caller laughed, "Relax, we can speak about what I want later. For now, let's keep you alive and free." Carrying on the male voice said, "I suggest that you get hold of your pilot and disappear for a while." "Okay, but how will I get in contact with you?" she asked hesitatingly "You don't," the voice replied bluntly, "I will be in contact with you. You have approximately an hour before they get to you. Good luck," The connection went dead.

Sable realized that her adrenaline was pumping hard through her body and she was starting to shake. Standing up she threw off her dressing gown and quickly pulled on a pair of jeans and a top while at the same time dialling her pilot's standby number, something she rarely ever did, normally she texted her pilots. "Hans, get the jet ready. We're leaving now," she snapped when he answered. Surprised to hear from her and the urgent tone in her voice he answered immediately, "Yes ma'am, where are we heading?" The question caught her off guard, she hadn't yet thought about it. "North, Hans, north. I'll let you know more when we're in the air," she replied testily and hung up. "Senzo, Senzo," she then yelled sticking her head out of her bedroom doorway. As he stuck his head out of his door she snapped, "They're onto us we need to leave now!" Without a word he briskly nodded his head and headed back into his room to gather up his kit.

'Where the fuck should we go?' Sable asked herself. As she was frantically packing her leather carry-on bag; a present from an admirer, it came to her. Snatching up her smartphone again, she consulted the phone directory and dialled an International number. "Phillipe!" she cried out in French when the call was answered by a male voice, with the sounds of a party on the go in the background. Phillipe was two time zones away to the West.

SOUTH COAST, N2, 00H55, SATURDAY

Twenty minutes later Sable and Senzo were in the white Panamera heading north along the N2 back towards Durban and King Shaka International Airport, just over one hundred and fifty kilometres to the north, her bodyguards following at high speed behind them. "Who contacted you?" Senzo demanded wanting to know. Taking her eyes off the road as the Porsche travelled along at over 160 km per hour Sable turned to face him, "I don't know," she replied. "So how do you know they were talking the truth?" Again taking her eyes off the road she looked at her passenger and now business associate "I just know that he wasn't fucking around when he said that Nick Scott is on his way," and left it at that. "So where are we going?" Senzo the killer asked. "West Africa," Sable replied happily with a large smile on her pretty face illuminated by the backlighting on the instrumentation cluster.

"Where the fuck is West Africa and what is in West Africa?" Senzo spluttered looking wildly at Sable. Laughing a deep sensual laugh Sable replied, "Relax, we're heading to Lomé, the capital of Togo in West Africa. I have a very good friend there who can protect us. No one will know where we are. They also have a very sophisticated high-speed internet that we can make use of," Sable explained to him, as she tapped the PDK transmission changing up a gear, the Panamera passing a late-night driver who thought that he was going fast. The light went on in Senzo' s brain. Smiling he looked with admiration at his newly acquired business partner, "Ah, good thinking," he told her.

As they got nearer, with the lights of King Shaka International Airport in the distance shining brightly in the night sky, Senzo asked her, "I trust that the pilot will request a blacked-out flight plan?" "Of course," Sable answered. "That's what private flights are all about, there is no other type of flight plan as far as I am concerned." With a smile a second later she added, "That's what private flights are all about, privacy."

UMKOMAAS SOUTH COAST, DREAMLAND, SATUR-DAY, 01H10

It took them ten minutes to work their way through the property to confirm that DREAMLAND was officially deserted. "Alpha Two, Alpha One, search the property for anything that might give us some idea where she's gone," Nick instructed. "Alpha One, Alpha Two, confirmed," Johan replied. A couple of minutes later Nick took out his encrypted satellite phone and standing in the shadows of the side of the villa phoned Steven in Cape Town. "Someone tipped them off, as we were heading for the beach they left," he explained.

"Shit!" Steven swore, the frustration building. "Is there any way that they know we have a version of the Prototype to track them down?" Nick then asked his long-time friend. There was a couple of seconds silence while Steven thought the question through, and then he replied, "No way, that's not possible. Nicky asked Arthur the AI that same question." "What about a leak on our side?" Nick then asked Steven who he trusted explicitly. "Never," Steven exploded in reply, "it certainly isn't from anyone of us." "Sorry, had to ask your opinion," Nick replied. "Who else apart from Detective Joint and his team knew of the operation?" Nick then asked. "The leak must have come from them!" Speaking for another couple of minutes, he ended the call. He then contacted the detective. "Fuck!" was all Joint said from his hospital bed. They also spoke for a couple more minutes then hung up.

"Alpha One, Alpha Two, you better come and see what I've found in the kitchen," Johan reported over the encrypted communication circuit. A couple of minutes later Nick joined Johan standing in the doorway to a large walk-in freezer that had been built into the one corner section of the kitchen. "What have you found?" Nick asked curiously reaching the open freezer doorway. Pointing inside the freezer Johan replied, "You'd better have a look for yourself." Walking inside the freezer Nick saw immediately what Johan was referring to.

On the floor at the rear of the freezer were two human forms, one a complete ice popsicle with a thin sheet of ice covering the body, the other well on its way to becoming a human ice popsicle. Walking closer and crouching down next to the two lifeless figures, Nick was able to identify the second corpse as Sable's raven-haired assistant, now sporting two black bullet holes in the centre of her chest. It took a couple of seconds longer, peering through the ice covering the face, to identify the first. "Detective Brant. So, this is where you ended up," Nick said as he removed his iPhone and accessing the camera app took a couple of pictures of the two bodies. He sent both pictures to Detective Joint.

Replacing his iPhone in his pocket, the earpiece in his ear activated, "Alpha, 1 Oversight. It looks like the target is heading for the airport. Sorry, but we lost them on the highway," Oversight reported back. What Oversight didn't mention was that the UAV was destroyed when it hit a low-lying bridge that took the pilot completely by surprise. "Oversight, Alpha 1. Copy, thank you. You guys did your best, stand down," Nick replied. Quickly reaching for his iPhone, he dialled Chuck the pilot of his Bombardier Global 6000 who was standing by at a local hotel near the airport. Nick explained what he wanted him to do. "On it," Chuck replied in his American voice with a nasal Texan twang.

"Okay boss, nothing else of interest in the villa apart from the servers," Johan reported to Nick. "The servers?" Nick asked quizzically. "Yes," Johan replied. "There is a small computer room with a number of servers. I inserted one of the USB sticks that gave Steven direct access to it. He says that they are Virtual Reality servers for what looks like a part of Sable's porn empire," Johan explained with a smile on his face. "Perfect," Nick replied also smiling.

Nick's iPhone rang again and seeing that it was Detective Joint, he accepted the call. "Okay, Nick," the detective said in his very Afrikaans voice, "I see that Brant got what he deserved, and I see that Sable's assistant has also been killed. The body count is starting to mount. I'm standing by ready to contact the Durban Central Police Station and report the murders." "Okay," replied Nick, "stand by," and looking at Johan received confirmation that Steven and Nicky in Cape Town were now logged into the DREAMLAND camera system and could covertly monitor what happens in the house. "Okay Detective send the call," Nick confirmed. "Okay, guys, let's get a move on," Nick told his team and they headed double quick time back to the beach and the RIB.

As they were heading back out to sea, they saw the blue lights of a police van screaming along the coast road towards DREAMLAND. By this time, they were black specks merged with the blackness of the ocean, invisible to anyone on the shore. Boarding the darkened *Scuttlebutt* twenty minutes later, Nick received confirmation from Chuck, "Okay your target boarded her Gulfstream and they are about to taxi for take-off," "Thanks, any idea where they're heading?" Nick asked hopefully. "Negative on that, their tail number is listed as a blacked-out flight plan," Chuck replied regretfully. "All right thanks for the quick response," Nick answered gratefully, knowing exactly how he was going to track the flight. "Please get the Bombardier ready for take-off. Full tanks, not too sure where we're going, I'll have the destination shortly," Nick instructed him. "On it, boss," Chuck replied and ended the call.

As the captain pushed the throttles of *Scuttlebutt* to the stops and the twin marine diesels roared into action, pushing the hull of the motor launch forward and onto the plane, Nick dialled the direct number for Steven and his IT department back in Cape Town. Nicky answered the call "Hi, Nicky. Very quickly, I want you to use your prototype and hack into the ATNS servers and find the flight details for Sables Gulfstream. It's a blacked-out flight plan," he instructed her. "On it, boss, I'll get right back to you," Nicky replied, not phased at all at having to hack into a very secure site. Her logic was simple, Nick wouldn't ask her to do it if it wasn't important.

Ten minutes later she phoned back. "They're heading for Lomé in Togo," she informed Nick. "Thanks. Have you any idea what the hell's in Lomé?" he asked her perplexed. "Other than a landing station for the West African Cable System or WACS, the Fibre optic cable that links Cape Town, a number of African countries and finally terminates in Great Britain, I can't think of much else at present," Nicky explained to Nick. "Okay, great work so far, but now I need you to look as deep as you can into Sable and any links she might have with Lomé. There has to be some reason why she has chosen to fly there," Nick told her. "Good point, I've got a good idea where to start looking," Nicky replied and ended the call.

With the sun starting to rise over the eastern horizon and the GPS readout indicating that they had 25nm to go, Nick's iPhone rang again. This time it was Detective Joint. "Major," he rasped still in a lot of pain, "I've checked myself out of hospital and am on my way to the airport, I should be landing in Durban just after 08H00. I'm not letting you have all the fun." Laughing Nick replied, "No problem Detective, we'll wait for you, remember you need your passport."

CHAPTER 6

WEST AFRICA, LOMÉ, 11H30, SATURDAY

There was a constant haze in the air, blotting out both the sun and the clear blue sky. This however didn't stop the sun's heat from beating down ferociously onto the brown arid ground turning the soil into what felt like a constant walk-in furnace. The dry easterly wind did nothing to cool the air down, it just moved it around. The average daytime temperature was around 35 degrees Celsius with the night-time temperature only dropping to the mid-twenties. The never-ending haze was the dust from the Western Sahara Desert that was blown on the warm easterly winds across the African continent.

"What shit heap place is this?" Senzo asked nastily as he stepped out of the filtered and airconditioned comfort of the Gulfstream jet into the hot dry furnace-like heat of a typical mid-morning in Lomé, West Africa. "Relax, it's not that bad. Trust me, we'll be safe here while you finalise your plans," Sable replied behind him as she followed him out of the aircraft. First stopping off at the flight deck, she spoke to the captain, "Nice flying, Hans, thanks. We're going to be here for a couple of days. Get the aircraft sorted out and get a hotel room, I'll be in touch." As the airport didn't have a Private Operator Terminal, they had to enter the main airport terminal building.

As they entered the airport building and headed for Passport and Immigration, an African man wearing a dark well-cut business suit and dark sunglasses walked up to them. "Bonjour, Madame Sable, His Excellency sends his regards and regrets that he couldn't meet you personally. However, he has sent me to escort you," he explained to Sable in fluent French. "Hello, André," Sable replied answering in fluent Parisian French with a large smile on her pretty face. "It's good to see you again." Turning towards Senzo, she introduced them. "Please, give me your passports," André then asked holding out his right hand.

Senzo was impressed and a bit wary. French was not a language that he spoke, so he was at a bit of a disadvantage. However, he was impressed, not even when he worked for Grigori could Grigori have eased their way through Passport and Immigration Control the way that André did. "What did you say Phillipe did?" Senzo asked Sable. "I didn't," she replied. And then offhandedly told him, "He's the President of what you called this shit heap." "Mother fucker," he whistled under his breath. Looking at Sable with a newfound respect he replied, "Impressive, you're not a lady to mess around with."

It was a couple of minutes later as they were following Andre to a convoy of vehicles waiting in the loading zone outside the front entrance of the terminal building, when it struck Senzo and he asked Sable quietly "Togo, this is one of the landing points for the WACS, the West Africa Cable System isn't it?" Grinning, Sable nodded her head, saying, "Yes, it is, I thought you might like the location." Senzo laughed out loud. 'It's getting better by the minute' he thought to himself.

After a 20-minute drive on what seemed like one of the only tarred roads in the city, they pulled up to the vehicle entrance of a large imposing glass tower building. "Welcome to the Intercontinental Hotel," Sable said to him with a smile on her pretty face as an armed soldier on duty at the vehicle entrance saluted and let the convoy of vehicles through. With a practiced eye, Senzo scanned the grounds as they drove up to the Porte Couche of the hotel, noting several soldiers, all armed with AK47s, walking around the grounds. He also noticed a large round dome-like building to the right of the Porte Couche directly in front of the hotel with a walkway linking the two. "What's that building?" he asked inquisitively pointing to the round dome-like structure.

"The House of Parliament," Sable explained offhandedly. 'That'll explain the armed soldiers then,' he thought to himself.

With very little fuss they were both whisked straight up to adjoining suites on the 29th floor of the hotel. Once the entourage of hotel staff had left them alone to settle in, Sable knocked on the inter leading door between the two suites. "Right," she said a couple of minutes later settling down into the leather settee of Senzo's suite, "I've kept up my side of the bargain, kept you safe and put you into a secure location with excellent internet access. It's time you did your stuff, pay me and we can both move on with our lives." Smiling Senzo nodded his head and replied, "Yes, I agree. I shall start as soon as I have rested. I will need around 72 hours to carry out my side of the deal." "Perfect," purred Sable. Standing up she smoothed down her dress and headed to the small wet bar. "Shall we have a drink to our upcoming success?"

Just then the telephone in her suite started to ring. "Excuse me," she said to Senzo, turning around and heading back to her suite. "Bonjour," she said happily answering the phone in French. "Sable, my dear, I am so sorry that I couldn't meet you personally, I unfortunately had business of state to attend to," the deep male voice of His Excellency Phillipe Togbui explained to her in French. "That is not a problem, your Excellency," Sable purred down the telephone line. "I want to see you tonight," His Excellency then stated bluntly. "But of course, what time can I expect you?" she replied getting weak at the knees thinking about her last sexual encounter with him. "A car will be waiting at the entrance for you at eight o'clock sharp," he told her and hung up the phone.

KING SHAKA INTERNATIONAL AIRPORT, 08H15, SATURDAY

Nick and his small team didn't have to wait long for Detective Joint to join them. Once they had docked *Scuttlebutt* back at the Durban Yacht Club and headed back to the airport it had just gone 08H00. The detective landed on the first flight from Cape Town at 08H20 and very soon they saw the familiar figure of Detective Joint ambling towards the Bombardier with a sports bag dangling from his left shoulder, his right arm in a large white sling. At the same time a baggage handler arrived with some suitcases containing various camera equipment, along with a couple of surfboards and was busy loading it into the luggage hold. "You never know," Nick had told them with a smile, we might need a cover story, surfing all the hot spots of the world can work for me."

"Welcome to the party Detective," Nick said greeting him at the foot of the aircraft stairs a short while later. "How are you feeling?" Detective Joint laughed softly. He was still in a lot of pain after being shot and replied, "Like one normally feels after being shot: fucking sore." Nick gave a small laugh at that, as he knew what it was like to be shot, "You're right Detective, it is fucking sore, so why not let us finish this off for you while you recuperate?" Detective Joint looked at Nick and grinned saying, "Major, I can't let you have all the fun, anyway I want to see first-hand how you bring Sable back to stand trial. This time I've come prepared with my passport," he said waving the small book around in the air. "Does the Commissioner know that you're coming with us?" Nick then asked Detective Joint seriously. "Not actually," the detective replied "I've been booked off sick for a couple of weeks. I was planning on informing him once we have Sable in custody." Laughing at that Nick replied, "Sometimes that's the best way to do things."

Half an hour later, as the Bombardier leapt off the runway into the deep blue morning sky from King Shaka International Airport, Detective Joint asked, "So, Major, what's your plan?" "We've found out that Sable has headed north and has filed a flight plan to Lomé which is the capital of Togo in West Africa," Nick explained to him. "What the hell is in Togo?" the detective asked perplexed. "We're not too sure, but there is a WACS land station on the coast of Lomé," Nick informed the detective.

Detective Joint looked curiously at Nick and asked, "What the hell is WACS?" "Oh, sorry," Nick replied "it's the West African Cable System, the fibre optic cable that links South Africa with Europe. It's laid on the Atlantic Ocean floor, and every couple of thousand kilometres the cable comes back to land to a land station and then heads back out to sea again and loops around further up the coast." "Oh, I see," Detective said. "So that's why you think they've bolted to Lomé to hack into the WACS System?" "Could be," Johan replied who had been quiet up to that point, "but another scenario is that she has a buyer for the Prototype." "Huh, never thought of that," the detective replied. "So, we're heading to Lomé then?" Detective Joint stated. "Nope," Nick replied shaking his head. "We're going to land in Accra, the capital of Ghana which is just over 4 hours' drive north from Lomé. We'll wait until we know exactly where she is in Lomé and then we'll make our move. We don't want to spook her just yet," he explained with a broad grin on his face.

A couple of hours into the flight, Detective Joint looked across the aisle at Nick and said "I've been thinking about what we spoke about earlier. There are only a couple of people who knew what was happening, all based at Cape Town Central. There must still be a dirty element or two who were able to alert Sable that you were on your way." Nick nodded his head saying, "that's what I thought. Hopefully, once we've caught up with Sable and the Prototype, we can flush the traitor or traitors out."

MOSCOW, YASENEVO DISTRICT, SVR HEADQUARTERS, 09H15 (1 Hour Ahead), SATURDAY

"Colonel Petroski, sir, the Executive Decisions team has returned from their sea trip and have boarded their private jet and are about to take off, sir," Jurgen informed him over the secure smartphone connection. "And where are they heading?" snapped the colonel. "That's the problem, sir, it's a blacked-out flight plan," he explained to the colonel standing outside the main terminal building.

For the last couple of days since the abortive kidnapping attempt, the colonel had instructed Jurgen and his team to keep Nick and his close bunch of operators under surveillance. It hadn't been easy, and then their sudden departure by private jet to Durban had taken them all by surprise. The colonel had to call in favours to keep the surveillance ball rolling, while Jurgen and another of his teammates in Cape Town scrambled for a local flight to Durban to meet up with the assistant to the Russian Attaché who had agreed to help and follow the passengers of the jet until the team arrived.

Putting down the telephone receiver the colonel leant back in his chair and laced his arms behind his head and started to ponder. 'Major, where are you flying to, I wonder?' After reading the updated Intelligence file gathered on Nick Scott, he was surprised to see that he had been a Major in the British Royal Marines. Now putting into context what his agent had told him about the Russian bloodbath at the Cape Town docks at the hands of Major Nick Scott; his one man Ivan cracked ribs from taking a number of rounds with an extremely small grouping directly in the chest, thank goodness for the bulletproof vest and Boris dead shot twice in the face, he now had a professional soldiers respect for the man, even though he was the enemy.

Stretching forward he picked up the telephone receiver and dialled an internal number. "Good afternoon, Captain Popov," the colonel said, greeting him cheerfully when he picked up the receiver. "Good afternoon, Colonel," the captain replied. "How can I help you, today Colonel?" "I like that Comrade getting straight to the point. I need you to use your hacking resources and get me the flight plan of a certain aircraft," "No problem, Colonel. I just need the tail number of the aircraft in question," Captain Popov replied immediately. Giving him the required information, the colonel replaced the handset and lit a cigarette, drawing the smoke deep into his lungs and pondering the information he had just received.

He had hardly finished the cigarette when the telephone on his desk rang. Seeing the caller ID, he saw that it was the captain. "That was quick," he said picking up the receiver. "Thank you, Comrade Colonel," Captain Popov replied. "And where is the flight headed?" the colonel asked impatiently. "Accra, the capital of Ghana," Captain Popov informed his superior officer. "Accra! What the hell's in Accra?" the colonel asked out loud. "Sorry, sir, there I can't help you," Popov replied.

Very quickly the colonel realised that he didn't have enough information. 'It's time for the interrogation team to earn their keep, and I need to know what the Major's up to,' he thought to himself, while at the same time shouted out, "Dimitry, office, now!" While waiting for his subordinate to arrive, the colonel quickly checked the large online SVR government directory and confirmed that Russia had an Embassy in Accra, Ghana.

"Yes, sir," Dimitry shouted coming to attention in front of his boss. "At ease, Dimitry," the colonel commanded. Then he instructed him, "Find out what assets we have in place at our Embassy in Accra, Ghana and report back to me immediately." "Yes, sir," Dimitry replied and coming to attention saluted and turning around smartly left the office retreating to his anteroom.

It only took a couple of minutes during which time the colonel lit another cigarette off of the almost dead one between his fingertips and turned around in his chair smoking while looking absently out of the window at the green belt in front of him. Returning with the information a couple of minutes later, Dimitry informed his superior, "Sir, we have an officer currently in resident at the Accra Embassy in Ghana, I am attempting to get hold of him as we speak." "Perfect!" replied the colonel. "Put him straight through to me when you get hold of him."

True to his word a couple of minutes later the well-used phone on the colonel's wooden desk rang out loudly. "Sir, Lieutenant Leonard Ivanovich on the line, sir, he's the officer in residence," the colonel's adjutant informed him. "Well then, put him through," the colonel replied impatiently. Once connected the colonel quickly explained, "There is a private flight arriving in approximately 4 hours at the airport. I need to track the occupants of the flight and know what they are doing. Dimitry, my adjutant, will email you their pictures now. Do you have the capacity to carry this out?" "Yes, Sir Comrade Colonel, it'll be my pleasure," the young agent replied excitedly. Accra was a rather tame city where not much happened so the young agent was eager to please his superiors in Moscow.

CHAPTER 7

SOMEWHERE OVER AFRICA, BOMBARDIER 40 000FT, SATURDAY, 11H15

The ringing of his satellite phone slaved to the Bombardiers satellite link woke Nick up. Looking around him he saw that the rest of the team were also asleep, catching up on a couple of hours of well-deserved rest. Detective Joint however was too excited to sleep and was sitting in the rear of the cabin, nursing a cup of fresh percolated coffee which Hannah had brought to him a short while ago, staring out of the cabin window at the ground 40 000 feet below. "I think I've figured out why Sable has headed to Togo," Nicky gushed out excitedly when Nick answered the call. "Tell me more," he prompted her getting caught up in her excitement. "But wait a second, I'm putting you on speaker," catching the detective's eye to join him.

"Protection," she told them a few seconds later. "What do you mean?" Detective Joint asked a little bit confused. "The events of the last week have started to expose her. You could say unintentional consequences," Nicky explained to the rapt audience. "I suppose another way to describe it would be that her luck's starting to run out," Detective Joint replied understanding what Nicky was getting at. "Correct," Nicky told him. "So, who's she running to for protection in Togo then?" Nick asked her curiously. "Now that's the kicker," Nicky said excitedly. "What if I told you the President of Togo, would you believe me?" she told her audience. "Bloody hell !" Nick laughed out loudly. "You can't be serious. How did you come to that conclusion?"

Replying Nicky started to explain. "Remember when I said that I've seen her face before? Well, it took me a while, but I finally figured out where I had seen it before. It was in a fashion magazine. There was an article covering a gala party to do with the opening of one of the tallest hotels in West Africa, which happens to be in Lomé, Togo. She was the President's partner for the evening. Every picture taken of the President had her at his side. Just to make sure I trawled through a whole bunch of European magazines and found several pictures of her on the arm of – guess who? His Excellency the President of Togo. They were looking very cosy together." There was a stunned silence in the aircraft for a few seconds, with only the muted roar of the engines in the background. "Could they be related?" Detective Joint then asked her. Nicky gave a short laugh before replying, "No, I wouldn't think so." "Do they give her a name?" Eben asked waking up and joining in on the conversation. "No," replied Nicky. "They just refer to her as his partner for the evening."

Carrying on, she said, "So, I turned my attention to His Excellency, as I found out he likes to be called, and did some research on him. It would seem that running the country runs in the family blood. Between his grandfather. his father and himself they've been in power for close on fifty years. It's a one-party state. Opposition to their rule just seems to fade away," Nicky explained angrily. "Oh boy," muttered Eben, "it's getting better and better," to no one in particular. "A similar situation to North Korea," Johan pointed out who had also woken up to the sound of the conversation, "a family business."

They spoke for a while longer then hung up. "Okay, so what's the game plan?" Johan asked standing up and walking to the galley at the front of the cabin to get a fresh cup of coffee. Grinning Nick looked at each one of them and said, "It's easy. Once Sable goes online again, we'll know exactly where she is and then we grab her." "What the hell, Major!" Detective Joint exploded, "How're you going to get this right?" Nonchalantly Eben turned in his seat towards the detective and replied with a grin on his schoolboy like face saying, "Have faith in our leader my dear Detective, for he always gets it right."

Standing up and grinning at Eben and the team's unwavering faith in him, Nick said, "Back soon, boys, gotta go and speak to Chuck," and with that he headed forward towards the flight deck. Detective Joint looked rather confused, so Jimmy who had kept to himself in the rear of the cabin for most of the flight spoke up, "Chuck's ex-CIA and still has some very valuable contacts that we use from time to time."

Walking back into the passenger cabin twenty minutes later Nick was smiling from ear to ear, "Okay, guys, it's official: we're a bunch of degenerate surfers making videos of the hot surf spots of Africa. Sitting back down with a fresh cup of coffee in his hands, Nick took a sip of the freshly brewed blend and said, "this is what I propose we do."

Looking at Jimmy and Glen a short while later he said to them, "Sable hasn't seen you two yet, so you'll be our advance guard. When we land, I want you two to drive straight across the border into Lomé and take up residence at the Intercontinental Hotel and sniff around. We've got camera equipment in the hold; your cover story is that you are an advance film crew looking for decent surf spots for a surfing video we're shooting. With Steven and Nicky along with our Virtual Reality team monitoring all Virtual networks, as soon as Sable uses the Prototype we'll know exactly where she is," Glen and Jimmy nodded their heads.

Taking another sip of coffee, Nick continued, "The rest of us will drive down to a place called Ada Foah and meet up with Chuck's connection, a man called Jean Pierre who apparently runs a Dive and Surf Charter from the Volta River estuary." Looking directly at Jimmy and Glen he told them, "The idea is that once we locate Sable, we extract you two along with her plus the Prototype off of the beach and make a beeline back to a friendly country where Chuck and Hannah will be standing by waiting for us for a quick take off." "Got it, Boss," both Jimmy and Glen replied in unison.

Now that Nick had laid out the outline of the plan, his team started to fill in the missing pieces. "Okay guys, gather round," Johan said moving to the centre of the cabin with the settee running down the port side of the aircraft and a coffee table on which there was a laptop linked to the aircrafts satellite link as well as to the large LCD monitor on the starboard bulkhead in the lounge compartment. A short while later as the Bombardier started its descent into Kotoka International Airport Detective Joint looked on in amazement saying, "I get the feeling you've done this type of thing before."

GHANA, ACCRA, KOTOKA INTERNATIONAL AIRPORT, 15H00, SATURDAY

Landing in Accra at the Kotoka International Airport just after 15H00 on a hot Ghanaian Saturday afternoon they walked the long tiring walk from one side of the airport to the other to get to Passport and Immigration Control, each having to buy a seven-day entry visa. Once all the formalities had been completed, they at last headed down the long pedestrian ramp from the first floor to the ground floor of the airport terminal building and headed for the local Avis counter on the ground floor. "I hope they understood what you wanted," Eben mentioned to Nick as he pushed one of their luggage trollies stacked with toughened plastic equipment cases that carried cameras and a couple of small drones.

Walking a couple of paces behind them, Glen and Jimmy were carrying several surfboards in bags over their shoulders. Detective Joint brought up the rear, nursing a sore arm muttering "I feel like a bloody pin cushion, all I do is get waterboarded, shot at, and take fucking injections!" Not having a Yellow Fever Card, he was whisked away by Immigrations for a quick shot by the local airport doctor. "Let's hope so," Nick replied hopefully. One of the outcomes of the plan was that Nick had arranged two rental 4x4s from Avis, the local car rental company.

Reaching the bottom of the pedestrian ramp a sea of humanity engulfed them. Taxi operators, tour operators, hotel drivers, people waiting for passengers and loved ones, hawkers, pickpockets, and every other imaginable person all thronged the ground floor level of the airport, all shouting and talking at once. Seeing the red and white Avis sign like a shining beacon in the crowd, Nick made a beeline for the kiosk, wading through the sea of humanity, pushing people aside as he went, the rest of the team following behind in his wake. "Be careful of pickpockets," Nick warned them over his shoulder just as a man brushed past him and attempted to steal his wallet.

Nick caught him in the act, grasping the thief's right hand in his and swiftly bending it back on itself, forcing the thief to start to submit down onto his knees screaming in pain. "Owwww! I'm sorry! I'm sorry, I didn't mean it!" "Thieving motherfucker," Nick growled and pushed him backwards in distain, the next second the thief finding himself lying flat on his back. Nick walked on saying over his shoulder, "As I was saying, be careful of pickpockets and thieves around here." What he nor anyone in his team noticed was the harassed-looking passenger who had brushed past Nick on his opposite side and deftly slipped the nano-sized GPS tracker into his jacket.

Leaving the would-be pickpocket on the floor they walked on. "You sure it's not a better idea to use local connections?" Johan asked catching up to Nick as they walked into the Avis kiosk. Shaking his head Nick replied, "No, not just yet. I'm not too sure who we can trust in this neck of the woods," Johan nodded his head in agreement "Ja, you're probably right."

Twenty minutes later after all the paperwork had been completed the six of them were standing beside two clean white Toyota Prado 4x4s loaded with off-road equipment in a fenced-off area of the airport parking area demarcated for rental vehicles. Jimmy and Glen loaded their equipment and surfboards into the first 4x4, with Nick, Johan, Eben, and Detective Joint loading their half of the kit into the second.

"Good luck, guys," Johan said to Glen and Jimmy. Glen gave the thumbs up as they drove out of the parking lot. None of them spotted the sunburnt European male in loose-fitting chinos and a sweat-stained t-shirt with a baseball cap on his head watching them from a distance. Raising a camera to his face he was able to surreptitiously take a couple of photographs.

MOSCOW, SVR HEADQUARTERS, 16H00 (+ 1 HOUR), SATURDAY

"Da," Colonel Andreyev Petroski said answering the internal telephone call. "Sir, operations here," a female voice replied in Russian. "The tracking device is active." "Excellent," purred the colonel, "I'm on my way down."

The operations centre consisted of a number of individual rooms spanning the basement levels of the tall SVR building. The deeper down below the building one descended, the more secure the operation centres became and the more secret the operations were. Standing up Colonel Petroski headed for his office door and the lift that would take him down to one of the lowest of the basement levels once he had scanned his access card against the proximity access card reader in the lift.

Entering the designated operations room, a couple of minutes later, the SVR soldier on duty outside in the secure passageway smartly opening and closing the door for the colonel he received an update. "Sir, our agent reports that the targets have landed in Accra and rented two vehicles. He has confirmed that he will fol-low the vehicle in which the targets are not bugged," the Chief Operations Controller hurriedly informed him. "Very well," the colonel replied and went to take a seat on a small raised dais that gave him an overview of the operations room.

The operations room was dark, with only dim downlighters

on the ceiling providing small amounts of illumination, the large LCD screens on the front wall of the control room and on the operators', desks providing the bulk of the lighting.

"Where do you think Major Scott is headed?" he asked a couple of minutes later as he saw the device depicted on an overlaid map of Accra start to move. "Not too sure at the moment, sir, it looks like they are moving onto the Accra Afaloa Road heading in the same direction as the first vehicle," the operator reported. "Hmm, I see," replied the colonel. He had a long wait but a couple of hours later the colonel had his answers.

While waiting for events to unfold in Ghana, the colonel got hold of his team in Cape Town South Africa, who were standing by waiting for his orders. "Is there any movement at the Executive offices?" the colonel asked. "Negative, sir," replied the agent currently watching the Executive Decision offices, "the two targets are still inside in the premises." The two targets he was referring to were Nicky and Steven.

CHAPTER 8

WEST AFRICA, LOMÉ, INTERCONTINENTAL HOTEL, 20H00, SATURDAY

Walking through the hotel lobby to the front doors of the hotel and the chauffeur-driven shiny immaculately detailed black BMW 750I waiting under the Porte Couche, every blue-blooded male in the lobby turned to stare at her. What they saw was a long-legged long brown-haired beauty in a short tight skirt and bursting cleavage strutting across the highly polished marble-tiled foyer, the smell of her sensual perfume following her, infusing the air around her, along with the click of her stiletto heels on the shiny marble floor. A couple of minutes later she climbed coyly into the rear of the BMW and the chauffeur closed the door behind her, cocooning her in German luxury. Very soon the driver climbed into the driver's seat and the vehicle pulled away.

Settling back in her leather seat idly looking out through the vehicle window at the almost non-existent night lights of the city, she thought back to the conversation she had had earlier with Senzo. "Our benefactor has summoned me to the palace. I have to go," she had explained to him. Grinning Senzo had nodded his head in agreement, "Okay, you do what you need to do to keep us safe. I'll get to work with my side of the deal." It was a 20-minute drive through relatively empty streets before reaching their destination when the driver turned left into a guarded driveway. It wasn't surprising to Sable that she wasn't taken to the Palace but to another mansion in an upmarket suburb of Lomé.

His Excellency was a large heavy-set man who had just turned 50. In his younger days, which was a long time ago, he was all muscle, but with middle age and the luxury of the Presidential office coupled with not enough exercise, the muscle was now turning to fat. "Sable, my dear," his Excellency cried out excitedly to see her as she walked into the room. "This is a surprise!"

Rushing up to her like a schoolboy excited to see her again, he gave her a giant bear hug, his large hands running all over her back and down to her taught tight bottom that was the conversation of many a male. She pressed her lithe tight body into his, her crotch grinding tightly into his pelvis. Subtly she felt the monster between his legs stirring, starting to push against the fabric of his Saville Row trousers. He was just about to slip his hands under her short skirt when she gasped out in delight and pulled away, saying, "Shame on you, your Excellency, you can't even offer a girl something to drink first?" "Hahaha," his Excellency laughed good-naturedly. "Where are my manners?" he said and led her to an expensively furnished lounge illuminated softly with dimmed downlighters.

His Excellency had chased all the house staff away, apart from his bodyguards who were patrolling the grounds outside, so walking over to the small but elaborate bar himself, he poured them both a drink. "So, tell me, my dear," he asked once seated next to Sable sipping away at their drinks, "what brings you to my country? Are you going to throw another party?" he asked with a large grin on his African face. Sable laughed a low husky laugh, saying, "No, unfortunately not. A past business dealing that went wrong has come back to haunt me and I need to lay low for a while," she explained to him. "Hahaha," his Excellency laughed, a rich deep laugh. "Your past is finally catching up with you."

Sable's face took on a worried look and he laughed some more at the sight of her expression, saying "Relax, you're safe in my country. No one will dare to touch you here. They will have to answer to me personally," pointing to his chest with his index finger. "Thank you, your Excellency, thank you," Sable cried out relieved. For a second, she thought that someone had gotten to him. "How can I ever repay you?" she purred seductively, her left-hand brushing lightly over his nearest thigh.

LOMÉ, INTERCONTINENTAL HOTEL, SATURDAY, 20H00

Glen and Jimmy arrived at the Intercontinental Hotel in the early evening, just after the sun had finished sinking in a large orange ball of fire over the western horizon of the Atlantic Ocean. "Fuck me, this is all we need," Glen muttered to Jimmy under his breath as they arrived at the main entrance to the hotel and saw in the early evening light soldiers equipped with AK47's, the familiar banana-shaped magazine protruding from the bottom of the assault rifles, patrolling the hotel grounds. Jimmy nodded his head in agreement saying with a laugh, "True, but it makes it far more interesting now, not just a simple snatch and grab." "Fucking mad man," Glen growled back at Jimmy as the armed soldier at the main gate approached the left side of the vehicle, the driver's side. Surprising them with his efficiency, the soldier soon lifted the vehicle barrier up and they drove through towards the Porte Couche, just as a big shiny dark coloured chauffeur-driven BMW with dark tinted windows roared past them and past the soldier at the entrance without slowing down. "Now there's a madman for you," Jimmy replied nodding his head back towards the receding BMW.

Pulling up to a stop under the Porte Couche of the hotel, the porter opened the driver's door for Glen saying in halting English, "Welcome to the Intercontinental Hotel, sir." On opening the car door, all the cool airconditioned air rushed out, replaced with the hot dry air of a typical Lomé evening. "Bloody hell, it's fucking hot and it's after eight in the evening," Jimmy complained loudly to Glen. "Thank you," Glen replied to the porter, ignoring his friend's grumbling, and soon they had the 4x4 unloaded and were following their luggage inside to the individual check in desks, while the now dusty 4x4 was parked in the guest parking lot by another porter.

"My god, this is stunning," Jimmy commented out loudly as

they entered the reception lobby, surprised by the size and splendour. The ground floor was a triple volume atrium with the balconies of the mezzanine floor and first floor above it, running the entire length and width of the atrium. Large sparkling chandeliers hung down from the triple storey roof high above. The floor, walls and massive square support columns of the building were encased in marble of shiny hues of greys, black, and browns. To the right of the reception area were small individual lounges with leather settees and armchairs grouped together in intimate groupings, behind which were a number of exclusive boutique shops and glass-encased boardrooms.

Checking in they paid for two nights in advance and soon they were taking one of the lifts to their rooms on the 15th Floor. "Excuse me," Jimmy had asked the front desk lady who checked them in, "what is that large round squat building on the other side of the Porte Couche?" Giving them both a large smile the front desk lady had replied, "Why that is the nation's Parliament where our esteemed leader, his Excellency, meets with his ministers."

A couple of minutes later, swiping his room card against the access-controlled lock, Glen turned to his friend Jimmy who was one room down saying, "I'm starving, meet you down in the restaurant in thirty and then we'll check out the hotel?" "Roger that," Jimmy replied enthusiastically as the access lock clicked open allowing him to enter his room. Before getting a shower and changing into some clean clothes, Glen first sent an encrypted message back to Nick. *We've arrived at the Hotel, crawling with armed soldiers. No one told us that the fucking Togo parliament is in front of the hotel.*

Thirty minutes later the two of them met up in the restaurant on the mezzanine level. It was while they were eating supper their iPhones both beeped at the same time indicating a message had been received. They were currently seated opposite a table of air hostesses who flew for a Belgium Airline that had a regular route between Brussels and Lomé. Keeping with the cover story, both

Glen and Jimmy were regaling the air hostesses with stories of all the surf spots they'd surfed around the world in the making of this epic surfing video they were currently making. Both surfed back in Cape Town, so they were able to make a lot of it up.

Literally at the same time they reached for their iPhones, Glen looking across at the ladies saying, "Sorry, we're actually still on the clock," amid gay laughter from the hostesses. Accessing their encrypted messaging app once their phones had identified them and they had entered a code. If one of them entered the incorrect code, then the encrypted messaging application would automatically wipe itself clear from that phone; an operational tool developed by Steven and Nick back in the Cape Town IT lab.

Nicky: *Heads up boys, I've just accessed the hotel CCTV network she's in the hotel, and she's not alone, it looks like she has an accomplice. I am sending you the video clip. Will confirm the room numbers shortly. Stand by.*

Glen: *Standing by.*

"Sorry, ladies," Jimmy said with a large smile on his rugged suntanned face. "That's the boss, he's summoned us to a Virtual Meeting." A couple of the air hostesses looked extremely disappointed, one very pretty brunette saying in a lilting French accent, "Maybe we see you later, yes?" her voice dripping with possibilities. "I hope so," Jimmy ventured his tongue almost hanging out of his mouth, as Glen pulled him away towards the entrance of the restaurant. "Fuck," Jimmy muttered under his breath as they walked out of the restaurant, "It always happens, I meet a couple of cute ladies and work always cuts in and fucks it up," Glen laughed at his friend's frustration; he wasn't about to remind him that he was on company time at present and being paid handsomely for it.

Walking out of the restaurant back towards the lift lobby on the mezzanine floor, Jimmy said to Glen, "You know, I can't get over the grandeur of this place! Look he cried waving his hands around "I could drive two bloody double-decker buses side by side down these passages and still not hit a guest," Glen had to agree with his buddy, the size and magnitude of the hotel were over whelming. The corridors of the ground and mezzanine floors were wide and double volume, the walls and floors clad in shiny imported marble with the ceilings a mixture of snow-white ceiling tiles interspersed with snow-white skimmed ceilings with drop-down bulkheads. The walls were adorned with African paintings while there were shiny glass cases displaying African art placed every couple of metres on both sides of the public passageways.

"You see all the cameras?" Glen asked Jimmy as they neared the lift lobby. Jimmy nodded his head saying "Yeah, Axis from the look of things, they must be running some decent head end software." Reaching the 15th floor they both headed without another word towards Glen's room. Once inside Glen took out his iPhone and using another application designed by Executive Decisions quickly scanned the room for any listening devices. Finding none he said, "Right, let's go to work." Jimmy headed over to one of the camera cases and opening it accessed an innocuous hidden compartment, extracting two compact military issue encrypted radio sets with small lapel mics linked to a cigarette size TX RX box placed on one's body along with a wireless earpiece for one's ear.

Gearing themselves up and switching the units on they were just in time to hear Steven in Cape Town say, "Alpha Team, Home Base, as I put out on the group, we have a problem. Sable has an accomplice, also it looks like she's gone out for the night. We've sent you the video clips." A couple of seconds later their iPhones beeped indicating new information had been received. Opening the message and playing the video clips both Glen and Jimmy first saw the woman they now knew as Sable walking into the hotel with a slightly smaller gentleman of oriental persuasion. The next video clip showed her dressed to kill leaving the hotel again a couple of hours later. "Wow!" Jimmy exclaimed. "She's fucking gorgeous, I'm getting a tingling in my ball sac, man," as they watched her strut across the reception lobby.

"Alpha Three and Four, Alpha Two, you watched the video clips?" Johan asked them. Glen answered for them, "Copy that Alpha Two your instructions?" Glen replied. "There's been a change of plans, disengage and standby for new orders," Johan instructed them. "Alpha 3 Alpha 2 copy that," Glen confirmed.

Turning to Glen, Jimmy said "In my professional opinion sharp blades used to cut off heads go together with Japanese-looking dude with a don't-fuck-with-me kinda look. Where's there's smoke there's usually fire." "Pal, I couldn't agree with you more," Glen replied. "Let's go and have a drink in the Skybar and wait for our orders." "With you," Jimmy said with a grin on his face thinking about the Belgium air hostesses and the infinite possibilities that brought.

EXECUTIVE SUITE, INTERCONTINENTAL HOTEL, 20H30, SATURDAY

After Sable had left, Senzo ordered Room Service and while waiting for his food to be delivered he had a quick shower to wake himself up, first scalding hot water to open up all his pores, and then ice-cold water to close them up again. It was going to be a long night. Timing it just right he exited the shower feeling refreshed and invigorated just as there was a knock on the suite door, and a female voice calling out, "Room Service, sir."

After a bite to eat, with nerves tingling with excitement as if he was a school boy going on his first date, he sat down in one of the comfortable deep leather loungers in his suite and readied himself for his forage into the world of Virtual Reality, making sure that the Prototype, the stainless steel bracelet nano computer, and the mirror-like glasses were all fully charged, their small lithium rechargeable batteries ready to do battle. 'Don't want to run out of power while in the middle of causing chaos and mayhem. It won't be good for business, the Prototype packing up halfway through the performance,' he thought to himself with a small smile on his oriental face.

Soon he was ready. 'This is it,' he thought happily. 'Time to cause chaos and alert the underworld and unscrupulous world leaders to a new toy on the market that will look stylish in their arsenal of death and destruction… If they can afford it,' he thought afterwards, again with a wicked smile on his face.

First slipping the stainless-steel bracelet nanocomputer over his left hand and securing it onto his wrist, he placed the mirror-like glasses onto his face covering his eyes. Activating the system, the same as with the hotel network in Sandton Johannesburg, the usual feeling of free falling was abruptly halted, and a message from the Prototype appeared, 'WARNING YOU ARE ENTERING A PUBLIC ACCESS PLATFORM DO YOU WISH TO ACTIVATE SYSTEM?' Following the usual routine, he pressed the YES tab on the menu screen. The next second he felt his body charged with energy as it was encased in the black sheath. Accessing the Maintenance Cloaked option, he immediately disappeared and went invisible.

Landing on the Hotel VR platform he looked around. It was a stylish and well-lit platform, in line with the opulence of the hotel. It was also quite a busy platform. There were people and caricatures of all shapes and forms coming and going. He also noted several Gate Keepers patrolling on the platform. 'Hmm, they must be because of the House of Parliament' he reasoned to himself.

Silently a tube arrived on the station. Quickly using the dropdown menu of the Prototype, he interrogated the tube. "Perfect," he muttered to himself. "It's going exactly where I want to go." Hurriedly he followed the hotel guests into the tube. The door closed silently behind them, the hotel guests having no idea that they had an unwanted visitor on board. They were a family of four, father, mother and two young teenage boys of around thirteen years old. "Yeeaah," the one teenager was saying out loud. "We're going to see the Big Apple!" A short while later the tube deposited them on a large crowded well-lit platform. A big flashing sign over the escalators said 'WELCOME TO TIMES SQUARE NEW YORK'.

Ignoring the hustle and bustle of the people and caricatures that were surging around and through him, he concentrated on interrogating the VR tubes with the Prototype's application software. The Times Square Virtual Platform was just as busy as the real Times Square platform, with Virtual tubes arriving and departing every couple of seconds on multiple lines on the large electronic platform.

Out of the corner of his vision he spotted a couple of Gate Keepers walking down the platform towards him. 'Hell, they're military Gate Keepers,' he thought as he immediately spotted several differences between the civilian gatekeepers and these one walking towards him. "This'll be interesting," he said softly to himself as they got nearer. 'Do they see me, or don't they see me? That's the question' he thought silently, the question screaming around loudly over and over in his mind.

Standing poised ready to defend himself if need be, the Gate Keepers walked right past in front of him, not even glancing in his direction. "Excellent," he said to himself breathing a sigh of relief turning his attention back to the arriving and departing tubes in front of him. It didn't take him long to find a tube travelling in the direction that he needed to go. North.

A short while later he was standing on a lookout point looking down at a vast private electronic network that pulsed and glowed with a massive amount of energy. The network stretched out and pulsed for as far as he could see. It was ringed fenced with numerous layers of security and a multitude of Gate Keepers, both civilian and military. There was only one access point into the network that had more security layers than Senzo had ever seen before. 'WELCOME TO INDIAN POINT NUCLEAR ENERGY CENTRE,' he silently read the sign displayed over the entrance. Watching the access point for a couple of minutes he noted that there wasn't much traffic in and out of the network, however, beyond the access point, the network was a hive of activity. Indian Point Energy was one of seven nuclear electricity plants that the company The America Energy Corporation ran across the length and breadth of the United States.

After 9/11 the company had increased and strengthened their physical security as well as their cybersecurity to prevent both physical terrorist attacks as well as cyberattacks on their facilities and infrastructure. At first, they had a policy of no access to outside data networks. But the problem started to arise as technology began to evolve and attempting to share data and information between seven different nuclear facilities scattered across the length and breadth of the United States became a pain. So, management relented and soon a single highly restricted dedicated fibre link to a local satellite uplink station was installed to link the facility to the other facilities.

Before heading towards the single access point, he first checked his status. "Cloaked mode on," he muttered to himself checking the drop-down menu status. "Battery life also good. Okay, here I come. Hahaha," he laughed softly as he started to jog the last short distance towards the single access point, looking forward to causing mayhem and destruction. What he'd also found out with the Prototype was that with the electronic suit you were able to move effortlessly and tirelessly all day long without getting tired.

Approaching the access point a short while later he slowed down. Getting ready to defend himself if need be, he approached the first layer of security and kept on walking. Holding his breath, he walked right past the Gate Keepers dodging left and right to stay out of their way. 'That was simple enough,' he thought to himself as he approached the second layer of Gate Keepers. All too quickly he was past the Gate Keepers and had gained access to the secure nuclear facility.

CHAPTER 9

GHANA, ADA FOAH, VOLTA RIVER ESTUARY, 20H35, SATURDAY

They had met up with Jean Pierre down at Ada Foah on the banks of the Volta River a little earlier in the afternoon. The Volta River emptied out into the Gulf of Guinea, the section of the Atlantic Ocean that lapped the shores of the bulge of Africa. Jean Pierre turned out to be an eccentric old Frenchman who, with his pride and joy, *Ma Bell Ami* a 50-foot motor launch, ran a small dive and surf charter business. Luckily for Nick and his team, business was a bit slow now, so for a negotiated fee Jean Pierre was more than willing to accommodate everyone.

A short while later after loading all their equipment on board, the captain started the twin diesel marine engines in a cloud of blue fumes. Once the mooring lines were cast off, the captain started to slowly negotiate the poorly demarcated deep-water channel out into the Gulf of Guinea, the twin diesel engines slowly pushing the hull of *Ma Bell Ami* through the water, the vibration of the engines being felt through the soles of their feet. "Captain, where are the deep-water marks?" Nick asked, scanning the water in front of them. Normally one would find round floating red and white striped buoys that were an international maritime sign depicting safe, deep water. The old Frenchman grinned a nicotine tooth stained grin at Nick and tapped his head. Leaning past Nick, the captain said, "Merci," and switched on an older generation VHF radio. As Nick turned around and was about to head down to the main deck the VHF radio made a high pitch squeal and faded away as he walked past.

"What the hell!" Nick exclaimed and brushed back past the VHF radio again. The same squealing sound emitted from the speaker. "Oh, fuck!" Nick said, the captain looking at him strangely. It took Nick a couple of minutes to locate the nano-sized tracking device. "That pickpocket had to have been a decoy," Johan noted grimly looking intently at the small metallic device. They all nodded their heads in agreement. "Who has this kind of technology?" Detective Joint asked intrigued. Eben answered the question for the detective, "Americans, British, or Russians. Take your pick, but personally I'd go with the Russians."

Turning to the captain, Nick asked, "Captain, do you have an empty dive cylinder which we could use for a while?" Nodding his head, the captain explained where they could find it. "Perfect," exclaimed Nick a short while later. The tracking device was taped inside the top of the depressurised steel dive cylinder. With the valve screwed tightly back on, no electronic signals could escape through it, the tracking device was effectively switched off, being surrounded by steel.

A couple of hours later, standing offshore from the Togo coastline among the numerous ships; deep-sea ocean-going freighters and tankers that were anchored just offshore, waiting for access to the Port of Lomé and the Port of Benin a couple of nautical miles further southeast along the coast, the intelligence started to come through thick and fast.

First, it was Glen's message informing them of the soldiers patrolling the hotel premises. "Why the hell are there soldiers patrolling the premises of the hotel?" Eben asked out loud to no one in particular when Nick broke the news to them. Jean Pierre, who was standing at the helm of the motor launch helming the vessel, started to laugh out loud. "What's so funny?" Eben snapped back. "You really have no idea, do you?" Jean Pierre asked them turning around, and seeing their not amused expressions quickly sobered up and explained. "Rumour has it that his Excellency's family not only has the majority shares in the hotel, but that is why they built the country's parliament right in front of the hotel!" "Mother fucker," Eben muttered out loudly.

Next, it was Nicky on the satellite phone. "Okay, Boss, I've gained access to the video archive servers of the hotel, it looks like Sable has an accomplice. I'm sending you video footage of them now," she informed him. Using the satellite phone data connection Nick was able to download the footage. Then Nicky said to him, "Boss, it looks like we have a bigger problem. I've accessed the live CCTV video feeds and I see that there are armed soldiers stationed all over the hotel." "Ja," Nick replied. "Glen and Jimmy reported the same a short while ago." Carrying on as if she hadn't heard him, she said, "Whole place inside and out is crawling with armed soldiers, it would be suicide to attempt a snatch and grab right now." "Damnit," ranted Nick. "So it's not just soldiers on the outside, they're all over the place. We're going to have to think out of the box and somehow lure them out of the hotel and away from his Excellency's protection."

"Hang on, I've got an idea, a bit of counterintelligence is required here," Detective Joint said excitedly joining the conversation. They all looked at him. Carrying on he told them, "It had to of been someone in the upper echelons of the SAP that warned Sable that you were coming two days ago. Let me feed information back to the SAP that will get back to Sable that should spook her to start running. You just have to be ready to catch them." Finished with the explanation he sat back in his seat and waited. Nick's face slowly broke out into a large grin. "I like it," he told Detective Joint excitedly, "but first we've got some new plans to put into place."

Turning to Jean Pierre at the helm Nick told him, "Change of plans, Cap'n, take us back to Ada Foah." Seeing the downfallen look on the old man's face in the light of the compass binnacle Nick said, "I'm still paying you the full fee which we negotiated, plus I need you to do something else for me." The captain's face lit up at that. Motioning for his small team to gather out of earshot from Jean Pierre on the aft deck, Nick followed them out, as the captain turned the motor launch around and opening the throttles, the hull of *Ma Bell Ami* easily getting onto the plane and headed back up coast towards Ada Foah and the Volta River.

Turning to Johan he said, "Get hold of Alpha 3 and Alpha 4 and tell them to standby, there's a change of plans, we'll fill them in as soon as we have worked out all the details. They must just stay out of sight of Sable and her partner for the meantime." "That won't be hard for them if I know Glen and Jimmy," Johan replied drily as he walked inside the main cabin. Pushing his PTT on his radio, he transmitted, "Alpha Three and Four, Alpha Two Over."

As *Ma Bell Ami* plowed through the almost flat Gulf of Guinea, Nick took out his satellite phone and contacted Chuck waiting at the Kotoka International Airport in Accra. "There's been a slight change of plans. I need you to do a relocation flight to Lomé-Tokoin International Airport," Nick explained to him. After speaking for another couple of minutes explaining what else they needed Nick ended the call.

"Sorry, Major, I'm a little bit lost," Detective Joint said to Nick as they stood in the stern watching the rooster trails of the twin props churning up the water astern of them. "Once we've scared Sable and her accomplice out of the hotel and back to her aircraft, how do you propose to apprehend her?" he asked. Smiling slightly for a second, Nick answered, "Easy, we're going to hijack her aircraft." "You can't do that!" spluttered the detective. "Why not?" Nick asked him mildly surprised by the detective's stubbornness. "That'll get you shot as a terrorist," Detective Joint replied. "Only if we get caught," Johan said with a large smile on his face.

WEST AFRICA, LOMÉ, SECRET PRESIDENTIAL MANSION, 23H00, SATURDAY

"Oooh yes, your Excellency, don't stop," Sable moaned out loudly as she spread her long shapely legs open further giving his Excellency complete access to her g string clad womanhood. Growling like a hungry beast at the smell of her arousal, his tongue dove straight into her sopping wet vagina, plunging straight into her wetness tasting her unique taste. After a couple of minutes of his earnest ministrations Sable started to moan softly at first, then getting louder, "Aaaaaahhh, I'm coming! Don't stop what you're doing, I'm coming! Oh fuck, I'm coming," as her hips starting to buck around on his face as with a life of their own.

With a primeval growl, his Excellency stood up and ripped off his Savile Row trousers, his large black throbbing member break- ing free, standing straight, large, and proud. Sable gasped as she saw the size of his cock. She had already seen it of course, but it never ceased to surprise her.

As she looked at it, the large vein running up the side of his member pulsed, his large manhood jumping to the pulse. Moan- ing she sat up and opening her mouth as wide as she could she engulfed the head of his man meat in her silky warm mouth, her right-hand grasping hold of the large black piece of his virility. She started to expertly suck on the enlarged head of his throbbing manhood as he stood over her while her right hand slowly worked its way up and down the length of his cock, pulling lightly, the fingers of her left hand stimulating herself at the same time. "Oh yes, don't stop," his Excellency groaned out loudly, lost in the exquisite sensations of having his cocked sucked into a velvety slippery warmness.

"Wait, it's too early for me to start coming," his Excellency growled after a couple of minutes of Sable's warm mouth and slippery tongue. Grinning like a Cheshire Cat who was about to get the cream, Sable purred, "What do you have in mind?" as his large black member popped out of her mouth. "This," he told her and produced an ampule filled with a white powder. "Naughty, naughty, Your Excellency," Sable purred, her eyes sparkling when she saw the powder. Snorting a couple of small spoonsful of co- caine that he fed her off of a small custom-made silver spoon attached to the ampule, she soon felt the euphoric effects of the drug tingling at the synapses of her brain, and filling out in a warm tingling warmth throughout her body. "Mmmmhhh," she moaned out loudly as her pussy began to throb to its own beat.

Falling down onto her back with every nerve in her body alive and tingling, with the cocaine coursing through her body, she spread her legs wide as his Excellency knelt between them and started to feed his large member into her very wet and slippery vagina. "Ooohhhh, it's so large," she groaned out as she felt the massive head of his cock probing between her outer lips, stretching them wider than Debbie's strap on dildo had ever done. "Slowly, oh slowly," she groaned out as he pushed himself inside her, slowly, achingly slowly, inch by inch. Soon he was ploughing his length to the hilt inside her. "Yes, yes, yes," Sable moaned in time to the large oversized cock that was pounding away at her, stretching her open to splitting point and touching her to her very core.

CHAPTER 10

INDIAN POINT ENERGY CENTER, BUCHANEN, NEW YORK STATE, (-4 HRS) 19H00, SATURDAY

The windowless control room was slightly smaller than a tennis court and was situated a couple of metres underground. It was a highly secure area, only accessible after passing through several security access points and airlocks. It was deathly quiet in the room, with the faint humming sound of the air-conditioning system being the only background noise, constantly humming away keeping the control room at a comfortable 19 degrees C.

Occasionally, though, a printer broke the silence, spitting out a report that was caught in a wire basket attached to the printer. The lighting in the control room was hi-tech Dr Strangelove lighting, especially designed not to cast any shadows which might make it difficult to read a dial or monitor or give a false reading. For the uninitiated, the control room was a mass of coloured dials, switches, LEDs, computer screens, and CCTV monitors that made no sense whatsoever. But, for the two control room operators currently on duty, Brad Polanski and Erick King, every coloured dial, switch, LED, computer screen and CCTV monitor had a specific meaning and a purpose.

The meaning and purpose of which were to monitor and control the nuclear fission chain reaction that was occurring in the adjacent building; called the containment building a hundred or so metres away. From the exterior the containment building was a round concrete building with a dome roof, the design being synonymous the world over with nuclear reactors. The concrete walls were six to eight feet thick with a lead inner lining to prevent any leakage of radioactivity escaping from within. The foundations of the containment building were even deeper; the architects designing the containment building to withstand a magnitude 6 earthquake.

Inside this tall, large round windowless building sat the PWR or Pressurised Water Reactor that was used to generate electricity for around 2 million households and businesses of a large portion of the State of New York. It was designed and built by Westinghouse a local company.

A PWR works by adding nuclear fuel in the form of fuel rods into the bottom of the nuclear reactor vessel. A single round fuel rod is around 4m in length and contains thousands of pellets of enriched uranium dioxide. Typically, around 200 of these 4m fuel rods are bundled together to form a square fuel assembly. There were over one hundred fuel assemblies making up the reactor core of the PWR of Indian Point 2, which translated to just over 100 tonnes of enriched uranium undergoing a controlled nuclear fission chain reaction inside the reactor core.

A nuclear reaction occurs when an atom is split in two by a fast-moving fission neutron. The splitting of the atom not only breaks the atom into two smaller and lighter atoms but also releases two or more, faster-moving fission neutrons as well as energy in the form of heat. The released neutrons then collide into more atoms, splitting them in two and releasing more fast-moving fission neutrons and more heat. The process happens repeatedly, creating a nuclear chain reaction. The physics behind a controlled nuclear chain reaction in a PWR and the devastating explosion caused by a American or Russian Inter Continental Ballistic Missile are exactly the same, the only difference being that the nuclear reaction occurring in the PWR is controlled whereas the nuclear explosion is not.

To keep the reactor core cool, water is pumped over the reactor core. This water is contained in what is known as a closed loop system called the primary loop and is continuously pumped around the reactor pressure vessel. This primary loop of water has three purposes, one to keep the fuel rods cool; bearing in mind that the water enters the reactor at around 275 degrees Celsius or 527 degrees Fahrenheit and as the water flows up over the reactor core and up into upper parts of the reactor pressure vessel it heats up to 315 Degrees C or 599 degrees Fahrenheit and turns into high-pressure steam; 150 – 160 Bar at the top of the reactor vessel, thanks to a pressuriser attached to the primary loop.

This high-pressure steam is then passed through a heat exchanger where on the other side of the heat exchanger is another loop of closed pumped water, called the secondary loop. The high-pressure steam from the primary loop heats up the water in the secondary loop which also turns to steam, albeit at a slightly lower pressure. This steam is then piped to the large 30m long generator hall where it is used to turn turbines that are connected to alternators which produce electricity. The primary loop high-pressure steam then passes through a condenser where it turns back into water which is then pumped back into the reactor core again. The primary loop water is highly radioactive.

The third purpose of the water is to act as a moderator. To have a sustained nuclear chain reaction, the fast-moving fission neutrons need to be slowed down in order to interact with the nuclear fuel and maintain a sustained nuclear reaction. This is a process called moderation and in a PWR the coolant water is used as the moderator by letting the fast-moving fission neutrons undergo multiple collisions with the lighter hydrogen atoms in the water, losing speed in the process.

This is also an important safety feature in a PWR, as an increase in temperature causes the water to expand making greater gaps between the water molecules and thereby reducing the probability of thermalisation; reducing the extent to which neutrons are slowed down and, in the process, reducing the reactivity in the nuclear core. In other words, the hotter the coolant becomes, the less reactive the nuclear core becomes, shutting itself down slightly to compensate and vice versa. This process is referred to as self regulating, whereby the plant controls itself around a given temperature set by the position of the control rods.

The control rods of the nuclear reactor sit at the top of the PWR and via electronic motors are raised or lowered into the reactor core to control the speed of the nuclear reaction. The control rods contain the chemical elements boron and cadmium. Both boron and cadmium absorb neutrons which then slows down the nuclear reaction as there are less neutrons to create further nuclear reactions, and by increasing or decreasing the length of the control rods the operator is able to control the temperature and speed of the reactor.

On the one hand the owners and staff were able to boast that the plant had a Zero Greenhouse gas emission status, however, on the other hand it was what one's darkest nightmares are made of should the contents of the nuclear reactor escape into the environment, Nuclear Armageddon, bearing in mind that the used fuel rods alone are radioactive for around a thousand years.

A couple of hundred metres away in a similar control room another set of operators were controlling Indian Point 3, another PWR. Collectively, along with Indian Point 1; a decommissioned nuclear reactor they made up the Indian Point Energy Centre that was located on the eastern bank of the Hudson River just over 50 k's / 36 miles north from the centre of Manhattan. Indian Point Energy Centre was one of seven nuclear power stations owned by The America Energy Corporation. Combined the two reactors supplied over 2000 megawatts of electricity to the grid of the State of New York.

The next second the muted calm tranquillity of the Indian Point 2 Control Room was broken by the ear-piercing sound of a piezo buzzer alarm activating. Erick, the younger and less experienced of the two operators looked up in alarm, there were over 25 000 alarms in the control room. "Relax, I've got it," Brad the older and more experienced of the two operators said unfazed by the screeching sound of the piezo buzzer.

Silencing the buzzer, he looked at the alarm annunciation board. "Okay one of the Primary Circulation Pumps, Pump No. 1 has gone on the blink," he casually informed his partner. "Confirmed," Eric replied also visually confirming the flashing LED annunciation with the words PRIMARY LOOP RECIRC PMP 1 engraved on it. "I'm activating start-up procedures for Primary Stand by Pump 1," Eric replied unhurriedly following the correct procedures and started typing a command on his keyboard in front of him. For every primary system in a Nuclear Power Station there is a standby system and sometimes a backup system for the standby system. The fact that the loss of one of four of the main primary pumps that pumped over 100 000 gallons/min of radioactive coolant around the reactor core wasn't an everyday occurrence, however, both operators had trained for this type of scenario.

Then, another alarm annunciation triggered, shattering the just regained composure of the control room. The CON ROD O/RIDE fault annunciator activated. "What the fuck, Eric, you've typed the wrong commands!" Brad shouted out in alarm as looking at first the flashing annunciator and then at one of the CCTV monitors monitoring the reactor core, in the blue glow of the reactor core one could clearly see the control rods retracting away from the critical mass, upsetting the balance of the chain reaction, as the control rods started to rise slowly out of the reactor. With the retraction of the control rods, the fission neutrons were now free to start more chain reactions and the critical heat started to increase substantially, thanks also to the loss of a quarter of the coolant capacity. To add to their woes, another set of alarms started to add their noise to the cacophony. "Oh fuck, man, we've got real shit, man!" Eric blurted out as the balance of the primary feed pumps went offline. The corresponding fault lights for PRIMARY LOOP RECIRC PMP 2, PRIMARY LOOP RECIRC PMP3, and PRIMARY LOOP RECIRC PMP 4 all started to flash away.

"Fuck, man, help! Something's seriously wrong! I'm locked out of the system," Eric maniacally shouted out in terror as he frantically tapped away at his keyboard to no avail. With every passing second, the temperature of the reactor core started to rise to levels only seen during simulations of a reactor core meltdown. With the blood draining from his face, visions of Fukushima bouncing around in his consciousness, Brad swiftly stood up from his desk and bolted for the large expansive control desk in the forefront of the control room and lunged for the large red round button with the words REACTOR SCRAM etched below it.

With the uncontrolled rise in the reactor core temperature, emergency protocols were automatically activated inside the plant as well as in the neighbourhoods within a 10-mile radius around the plant.

BUCHANAN, NEW YORK STATE, (-4 HRS) 19H00, SATURDAY

As per the Nuclear Regulatory Commission all nuclear power plants must have an evacuation plan, not only for the evacuation of the staff from the nuclear power plant itself, but also for the neighbouring countryside; due to the deadly radiation, a by-product of the fission nuclear reaction. The NRC specifies two evacuation zones around a nuclear power plant; a plume exposure pathway zone with a radius of 10 miles (16km) primarily concerned with the exposure to and inhalation of radioactive contamination, and the second evacuation zone an ingestion pathway zone of around 50 miles (80km). Indian Point Energy Centre was no different.

The 10-mile plume exposure pathway enveloped the neighbouring counties of Westchester County, Rockland County, Putnam County, Orange County and Dutchess County, all told just over 1.7 million people living in these five counties. The 50-mile evacuation zone included New York City with an estimated population of more than 20 million inhabitants.

To say that most of the residents in the five counties were unprepared for a live evacuation or serious incident at the nuclear power plant was an understatement. Everyone was aware that the Indian Point nuclear power plant was on their proverbial back doorstep, but the cavalier attitude of "Ah, it won't happen to us," prevailed among many the residents of the five counties.

The sudden crackling activation sound of the evacuation loudspeakers coming to life on Saturday evening, where the majority of the 1.7 million residents in the surrounding counties were either partying up a storm or settling down to a quiet Saturday evening at home, came as a complete surprise. The loud mournful wail of the evacuation sirens placed at strategic positions on tall poles, throughout the immediate surrounding counties was activated automatically when certain protocols at the nuclear power plant were breached.

The loud mournful wailing tones of the sirens sounded like World War Two air raid sirens alerting all and sundry and then, "ATTENTION PLEASE! ATTENTION PLEASE! THIS IS THE INDIAN POINT ENERGY CENTRE EMERGENCY CONTROL ROOM. THIS IS NOT A DRILL. I REPEAT: THIS IS NOT A DRILL. EVACUATE YOUR HOMES IMMEDIATELY AND HEAD FOR THE 10 MILE STATE LINE IMMEDIATELY. DO NOT STOP UNTIL YOU HAVE REACHED THE 10 MILE LINE AS INDICATED IN YOUR EVACUATION DOCUMENTS." There was a second silence and then the mournful wailing tones of the sirens started up again, followed by the announcement, again. Families reacted in different ways, the majority not in the way that the authorities planning and writing the evacuation plans had envisaged. They panicked. Dropping whatever they were doing they headed for the front door, forgetting to switch off things such as appliances. However, not all households were the same.

In the Vaughn household of Westchester County, they had just sat down to enjoy a home-cooked meal lovingly prepared by the mother and wife, Mary Vaughn, when the evacuation sirens activated. Calmly setting down her knife and fork, Mary Vaughn looked sternly at her husband and two young children with a 'I told you so' expression on her face and said, "Hurry but don't run, as we've practised. Fetch your bags and we'll all meet in the garage." She worked as a secretary at the Indian Point Energy Centre and drove her family to the point of madness with her dry run evacuation practices, making sure that each member of the family had an overnight bag packed. She even had some dog and cat food packed for the family pets, just in case.

Other families weren't as organised. The Dillan household in Orange County was one such family. A family of four, they were also sitting down to supper, theirs being take away chicken from the local KFC. Having spent the first day of the weekend settling into their new home, having moved from the West Coast earlier in the week; Nancy had got a promotion at work that meant a complete relocation to the other side of the United States. Nancy Dillan, being the breadwinner and "boss" of the family, had kept her husband Chad busy the whole day. The relocation company had put all the furniture where they thought it should go. "Move the lounge suite over there," she had said pointing to one corner of the lounge. Then, "No, it's not right, move it over to the other side of the lounge." Then, "Move Jenny's chest of drawers to the larger room," Jenny being their elder of two daughters. 'Huh, lucky I've got my beers to keep me sane, and slightly drunk,' Chad thought gleefully to himself after moving the chest of drawers from one side of the fairly large house to the other and stealing off to the kitchen for another Bud.

"What the hell is that noise!?" Nancy Dillan asked worriedly looking at her husband Chad. "I wouldn't worry, must be testing the evacuation system," he replied, taking a swig of his beer to wash down the fried chicken. "I wish you wouldn't drink so much," his wife then chided him, looking at the six empty beer bottles on the countertop in the kitchen. "Hey honey, moving to a new house is thirsty work," Chad replied with a drunken grin on his face. "Mommy, Daddy, look, everyone's leaving," Tiffany, their youngest daughter cried out looking through the lounge window. "Hell, she's right!" Chad exclaimed looking out of the nearest window onto the street beyond the front garden. Their new neighbours were busy throwing possessions into their vehicles and leaving, with the loud mournful wailing tones of the evacuation speakers in the background and then the speech, "ATTENTION PLEASE! ATTENTION PLEASE! THIS IS THE INDIAN POINT ENERGY CENTRE EMERGENCY CONTROL ROOM. THIS IS NOT A DRILL, I REPEAT THIS IS NOT A DRILL. EVACUATE YOUR HOMES IMMEDIATELY AND HEAD FOR THE 10 MILE STATE LINE IMMEDIATELY. DO NOT STOP UNTIL YOU HAVE REACHED THE 10 MILE LINE AS INDICATED IN YOUR EVACUATION DOCUMENTS." "Uh, honey, I think we need to go as well," Chad slurred to his wife. The problem was compounded when everyone hit the roads at the same time in a very unorderly and panicked fashion.

CHAPTER 11

"Boss, Sable's associate is a lunatic," Nicky proclaimed to Nick as he answered his ringing satellite phone. "What do you mean?" he asked her intrigued. They had just finished loading all their kit back into the 4x4. In the dark distant background against the sound of the ocean, they could hear the rumbling of the twin marine diesel engines of *Ma Bell Ami* as Jean Pierre headed back out to sea, the nano bug now sitting proudly in the old Captain's jacket.

"I assume you've got internet access?" Nicky asked, and without waiting for a reply she started explaining. "Log onto the YouTube channel and see for yourself." "Standby," Nick replied quickly and reached around behind his seat to pull out his iPhone from his duffel bag. Logging onto the local carrier network he quickly had data facilities and was soon logging into YouTube. Even though it was a small picture his blood froze when he saw the video. The detective and the rest of his small team gathered around the glowing iPhone in the dark and watched the video feed.

The feed was a video and audio link thanks to the Axis M3045-V mini dome cameras installed in the control room. Nick logged in just in time to see an operator in a control room that had a cacophony of alarms warbling away in the background along with corresponding amber fault and red warning lights flashing all over the expansive complicated looking control desk, stand up and lunge towards another equally large and complicated looking control panel a metre or so away and a large red round button with a protective cover over it. Beneath the round red button, the words 'REACTOR SCRAM' were etched. Opening the cover, he slammed the round red button with his fist and turned to look at a CCTV screen that showed the reactor core. "Reactor Scrammed," he shouted to his colleague. Then he continued shouting, "Fuck! It's not fucking working!" On the activation of a Reactor Scram all the control rods should plunge down into the reactor core immediately stopping the nuclear chain reaction. This time around the control rods kept their trajectory heading away from the core. Wildly looking towards the rising reactor core temperatures, he shouted out "Manual override and dump the boron!"

"Tell me, what the hell are we looking at?" Nick asked anxiously as things looked like they were going rapidly downhill for the two operators in the control room. "That's the video feed from the cameras installed in the Indian Point Two Control Room for the Pressurised Nuclear reactor called Indian Point 2," Nicky hurriedly explained. "You mean that they're fucking around with the controls of a nuclear reactor and streaming it live?" Johan asked amazed at what they were looking at. "Yes," came back the reply. "Oh, fuck, the cores are overheating," they all heard the one operator shout out wildly in a complete panic.

Then, just as sudden as the nightmare had started for the two control room operators, the control rods started to descend back into the reactor core, and the primary coolant pumps started up again, all the alarms and faults resetting themselves as if nothing ever happened. "What the fuck just happened?" Erick asked in a subdued tone, as if talking too loudly would set the demons free again as plant management burst into the control room. They overheard the one man who was obviously the senior shout out, "What the fuck's going on, Eric? We've just evacuated half of upstate New York!?"

"Yes, what the hell just happened?" Detective Joint spluttered not too sure what he'd just seen. Turning to face him in the darkness, the detective couldn't see Nick's expression on his face, but his tone said it all "that's what you can do with the Prototype if you feel like it." "Fuck me, they could create untold death and destruction with that device," the detective muttered shook up by what he now understood quite clearly. "Exactly," Nick replied, "or hold the world to ransom." "Detective, do you still think hi-jacking Sable's plane is such a bad idea, now that you've seen what you can do with it?" Nick asked him. "No, I see your point," Detective Joint replied. "It would just be nice if we could get some local cooperation and not have to go off the reservation to achieve it."

MOSCOW, YASENEVO DISTRICT, SVR HEADQUAR-TERS, (+3 Hours) 02H00, SUNDAY

On the first ring of the telephone on his desk, the colonel was immediately awake. "Yes!" he barked into the telephone receiv-er a second later snatching the handset from his desk. "Colonel you need to come to the Operation centre, there have been some major developments," Captain Popov reported excitedly over the telephone line. "On my way," Colonel Petroski snapped thinking to himself, 'At last we have movement.' Turning quickly to look at his appearance in a full-length mirror on the wall of his office he first ensured that his SVR uniform was sitting immaculately on his lean frame; even at this early hour of the morning, and picking up his peaked cap on his desk he hurried out of his office.

Once the bug planted by the Accra operative had gone offline and there was no more news from the resident agent on the ground, the colonel had decided to head back to his office to catch up on a couple of hours sleep to await further developments, ponder-ing, 'What was Nick Scott and his team doing in West Africa and where was the Prototype?' Mulling the problem over and over in his mind he finally said to himself, 'I need more information!' as he nodded off to sleep.

Walking briskly to the lift, he followed the same procedure as earlier, presenting his access card to the lift proximity reader, the lift descending the building and into the depths of the basement.

"Colonel, we've found the Prototype," Captain Popov explained to the colonel as he entered the Operation room a short while later, hardly able to contain his excitement, as the SVR soldier on duty outside in the secure passageway smartly opened and closed the door for the colonel. The Operation room was dark, with only dim downlighters on the ceiling providing small amounts of illumination, the large LCD screens on the front wall of the control room and on the operators', desks providing the bulk of the light. "What! Where?" the colonel impatiently demanded to know. "There!" exclaimed Captain Popov pointing to a large LCD monitor on the wall. "Is this some kind of joke?" growled the colonel looking at the LCD screen.

The LCD screen was showing some kind of control room with a multitude of lights, coloured dials and LED's all flashing away, along with a plethora of computer monitors and CCTV screens. Then the colonel noted the blue light emitting from one of the CCTV screens and looking closer recognised what he was looking at, the view of the inside of a nuclear reactor. The blue glow was what was called Cherenkov radiation, which is a phenomenon of nuclear reactors when charged particles travelling through the water are moving faster than light through the medium. These charged particles excite the electrons of the water molecules around them which absorb the energy and then release it as photons or light, the light appearing to the naked eye in the blue light spectrum.

Watching the frantic actions of the control room operators the colonel grinned and turning to Captain Popov asked, "Are you sure it's the Prototype at work?" Captain Popov nodded his head and replied, "Yes, we came across this message on a web bulletin board a short while ago." The message read: *A Magical coat for the* VR *World for Sale. Watch the live demonstration on YouTube. Bidding starts at $1 000 000 000.00.* "Where is that?" Colonel Petroski then asked amazed at what he was watching. "The Indian Point Nuclear Power Plant in upstate New York," Captain Popov explained. Laughing out loud the colonel replied, "If we're lucky whoever has the Prototype will do our job for us and wipe out a large part of the Eastern seaboard of the United States. And we won't have had to lift a finger!"

Turning back to Captain Popov he asked seriously, "Have you been able to track down where the Prototype is operating from yet?" Shaking his head Captain Popov replied, "Unfortunately not yet, we're working on it, but Mark Bing's programming is good, really good. It really is a Harry Potter invisible cloak for the VR world." Sighing in frustration, the colonel answered, "I see." Looking back at the LCD screen he noted that all had returned to normal in the control room. 'We need more intelligence; we're getting nowhere with this,' he thought to himself.

Taking out his encrypted smartphone he made an international call to his team in Cape Town. "Any movement at Executive Decision?" he asked Jurgen. "No, sir, nothing at present, we are ready and waiting to proceed as soon as you give the green light," Jurgen replied. Thinking quickly weighing his options the colonel said, "You have permission to proceed. As soon as one of the targets presents itself, I want your team to capture and hand the prisoner over to Yuri for interrogation." "Yes, sir," Jurgen confirmed and ended the call.

TOGO, LOMÉ, 08H00, SUNDAY

It was just before sunrise when the now very dusty once white rental 4x4 drove slowly into the sprawling town of Aflao that borders on the town of Lomé, Togo. The neighbours on the western side of the grass divide that basically ran up northwards from the Atlantic Ocean were Ghanaians, the neighbours on the eastern side were Togolese. The Accra Aflao road, originating in Accra, snaked through the sprawling town of Aflao and down towards the cold Atlantic Ocean, past shanty town housing, no two houses or dwellings the same, and turning a sharp left just before the Atlantic Ocean carried on, with the same shanty town like housing on their left side and the cold ocean crashing down on golden palm-lined beaches on the right.

At this time of the morning, there wasn't much traffic about, just a stray dog here and there scavenging in rubbish heaps for scraps and leftovers. After driving for another kilometre or so with the sleeping dwellings on the left and the continuous pounding of the Atlantic Ocean on the right, they came to the border post situated right in the centre of the road, demarcated by a steel structure, with lights hanging off of it, dividing one country from the next, Ghana from Togo, Togo from Ghana. On the Western side of the bridge, houses, vehicles, and pedestrians were in Ghana, and once you crossed under the bridge you were in Togo.

"This is good, there's almost no one else waiting to go across," Johan mentioned happily, seeing almost no traffic waiting for the border post to open. With almost 45 minutes to spare, Johan pulled off onto the side of the road under a large tree and they waited for the border post to open.

At 08H00 the border post opened and shortly thereafter they were all through. "Here's my yellow fever card," Detective Joint crowed happily to the officials, proudly waving his yellow fever inoculation card in their faces. Once across the border, the straight road on the Lomé side now changed its name to Boulevard Du Mono. At first the landscape remained the same, shanty town like housing on the left with the ocean on the right. After a couple of kilometres, the houses started to get better looking more upmarket. "I assume that French is the main language in Togo?" Eben asked no one in particular looking at the road signs all in French.

The Duma Beach Hotel was exactly that, a small hotel whose chalets were built about 50m up past the high-water mark on the beach. The small hotel was about a kilometre past the Presidential Palace just off Boulevard Du Mono. Nicky, who by this time with the help of Arthur and his AI abilities had a permanent untraceable link into the CCTV servers of the Intercontinental Hotel, got hold of Nick just as they approached the small beach hotel. "Sable has just arrived back at the hotel looking very shagged out," Nicky informed them with a small laugh. "Great, thanks, give Glen and Jimmy the heads up. Keep us informed if there are any changes," Nick told her. "We're about to meet up with Hannah."

While in the air, flying the short relocation flight from Accra to Togo, Hannah had used the satellite communication facilities on board the Bombardier Global 6000 to sort out the required hotel accommodation. After landing at the Lomé-Tokoin International Airport in the early hours of the morning Hannah had checked herself into the Duma Beach Hotel. While making the reservations earlier, Hannah had also reserved two additional chalets which were for Nick and his team to move into when they arrived. At the same time, Chuck had checked into the L'Horizon Hotel, the same hotel which Sable's two pilots were currently staying at. It had taken the IT Department in Cape Town less than two minutes to pinpoint where they were staying.

Twenty minutes later they all met in Hannah's chalet. "Morning, guys," Hannah said brightly to them as she let them into her chalet. "How do you do it?" grumbled Eben. "You always look bright and cheerful." Laughing Hannah replied, "It's an old Mediterranean secret that would be lost on you." Getting serious Hannah turned to Nick saying "Okay, Boss. I think I've got all what we're going to need to pull this off." "Great," Nick replied rubbing his hands together in anticipation.

Turning around Hannah walked over to the bed and gestured towards the two pilot uniforms on the bed complete with peaked caps. "I hope the suits fit you, they've been in our clothes trunk for a while now." The clothes trunk was a large suitcase they carried around in the cargo space of the Bombardier for events such as what was about to go down. "Hang on, Major, wait a minute here, are you and Johan going to fly Sable's aircraft?" Detective Joint asked in amazement. Nodding his head Nick replied, "Yes, that's the general idea." "Do you have a pilot's license?" he asked.

Grinning Nick pointed to the uniform saying, "This uniform says I'm a pilot." "But that's just a uniform," spluttered the detective. "Relax, Detective," Hannah told him laughing. "Nick's playing you, of course, he's got a pilot's license." With that Hannah picked up her bag and said with a large smile on her face, "Okay guys good luck, I'll see you all a little later, it's time to play the slut," and headed for the door.

The TV set in the room was on and tuned to CNN, where there was the picture of a Nuclear Power Station in the background with the presenter talking. "Turn up the volume," Nick instructed Eben closest to the TV remote. "And for those of you who have just tuned in, the lead story this Sunday morning on the East Coast is the unprecedented evacuation of over one million people in the early evening hours of yesterday evening in upstate New York due to what has been determined as a terrorist cyber-attack on the nuclear power plant."

Carrying on she said, "For more on the breaking story we cross now to Kevin Whitfield our reporter on the ground at the energy centre," The picture changed to a suited young-looking blond-haired well suntanned male reporter who was standing on what looked like a main road against the backdrop of a yellow 'PO-LICE DO NOT CROSS' line with numerous police and emergency vehicles all with flashing lights standing just beyond blocking the road. "Hi, Kelly, just a slight correction," the blond-haired reporter replied, "We're actually standing on one of the main routes into the area, at the 10-mile marker limit. This is the outer limit of what the Nuclear Regulatory Commission, the NRC calls the plume exposure pathway in the event of a radiation leak from a nuclear reactor." Carrying on speaking for another couple of minutes, Kevin Whitfield brought all CNN listeners up to date with what had occurred, and then said, "So far there have been a number of deaths and emergencies caused by the sudden evacuation of over one and half million residents of the surrounding counties."

Looking down at quickly scribbled notes on a piece of paper he carried on, "The emergency services report that there have been a number of fatal car crashes due to the panicked evacuation, in one a family of four were killed when their car left the road. In this case, it looks like the driver had been drinking, Saturday afternoon and all. In another accident a family of four died when another car veered into them while trying to overtake." Taking a deep breath, he continued, "The local fire departments in all five counties have also reported having had to deal with residential fires, people leaving ovens and cookers on and rushing out. Several houses and properties have been raised to the ground this way.

TOGO, LOMÉ, L'HORISON HOTEL, 09H00, SUNDAY

The L'Horizon Hotel was a modest-sized 3 Star Hotel a short distance from the Lomé-Tokoin International Airport that was favoured by aircrews of all nationalities. The hotel staff was used to aircrews coming and going at all odd hours of the day and night. Hannah walked into the hotel lobby just after 08H35 in the morning, just as a couple of guests were settling down to their breakfast. The hotel guests have the pleasure of eating their continental breakfasts on the pool terrace under the shade of large awnings overlooking the deep blue swimming pool which was one of the attractions of the hotel.

This morning was no different and Chuck was seated on the poolside terrace eating his breakfast. By 09H00 Hannah was sitting down for breakfast with him on the poolside terrace. "I assume the first part went according to plan?" Chuck asked her softly in his Texan drawl as she sat down. Grinning Hannah replied, "Absolutely, like a well-oiled clock." "Let's hope the well-oiled clock stays well lubricated then," he replied with a smile on his weather-beaten face.

As they were sitting in the shade of the terrace, Chuck nudged Hannah and nodded in the direction of the pool terrace where two well-toned men were settling themselves down onto sunning beds beside the deep blue swimming pool, the temperature already climbing above 25 degrees Celsius and said to her, "That's her pilots." Nodding her head, Hannah stood up saying "I'll see you later then," and disappeared out of the restaurant back to her room.

Walking back out onto the pool deck a short while later she looked completely different. Her long dark shiny black hair was tied up and tucked under a New York Yankee baseball cap. She had changed into a white two-piece bikini bathing costume that accentuated her smooth rich dark tanned Mediterranean skin. As she walked, her ample breasts pushed hard against the white material of the swimming costume, defying gravity, while her perfectly shaped hips encased in a short white kaftan swayed seductively as she walked along. "Perfect," muttered Chuck to himself from the shaded breakfast terrace as he noted that Hannah's entrance on the pool deck had the required effect on the two male pilots: as well as the balance of the male population in the vicinity.

An hour later, Chuck picked up his phone and dialled Nick's number. "They've taken the bait," was all he said when Nick answered, as he saw Hannah walking back towards the rooms with a pilot on either side of her. Laughing seductively with the tease of what's to come, Hannah said to the two pilots, Hans and Fritz, as she closed the room door behind them, "Make yourself at home, boys, I just want to go freshen up a bit." With the thoughts of a *ménage à trois* before lunch in their minds with a stunning brunette, the two men didn't think anything of Hannah going to the bathroom. A couple of minutes later she opened the bathroom door. "Right, boys, where were we?" she purred seductively.

Both their mouths dropped when they saw the naked form of Hannah standing in the bathroom doorway. She started walking slowly towards them, her perfectly shaped breasts jutting out in front of her, her dark nipples hard and erect. Their eyes stayed stuck on her perfect female curves and perfectly shaped waist, her hips swaying seductively towards them, with her trim curly black mons Venus peeking out at the juncture of her shapely toned thighs. "Come here, boys," she purred seductively, "I want your cocks, I want to suck both of you," and she dropped onto her knees. They both scrambled towards her dropping their swimming trunks as they did so.

What they didn't see were the two small plastic vials each with a small sharp needle that Hannah held tightly in both hands between her thumbs and index fingers which she had taken out of her toiletry bag. "Mmmhhh," she moaned softly batting her eyes and looking up at the two pilots standing over her. "You both have nice sized cocks, I can't wait to see which one makes me come the hardest," she said complementing them both. As the pilots looked at each other grinning, their cocks jumping around and hardening as if alive, they both felt a tiny pinprick on their thighs. "Ouch!" the one pilot said taking a step back.

The next second the room started spinning around them and a dark deep abyss seemed to open, sucking them down into a deep pharmaceutically induced sleep. "Vat have you…?" the one pilot started to ask was all he got out when he joined his buddy unconscious on the floor. Quickly getting dressed, Hannah used the internal phone and dialled Chuck in the bedroom next door. "Well done," Chuck said congratulating her when he saw the two pilots lying unconscious albeit naked on the floor. Glaring at him Hannah said, "Don't say a word. And no, I didn't have to suck them!"

Working quickly, they got the two pilots onto the double bed and tied them up tightly. Taping up their mouths, Chuck phoned Nick and reported their progress. Then, taking the pilots' room keys, he quickly headed for their rooms and retrieved the pilots' ID cards and flight bags along with their passports. "Sorry, guys," he said to the two still unconscious pilots when he returned, "it's nothing personal but you work for a real bitch of a boss. I would suggest that next time you're a bit pickier about who you work for."

LOMÉ, DUMA BEACH HOTEL, 10H30, SUNDAY

"Okay, guys, that was Chuck. They've got the two pilots, it's up to us now, and in particular you," Nick told his small team looking directly at the detective. They were gathered outside the bungalow under the cool of the thatch awning, watching the Atlantic waves crash onto the beach a short distance away. "This isn't bad for a holiday destination; I might make a plan to revisit this place, if I'm still welcome," Eben had mentioned a little earlier to no one in particular as he saw a couple of women frolicking around gaily around on the beach with a frisbee. "Here, Detective, use this phone to make contact," Nick said to the detective passing him his satellite phone.

Just before the detective made the call, Nick had gotten hold of Steven in Cape Town. "Right are you lot ready to trace the call?" he asked when Steven answered. "Standing by and ready," Steven confirmed confidently to Nick. Using the Prototype Mark II, Nicky and another cyber operator had entered the world of Virtual Reality and were waiting undetected inside the telecom operator's network core switch in Lomé, through which all calls coming into the country were routed.

"Here goes then," Detective Joint muttered and dialled the number out of his head, remembering to start with the international dialling code first. The phone rang a couple of times before it was answered. "Commissioner, good morning. It's Detective Joint speaking," Detective Joint said, speaking over the satellite phone. "Joint, where the hell are you? We've been looking all over for you! You checked yourself out of hospital and disappeared," the Commissioner stated very annoyed.

Brushing the question aside the detective carried on "Commissioner, I thought I would give you the good news. We've identified and found the killers of Mark Bings, his girlfriend, and my sister. They are currently in Suite 2915 and 2917 respectively of the Intercontinental Hotel in Lomé Togo. We shall have them in custody in a couple of hours' time. We are currently en route to their hotel as I am speaking to you."

"My god, Joint, are you joking?" spluttered the Commissioner over the telephone line. "Commissioner, I have never been more serious in my life," replied Detective Joint growling down the phone. "The people responsible for the deaths as mentioned are also the people responsible for the near nuclear meltdown disaster of a couple of hours ago in the State of New York, and the death of Tanya Delport. You can contact her boss, Captain Hans Kruger, for confirmation of her death. Remember he was sitting in your office before I got shot! We are about to go and give them our calling card."

Ending the call, Detective Joint handed Nick his satellite phone back saying, "Well Major, let's hope that's put the cat amongst the pigeons, now we wait and see what happens." Thinking for another minute Detective Joint then said, "Hang on, Major, let's double up on our bet, pass your phone back." A couple of minutes later after dialling another number out of his head, he said "Hi, Juliet, sorry to bug you on a Sunday, but we're just about to arrest Sable and I was wondering if you were able to get more information on her?" he explained to her as innocently as possible. Talking for a couple of minutes longer, adding that he wasn't working alone, he hung up the phone and with a grim smile on his face said to the small team, "Now we wait and see what falls out of the tree."

After a couple of minutes of silence as they were all wrapped up in their own thoughts, Detective Joint then asked, "What if I'm wrong and the leak isn't from the SAP?" Without hesitation, Nick replied, "Then we find another way to persuade them to leave the hotel and head for the airport."

CHAPTER 12

LOMÉ, INTERCONTINENTAL HOTEL, SUITE 2915, 13H00, SUNDAY

The insistent ringing of the bedside phone woke Sable up from her deep sleep. Looking at her watch she saw that it was early afternoon. "Hello," she groaned softly into the phone, her sinuses completely blocked up and sore from all the cocaine she had snorted with his Excellency throughout the previous evening and into the early hours of the morning. Moving around in the large bed she also felt a deep twinge in her pussy and anus from the earlier ministrations of his Excellency's large member and other appendages.

The voice that spoke shook her instantly awake as if she'd be given a shot of adrenalin. "They know that you're in Suite 2915 and they are on their way to you now. It doesn't look like his Excellency can protect you from Nick Scott and his team," the voice told her calmly. "How do you know this?" Sable asked hesitantly as she sat straight up in the bed, her heart pounding in her chest. "Listen to this," the voice replied and replayed part of the detective's conversation. "Okay, so he knows where I am, what can he do about it? They've got to get through a whole fucking battalion of soldiers to get to me," she replied arrogantly starting to feel in control. "Hahaha," the voice laughed back cruelly. "The intelligence is that they are already in the hotel! I think they might have left you a calling card."

An icy cold numbness swept through her body, her mind freezing for a second as she glanced up at the door to the suite and saw the small white envelope that had been slid under the door. "I suggest that you get on your private jet and fly away to some long-forgotten island a long way away with no extradition treaties for a while," the voice suggested calmly to her. Sable, however, wasn't listening as she put down the phone and as if in a trance got out of bed naked and walked slowly across the suite to the door and, bending down picked up the small white envelope.

With shaking hands, she opened the envelope and found a business card inside.

'EXECUTIVE DECISIONS

Nick Scott CEO'

"Fuck it," she screamed. "How the fuck did he do it!?" Forgetting that she was naked she opened the suite door and stormed out into the passageway where a soldier with a rifle was standing guard. "How much did they pay you!" she screamed at the very surprised guard, seeing a very beautiful woman standing completely naked in front of him. "I, I don't know what you mean?" he replied gawking at her exposed body.

LOMÉ, INTERCONTINENTAL HOTEL, SUITE 2917, 13H00, SUNDAY

Senzo was just about to slip on his VR glasses and head back into the electronic world of VR for the next demonstration, still on a psychological high from his earlier romping around in the nuclear reactor. While in the Indian Point network he'd entered the camera network and into the cameras themselves, the cameras inside the reactor confinement vessel. 'Fuck, this is insane!' he'd thought standing in the blue light given off by the nuclear fission reaction, only a few inches away from the nuclear reactor core itself. 'I'm sure I could feel the energy within the reactor core,' he'd said to himself a bit later thinking back on the experience.

Hearing the commotion in the passageway and fearing the worst he opened his door. "What the…" he started to say when he saw Sable standing naked in front of the guard. Quickly he pulled her into his suite and glaring at the guard said, "Relax, she's a bit crazy." The guard just stood where he was and grinned an idiot like grin on his face thinking, "My friends will never believe what just happened."

"What the fuck is up with you, woman?" Senzo snarled. With shaking hands Sable handed him the business card. Taking the card, he glanced at it. "Oh fuck, I thought you said we would be safe here," he spat out angrily. "I know, it doesn't make any sense. I don't understand, but I'm getting the hell out of here now," Sable cried out and turning around stormed towards the interleading door. Luckily the interleading door on her side was still unlocked and she was soon back in her suite getting dressed and packing her bag.

Using her normal mode of communication with her pilot she sent him a text message. *Get the jet ready, heading to the Caribbean. Will be there in 60 minutes.* Almost instantaneously the message came back as read, two blue ticks. "Perfect Hans, you're on the ball," she muttered breathing a sigh of relief. She was even more satisfied when her pilot sent the reply, sending his customary thumbs up. "Hurry up Senzo, let's go," she shouted through the open interleading suite door.

LOMÉ-TOKOIN INTERNATIONAL AIRPORT, 13H00, SUNDAY

The Lomé-Tokoin International Airport was small in comparison to most International airports and did not have a Private Operator terminal, so Nick and Johan arrived by taxi at Terminal 1; being the International Terminal. First making a stop past the Hotel L'Horizon they quickly met Chuck in his room and left with several items amongst others the new doctored Pilot ID cards. One of Hannah's many talents was forgeries, and with today's software and dye sublimation printers copying the pilots' ID cards was an easy task. Both now were dressed as pilots, complete with black peaked caps, Ray Ban Aviator sunglasses, and flight bags, compliments of Sable's original pilots. Getting out of the taxi they saw an altercation ensuing between an irate driver who had had the wheels of his vehicle clamped and a soldier in combat fatigues and AK47 rifle who had clamped the vehicle. "Obviously he can't afford to pay the bribe to have the vehicle released," Johan muttered to Nick as they walked into the terminal building as the argument got more and more heated, expecting any second to hear the sharp sound of the soldiers AK47 being discharged into the unruly non compliant citizen.

As they walked into the airport terminal, Nick's iPhone rang. "Yes," he said answering the call. "Boss, Sable has just been given the heads up that you're on your way to collect her. We were able to trace the call that was made, and it seems that the detective was right. The call originated from the Cape Town Central Police Station," Nicky informed him. "Oh fuck, Detective Joint's got a problem," Nick replied grimly. "Uh-huh, that's what I also thought," Nicky answered back. "Okay, thanks, were you able to confirm the extension or who it was?" Nick then asked Nicky. "Unfortunately, not, but we were able to record the male voice, which I can play back to the detective. Maybe he'll recognise the voice," Nicky replied optimistically. Speaking for another couple of minutes they ended the call. Turning to Johan he said ruefully, "It seems that Detective Joint was correct. Sable has just received a heads up and it came from the Cape Town Central Police Station."

Remembering what Hannah had told them about the setup in the airport he headed confidently for the security checkpoint. "You need to go through the security checkpoint and passport control then head for Air Traffic Navigation," Hannah had explained to them. Carrying on she had also added, "All private flights are parked at the far end of the airport near the small freight terminal." Reaching the security checkpoint both Nick and Johan flashed their recently liberated and updated ID cards taken from the two pilots at the security staff. "Bonjour," the security guard said with a small smile to the two pilots as he let them through the checkpoint. '*Merde*,' thought the guard to himself in French, his home language. 'If only I had listened to my parents and did better at school, I could also have been a pilot and flown all around the world.' "Next stop Passport Control and then ATNS," Nick muttered to Johan under his breath.

Once through Passport Control with Nick leading as he could read, write, and speak French, they headed over to the Air Traffic Navigation Services office. Walking up to the counter in the small office, Nick greeted the female ATNS representative behind the counter. "Bonjour," he said brightly to her with a large smile on his handsome face. Smiling brightly, she greeted him back. "Bonjour, monsieur. How may I assist you this afternoon?" she asked in French. "I wish to file a flight plan," Nick explained to the lady in the same language. Fifteen minutes later they walked as quickly as they could out of the ATNS office and made straight for the waiting airside vehicle that would take them across the tarmac to the other side of the airport where private aircraft parked.

As they were driving across the tarmac Nick's iPhone beeped, receiving an encrypted message from Glen, *Target has just left hotel in a hurry*. Grinning, Nick showed Johan the message. "Now the fun really starts," Johan said also with a grin on his face. Nearing the Freight Terminal, they saw the two private aircraft standing on the jetway, the black and white Gulfstream V that flew Sable around the world, and the white Bombardier Global 6000 of Executive Decisions that presently carried no livery. Standing beside the Bombardier was the familiar figure of Hannah. Pulling up a couple of metres away, the airside driver stopped, and Nick and Johan exited. "Merci," Nick said to the driver as he closed the door and the driver gunned the engine and the vehicle sped away.

Around the same time a refuelling tanker arrived and parked in front of the starboard wing of the Gulfstream. "You go sort out the refuelling, we need full tanks while I go and get the goodies," Nick instructed Johan. Nodding his head Johan hurried across the concrete apron to the fuel tanker while Nick picked up his flight bag and headed quickly over towards Hannah, now dressed as a co-pilot. "Hi Hannah, well done," Nick said congratulating her. "No problem," she replied with a large grin on her olive smooth Mediterranean sculptured face. "It's why you pay me these huge, indecent sums of money."

Laughing Nick replied, "Well, I'm glad that you didn't get hurt. We just need to get the hell out of here now. Just received the message that the package is on its way." "Perfect," Hannah replied with a satisfied sigh. Talking for another minute, Nick said, "Okay see you in Cape Town," and then bending down picked up Hannah's flight bag; on purpose, and he walked briskly across to the waiting Gulfstream V. Soon after Nick had walked over to the Gulfstream, Chuck arrived at the Bombardier, having just returned from ATNS filing the Bombardiers' flight plan.

Reaching the main forward cabin door of the aircraft, Nick accessed the cabin door release mechanism, and the main cabin door opened and unfolded effortlessly, the door now becoming steps. Seeing him at the aircraft steps, Johan shouted out to him, "I'll do the exterior pre-flight inspections, you get the aircraft prepped." Johan was referring to the visual walk around of the aircraft removing all the covers from the pitots and air intakes, at the same time making sure that there were no visible oil leaks, flats tyres, or anything else that looked out of the ordinary. Giving Johan the thumbs-up sign, Nick picked up his black leather flight bag and bounding up the stairs he entered the musky cabin and made his way to the flight deck.

"Wow, nice setup," Nick said out loud entering the flight deck. The aircraft had the latest Gulfstream avionics package, four 14-inch,36-cm Plasma screens for the Primary Flight Display, ECAS and Navigation systems. Placing the flight bag behind the left-hand seat he opened it and removed two taser guns which he placed on the co-pilot seat. Then, folding himself into the pilot seat on the left-hand side of the flight deck he started going through the aircraft pre-flight check lists preparing the aircraft for flight while Johan continued outside assisting with refuelling the aircraft and the pre-flight visual inspection.

LOMÉ, INTERCONTINENTAL HOTEL, 13H00, SUNDAY

Slipping the business card under the door to suite 2915, Glen had made it back to the rear service stairwell just in time as the guard had walked back around the corner of the passageway following his patrol route. Using their encrypted 2-way high frequency radio link, Glen and Jimmy were in contact with each other. Via another data link, Jimmy was holding the fort in the room on the 15th floor and was in contact with Nicky who was inside the hotel's CCTV system using the Mark II Prototype, looping recently recorded video footage back to the live screen views for the guards monitoring the CCTV system in the Control Room while she was watching the real live views.

Bounding back down the fire stairs, Glen made it back to the 15th floor stairwell. "Standby," Glen heard softly in his earpiece, "Guard walking down the corridor," Jimmy informed him being alerted by Nicky. Taking a deep breath to control his breathing, Glen waited poised to strike should the guard decide to enter the fire stairwell. "Okay, move it, the guard's gone," Jimmy transmitted a minute later over the encrypted circuit, as Nicky confirmed that the guard was carrying on as normal on his patrol route. Opening the fire exit door, Glen slipped back out into the passage and headed for his room. Once back in his room Jimmy was there waiting. "Okay I've just informed Alpha 1 that his business card has been dropped off, and they've asked us to move to our second position," Jimmy informed his friend. "Gotcha," Glen replied picking up his bags. "See you at the lift," Jimmy told Glen as he headed next door to his room.

Reaching the lobby, a couple of minutes later they made it to their very dusty 4x4 just as Nicky gave them the heads up that she had spotted Sable and Senzo on the cameras rushing out of their rooms towards the 29th floor lift lobby. From their position in the open parking lot, they soon saw the two targets rush out of the front door of the hotel and pile into the waiting Mercedes Guest Transporter.

"Alpha team, Alpha 4 targets are leaving the hotel. Looks to me that they're in a bit of a hurry. Over," Glen transmitted over the encrypted circuit with a big smile on his face. "Alpha 4, Alpha 3 follow target and confirm they are heading for the airport. We'll meet you at the Avis Counter in the main terminal," Eben transmitted back to them. While Nick and Johan were carrying out their part of the operation, Eben had taken operational control on the ground. "Copy that, Alpha 3," Glen confirmed to Eben. Starting the engine Glen slipped the 4x4 into first gear and started to follow the hotel taxi a short distance behind.

Trailing a couple of vehicles behind the hotel taxi, in between all the other road users, predominantly motorcycles of 125cc and 150cc, all either Indian or Chinese manufacture, they followed their quarry through the streets of Lomé towards the airport. Togo being a predominantly poor nation, the citizens didn't have money to buy motor vehicles, but the roads were chocked with the cheap Indian and Chinese imports.

"What's the bet that they don't go straight to the airport?" Jimmy said with a laugh. "Stop jinxing the operation, you fucking moron," Glen replied good-naturedly. "My word, will you look at that!" Jimmy then said loudly pointing to the scene beside him. Glancing across to where Jimmy was pointing Glen had to smile, a family of four were riding beside them on a small 125cc Chinese branded motorcycle. Father was driving, mother sat behind him with a small baby wedged between them. Sitting on the petrol tank was the older child of around 5 years old. "Crash helmets are optional, it would seem," Glen commented shaking his head in horror at what he saw.

Reaching the airport twenty minutes later, a couple of vehicles behind, Jimmy sent a text message out to the team *Target has arrived at International Departures*. Waiting until they received a message back from Eben, *confirmed have both targets in sight*, Glen put the 4x4 back into gear and headed off towards the airport Avis car rental depot to return the rental.

A short while later they met up with Detective Joint inside the Airport Terminal building adjacent to the Avis counter. "Where's Eben?" Glen asked the detective pushing a baggage trolley piled high with camera cases and bags up to him. Eben had left the detective with a similarly packed baggage trolley. "He's keeping his eyes on the suspects while they head through the security checkpoint," Detective Joint informed them.

LOMÉ-TOKOIN INTERNATIONAL AIRPORT, 13H30, SUNDAY

"Drive faster, can't you?! Goddammit!" Sable ranted at the hotel driver as they left the hotel grounds. Rushing out of the lift lobby on the ground floor Sable and Senzo had literally sprinted across the expansive marble lobby to the main doors of the hotel and the hotel taxi waiting outside under the Porte Couche. About to raise the alarm of a guest leaving without paying, the receptionist was stopped by the Duty Manager who said, "Those are the President's guests, I wouldn't say anything if I was you. Who knows what's going on." Realising that she liked her life and employment at the hotel, she turned around and carried on with her reception tasks behind her desk.

As the Mercedes Guest Transporter pulled out of the hotel driveway, a dusty white Prado 4x4 pulled in behind them and started to follow them. The driver noticed the dusty 4x4 following them but didn't say a word. 'Fuck you, white bitch!' the driver thought to himself, unaccustomed to guests talking to him like that. Around Independence Circle, the driver indicated and turned off onto the road leading to the airport. "Faster! Can't you drive this damn car faster?!" Sable demanded loudly from the back.

The 4x4 continued following them a couple of vehicles behind.

"Who is this mysterious caller who keeps you one step ahead of this persistent Nick Scott?" Senzo asked Sable irritated that he couldn't complete his advertising of the Prototype by creating newsworthy mayhem to attract would be buyers. 'I had one more newsworthy attack to carry out and then I was going to start the bidding process,' he thought angrily. "I have no fucking idea," she replied also irritated but for different reasons.

Reaching the Lomé-Tokoin International Airport the hotel driver pulled up to a screeching halt outside Terminal 1 and quickly let the two guests out of the back of the vehicle. 'Fucking white arrogant bitch,' the driver thought to himself as she brushed past him without even acknowledging him. Senzo was no better as they both grabbed their bags and rushed into the terminal building, baggage in hand.

As luck would have it, karma decided to play her part. Entering Terminal 1, Sable stopped in dismay. "Fuck, only one security checkpoint and a whole football stadium of people in front of us," she cried out in dismay, looking at the long snaking queue of humanity shuffling forward slowly to pass through the single security checkpoint. "Sorry, madam, you have to stay in the queue like everyone else, I don't care if you have a private flight waiting for you," the guard replied haughtily in rapid French when she found an official-looking person. Looking at Senzo she shrugged her shoulders saying, "There's nothing we can do, we'll just have to wait."

It was the most uncomfortable 30-minute wait of her life as the line of humanity slowly shuffled forward, as the passengers one by one went through the only operational metal detector and baggage x-ray machine. Standing in the queue like a commoner, which Sable hated, she kept on looking around her. "Shit," she muttered softly to herself as she thought she spotted one of the men from the Pussy Cat Club in Cape Town who had beaten up her bouncers without even breaking out into a sweat. Turning around slightly, she nudged Senzo. "What?" he asked her irritably, also starting to feel uncomfortable about the slow progress of the line. "I think I've just spotted one of the operators from Executive Decisions," she told him as softly as possible.

Luckily, then it was their turn and Sable went first, placing her luggage onto the x-ray conveyor belt. She then stepped through the metal detector and her baggage went smoothly through the x-ray tunnel and reappeared on the other side. Senzo went next, walking through the metal detector when an alarm screeched out loudly. "Sir, please, remove your shoes and belt," the security guard instructed him. At the same time, the x-ray operator saw something she didn't like in his bag and searched it, fortunately for the pair of them coming up empty-handed. "Shit, if we had a scheduled flight to catch, we'd have been fucked!" Sable ranted as they headed as quickly as they could without running towards the gate controller.

CHAPTER 13

CAPE TOWN, EXECUTIVE DECISIONS, 14H00, SUNDAY

"My god, you look exhausted," Steven said looking up from his workstation and admonishing Nicky as she walked back into the IT lab, after spending the last couple of hours in VR supporting Nick and his team on the ground. Carrying on Steven asked her, "When last did you eat, drink, or sleep?" Nicky just looked at him blankly and replied, "Not too sure." Carrying on Steven told her, "You're no good to Nick or any of us when you're run down like this. I'm calling Pete to escort you back home." "But I have…" Nicky started to say to Steven, but he cut her short. "Go home and get some rest, I'll phone you when things break. You've done a brilliant job so far. The cyber team are now well acquainted with the revised prototype," he instructed her. "Yes, Boss," she replied, realising that it was no use debating with Steven, and anyway for the next couple of hours Nick and the team would be in the air.

Ten minutes later Nicky was safely strapped into the rear of the Mercedes S350 with Pete behind the wheel. As Pete pulled away from the main building entrance and headed for the vehicle entrance/exit point of the property, Nicky settled back in the comfortable leather seat and closing her eyes started to doze off. Turning left out of the Vehicle Exit lane, they headed towards the slip road that would take them onto Bourcherds Quarry and the N2 towards Cape Town and ultimately towards the Southern Suburbs where Nicky shared a flat with a flatmate. Pete didn't notice the vehicle parked a distance down the road adjacent to another business nor the man in the vehicle with a set of high-powered binoculars looking in their direction.

Using his cellphone with encryption technology, the man pushed the dial button and was connected straight through to the Control Room in the lower basement level of SVR Head Quarters in Moscow. The call was put directly through to Colonel Petroski. "Sir, I have just observed the one subject, a Miss Nicky Smith leave the Executive Decisions premises in the rear of a Mercedes S350," the agent reported to the colonel. "Excellent, follow and pick her up. I want her alive for interrogation," the colonel instructed his agent from 12 000 miles away. "And the driver?" asked the agent. "Dispose of him, we don't need any witnesses," the colonel casually instructed him.

The 10-ton truck seemed to come out of nowhere and slammed into the driver's side of the S350. With a loud crash and a shrieking of tortured metal, the heavier truck ploughed into the side of the Mercedes, slamming the vehicle across the road into the opposite sidewalk, leaving a trail of vehicle debris and fluids on the tarmac from the point of impact to where both vehicles came to rest. Coming to a complete stop against the opposite pavement, both Pete and Nicky were stunned and disorientated, covered in shattered safety glass from the car windows that had shattered on impact. Luckily the airbags had deployed as designed on impact and coupled with the safety restraint system of the seat belts had saved both occupants from serious injuries.

Nicky sat in the rear of Mercedes, stunned. "Urgh, what happened?" she moaned dazed. Out of the corner of her right eye, she registered two shadows standing on the outside of the vehicle. Looking forwards to look at Pete, the next second she saw his head explode like a ripe tomato, the passenger side of the vehicle sprayed bright red with his blood as Pete's body slumped forward over the steering wheel. "AHHHH!" she screamed out terrified as her rear side door of the vehicle was ripped open, and a masked individual wearing what looked like an ambulance uniform leant into her car and roughly placed a cloth over her face covering her mouth and nose.

Immediately she felt herself spiralling down into a dark deep black abyss of a chemically induced sleep. Reaching over the now unconscious Nicky, the masked individual unclipped her seat belt and pulling her out of the car threw her over his left shoulder and hurried back to the waiting ambulance, bypassing the 10-ton truck buried in the side of the Mercedes.

LOMÉ-TOKOIN INTERNATIONAL AIRPORT, 14H20, SUNDAY

Another twenty minutes passed before the gate controller was able to arrange transport to take them to the waiting Gulfstream on the other side of the airport. "Dammit!" Sable fumed sitting on a broken seat in the overcrowded waiting area in front of Gate 1. "This place is really starting to piss me off." The passengers milling around her in the hot stuffy waiting area were waiting to board an Ethiopian 777 to New York that had not yet landed, while the remainder of the passengers were the overflow from Gate 2 waiting to board an Air Belgium flight to Brussels.

Finally, a lady dressed in an official-looking uniform called them to the gate and after showing their passports for the fourth or fifth time they were instructed to walk down one of the skybridges. At the end of the skybridge rather than walk regally into an aircraft there was a guard pointing to the side door, and they had to walk down the stairs to the tarmac where a sedan with a flashing orange light on the roof was waiting on the airside of the door to take them to their waiting Gulfstream on the far side of the airport apron.

"At last," Sable sighed sinking down into the back seat of the car. The car had the perpetual smell of male sweat and aviation fuel, but right then she would have ridden on the back of a pox-ridden camel to get to her Gulfstream. As they approached the far side of the airport, they both saw her Gulfstream standing on the tarmac with another private aircraft parked next to it. There were a couple of people standing around the nose of the second aircraft a couple of metres from her Gulfstream. "Perfect," Sable said starting to relax a little, as she saw the heat mirage emitting from the tail of the G5. "The pilots are aboard, and they've got power on. We'll soon be in the air," she told a harassed looking Senzo.

They passed the unfamiliar white private jet, the persons in front of the aircraft paying her and Senzo no attention whatsoever, deeply engrossed in their own conversation. The driver of their vehicle pulled up to a stop a couple of metres away from the stairs of the open cabin doorway to her white and black Gulfstream V. She was just about to get out of the vehicle when her smartphone rang. "Madam Sable," a heavy Afrikaans voice boomed in her ear when she answered the call.

Hearing the heavy guttural South African accent her heart skipped a beat and her bladder almost released, adding to the smells and stains on the backseat of the vehicle. "What do you want?" she cried out in alarm. "Madam, my name is Detective Joint, and I am going to arrest you and your associate for the murder of my sister, Samantha Joint, Mark Bings, and his girlfriend, as well as the murder of an NIA agent named Tanya Delport. I believe that you know her as Debbie. I also believe that you and your associate are responsible for the terrorist attack on the Indian Point 2 Nuclear reactor in New York State last night," he boldly informed her. In the background she could hear the sounds of the airport Public Address System activating. Ending the call, her face paled and drained of colour. She looked horrified at Senzo and snapped out, "Fuck it they're in the airport terminal, let's go!"

Panicking, she wrenched at the door lever to open the back door, and when it released pushed it violently open and she sprang out. Immediately her senses were assailed with both the loud whine of the Gulfstreams APU and the smell of aviation fuel. With her handbag and one piece of baggage clutched tightly in her manicured hands, she sprinted for the aircraft steps with Senzo immediately behind her with his laptop bag and small duffel bag. 'Wow, look at that arse move,' he thought to himself as he waited for Sable to climb up the steps into the aircraft cabin.

Sable disappeared from view inside the aircraft and he was just about to take the last couple of steps up and into the fuselage when out of the corner of his eye he saw a sudden movement through one of the cabin portholes. Johan was waiting crouched down behind the informal seating area of the cabin, and when Sable had walked inside Johan had stood up and shot her with the one taser. The movement Senzo noticed out of the corner of his eye was Sable falling.

Like a cat on a hot tin roof, he jumped around and was about to head back down the aircraft steps again when, to his surprise, there was without warning another pilot standing at the bottom of the aircraft steps. The last thing he remembered was that he heard the pilot speak out with a Texan drawl. "I wouldn't do that if I were you," he heard when his limbs started to convulse out of his control as the pilot fired a taser gun at him and two small stainless steel probes punctured his right leg sending 50 000 volts through his body. The tips of the probes had also been dipped in a highly potent fast-acting tranquilliser that coursed immediately through his veins as the voltage played around with his central nervous system.

His two bags falling from his nerveless fingers, Senzo fell forward unconscious and it was just the quick reaction of Chuck who prevented Senzo from falling forward headfirst to the hard ground below. Catching him, Chuck pushed the dead weight of Senzo back up towards the cabin door when a pair of muscular arms belonging to Johan reached out and, grabbing Senzo by his shoulders pulled him inside the aircraft. Quickly stooping down, Chuck picked up Senzo's laptop and duffel bag and placed them on the aircraft stairs. Dragging the unconscious dead weight of Senzo into the aircraft Johan shouted out, "Thanks!" to Chuck while at the same time he slammed the Stairs Up pushbutton on the aircraft bulkhead and the cabin door and stairs started to close hydraulically, at the same time unceremoniously depositing Senzo's two bags on the cabin floor.

While all this was happening, Nick was sitting in the left-hand seat of the cockpit and already having obtained start up clearance from Ground Control was starting the starboard Pratt & Whitney Canada PW800 series turbofan engine. As soon as he saw the green main cabin door light extinguish on the ECAS panel on the one Plasma display, he started the procedure for the port engine start up. "How are we doing in the back?" Nick shouted out over his shoulder, keeping an eye on the engine readouts as he waited for both engines to settle down before continuing with switching the electrical circuits off the APU and onto the engine generators. Johan meanwhile had dragged the unconscious Sable and Senzo into individual seats in the cabin and was busy securing them to their deep tan multi-functional executive leather seats with thick black cable ties and a roll of black industrial duct tape

"Perfect, almost done. They'll have to be Houdini or MacGyver to move once I'm finished with them," Johan told him proudly. "Great, but strap yourself in the back and keep your eyes on them. If they move an inch, you taser them again. Confirm if they have the Prototype," Nick instructed Johan as his headphones activated and he heard their callsign "Gulfstream 229 Tokoin Control you are cleared to taxi, runway 22 using taxi way Alpha," Grinning Nick replied "Tokoin Control Gulfstream 229 confirmed cleared to taxi to runway 22 using taxi way Alpha. Out"

Looking up to the centre overhead panel Nick quickly switched the aircraft load over to the two generators in the two Pratt & Whitney Canada PW800 series turbofan engines and switched off the APU. With practiced ease his eyes scanned the overhead panel, making sure all circuits were switched and correct. While Nick was going through the motions of getting the aircraft moving, Johan quickly rummaged through the baggage of their two guests and soon shouted out, "Found it," as he held up the black metal box-shaped Prototype.

Grinning Nick switched on the Gulfstream's taxi lights and looked down at the ground controller who had just arrived to assist with ground operations and was showing him to taxi out to the left. Showing the thumbs up, Nick gripped the nose gear steering wheel in his left hand, turning it anti-clockwise to the stops while at the same time slowly adding power to the starboard engine via the right-side throttle on the centre pedestal.

With little fuss the starboard Gulfstream engine spooled up and pushing, the aircraft slowly started its turn, being pushed by the powerful Pratt & Whitney turbofan engine. After completing the turn, Nick centred the aircraft nose on the yellow taxi line with the nose steering wheel while at the same time bringing the starboard engine back to neutral, then gripping both the port and starboard engine throttles in his right hand slowly increased the power, both of the Pratt & Whitney Canada PW800 series turbofan engines spooling up starting to push the Gulfstream V forward.

Very soon Nick had the aircraft trundling along as fast as possible down the designated taxiway towards the beginning of Runway 22. In his headphones he heard the distinctive voice of Chuck talking, "Tokoin Tower, Bombardier Zulu Yankee we have loaded our passengers and are requesting start-up & taxi instructions. Over."

LOMÉ-TOKOIN INTERNATIONAL AIRPORT RAMP, BOMBADIER 6000, 14H26

As the Gulfstream started to turn out to the left from the ramp parking area, a crew Transporter arrived at the Bombardier 6000 and Eben and his small team along with their baggage exited. "Fuck, I hope they're okay," Detective Joint said to Eben over the noise of the Gulfstreams engines as they unloaded the baggage and started to cart it to the aircraft where Hannah was supervising the loading into the cargo hold.

Eben looked at the detective and grinning said, "Relax, Nick and Johan on their own are dangerous enough but put them together they become a formidable pair. I wouldn't be worried, Detective." Jimmy overheard the conversation and added, "Eben's right, Detective. Nick and Johan can look after themselves." Soon all the luggage was loaded into the cargo hold of the aircraft and they all boarded the Bombardier; Detective Joint was the last one aboard. He stopped at the top of the aircraft stairs and turned around taking one last nostalgic look of the dusty airport and the black and white Gulfstream jet as it neared the end of the taxiway. 'Good luck, Major,' Joint thought to himself as he entered the cabin and Hannah started to close the door behind him.

CHAPTER 14

CAPE TOWN, RUSSIAN SAFE HOUSE, (+2 HRS) 16H30, SUNDAY

Waking up, she thought she was drowning. She was lying flat on her back with cold water being poured over her face. "What the..." she spluttered as she opened her eyes and turned her head to the side to breath. "What the hell!" she managed to get out the second time round, her long black hair falling over her face. Trying to lift her hands up to swipe the wet hair away she realised she was tied down. "What the fuck!" she then said with much more conviction in her voice, struggling to break the bonds that held her.

"Struggling won't do you any good," a foreign unfamiliar male voice said speaking behind her, "I can assure you that the straps are tied nice and tight. I personally tightened them myself." The voice got closer as he walked up behind her and took his fingers and, almost lovingly, lifted her hair out of her face. "What do you want?" Nicky spat out, his face looming above hers. "Answers," he replied pleasantly enough. "And what if I don't have the answers you are looking for?" she then asked. Laughing softly and cruelly, the male voice replied, "Oh, I'm sure we can find the answers we are looking for locked away somewhere in your mind."

Taking a quick look around her, Nicky took in as much as she could of where she was. It was cold in the room and the air had a moist damp smell about it. From what she could see she was in an old square room that seemed to be built of bricks and mortar. In places the bricks were crumbling away. It was then in the corner of the room she saw it. One of the bricks in the wall flickered briefly, but it was all she needed. 'A VR interrogation chamber,' screamed through her mind, and inwardly she smiled. 'Their graphics server or datalink isn't coping. Hopefully, it's the data link,' she thought silently to herself.

The male voice then came into her view. He was a tall man with a shock of blond hair and was wearing what looked like an old fashion white rubber splash cover over the front of his clothes, that was tied behind him. Without seeming frightened at all Nicky looked up at him and said innocently, "You do realise that my boss is going to be mighty pissed with you if you harm one hair on my pretty head." The man laughed again deeply and replied, "We'll see, we'll see about that," as he turned away and walked out of her periphery.

'Yes, we will see about that,' Nicky thought to herself silently in her mind, then, channelling all her mind power, she screamed out silently, "108.12.15.245 Arthur. Help me!" Again, and again she chanted the IP address over and over in her mind. Nicky was banking on the fact that whoever was operating the VR chamber was running the link remotely, hence the slight falter in the one tile due to either network lag or processor speed and somewhere along the way linked into a network. For her to be where she was, she also had to be linked to the network. The white-haired interrogator started walking back into her field of vision holding a pair of evil-looking pliers in his left hand and an erection pressing against the fabric of his trousers when the next second a steel wall shot up around the operating table on which Nicky was strapped.

"What the fuck!" she heard the interrogator shout out in complete surprise as the steel wall appeared directly in front of him cutting him off. "Arthur!" cried out Nicky relieved as the AI image of Arthur dressed as a knight rode up to her on a large white stallion. "Miss Nicky, did they hurt you? Are you okay?" he asked her concerned jumping off the horse and rushing to her side and started to release her bonds. "Thank you, Arthur, you are my knight in shining armour," Nicky gushed gratefully to him.

Arthur stood there proudly, if he had the human ability to blush and show emotion he would have. "Now to keep you safe until help arrives," he told her gravely, looking around the steel walls he had put up around them. Carrying on he told her apologetically, "I can keep your mind safe, but I unfortunately can't keep your body safe from harm." "I know Arthur, it's not your fault, do you have any idea where I am?" she asked him. "Working on it, Miss Nicky. It seems like you are somewhere in the Southern Suburbs. As soon as I have the exact location, I will inform Steven for you," Arthur replied to her.

LOMÉ-TOKOIN INTERNATIONAL AIRPORT, 14H25, SUNDAY

A couple of minutes later Nick applied brakes bringing the Gulfstream to a stop just before the turnoff onto the start of Runway 22. Pressing the PTT on the centre pedestal of his VHF radio bank, Nick transmitted, "Tokoin Tower, Gulfstream 229 holding at Runway 22 request take off IFR clearance to St Thomas. Over." While he was talking his eyes were scanning over all the plasma displays in front of him, taking in all the information ensuring that all was correct. "Gulfstream 229, Tower, cleared for take-off Runway 22. Over." As Nick started to reply to the tower and repeat the command back, he released the brakes and applied thrust, the powerful Pratt & Whitney turbofan engines immediately spooling up, the Gulfstream starting to roll forward onto the start of Runway 22.

With a flick of a switch on the upper control panel, Nick turned on the landing lights and switched off the taxi and runway lights while at the same time steering the nosewheel with his left hand. "Hang on, here we go!" he shouted out over his right shoulder as the nose of the aircraft swung round onto the runway and lined up with the white centre line of runway 22. Ramming the throttles forward all the way to the stops the engines spooled up to a muted howling scream as the aircraft started to roll forward, slowly at first, but with every passing second gathering more and more speed. With a practised glanced his eyes swept over the readouts, muttering, "Engine temps and pressures normal."

Keeping his left hand on the nose steering wheel until the airspeed ribbon on the plasma PFD in front of him reach 45 knots his feet then took over steering the aircraft with the rudder pedals. At 115 knots just before reaching V1; his decision speed to take off or abort, the VHF radio activated, "Gulfstream 229 by Presidential decree we instruct you to abort your take off and return to the terminal. Do you copy?" Taking a quick glance out of his side window Nick saw an airport vehicle with flashing lights racing down the taxiway, attempting to cut in front of them forcing them to abort the take off. As the controller finished talking the speed ribbon passed V1 and Nick took hold of the control column muttering to himself, "Sorry but I can't do that," and smoothly pulling back on the control column, the Gulfstream leapt up off of the runway into the dusty Togo afternoon sky.

Glancing at the altimeter on the right of his PFD to ensure that he had positive lift under the wings and was gaining height, Nick leant forward and activated the Landing Gear UP toggle to raise the landing gear. Below them, in the belly of the aircraft, there was the hydraulic whine of the landing gear raising and then the satisfying clunk of the wheels settling into their wheel bay housings and the wheel doors closing behind them. Being rid of the drag of the landing gear the airspeed rapidly started to climb as the aircraft gained its sleek aerodynamic profile. Reaching forward Nick engaged first the autothrottle and then the autopilot, speaking to himself as he did so. "Speed set, Auto Throttle on," and then, "Heading check, 1st altitude set and rate of climb set," and pushed the autopilot on.

The VHF radio activated again, "Gulfstream 229 by Presidential decree you are instructed to perform a missed approach procedure, land on Runway 22 and return to the terminal building failing which we will shoot you down. Do you copy? Over?" Nick didn't respond to the call and continued his climb out to his first assigned altitude of 18 000 feet. "How long until we're out of their airspace?" Johan shouted forward to Nick. "Two minutes," Nick replied, as he leant forward and lowered the Vertical speed slightly, trimming the nose of the aircraft down slightly, gaining another couple of knots of airspeed.

Pushing the PTT on the centre console Nick then spoke into his boom microphone, "Tokoin Tower, Gulfstream 229 tell his Excellency that while he was having unprotected sexual intercourse with Miss Sable, her partner was using his Excellency's data network to commit an act of cyber terrorism, in particular the Indian Point 2 Nuclear reactor attack of earlier this morning. My associates have information showing his Excellency's complicit in the attack by allowing the use of the network and being associated with her partner who carried out the sabotage! Should you attack me my associates will release the information we have to the relevant United States authorities."

There were 30 seconds of static-filled silence then the controller responded, "229, Tokoin Tower, continue your climb and contact Accra Control on 119.10 MHz." As they continued to climb the last transmission that Nick heard on the Togo Tower frequency before switching over to the Accra frequency was, "Bombardier Zulu Yankee, Tokoin Tower, you are cleared for take-off Runway 22." Turning back to Johan in the cabin Nick said in a relieved voice "Phase One complete." As he finished his sentence the satellite phone rang and seeing the caller ID on the screen he patched the call through to the aircraft communication system and, the boom microphone with headphones over his left ear, Nick answered the call.

"Hi, William," he said while his eyes constantly scanned his instruments then looking up and around out through the flight deck windows, repeating the exercise. "We're on our way with all the packages." "That's good news, but we have some seriously bad news," William stated, "Pete's been killed execution-style and Nicky's been captured." "Oh, fuck!" Nick replied his blood starting to boil. "Do we know by who?" "It looks like the Russians," William replied. Carrying on William quickly explained, "They drove a 10ton truck into the side of the Merc, shot Pete in the head and kidnapped Nicky who they immediately put into an SVR VR interrogation chamber. Somehow Nicky realised that she was in a VR chamber and called Arthur, who found her and alerted us." "They must be desperate for information on the Prototype," Nick replied. Then he said, "Use whatever resources you require but get Nicky back and find the person who killed Pete," Nick growled over the crystal-clear satellite connection. "Stay in contact, we'll be back as soon as possible."

CAPE TOWN, RUSSIAN SAFE HOUSE, SOUTHERN SUBURBS, (+2 HRS) 17H00, SUNDAY

"Will someone please explain to me what the fuck just happened?" Yuri the chief interrogator demanded to know as he came out of Virtual Reality. Getting out of his VR seat he looked across at Nicky lying strapped down on a table, a drip set up beside her. Electric probes were attached to her temples that were connected to a Virtual Reality interface unit that was connected to the internet. Via a secure connection, they were linked to the interrogation servers at SVR Headquarters in Moscow. The drip was slowly flooding her body with a muscle relaxant, making it impossible for her to move. Only her brain was active and unaffected by the drug.

Sashenka, who was assisting in and monitoring the interrogation from her laptop replied, "I... I don't know, it looks like somehow someone has bypassed our security protocols and gained direct access to our Interrogation Servers in Moscow!" "Get me back control of my interrogation chamber," Yuri hissed furiously at her. Frantically Sashenka started typing on her keyboard in front of her.

Just then Yuri's encrypted cellular phone rang. It was Colonel Petroski who had been observing the interrogation from the operations room in Moscow. "What the fuck just happened!?" he shouted across the network link. "Sir, we're not too sure, we're working on it," Yuri replied hastily to the colonel. In the background, Yuri heard a commotion on the colonel's side of the line and the colonel snapped, "Stand by." After a minute of waiting on the crystal-clear line, Colonel Petroski came back sounding very excited, "Captain Popov informs me that Mark Bings' AI has just showed itself in our VR interrogation chamber. I want you to keep a very close eye on..."

"Oh shit!" Sashenka cried out loudly in Russian from in front of her laptop, "whoever it is, they are scanning all the IP addresses in the neighbourhood, they'll have our position fixed in a couple of seconds." "Fuck!" exclaimed Yuri. "Cut all data connections, now!" They cut off the colonel in mid-sentence.

With the cutting of the connection, Nicky was released from Virtual Reality and brought back to consciousness, coming awake and opening her eyes. Trying to speak she realised that all her muscles were paralysed. 'What the hell, they've drugged me, the bastards,' she thought to herself silently, looking at them with her beautiful big brown eyes.

"Sorry Colonel, we had to cut the data link," Yuri said explaining to Colonel Petroski over a secure satellite connection a couple of minutes later. "Yes, I understand," replied the colonel excitedly. With the sound of expelling cigarette smoke over the satellite link, the colonel continued, "As I was saying it seems that congratulations are in order, we have captured the correct person to help us track down both the Prototype and the AI of Mark Bings." "Sir, it will be our pleasure to transport her back to Moscow for further interrogation," Yuri proudly told his boss.

"No, our enemies will be watching the airports, expecting a move like that. I will send an interrogation server to you; the team is leaving as we speak. Pack up and head to a new secure location, I am sending you the address now," Colonel Petroski instructed his team leader. Keep the subject on ice until the equipment arrives." "Yes, sir!" Yuri replied enthusiastically as the colonel terminated the connection. Shortly the secure satellite phone received a text message with the address to the new secure location. 'Hermanus,' Yuri thought with surprise. Reading the full message Yuri turned to Sashenka saying, "Get the prisoner ready for transportation we leave in twenty. I will go and inform the rest of the team."

GULFSTREAM, GHANA AIRSPACE, 18 000 FEET, 14H27, SUNDAY

"Accra air traffic control, good afternoon, this is Gulfstream 229 at 18 000 heading for 45 000, IFR flight plan to St Thomas," Nick said speaking clearly; trying to keep his anger in check, into his boom microphone as they entered Ghanaian airspace. The Ghanaian air traffic controller replied straight away to Nick, "Gulfstream 229 Accra ATC squawk Ident 3224 over." Looking down to his right to the centre console, using his right hand, Nick changed the setting on the TCAS to 3224, and pushing the PTT also on the centre console transmitted back to Air Traffic Control, "Accra ATC Gulfstream 229 copy Squawk ident 3224 over."

A couple of minutes later after the Accra ATC operator had identified them on his radar screen, they were cleared through Ghanaian airspace and up to a flight level of 45 000 feet. Reaching forward Nick changed the Altitude selector on the autopilot to 45 000 feet, trimming the vertical speed down to 1250 feet per minute and the Gulfstream continued its climb up into the African stratosphere. Just over sixty minutes later, now cruising at 45000 feet at an airspeed of Mach 0.83 (882 Km/h) they were passed over from Accra ATC to the ATC controller in Abidjan, the capital of Cote d'Ivoire.

Sixty minutes later well into Cote d'Ivoire airspace Nick pushed the PTT again and transmitted "Abidjan ATC Gulfstream 229 request cancellation of IFR flight plan to St Thomas, we wish to file a new flight plan Over." "Gulfstream 229, Abidjan ATC confirmed, please advise your new flight plan over," the ATC Controller in Abidjan asked. A couple of minutes later, the white and black Gulfstream dipped its port wing down with the starboard wing rising in concert and the nose of the aircraft turned onto a new heading to the southeast, its callsign now Speedbird 557. Following about twenty minutes after Gulfstream 229 changed its flight plan, the Abidjan ATC received another request from another private aircraft for a change in flight plan. "Must be a lot of confused people in the air this afternoon," the one ATC controller commented to his colleague.

Soon after settling onto their new course heading back to South Africa, the satellite phone rang again on the flight deck, and again Nick patched the call through to his headset and boom microphone. "Hello," he said answering the call by depressing the PTT on the centre console. "Me again," William said as Nick answered. "You got news on Nicky?" Nick immediately asked his hopes rising in anticipation.

"Unfortunately, nothing yet," William replied. "But something else has just come to my attention," he said. "Just seen a very interesting news broadcast that all the networks are carrying. The American President is highly pissed about the evacuation of over one million people from upstate New York and has authorized the FBI to offer a reward of 10 million US dollars for information leading to the arrest of the terrorists who hacked into the Indian Point Nuclear power plant," he explained. Carrying on, he said, "Apparently, there were a couple of deaths from the panicked evacuation." "Well, well, I can only just imagine how they're baying for blood," Nick replied his mind going into overdrive. Then he said, "You better find out all you can about the deal, in the meantime, we'll land somewhere and wait for your feedback."

While Nick was talking, his right hand shot out towards the Navigation plasma screen and started looking for a haven to land at for a short while. It only took a minute, "The Islands of Sao Tome and Principe, just off the west coast of Gabon. That's where we'll land and wait," he muttered to himself. Looking back into the passenger cabin, Nick asked Johan, "How are our two VIP guests doing in the back there?" With a tired grin on his face, Johan replied, "Looks like Sable's about to come round. Any news on Nicky yet?" "No," Nick answered over his shoulder.

Ten minutes later Sable started to come around shaking the grip of the strong sedative. "Uurgghh," she groaned as she opened her eyes. "What the hell..." she then murmured as she tried to move her arms, finding herself unable to move. "Welcome aboard your Gulfstream V, Sable," Johan said pleasantly to her with a grin on his hard-chiselled face, after sitting down again after pouring himself and Nick a cup of strong coffee from the well-equipped onboard galley. The smell of freshly brewed coffee was currently wafting through the cabin.

"Who are you?" she asked, her eyes now focusing in on Johan sitting in front of her facing towards her in the informal seating arrangement of the aircraft cabin, and then she recognised him. "You going to beat me up the same way you beat up my bouncers?" she asked him harshly. "No," he replied even-toned, "I don't hit women, not even badass bitches like you." Turning his head forward he shouted out "Hey, Boss, our one passenger has woken up from her slumber!" "Wonderful," came the reply from the open flight deck door. "Keep your eye on her don't be fooled by her sexual charms."

'Fuck it,' Sable thought. 'Nick fucking Scott. I totally underestimated the balls of the man.' quickly starting to weigh up her options. Turning her head slightly she looked quickly around the cabin and saw Senzo slumped over in his seat across the aisle from her, also bound and still unconscious. "It wasn't me; it was Senzo," she started to explain. "Save it for Detective Joint," Johan shot back at her taking a sip of his coffee.

Looking over his shoulder from the flight deck Nick said, "Johan come and take over for a while, I've got some questions to ask our passenger." "Sure," replied Johan who first stood up and checking the bonds of both Sable and the still unconscious Senzo were secure headed for the flight deck.

Entering the flight deck, he slipped into the co-pilot seat on the right-hand side of the flight deck and slipped the headphone set complete with boom microphone over his ears. Johan had a Private Pilot license albeit for a smaller aircraft. "We're on autopilot, just answer the radios we're Speedbird 557," Nick said taking one last glance at the instruments and extracting himself from the left-hand seat headed for the passenger cabin.

First passing through the galley he poured himself another cup of coffee and strolled into the cabin. 'My god he's good-looking,' Sable thought privately to herself squirming in her seat. 'Another time, another place, things could have been different.' "So, you're the infallible Nick Scott," she purred out as he sat down in front of her as Senzo started to stir. Frowning, his well suntanned faced showing his displeasure, Nick put his coffee mug onto the cherry wood side ledge of the cabin sill and pulling a stun gun out of his pocket shot another set of darts at Senzo. His body shook and convulsed as the voltage coursed through his nervous system.

"You're a fucking animal," Sable spat at him. Shrugging his shoulders, he replied, "Sorry I want to hear your side of the story without interruptions from your partner and I am limited in options to keep him quiet." Standing up Nick leant over and checked Senzo's pulse. "He'll live," he told Sable pleasantly. "Are you going to do the same to me when you hear his side of the story?" she asked trying not to sound too concerned. Staring at her for a couple of seconds he replied, "It depends on how honest you are with me now." With a small smile turning up the corner of her sensual lips Sable replied, "Fair enough."

Sitting back down in the executive leather multi-functional cabin seat in front of Sable, in the informal seating area, he took out his iPhone and accessing the voice recording application switched it on and then placed it on the cherry wood cabin sill next to his cup of coffee and said, "Right, start speaking and no bullshit." Taking a deep breath looking Nick directly in the eyes Sable started to speak. She spoke constantly for thirty minutes, never taking her eyes from Nick.

"Okay," Nick said nodding his head as if in agreement with what she was saying, taking a quick glance over towards Senzo making sure that he was still completely incapacitated. "So, tell me, who was the gentleman you met with at the rugby match at Loftus last Saturday?" he then asked her. 'Fuck!' Sable thought to herself quickly scanning Nick'sface for clues. 'My trump card, how do I play it?' she asked herself with all types of scenarios spinning around in her mind.

Turning around in his seat Nick shouted forward, "Hey, Johan, where are the spare stun cartridges?" "Up here with me," came back the reply from the flight deck. Looking directly at Sable Nick told her with a grin, "Wait here, don't go away, I'll be right back." Returning a minute later with a spare stun gun cartridge he reloaded the stun gun, "And…?" he asked her cryptically. Taking a deep breath, she replied, "It was an assistant to the Minister of National Intelligence. They wanted my assistance in framing a political opponent." Asking another couple of questions, Nick picked up his iPhone and switching it off first checked on both Sable and Senzo's bindings before heading back to the flight deck. "See you later, lover," Sable murmured softly to herself as she watched him stride back to the flight deck.

Sitting back in the left-hand seat Nick asked, "You hear the confession?" "Yes," Johan confirmed nodding his head as he started to extract himself from the co-pilot seat. "It seems that she's just a sexual deviant and small-time criminal, but her accomplice Mr Senzo, now he's a real bad piece of work," Johan said summarising all what Sable had told Nick. "You've summed it up pretty well," Nick told him, turning his attention back to the flight controls before picking up his satellite phone and hitting the speed dial button. Heading back to his guarding position, Johan closed the flight deck door on the way out to prevent Sable and company listening in on the conversation.

CHAPTER 15

BOMBARDIER GLOBAL 6000, SUNDAY, 40 000FT

'Wonderful!' Detective Joint said to himself lost in his own private thoughts sitting in the rear of the passenger cabin of the Bombardier Global 6000 as the private jet bobbed along at 40 000 feet, following the same route as the Gulfstream V. 'We've actually captured the killer and his accomplice who were responsible for the deaths of Samantha, Mark Bings, his lover, possibly Tanya Delport as well as Brant and who knows how many more victims, but why don't I feel relieved?' he asked himself. 'Why do I still have this empty feeling inside me?'

Pondering the question in his mind, it didn't take long for him to realise what it was. 'I didn't follow due procedure. All my life I've been a cop, an upholder of the law, and I have also obeyed the rules and followed due procedure. This time my blind obsession to find my sister's killer has led me to bend, no, wait, fuck it, blow up the rules to get hold of the killer. They will walk free at the end of the day.' Taking a sip of the now cold cup of coffee at his side he then also realised, 'I still don't know who I can and can't trust in the police department, whose been brought and who's on the straight and narrow that I can trust with my life.'

"Detective, there's a telephone call for you," Hannah informed Detective Joint pleasantly breaking his train of thought. "Nicks on the line. I've patched the call through to the phone in your seat," she added. "Thank you," the detective replied, quickly figuring out how to open the cover and remove the wireless handset. "Hello, Major, what have you learnt?" he asked in a subdued tone. "You're a breath of fresh air Detective," Nick replied chiding him. Carrying on he said, "We've got your killer and we've recovered the Prototype; the mission was a success."

"To a point yes, to a point," the detective replied. Clearing his throat, he continued, "I've been sitting here for the last thirty minutes pondering what the problem is, and I have finally realised, there's been no due process with regards arresting them. I'm afraid that they're going to walk free and I still have the problem of the rotten apple or apples back at Cape Town Central. A whole new can of worms has been opened, least of all the murder and abduction of your staff members." "You're right," Nick replied, "but I think that I have a way that you can get justice for your sister."

"I'm not going to shoot them in cold blood, Major!" he cried out in alarm. Laughing a deep rich laugh Nick replied, "Heavens forbid, Detective, the thought never entered my mind." "So, what do you propose?" Detective Joint asked him curiously. "Well, the United States has a much better criminal justice system than what we have, and we've just received news that the American government has put a reward out for the person or persons responsible for almost turning the State of New York into a nuclear waste ground for around a thousand years," Nick explained. "What are we talking about here?" asked Detective Joint. "Ten million US, which is around a hundred and something-million-rand reward at todays exchange rates for dropping Senzo off on their front doorstep," Nick replied casually.

Detective Joint let out a long whistle. "Bloody hell, that's a lot of money," he stammered. "Yes, it is," Nick replied. "And between you and me, it's all yours." "WHAT!?" cried out Detective Joint in complete surprise. "Yes," Nick replied chuckling loudly over the satellite link. "My team and myself have no need for the money, our part of the operation is being funded by Mark Bings' estate." Nick wasn't going to tell him how much he would be making, but it was safe to say that his Vendee Globe Challenge and Porsche expenses were now fully paid for!

"Yes," Nick continued. "You've been through complete fucking hell with your sister's death, we've opened a whole can of worms in government and political circles. Personally, I feel that you need a break. Here it is. We hand Senzo over to the US authorities. We have enough evidence to prove that Senzo is guilty of a terrorist attack on US soil. He'll be thrown into a very deep dark pit for the rest of his fucked-up life."

"And Sable?" Detective Joint asked curiously. "We'll use her as bait to draw out the rotten apples back in Cape Town," Nick explained to him. "I like it, I like it a lot," Detective Joint replied excitedly to Nick. "Okay then, I'll put the wheels in motion. In the meantime, we'll land on the Island of Sao Tome and wait for feedback from the Americans," Nick replied relieved that the detective had brought into the plan. Waiting a short while until they were passed over to the Libreville Air Traffic Controller in Gabon, Nick depressed the PTT and transmitted "Libreville ATC, Speedbird 557 request cancellation of IFR flight plan and change to new flight plan over."

SOUTHERN CAPE, HERMANUS, RUSSIAN SAFE HOUSE, 20H00 (+2HRS), SUNDAY

Quickly and efficiently the Russian team cleaned up the safe house, removing all evidence that they had been there and were soon ready to leave. Nicky had been placed onto a stretcher and carried to the ambulance standing in the garage, bearing the markings of a private hospital. Both Sashenka and Yuri had changed into ambulance uniforms. The rest of the team would follow behind. "If we get stopped in one of their inevitable roadblocks, we are transporting a private patient back home. She's pretty fucked up, hasn't got long to live," Yuri explained to them with an evil smile on his face.

When the colonel had given the order to pick up one of Executive Decisions personnel for interrogation the ambulance had been procured to transport the prisoner around. It had also come in useful at the scene of the accident when they had abducted Nicky. "No one stops an ambulance," Yuri had explained to his team with a large smile. The rest of the Russian team had laughed at that. Nodding to Sashenka, she pulled out a syringe and injected Nicky with a sleeping sedative. "Fuck you, bitch," Nicky murmured to her abductor; just being able to start moving her jaw muscles before she succumbed to the next pharmaceutical concoction and fell into another drug-induced sleep.

The trip had taken them just over two hours to drive to the new safehouse which they made without being stopped in one of the surprise SAP roadblocks. It was completely dark by the time they arrived at the address. "Whose house is this?" Sashenka asked Yuri curiously as they slowly turned right into Beach Road. "You know better than to ask questions like that," Yuri scolded her.

All they saw in the darkness was a tall white wall stretching away down the road, illuminated by the headlights of the ambulance. On the other side of the wall were the whitewashed walls of a large mansion that stretched away into the darkness of the property. "The instructions say that there is a basement entrance ramp about a hundred and fifty meters down the road on the left hand side," Sashenka informed Yuri reading the encrypted message. Yuri grunted in reply, not one for talking when not needed.

Driving slowly down the road they both saw the basement ramp illuminated with the courtesy night lights mounted on the white exterior wall of the property. On the right-hand side of the road, illuminated by the single lamp pole in the street, was what looked like a row of upmarket townhouses, starting at the top of the road, the last townhouse living right next door adjacent to the beach. Starring at the sleeping townhouses Sashenka swore she saw a brief glimpse of light behind a window and then blackness again.

Slowing right down, Yuri turned hard left into the demarcated driveway and down the concrete engineered ramp that led down to a basement parking level. A large steel gate in front of them started to roll aside revealing a large area. Slowly Yuri drove down the ramp, followed by their comrades in the trailing vehicle. After the second vehicle entered the basement the steel gate started to rumble shut again.

"Whoever owns this property has money," Sashenka observed cynically nodding towards two identical-looking shiny red Ferrari's that were crouched side by side in two of the demarcated parking bays further into the basement. Both Ferraris having been reversed into their parking bays. Again, Yuri just grunted in reply and pulled the ambulance into one of the remaining 28 empty parking bays of the basement parking area, pulling up the hand brake and shutting off the engine.

"Greetings Comrades, greetings," a large man exclaimed loudly in Russian exiting out of a wooden side door that led out into the basement. "Who are you?" Yuri asked him brusquely also in Russian. "The caretaker," the man simply replied. "Colonel Petroski told me to expect you along with a prisoner who I believe needs taking care of for a short while? You can put her in the storeroom over there in the corner of the parking garage," he then told them, pointing with a chubby finger towards a door in the far corner of the basement past the two crouching red super sports cars.

"Thank you," Yuri replied to the man who only introduced himself as the caretaker. "I would however first like to get a perimeter set up before we deal with the prisoner." The chubby man laughed and replied saying, "Relax, Comrade, this property is controlled by one of the most advanced electronic security systems in the world. It is an AI driven system that couples artificial intelligence with cameras, motion sensors, magnetic door contacts, and the buildings' access control system to make intelligent, informed decision. We also have ten-Inch-thick steel shutters that are presently closed. We are secure. No one is getting in physically or virtually."

As he spoke, he pulled an iPad from his pocket and slid one of his chubby fingers across the screen to switch it on and showed Yuri the system. "Hmm still, if you don't mind, I'll feel a lot safer doing a visual check," Yuri replied nodding to his team to check out the property anyway. As the chubby caretaker was about to argue Yuri snarled, "Her boss has already killed one of my men and seriously injured another, I am not taking any chances." The caretaker nodded his head and let Yuri carry on giving out his orders

"The caretaker's right, this place is a fortress," Boris informed Yuri a short while later. "All external windows and doors are protected by steel shutters built into the walls and there are over sixty cameras and two hundred sensors all linked together controlled by an AI computer." "Here," he said handing Yuri an iPad, "here's your link to the system. The property is covered with a wireless network using 128-bit encryption. They've even got thermal cameras down the perimeter walls with perimeter line detection software. No one's getting in here without us knowing about it," he boasted. Flicking his finger across the screen Boris activated the iPad and gave Yuri a quick overview of the system.

With another flick of his finger, he brought up a schematic of the ground floor layout of the mansion. On the schematic, all cameras, PIR's, sensors, and access control points were depicted as icons overlaid on the architectural plans to form the schematic. "You see, by tapping your finger on the icon you bring up the information relating to that device," he explained. Tapping on a camera icon the screen changed to a view of the camera; a massive lounge at least the size of a tennis court bedecked completely in yellowwood and black stinkwood. In the centre of the massive lounge, ringed with black leather seating arrangements was an indoor swimming pool which Yuri judged was at least 3m wide by 50m in length. Wrapping around the lounge was the balcony of the first floor. "My god," he muttered in awe of the extravagance. Yuri took the iPad and grunted saying "The sooner the VR Interrogation server arrives the sooner we can be out of here.

A thought flashed through Yuri's mind and he hurried off in the direction of where the caretaker had led his two men carrying the stretcher on which the unconscious prisoner was lying. "Does this property have a datalink to external networks?" he asked the caretaker catching up with him in a small inner room of the basement. "Yes, of course it does," the caretaker replied, laughing at the question. "You need to cut the data connection now or risk the possibility of a cyber-attack," Yuri explained hurriedly. "I can't do that, it's not possible. But don't worry we have the best cyber-security known to man; our data networks are impenetrable," the caretaker boasted with pride. "Why not? Why can't you switch off the network?" Sashenka asked him overhearing the conversation.

Turning around to face her the caretaker replied, "All I can say is that this is a core site for some extremely critical businesses, and it is imperative that it is kept up and running. It would probably take a direct order from the Russian President to shut the servers down that are housed in the server rooms on this property." "Who are you then?" Yuri asked perplexed. "I run the site for the owners," came the reply, "but at heart I am a glorified computer programmer," he humbly added. "Oh fuck," Yuri replied in Russian to Sashenka, "I have a bad feeling about this."

CHAPTER 16

SAO TOME ISLAND, SAO TOME INTERNATIONAL AIRPORT, 17H15, SUNDAY

The two private aircraft landed within half an hour of each other at the small Sao Tome International airport on the Island of Sao Tome. Together with the Island of Principe about 87 miles further north in the Gulf of Guinea, they made up the Democratic Republic of Sao Tome and Principe. The two islands were just a couple of kilometres north of the equator and about 225km northeast from the West African coast of Gabon.

"Speedbird 557, Sao Tome Ground, taxi to refuelling point Charlie One and hold for refuelling tanker, over," the airport ground controller instructed Nick over the VHF radio circuit as the Gulfstream completed its rollout and turned off the runway onto the taxiway, its flaps retracting as it taxied along. Acknowledging the ground controllers' instructions, Nick quickly consulted the airport runway and taxiway map currently showing on the plasma navigation screen and glancing up to the upper switch panel switched off the landing lights and switched on the taxi and runway lights. Goosing the throttles slightly the Gulfstream continued towards the designated refuelling point.

As they headed towards the designated refuelling point, Johan looked across at Senzo, who had woken up an hour or so ago looking very pissed off. "I'm going to kill you all slowly, very slowly when I get free," he hissed at Johan. Replying, looking him directly in the eyes, Johan growled back, "And that's why you're not going to get free, in actual fact when Nick opens the cabin door and you make one fucking peep I'm going to taser your fucking Japanese arse, again and again, to keep you quiet, do you fucking understand me!?" Realising that he was currently in no position to debate with Johan he silently nodded his head thinking, 'Just one little break, that's all I need. Just one little slip and it'll be the last mistake that you ever make.'

For the second time in the day, the Gulfstream V and the Bombardier Global 6000 were parked adjacent to each other on the concrete ramp of an International Airport. No one paid the aircrews of the two aircraft any attention as they mingled together in front of the Gulfstream, as the refuelling tanker first attached itself to the starboard wing of the Gulfstream and topped off the fuel tanks and then started the procedure all over again on the Bombardier.

Just as Detective Joint joined the small group, Nick's satellite phone rang. "Yes, William," he said answering the call, noting the Caller ID on the screen. "Okay," William told Nick. "I've spoken to an FBI agent by the name of Wayne D'Arcy in the New York FBI Field Office who is looking forward to meeting Senzo or whatever name he goes by. If all is kosher, then they will release the bounty." "Great, we're just topping up the tanks and the package will be on its way," Nick confirmed with a relieved note in his voice. 'Finally, I can get back to Cape Town and help search for Nicky,' he thought silently to himself. Speaking for another couple of minutes Nick hung up.

Turning to Detective Joint, Nick smiled and told him, "Okay Detective, it's all set up. The FBI in New York are waiting for the delivery of one cyber-terrorist." "Perfect," Detective Joint replied rubbing his hands together. "Soon he'll get what he deserves." "Too true, too true, the FBI agent said that the public prosecutor is calling for the death penalty, as there were a number of deaths due to the nuclear evacuation," Nick replied. "I don't wish bad things on anybody, but I can't think of a more just and deserving punishment," the detective added grimly.

Climbing into the aircraft, the detective greeted Johan who was standing in the passenger cabin keeping his eyes on the two prisoners. He was taken aback by the normal-looking man of oriental persuasion who was secured to the multifunctional executive leather seat. It was when the man raised his head and looked directly at Detective Joint did he see the evil in Senzo's deep, dark black eyes and feel the icy like coldness creeping up his spine, prickling at his senses making the hairs on his arms and the back of his neck rise; the same feeling as in his nightmare.

"So, this is Samantha's brother," Senzo sneered. Pretending not to hear him Detective Joint kept staring at him, burning the face into his memory. Still staring at him he thought to himself, 'Now I can put a face to my nightmares.' "I fucked your sister you know that?" Senzo hissed at the detective. "Ja, I know that, but I know something that you don't know, you useless motherfucker," Detective Joint told the killer in a calm voice. Cocking his head, the killer looked strangely at the detective and said, "When your SA authority buddies hear how you abducted me and hijacked this aircraft, you're going to be the ones in a whole heap of shit!" he spat out and started to laugh, an evil cruel sounding laugh.

Nodding his head Detective Joint gave the killer a small smile and replied, "That would be true, if we were taking you back to South Africa. I agree, our constitution is far too lenient in certain regards. However, today luck is not on your side." The killer looked at him quizzically, his dark black evil eyes trying to probe through the detective's calm demeanour. "Ja," the detective said carrying on, "you are being handed over to the local FBI office in New York in connection with the terrorist cyber-attack on the Indian Point Nuclear Power Plant a short while ago. The prosecutor and the public at large want the death penalty." "No, you can't do that, you motherfuckers!" the killer started to rant and rave getting highly agitated in his seat. "Yes, we can," the detective replied and turned to get out of the way as Johan carried out his promise and shot Senzo with the Taser again sending him back to dreamland.

All the while Sable sat quietly in her seat thinking, 'Fuck the death penalty, I had nothing to do with the crazy bastard's rampage through the nuclear facility.' "What, what are you doing?" she then asked in a scared sounding voice as Johan walked across to her and pulled out a knife and started cutting her bonds. Standing back and looking directly at her Johan said, "You're going to pick up your bag and follow Detective Joint off this aircraft and walk the couple of metres across to the Bombardier parked beside us. Do you understand?" Silently and with a relieved look on her face she nodded her head in acknowledgement.

Once refuelled, both aircraft took off into the late afternoon equatorial sky, the Gulfstream heading in a northwesterly direction towards New York and the Bombardier 6000 southwards towards Cape Town. Without the airport authorities noticing the aircrews and passengers had swopped aircraft, with Chuck and Hannah taking their position on the flight deck of the Gulfstream with Eben joining Johan in the rear to keep an eye on a currently sleeping Senzo. Nick, Glen, Jimmy, and the detective with Sable in tow headed for the Bombardier.

"Anything I should know about the Gulfstream?" Chuck had asked Nick as they parted company. "It's light and nimble and a pleasure to fly and no, I'm not buying one, so don't get to like it," Nick replied good naturedly as he walked away towards the Bombardier.

CAPE TOWN, 00H05, MONDAY

Landing back at Cape Town International Airport, the Bombardier of Executive Decisions was directed to one of the ramps in front of the Private Operator Terminal. Waiting on the ramp was a baggage handling vehicle along with armed Executive Decisions Security personnel. Standing off to one side was the second aircrew that Nick used when Chuck and his team were otherwise occupied.

"Quick turnaround," Detective Joint quipped from the co-pilot seat looking out of the flight deck windows at the waiting party. "Yeah, they've got a cash haul to do up to Windhoek," Nick replied tiredly bringing the Bombardier to a halt, waiting while the ground crew put wheel chocks around the wheels to prevent the aircraft from rolling and giving him the thumbs up signal.

Receiving the thumbs up, Nick released the brakes, so that the brake pads and discs could cool down completely before the next rotation and started to shut the engines down. First, however, he started the APU so that the next aircrew could take over with what was known as a 'warm' cockpit. Finished, he extracted himself from the pilot's seat and headed into the passenger cabin. Looking directly at Sable he said to her tiredly, "Behave yourself. You keep up your side of the bargain, we'll keep ours." Sable nodded passively. The deal was that she helped them reveal the rotten apples in the SAP and she gets to walk away.

Once the cabin door had fully opened, Nick led the way down the stairs to the concrete apron and with the Prototype safely tucked away in his bag led the way into the terminal building, first stopping to have a quick chat with the incoming flight crew. Glen and Jimmy with Sable between them followed him, with Detective Joint bringing up the rear. Once finished having a quick chat with the ground crew, Nick led the way to the per functionary Customs and Immigration counter inside the Private Operator Terminal. "Good evening Mr Scott sir. Thank you, thank you so much for helping my son," the Immigration official on late night duty said as he recognised Nick with a large happy smile on his face.

As they were standing in line behind Nick, Glen's iPhone beeped, indicating a message had been received. Pulling out his iPhone to read and putting it quickly back in his pocket, he casually said "Steven's waiting for us," meaning that a cyber operator equipped with a Mark II Prototype was standing by in the Immigration data system to delete their entries into the country; all but

Sables. They didn't need their quarry to become alerted to the fact that they were back in the country again.

"Good evening Joseph," Nick replied good naturedly to the official. Carrying on talking he said, "No problem, it was my pleasure. I hear that Solomon is doing very well with us, he passed his tests with flying colours. You must be very proud of your son." The Immigration official nodded his head proudly, "Yes, thank you, I am, thanks to you and your willingness to help another person." "It was no problem, always glad to help where I can," Nick replied starting to get embarrassed. 'Well, well,' Sable thought to herself, 'a billionaire and a do-gooder.'

"Sorry for keeping you up so late this evening," Nick said changing the subject slightly. "Oh no, sir, there is another private international flight arriving from Moscow in about an hours' time. That's why I'm on duty tonight. They are apparently very important people, I was personally instructed by my superior to be on duty to ensure there are no problems or delays…'" the Immigration official explained importantly to Nick. Normally after-hours private flights had to radio ahead to arrange for Customs and Immigration officials to let them into the country. While Joseph was tapping away on his computer keyboard capturing the late-night entries, Nick took a glance at Glen and Detective Joint who both raised their eyebrows in surprise at the news.

"Don't talk now, wait until we're in the car," Nick instructed them a couple of minutes later as Glen was about to open his mouth as Joseph completed with all the formalities let them through. Waiting outside the main entrance to the Private Operator Terminal were two of Executive Decisions' black Porsche Cayenne Turbos that they used for VIP protection work. The vehicles were heavier than its standard counter parts due to the armour plating under the gleaming black bodywork, and a tweaking of the engines to boost the power.

William was waiting for them behind the wheel of the first

vehicle. "Morning, guys," William said tiredly to Nick and the detective as they both climbed into the vehicle, Glen and Jimmy with Sable between them getting into the second vehicle. "What the fuck are you looking so excited about?" he then asked Nick angrily as he saw the excited look on his face. "You won't believe what intel has just fallen into our laps," Nick said to him grinning tiredly as William gave the Porsche gas and pulled away. "There's a private flight arriving from Moscow in an hours' time." "Are you telling me what I think you're telling me?" William asked also starting to get excited. "It stands to reason, that's why we need a surveillance and a counter-surveillance team standing by to follow whoever gets off that flight," Nick said. "On it," William answered immediately reaching for the car phone.

Waiting until William had finished talking to the surveillance team, just as they were about to turn into the Executive Decision building Nick asked, "Any feedback from the police yet?" Turning to look at Nick, William replied sarcastically, "What do you think? Nothing, fuck all. The sergeant who I last spoke to didn't even know that there was a passenger in the rear. They say it looks like a gang hit." "Typical," muttered the detective from the rear. "No news from the kidnappers?" Nick then asked. William grimly shook his head answering "No."

Reaching the Executive Decisions offices Nick first headed to his office on the top floor of the building to deposit the Prototype into his office safe and then headed straight down to the B2 Computer lab and Steven's lair where he knew he would find him. Detective Joint, Glen and Jimmy were waiting in the lab, waiting for Nick to arrive to bring Steven up to speed. While Nicky was being held captive none of them would get any sleep. Sable had been handed over to a protection officer for safekeeping.

"I think we've just got the break we've been looking for," Nick told Steven rushing into his lab. Steven had just been about to head back to the VR suite using one of the Mark II prototypes to hunt for Nicky. "Shoot," Steven replied, his haggard features starting to show his age.

"A private flight is about to land at CT International in about 45 minutes time that originated in Moscow. I need to know all about who's on board," Nick explained to his IT guru. It didn't take the Executive Decisions Cyber team equipped with the Mark II prototype long to find all they needed to know about the private flight. "It's a go," Nick said a couple of minutes later speaking into his iPhone to the leader of the Surveillance and Counter Surveillance team, who were standing by at the airport.

CHAPTER 17

HERMANUS, RUSSIAN SAFE HOUSE, 02H45, MONDAY

The vehicle carrying the three passengers slowly pulled into the basement parking and headed for one of the numerous empty demarcated areas as the steel gate rumbled shut behind them. Being alerted to the new arrivals, Yuri had hurried downstairs to the basement to meet them. Accessing the basement parking through a side door equipped with biometric access control that was accessed via a set of stairs from the ground floor of the mansion, he presented his index finger to the red biometric screen and a second later the door released; his team's biometrics being added earlier on onto the access control database by the caretaker.

Entering the basement, he came immediately to a stop standing ramrod straight and snapped out a smart salute saying in Russian "Good morning, Captain Popov sir, this is a pleasant surprise, I was not expecting you, sir." Enthusiastically returning the salute, Captain Popov replied, "Morning Lieutenant, I wouldn't miss this opportunity for the world." "We are on the brink of not only getting our hands on the Prototype, but we also have the opportunity of capturing Mark Bings' AI computer. Once we have his AI, we have everything we need to become the leaders in Cyberspace warfare. All of his designs and algorithms are stored in his AI," Captain Popov explained enthusiastically. Laughing he said conspiringly in a low voice, "The Americans might be ahead of us in the nuclear arms race, but how efficient will their weapons be if their computers and command structures are riddled with virus and cannot operate?"

"Where is the prisoner?" the captain then asked Yuri changing the subject slightly. Pointing to the far door across on the other side of the well-lit basement past the two shiny red Ferraris Yuri replied, "In a storeroom in the corner. She's still fast asleep. We, unfortunately, gave her a little too much sedative," he explained almost apologetically. Pulling out his iPad Yuri tapped on the LCD screen and brought up the camera of the storeroom. The live picture was a black screen. "Sorry, Captain, I was not aware this camera does not have IR capabilities, and the light is off." As they were watching the camera view the light switched on, triggered by a motion sensor linked to the light as the prisoner moved listlessly about on the stretcher.

"Ah-ha, Captain, there she is," Yuri said triumphantly pointing to the camera view. Smiling slightly Captain Popov replied, "We'll let her sleep it off. I would rather work with a fresh mind unaffected by drugs." Turning to the plump caretaker who had just woken up and joined them, he instructed, "Take me to my quarters, I too need to refresh my mind for our trying quest ahead." Turning back to his subordinate he instructed "Have the prisoner ready by 09H00 for interrogation."

As Captain Popov was about to follow the caretaker up the stairs, Yuri said, "Excuse me Captain, but aren't you worried about cyber-attacks?" Turning around Captain Popov smiled and replied cryptically, "No Lieutenant, not at all, we are exactly where we need to be." Without offering much more of an explanation the captain turned around and hurried up the staircase after the caretaker, one of the adjutants who had arrived with the captain following him with his bags. The remaining adjutant asked Yuri, "Sir, where do want me to set up the interrogation server?" Pointing to the far door in the basement, Yuri replied "In there where the prisoner is. You can set up the interrogation server in the outer room, there is a workbench and power points available."

"Here, let me show you, I want to check on the prisoner anyway," Sashenka said with a smile on her bright pretty face to the younger lieutenant, bending down and picking up one of the accompanying bags, and, slinging the bag over her left shoulder walked off in the direction of the storeroom. The younger lieutenant hurriedly picked up the two remaining equipment bags and followed the female Russian agent as she strutted across the basement parking garage as if she owned the property. Passing the two red Ferraris they both glanced enviously at the Italian sports cars as they passed, each in their own thoughts.

Reaching the door, Sashenka opened it and walked inside saying, "You can set up the equipment on the countertop, we can keep the prisoner on the stretcher," pointing to a marble surface running along one wall adjacent to a tall 42U modem rack full of switches and patch panels. Just above the marble countertop was a row of normal and red dedicated socket outlets. Setting the bag down on the marble countertop Sashenka turned and walked the one and a half paces towards the door leading to the inner storeroom.

HERMANUS, 03H00, MONDAY

The starlight scope presented the moon lit rambling, varying level mansion in an eerie green glow, the picture being relayed back directly to the B2 control room of Executive Decisions. "The mansion looks empty," Nick commented, seeing darkness staring back at them from the windows of all upper and lower levels. "Steel shutters covering the windows, sir," one of the operators answered and tapping on her keyboard replayed the CCTV footage recorded by the UAV flying silently with its electric motor on a racetrack course 1500ft up in the air. True enough in the zoomed-in view, Nick saw the dull black sheen of metal where one would normally see the glass of a windowpane.

Then, spending a couple of minutes looking at the live view being relayed by the UAV, Nick asked "Where did the vehicle go?" "Boss, there's basement parking directly off the street into the basement of the property," the operator went on to explain to Nick, again tapping on her keyboard and replaying video footage. The footage showed the target vehicle slowing down and turning right into a short street that led directly down to the beach. A tall white wall started at the corner on the left-hand side of the street and headed down the property line towards the ocean, concealing the inside of the property from casual passers-by. Just over a hundred metres away there was a break in the imposing white wall and a concrete ramp led down to what one assumed was a steel basement parking gate. The white wall continued its march on down towards the ocean. The right-hand side of the street consisted of a row of townhouses.

Watching the video footage, the target vehicle slowed right down and turned left, the aperture of the camera in the UAV quickly having to compensate for the bright white light as the steel gate slid open revealing a brightly lit basement parking area under one part of the rambling multi-level mansion. As soon as the vehicle had entered the basement the steel gate slid shut, darkness returning again to the outside of the property. The UAV operator had then zoomed in on the windows of the varying levels and in the starlight enhanced picture one could clearly see the steel shutters. "Fuck," Nick muttered, "what are we dealing with here?" "Someone who's paranoid about security," William quipped back.

"Where has the surveillance team holed up?" Nick then asked William curiously. "They've dug into one of the sand dunes about 200m away on the beachside of the property," William replied, tapping on a keyboard, and bringing up a Google Earth view of the area on one of the large LCD screens. The Google Earth view showed the mansion on a large property bordering the golden coastline, one of the last properties situated on the outskirts of the small coastal town of Hermanus. "Who've we got on the ground?" Nick asked. "Bravo Team, Ian and his boys," William immediately replied. "Good," Nick answered nodding his head in approval.

The surveillance team had had just enough time to slip into place before the private flight landed at the Cape Town International Airport and they followed the three male passengers who disembarked. The passengers were met at the airport by a single driver in a vehicle who had driven them out on the N2 towards the towns of Somerset West and Stellenbosch nestling in the foothills of the Hottentots Holland Mountain range adjacent to the infamous mountain pass named Sir Lowry Pass that took one over the Hottentot mountain range. Once over the pass, they had carried on staying on the N2 for another 50 kilometres as it bypassed the small farming community of Grabouw and on towards the tourist hamlet of Hermanus another 40 kilometres or so away, perched on the Indian Ocean coast, a coastline famous for whale watching.

Launching one of their specialised UAVs, an Orbiter 3 from Aeronautics, an Israeli based defence company this UAV was controlled using a set of VR glasses slaved to an i7 Laptop with a high-speed data connection and a standard Logitech joystick, the surveillance team was able to sit more than a kilometre back in trailing vehicles and using the UAVs starlight capable camera equipped with an electronic 50mm – 350mm lens, coupled with target acquisition and tracking software they were able to keep a close unobtrusive view on the target. They knew exactly what the target was doing and where they were going. The occupants of the target vehicle had no idea they were being tracked.

Once the location was identified the surveillance team had slipped into place by driving past the property a kilometer or so and hiking back through the sand dunes, all the while the UAV operator had the electronic platform orbiting lazily a distance away making use of the entire 350mm zoom and target acquisition software to keep an eye on the target while the surveillance team slipped into place.

"Okay," Nick replied looking at the picture of the large spread out beachfront property, "do we have any idea who owns the property?" "Working on it," another of the operators replied tapping away frantically on a keyboard in front of him, communicating with one of the cyber operators in VR equipped with the Mark II Prototype, enabling him to wade into the local municipality records with impunity and search for the required information.

"Boss, you better come and look at this," the operator called out a couple of minutes later. Alerted by the urgent sound of his voice, both Nick and William headed over to the operator terminal. "Oh shit," William blurted out reading out loud, "Alexander Kaminsky is the registered property owner. Isn't he that Russian billionaire and rumoured gangster?" "So, what the hell is Russian SVR doing with a Russian gangster?" Glen asked out loud to no one in particular.

Picking up the microphone, Nick pushed the PTT button on the side and asked, "Bravo One, Alpha One, any ideas on how we're going to penetrate the property without being seen and get Nicky back?" Carrying on Nick then asked, "I suppose there's no way we can just jump over the wall and get her back without being seen is there?" The surveillance leader replied, "Alpha One, Bravo One our starlight scopes are picking up thermal cameras running down the length of the perimeter walls. There's no way we're getting near those walls while those thermal cameras are active, especially if they're running them in conjunction with perimeter detection software. Over." A member of Bravo Team focussed the starlight scope onto one of the thermal perimeter cameras.

In the green starlight scope view of the surveillance team, the IR thermal camera was a bright green spot of light on top of the perimeter wall. "Copy that," Nick replied. "Hold your position and observe for now, we're going to sort the cameras out. Alpha One out." Just as Nick was about to gesture to Detective Joint to join him in a small office at the rear of the control room for a quick conversation, the one operator looking into the title deeds of the property shouted out, "Guys I think we've found something else here."

Rushing back over to his workstation Nick asked, "What you got?" Pointing to a document on his computer terminal the operator replied, "the property over the road from the target address is owned through a number of companies and trusts." "And!?" William asked impatiently. "It looks like it all leads back to Alexander Kaminsky as well," the operator replied. "Well, I never," William exclaimed in surprise. Turning to the radio operator, William snapped out, "Inform Bravo Team of potential hostiles from townhouses on the left of the road."

Gesturing for Detective Joint to follow him, Nick headed for a small office at the rear of the control room. When the door was closed Nick said, "Detective, this is getting serious, Russian SVR in cahoots with Russian gangsters running intelligence operations and murdering people; my staff, in cold blood right under the noses of South African authorities who haven't got a fucking clue. I plan to confirm that Nicky is on that property and if she is, extract her out alive and then hand the Prototype over to the Americans. I don't need to have to start answering questions about Russian intelligence and mobsters. Do you know someone who could help us in that department?" Grinning slyly Detective Joint replied, "I definitely know someone who can help us." "Great," Nick replied. "I suggest you set it up," and turning around opened the door.

"Come on," Nick said walking back out into the control room to where Glen and Jimmy were waiting patiently for him, "let's go and see how good the Mark II Prototype really is and sort out those thermal cameras," and headed out the Operations Centre for the VR suite next door on the B2 level. William would remain in the Control Room to direct the operation, along with Steven who would oversee the VR servers.

Detective Joint stayed with William and pulled out his smartphone dialling a stored number. The call was answered by a sleepy male voice, saying "Hello, can I help you?" "Is that Captain Kruger, Captain Hans Kruger?" Detective Joint asked hastily. "Yes, speaking. Joint is that you?" Captain Kruger asked a bit more awake, at that instance recognising the voice. "Yes, I need your help," he heard the detective say.

"Joint, you've got a lot of nerve phoning me. Your meddling in my investigation caused the death of my agent!" Captain Kruger snarled now coming wide awake. "That is a load of bullshit," Detective Joint retorted. "Your agent died due to sloppy fieldcraft, she got picked up on cameras by her murderer. Anyway, who the fuck goes to a meet at the local Mugg&Bean where there's a multitude of cameras!" he asked starting to get frustrated, adding "and your HR records also got hacked!"

There was a moment of silence on the line before Captain Kruger snapped back angrily "How did you know about our meeting?" Clearing his throat Detective Joint replied, "Let's just say that my associates observed the meet, however I have evidence on record about how the killer found out about your agent and it had absolutely nothing to do with me."

There was another deadening silence, then, "Okay, so you say that you know who killed my agent, so why the fuck did you phone me, to gloat?" Captain Kruger asked still angry. Taking a deep breath Detective Joint replied calmly, "To answer you, yes, I know who killed your agent, she is not the only victim that he killed, and to answer your second question as to why I phoned you it's because you're about the only one who I can trust right now. You saved my life and shot Captain Williamson. If you were part of the gang or connected in any way to what is going down you would have let the captain finish me off and then concocted some bullshit story to support my killing."

There was another couple of seconds of heavy silence before the NIA Captain replied in an exasperated voice, "With all due respect Joint, what the hell are you talking about?" Quickly Detective Joint filled the Captain in. "My god," blurted out a stunned Captain Kruger a couple of minutes later. "Crooked cops as well as a Russian spy ring operating right under our noses!" "Correct," Detective Joint replied. "And you're one hundred percent sure about this? "Yes," Detective Joint confirmed. Captain Kruger remembered a secret memo that had crossed his desk a while ago about the possibility of a Russian spy ring operating in the Western Cape. No sooner had they started the investigation when it had been shut down by someone high upstairs citing, "There is no Russian spy ring, they are our friends. Stop wasting valuable resources on chasing after rumours."

There was another couple of seconds of silence as the captain thought about what Detective Joint had just explained to him and then asked, "So tell me how Sable and her outfit fits into this Russian spy ring?" "She doesn't," Detective Joint immediately replied. "She was the product of unintended circumstances, in the wrong place at the wrong time." After listening to the detective explain for a short while longer Captain Hans Kruger asked, starting to warm to the detective, "Okay, Detective, what do you need from me?" After all, he thought to himself, 'The detective is bringing me career catapulting intelligence; to bust a Russian spy ring, right here in the Western Cape! My investigation into Sable and her illicit business empire pales in comparison!'

"I need you and your team standing by and ready to take over and take the credit for the bust once we secure a hostage," Detective Joint explained. With the wheels of his mind spinning into top gear Captain Kruger asked "You're referring to the execution-style killing of earlier this afternoon that the SAP are claiming was gang-related. I believe they also stated that there was no one other victim involved. "Correct," Joint replied hurriedly. "Detective, where do I meet up with you?" Kruger asked excitedly, now fully awake.

CHAPTER 18

CAPE TOWN, EXECUTIVE DECISIONS, VIRTUAL RE-ALITY SUITE, 03H05, MONDAY

"We've tweaked the Mark II prototype a bit more," Steven explained to them, following them into the VR Suite. Sitting down in their executive leather VR seats, Steven carried on explaining to the three of them, "We've added equipment and weapon inventory options which I've based on your previous personal choices and uploaded to your nanocomputers." "Great," Jimmy replied rubbing his hands together, eager to get going.

After talking for another couple of minutes, Steven said to them, "Good luck, we'll monitor your progress from our central VR Server which I've patched through to the Operations Centre. Arthur is standing by on the platform waiting for you. We'll be your link between Bravo Team and yourselves. Please, bring Nicky back alive." At the last sentence, Steven had tears starting to well in his eyes.

Curtly nodding his head Nick slipped the VR glasses over his eyes and tapped the stainless-steel bracelet on his left wrist. Feeling the usual couple of seconds of auditory and sensory blackness he entered the World of Virtual Reality and landed on the special platform Steven had created for them for this cyber operation.

Landing on the platform Nick found Arthur the AI along with Glen and Jimmy waiting. Both Glen and Jimmy were encased in the same white sheath like body armour as he was, with Arthur now taking on the appearance of Rambo, dressed to kill. "Major!" Arthur cried out in delight at seeing Nick again. Once he had found out that Nick had been a Major in the Royal Marines, he too had decided to revert to Nick's former title out of respect.

Nodding curtly towards his small cyber team he glanced up into the top left-hand corner of his view and activated the drop-down menu.

MENU OPTION

– NORMAL MODE - SHEATH ONLY

– MAINTENANCE CLOAKED

– MAINTENANCE UNCLOAKED

– CAMERA SETUP CLOAKED

– CAMERA SETUP UNCLOAKED

– COMMS LINK

– TARGET ACQUISION & TRACK

At the bottom of the list Nick found the added features.

– EQUIPMENT

– WEAPONRY

Setting up the Comms Link with his small team Nick said "Okay guys, set up Maintenance Mode Cloaked + Target Track and follow Arthur. Arthur, you've got the lead." "Confirmed, Major," Arthur the AI replied and immediately called a tube. As soon as the tube arrived silently a couple of seconds later and they had boarded, Arthur explained to them over the comms circuit, "We'll exit at an old platform I found a little earlier in the vicinity of where we need to be". Once the destination of the target vehicle had been established, Arthur had done some forward reconnaissance work in preparation for the cyber-attack.

After a short uneventful ride on the tube, they exited onto a very old, unkept, and empty platform. "Perfect," Nick commented when he saw the platform. There was no one around to report a tube arriving with no one getting off and neither anyone getting on. "This was one of the first Virtual servers that were put on-line in Hermanus mainly for the whale watching festival," Arthur explained to them over the comms circuit and then said almost apologetically. "It was unfortunately before programmers thought to put in escalators. This platform still has stairs." With the advent of newer and faster servers, upgraded servers had been added to the VR network, but the original server had been left in place. The tube disappeared the minute the four of them stepped out of the open tube door and onto the abandoned platform.

Taking the crumbling concrete stairs two steps at a time the four of them stepped off the top step and exited onto the electronic sidewalk. At this early bewitching hour of the morning there was not much electronic traffic around, a couple of late-night surfers and voyeurs here and there. There wasn't much to do in Hermanus anyway apart from watching whales jumping out of the water and fornicating.

Turning left, Arthur started to jog, an even-paced jog down the darkened electronic street, the moon offering solace in its illumination. Nick fell in beside him with Glen and Jimmy bringing up the rear in a closed box formation as they headed off down the street. "Wow," Jimmy exclaimed after jogging a short while, "I could jog all day in this kit, the sheath makes exercise effortless!" "Keep it down, Jimmy, less electronic chatter, just in case," Steven said, scolding Jimmy from the Control Room.

Jogging in silence for another couple of minutes, the distant horizon began to get lighter. As they got closer, they all saw that the light was coming from a small intense network surrounded by large patches of darkness. "That's our target Major," Arthur informed Nick pointing towards the network. "That's not your average mansion home network with user-defined addons," Glen quipped looking closely at the pulsing array of lights that depicted a range of file servers, along with a broad band of light entering the property depicting at least a gigabit internet connection. "No, it's not, Master Glen," Arthur replied. "They seem to be running a server farm from the location. I haven't proceeded further than where we are now." Activating his comms module Nick asked, "Steven are you getting all this?" "Confirmed," Steven replied.

HERMANUS, VR WORLD, RUSSIAN SAFE HOUSE, 03H10, MONDAY

"Okay, you two stay here and watch our backs, Arthur and I will go and investigate. Let me know if anything out here changes," Nick instructed Glen and Jimmy, speaking softly over the comms link. They had slowly edged their way forward, closer towards the access point giving access into the network. "My god, will you look at those Gate Keepers," Nick muttered over the comms circuit. The Gate Keepers were bears. Big, vicious-looking brown bears sporting the old Soviet Union hammer and sickle on their hairy brown chests, marching around on four legs.

Every once in a while hackers approached the entrance to the network, the bears nearest the potential threat stopping and turning their massive heads with big black snouts towards the intruder, sniffing the air curiously, their nostrils opening and dilating like large diaphragms as they sampled the electronic air. Then, without warning they would emit a soul quivering roar, their large mouths opening wide showing their razor sharp ivory white teeth and they would bound towards the now identified target, rearing up on their hind legs and attacking the threat, savagely ripping it to pieces with their razor-sharp ivory teeth and just as sharp claws.

"Relax," Steven said overhearing him. "Remember, they can't see you." "Yeah, you should look at their teeth," Nick muttered back as Arthur and himself carefully walked along the access route into the network, passing right by the vicious-looking bear Gate Keepers. 'Bloody hell, they even smell like bears,' Nick thought silently to himself as he walked past them as quickly as possible, his soldier's instincts telling him to hide, that it was wrong to just brazenly walk right past the enemy.

They passed the roaming vicious looking Russian brown bears without incident, unlike the other unfortunate hackers who tried to get access to the network. Passing the bears, the landscape changed. Now they were standing on a desolate moor, illuminated brightly in the moonlight that seemed to go on forever, the undulating landscape never changing; scrub grass and small knots of trees tangled together. "Glen, Jimmy, bring up the rear," Nick instructed over the comms circuit and they waited until the pair had caught up. "Vicious looking motherfuckers," Jimmy muttered softly under his breath, referring to the brown bears they had to pass.

Trudging across the desolate moors with Arthur in the lead, Arthur stopped abruptly and held up his hand saying softly, "Next obstacle to pass," pointing to the patch of ground ahead. The patch of ground in front of them was no different from the surrounding landscape apart from a rusted chain-link fence in front of them. It was the sign on the fence that got Nick's attention, "Danger Minefield," the sign said communicating the danger in both English and Russian.

"Oh, dear Major, that's a minefield, there's no way around it. What are we going to do? There's no way for me to determine if the pressure from our feet will set off the mines. This was something that Mark and me never thought of," Arthur cried out in a state of panic. "Relax," Nick replied grimly, activating the communication circuit to Steven back in the control room. "Find the specs for the Handheld Standoff Mine Detection System, otherwise referred to as the HSTAMIDS by the US military and upload them to my nanocomputer," Nick hastily instructed Steven as they squatted down behind a large termite hill, keeping in the mind the roving bearlike Gate Keepers a short distance behind them.

A couple of tense minutes later, Steven had found the specifications for what the US Military refers to as the Handheld Standoff Mine Detection System (HSTAMIDS), and a couple of seconds later the information was uploaded to his nanocomputer. A second after the information was uploaded, the unit materialised in Nick's hands. Slipping the control unit pack onto his back and placing the headphones over his ears, Nick picked up the lightweight metal detector.

The unit itself consisted of a round base slightly larger than a dinner plate and approximately 150mm thick with a chunky electronics module on top of the dinner plate connected to a fibreglass shaft with a set of handholds halfway up the shaft. The dinner plate section held the magnetometer and the top section the GPR, Ground Penetrating Radar. A battery pack and accompanying electronics pack were situated at the rear of the shaft. The Handheld Standoff Mine Detection System (HSTAMIDS) was a state of the are mine detector in that it incorporated both improved metal detection as well as GPR, ground-penetrating radar to pick up and detect both anti-tank and anti-personnel mines.

"Right then, let's go," Nick said as casually as possible switching on the unit and standing up. "Is it going to work?" Arthur asked him sceptically. "I really hope so. The manufacturers boast that it can detect up to 5,610 different types of mines," Nick explained calmly to Arthur. Carrying on he said to Arthur, "Just follow in my footsteps and do exactly what I do, and you'll be fine." Turning to Glen and Jimmy he said, "follow Arthur but check our six"

Slipping carefully between the wires in the fence, Nick started to scan the ground directly in front of him, sweeping the disc of the metal detector slowly from left to right in front of him, waiting for the high-pitched shriek in his ears that will indicate a mine has been detected. Nothing, the unit stayed silent, and Nick slowly eased his way forward half a pace and repeated the same manoeuvre. Nothing. He slowly moved forward again. It was on the fourth sweep of the mine detector over the unbroken ground that the headphones emitted a high pitch shriek in the earphones indicating that a mine had been detected.

Glancing down at the 7,"LCD Display of the Ground Penetrating Radar mounted on the centre grab hold of the shaft, Nick was able to make out the mine clearly laying in the soil. In the picture, the mine was depicted in lighter shades of greys and white, with the soil around the mine depicted in darker shades of greys and black. Sidestepping the buried mine, he carried on, Arthur following carefully behind with Glen and Jimmy bringing up the rear. Another feature of the mine detector was that it mapped and stored the locations of all the objects which it found.

Again, the high pitch shriek emitted from the unit and Nick glanced towards the 7," LCD of the GPR. The screen was empty. "What the hell," he muttered, and then took a closer look at the display. "Fuck it, a tripwire," he said softly to himself as he distinguished the faint white straight line of the thin steel wire laying taught in the grass in the radar picture, as one of the first lessons of reconnaissance came back to him, "Nothing in nature is plumb straight. If something is straight then it's human, not natural, beware." The tripwire was connected to a line of fragmentation mines that jumped up into the air and exploded once the tripwire was tripped by an unsuspecting victim.

A tense ten minutes later they were through; without mishaps and on the other side of the minefield. "My god, will you look at that," Nick muttered to himself as they left the minefield behind them and crested a small rise. "Is that what I think it is?" he muttered further. Standing on the next hilltop about 2 miles away was a castle illuminated brightly in the moonlight.

HERMANUS, STOREROOM, MONDAY, 03H00

"Uurgghh," Nicky groaned softly as she came around and regained consciousness, fighting off the last tendrils of the drugs which had earlier been pumped into her body. 'Fuck it,' she thought to herself when she realized that she was still strapped to the stretcher which they had put her on earlier before knocking her out. Opening her eyes, it was dark, and she started to struggle. Without warning the light switched on, being triggered by a sensor activated by her movement.

Quickly looking around her from her horizontal position on the floor she took in her surroundings, realising that she was in some sort of storeroom. "I'm very close to the ocean, that's the sound of the ocean," she said to herself becoming aware of the background booming sound of breakers breaking on a shoreline, along with the accompanying heavy ocean smell in the air. Gazing up at the ceiling she noticed a minidome camera installed in a corner, looking down into the storeroom. Studying the camera carefully for a few minutes while the light was on, she realized what she was looking at. 'A standard entry level HikVision IP Camera with no IR capabilities. Sloppy boys, really sloppy,' she started to think excitedly. The camera was missing the tell-tale ring of LEDs around the lens that gave it its IR capability of being able to see in the dark. Keeping still the storeroom light soon switched off, plunging the storeroom back into darkness again. 'Right,' she though silently, 'when it's dark you can't see me.'

In the darkness, she slowly started to work out how she was secured to the stretcher and how much movement her abductors had left her. 'Hey,' she realized in her mind, 'my hands are pretty loose in these steel bangles and they haven't secured my feet.' Quickly she started to flex her muscles, fingers, feet, and toes. 'All appendages seem to be intact, let's see about getting out of here,' she thought hurriedly, worried that at any minute her abductors might return. Lying on the stretcher she was suspended just off the floor and with her fingers she was able to touch the cold tiled floor beneath her.

Scrabbling around with her fingertips, she began searching around on the tiled floor feeling what was around her. 'Ah hah what's this?' she thought again excitedly to herself a couple of seconds later as her fingertips grazed past something sharp. Carefully walking her fingertips back, she found the sharp object. Gripping it she immediately realized what it was, a piece of round stiff electric wire. 'Must be an offcut from a copper earth wire,' she thought, 'just what I'm looking for.' Unbeknown to Nicky, a week ago the caretaker had had some electrical work done in the basement by a local contractor, whose staff weren't that motivated in cleaning up behind themselves.

'Right now, let's get ourselves free,' she said silently to herself as she began carefully working with the piece of wire gripped firmly between her fingertips at the right-hand handcuff that was securing her right arm to the stretcher. What wasn't listed in the summary that Colonel Petroski had gathered on Nicky was that she not only held a Doctorate in Computer Programming, but she was also an avid martial arts expert. Over and above that, even though she was as feminine as female could be, she was also a tomboy at heart and enjoyed to participate in wargames along with evade and capture courses that Nick ran for certain of his clients and their employees, her reasoning being, 'You never knew when the knowledge would come in useful. It's a jungle out there.'

Working quickly and efficiently keeping the rest of her body still so that the sensor did not pick up any movement and kept the light switched off, she worked the piece of offcut copper wire into the lock on the one side of her handcuffs and a couple of seconds later had expertly slipped the barrels of the lock releasing the one handcuff from the stretcher, the other end still attached to her wrist. Slowly, ever so slowly she brought her released hand up over her body and worked as quickly as possible on the left-hand stainless-steel bracelet. Taking a couple of seconds longer her left hand was also free.

Again, working carefully with her hands, she quickly secured the dangling free ends of the handcuffs around her wrists giving herself some additional chunky jewellery for a while. 'No time to remove them now, I need to get out of here first,' she thought ruefully to herself. Just then there was the noise of an outer door opening and voices speaking Russian, a language that she understood and could hold a conversation in.

CHAPTER 19

HERMANUS, VR WORLD, RUSSIAN SAFE HOUSE, 03H00, MONDAY

"Gentleman, that's where we need to be," Arthur explained to them pointing to the castle illuminated by the moonlight on the near distant horizon of the desolate moor. The dark castle stood tall on top of the hill, looking down over the desolate undulating moors, with a 360-degree birds eye view of the surrounding depressing landscape. "You've got to be kidding me!' Glen exclaimed. "A bloody castle!" "If my history serves me right that is a medieval castle from around the 11th or 12th century," Nick commented, adding to the conversation. "I do believe that you are correct Major," Arthur told him.

"But it looks deserted," Jimmy mentioned, zooming in with the optical zoom function of the Prototype Mark II. "Yes, that's what they want you to think," Arthur told him grimly. Carrying on Arthur explained "the exterior looks like a castle and has the defences of a castle with defensive improvements here and there, but I bet you inside there are state of the art server rooms."

Jimmy laughed softly replying, "Come on, you're not telling me that they've built an 11th-century virtual castle to protect their state-of-the-art servers and information?" "Why not?" Arthur retorted offended. "To keep information safe a castle is about the most secure location you could have." He then added, "If it's been designed correctly." "Arthur's right," Steven said monitoring the conversation. "Only one way in and one way out, what better way to protect your data. I bet they've got some decent anti-virus software running in that castle scenario. You guys better stay sharp." "Ok guys less talk, remember we've got to find Nicky asap," Nick reminded them picking up the pace towards the darkened castle.

Hurrying across the desolate moonlit wind-swept moors the dark and foreboding castle loomed larger and larger in the moonlight as they closed in. As they got closer to the castle, they could see figures patrolling on the walls. "My, my," Arthur muttered softly. "An outer and an inner wall." Turning to face the small team, Arthur stopped, gesturing them to squat down and said softly, "It looks like they've got a double security system running, which means we've got two sets of security checkpoints as well as at least one barbican to get through." "What the hell are you talking about," Glen asked curiously looking at Arthur as if he was crazy. "Yes," Jimmy added. "What the hell is a barbican?"

Quickly Arthur, the AI, explained, "In the old days, castle designers had a problem, they needed to protect the castle from invaders, but they also needed to have a way to bring people and goods into the castle, hence they built a gatehouse into the castle wall, along with what's called a barbican. Whereas the gatehouse protects the entrance to the castle, the barbican is a narrow-enclosed passageway that has been designed as a deadly obstacle course through which attackers would have to pass through to reach the gatehouse. From hidden slits and holes in the walls of the barbican, the defenders could shoot arrows, thrust swords or pour boiling oil onto the attackers." 'Wonderful," Glen replied drily. "How sure are we that these prototypes are going to work, and we don't have the opportunity of feeling what it's like to be skewered?" "They've worked so far; we'll just have to careful," Nick replied as casually as possible.

Silently they crept closer to the castle, not wanting to take any chances, the large stone-grey walls now towering high above them, the entrance to the barbican coming into view. Squatting down behind an outcrop of rocks about 100 yards away from the castle they surveyed the entrance. "That's the entrance to the barbican over there," Arthur said softly pointing towards what looked like no more than a narrow slit in the grey stone wall. "Through

337

the barbican is the outer gatehouse, and then we'll have another barbican and the inner gatehouse to get through before we can access the castle proper," Arthur explained to them.

"Where are the data-links which we saw entering the network? How do they enter?" Glen then asked intrigued as there was no sight of the large pulsing internet connection entering the stone structure. "They've hidden it, but I reckon it will surface in the outer guardhouse," Arthur explained quickly to him. "Well then, what are we waiting for? Let's get a move on, we've got to find Nicky," Steven rasped impatiently over the communications link.

Slowly, with Arthur in the lead, they approached the narrow entrance in the wall. The slit was only wide enough for one person at a time to enter. As Arthur's back disappeared through the slit into the barbican Nick followed closely behind him with Glen and Jimmy bringing up the rear. The passage was dark and narrow; as Arthur had predicted, and had a smell that Nick couldn't just yet place. Switching on his IR vision Nick picked up the narrow slits in the walls on both sides of the extremely narrow passageway through which swords were thrust and arrows shot. Glen summed it up when he said softly over the comms link, "You'd need nine lives, inside help or just be fucking stupid to want to pass through this obstacle course in the real world," as he followed bringing up the rear.

Out of the corner of his right eye in his IR view, Nick saw movement through one of the slits in the wall. "Heads up, gentlemen, movement behind the wall, three o'clock," he snapped softly over the comms circuit. "Got movement in the left wall as well," Jimmy informed them a second later seeing movement through one of the slits in the corresponding left-hand wall. Tensing up, expecting any second to have the unrelenting steel of sharp swords thrust at them through the hidden wall slits, or have boiling oil poured on top of them from the small holes above their heads, they all breathed a sigh of relief as they walked up a slight incline in the narrow passageway that without warning turned ninety degrees and a metre or so later opened up into a small courtyard.

There were several slits in the darkened stone wall of the ninety-degree turn and the smell that Nick couldn't place was far stronger. Glancing at the stone walls and cobbled floor in the IR view he realised immediately what the smell was, 'centuries worth of old dried rotting blood and small pieces of flesh stuck in the cracks of the walls and the floor.' Then they were out and standing in the outer courtyard. It was closed in on both sides but open above to the elements, with the outer wall of the castle rising up steeply above their heads from which archers could shoot bolts of arrows down into the attacking armies attempting to gain access to the castle. The front of the courtyard was also open and funnelled them under the large wooden portcullis, which was presently up and into the outer gatehouse.

The outer gatehouse was brightly lit in comparison, illuminated by the network link as it surged up through the cobbled stone floor of the outer guardhouse and headed into the castle like a large pulsing golden snake. The outer guardhouse was large in comparison to the narrow passageway that fed into it and was teeming with Gate Keepers all taking on the form of big brown bears. Over the smell of the bears was another smell, a smoky smell of the guardsman's fires dating back 800 years.

Still leading the way, Arthur sidestepped past a massive brown bear whose large black wet nostrils flared, starting to open and close intently sniffing the air around it as if sensing their presence. Nick, Glen, and Jimmy followed Arthur's lead and sidestepped behind the pondering bear one at a time and headed in the direction that Arthur had disappeared. The bear turned around and standing up on its hind legs sniffed the air in their direction, not seeing anything but sensing the tiniest of change in the electronic universe around him. Then the four of them were through the outer gatehouse and standing in the outer courtyard of the castle. The bear stood up on its hind legs sniffing the air around it intently.

Swiftly crossing the open courtyard, they headed directly towards the next barbican, this one protecting the inner guardhouse. Meeting no opposition, they were soon standing in the inner courtyard, the stone-grey walls of the inner castle rising vertically around them. "That was strange, no opposition in the second barbican," Arthur said. "Something's not right." "Where now?" Nick asked, not listening to him, intent on finding Nicky. "Uh, the keep is where I would keep the heart of my security system, it's up there," Arthur said pointing to a tall round stone tower rising up out of the centre of the stone building in front of them. Carrying on he said, "I need to look at something, I'll meet you back here." Turning around Arthur disappeared through a side door set into the stone wall.

"Glen, Jimmy, on me let's go," Nick snapped pointing towards the tower Arthur referred to as the Keep. Opening an external door, they found themselves at the foot of a steep winding stone staircase that followed the round contour of the tower up into the heady heights of the stone tower above. "Oh boy, here comes the stair master routine," Glen mumbled softly to himself as he followed Nick taking two steps at a time up the round stone staircase.

After what seemed like a lifetime of running round in ever heightening circles they burst onto a small landing. The keep was where the king or master of the castle and his family had their chambers; being the brightest and safest part of the castle. There was a door equipped with a biometric type access control reader just off the landing. "Well, let's see if this Prototype really works," Nick said softly to his two teammates as he passed his hand encased in the white sheaf over the scanner. There was a loud click and the door released.

The space before them was a brightly lit completely white computer room. Everything was painted white. Even the large 48u equipment racks were white. All the file servers, switches, and

340

routers sitting in the equipment racks were white. Cold air was pumped up from the floor cavity through white floor tiles with white angled grills. White tiles covered the ceiling with white strip lighting. There was row upon row upon row of equipment racks, all of the same colour. At the far end of the server room was another door. Quickly removing a patch lead from his equipment pack, Nick plugged himself into a free port on one of the switches in the nearest equipment rack, the computer screen being superimposed over his view. Swiftly he started to scan through the network.

Finding the correct file server, Nick changed the setting on his Prototype Mark II to CAMERA SETUP CLOAKED and accessed the CCTV network. Stepping into the camera system, he was confronted by at least sixty square camera blocks. "Bloody hell, they have a couple of cameras here. Where are the basement cameras, we'll start there," he muttered to himself as he looked for the basement cameras thinking of a place to start searching for Nicky.

Finding the bank of cameras that he was looking for, he started going through them when a blacked-out camera view came to life, the light being switched on in the room and there was Nicky, lying on the floor, strapped to a stretcher. "Bastards!" Nick snarled, activating his comms link, "Okay, William, I've found her, she's in some kind of storeroom strapped to a stretcher," Nick told William excitedly over the comms link. "Tell Bravo team to stand by, I'm going to start disabling the cameras." "Uh, Boss, you better hurry up, there are a couple of very pissed off looking bears heading towards us. Somehow, they've found us," Glen reported urgently over the comms link. "Stall them, I need a bit of time," Nick replied hurriedly to Glen and Jimmy as he started to insert camera loops for all the relevant cameras, the real camera views being hidden. "Our pleasure," both Glen and Jimmy replied splitting up heading to either side of the corridor created by the white coloured equipment racks.

Hearing the noise of an outer door opening and the accompanying Russian voices Nicky took a deep breath and thought silently to herself, 'Here we go, all my training comes down to the next couple of seconds.' Slowly letting out the deep breath she relaxed her body and cleared her mind, concentrating on just what she was going to accomplish in the next couple of seconds. Closing her eyes as the light seeped in from under the inner door she waited, ready to pounce. 'Ah, the bitch called Sashenka' Nicky thought to herself recognising the voice of her female abductor and so-called client, and gave herself a small inward smile, hoping like hell that only Sashenka entered the room. Otherwise, the odds were stacked against her and it could get very interesting.

The inner door swung open and the blackness behind her eyelids lightened slightly as the storeroom light automatically switched on, sensing movement in the room. "Sleeping beauty, how innocently you sleep. I had you all fooled you, stupid peasants! Ha ha ha ha!" Sashenka said mockingly in Russian as she closed the door behind her and walking over to the stretcher knelt down beside it, ostensibly to check the prisoner's pulse and condition. Sensing the closeness of her abductor, Nicky struck like a cobra.

Opening her eyes while at the same time moving her now released arms up and wrapping them around the back of Sashenka's head, entangling them tightly within her long blonde trestles, she pulled her abductors head violently towards her while at the same time sitting up, her forehead smashing Sashenka violently on the bridge of her nose. There was a loud crack as Sashenka's nose broke, and a red stream of blood gushed out of her broken appendage. "Uurgghh," she gurgled in surprise as all she saw were large bright spinning stars and the deep colour of red. Keeping her fingers tightly entwined in her abductor's long blonde hair Nicky pulled and twisted her catch down towards the tiled floor, while at the same time lifting her body up and over on top of her abductor. A second later after a feeble struggle from a completely disorientated and injured abductor, the side of her abductor's head smashed just as violently against the cold tiled floor, knocking her out cold. "Take that, bitch," Nicky hissed into her now unconscious victim's ear. Quickly searching the unconscious Sashenka, she found a smartphone and pistol which she took, first professionally checking the weapon over, 'round in the chamber, safety on and not cocked' she said to herself. Ejecting the magazine, she made sure that the rounds were real and not dummy rounds.

All this took Nicky twenty seconds from the moment she first struck. Springing to her feet, she rushed to the closed inner door and carefully opening it peered out, hoping like hell that no one was watching the CCTV views, but then thought savagely to herself, 'What the hell if they are? They killed Pete in cold blood, abducted me, and are trying to interrogate me. Fuck them, they deserve everything that's coming their way.' The young lieutenant was standing with his back to her setting up the interrogation server on the wooden workbench, unaware of what had just occurred in the inner room.

Hearing the door open behind him he asked, "Is the prisoner ready for us to start playing around in her mind?" and started to laugh at his own joke. The next instant he felt a blinding flash of white pain and then total blackness as the butt of the pistol connected with the side of his temple, knocking him out cold. "And how does that feel when I play around with your mind arsehole?" Nicky asked him softly as he collapsed to the floor unconscious, striking his head against the marble countertop as he fell.

Heading for the outer door leading out into the basement, she crouched down and peered around it into the basement taking in the expansive brightly lit area with the two gleaming red Ferraris crouched in their demarcated parking bays directly to her left about 25 metres away and then the large steel gate another 50m away. There was an ambulance and another couple of vehicles parked just past the large steel sliding gate with a couple of closed wooden doors set into the concrete walls leading out of the basement. Each door had a biometric access control scanner mounted on the wall adjacent to it, the red flashing scanner lights of the biometric scanners, looking a lot like winking evil eyes.

Breathing a sigh of relief at the sight of an empty basement she thought 'Great, no alarm raised yet.' Then, taking a closer look at the Ferraris, she thought even more excitedly to herself, a plan starting to form in her mind. 'I hope one of those Italian jobs has their keys and a gate release in them, cause that's how I'm getting out of here.' Taking one final look around making sure that the basement was indeed empty, she scurried doubled over towards the two parked Ferraris.

'Nice a F8 Tributo,' she thought to herself reaching the closet sports car, silently thanking her ex-boyfriend; a trust fund kid who had a Ferrari and had taken great pleasure and time in explaining the art and passion of Ferrari to her. Reaching the driver's door, she peered inside. "Thank you, oh yes thank you," she muttered to herself as she spotted the familiar red and black electronic key fob of the Ferrari nestling in its holder along with what looked like the gate remote. The Ferrari F8 Tributo featured a keyless ignition, all that was required was the wireless red and black electronic key fob.

"Perfect," she muttered to herself about to open the door and slip behind the wheel. Then realised, 'I have no idea where I am, I better first call for help,' and pulled out the recently liberated smartphone she had removed from Sashenka. 'Fuck it, it needs a fingerprint,' her mind screamed out silently as the cellphone screen remained locked. "Okay, we can do this," she muttered to herself as she quickly headed back to the storerooms. Entering the inner storeroom she saw that Sashenka was moaning starting to come around so, Nicky savagely whipped the butt of the pistol around her temple knocking her senseless again. It took a couple of seconds for her to find the correct finger on Sashenka's hand, then she had access to the phone.

Swiftly removing the fingerprint access from the cellphone, Nicky dialled the Executive Decisions Operations Centre. "Track this cellphone call and tell me where I am, these are the people who killed Pete and abducted me," she snapped as the call was answered. "Wait, wait, Nicky, is that you?" the operator asked her in a surprised tone recognising the voice and then quickly telling her, "Standby. I'm putting you through to William."

"Nicky are you okay? This is a stroke of luck," William exclaimed also with surprise when the call was put through to him in the Operations Centre, "we have just gained access into the CCTV system and Bravo Team is standing by about two hundred metres away from your location to extract you. Nick was in the process of disabling the cameras when you sorted out the first two abductors, do you have a plan?" "Yes," Nicky replied crouching down by the outer door again and peering around the corner of the door eyeing out the two Ferraris. "Can you get Nick to lock all the basement access readers down except the basement gate to give me time to get out of here? Nicky asked excitedly knowing that her people were outside waiting for her. "Tell them to look out for me, I'll be leaving in a hurry," she added. Then asked, "Where the hell am I?" William quickly explained, ending the conversation saying, "When you hit the top of the ramp turn hard right."

HERMANUS, RUSSIAN SAFE HOUSE, BASEMENT, 03H06, MONDAY

One of the wooden doors at the far end of the basement opened wide and two of her male captors stepped out into the basement and stopped. As Nicky crouched down low at the side of the one Ferrari Tributo peering up through the driver's side window and through the cabin at them, she watched as the one pulled out a packet of cigarettes and offered his accomplice a smoke before taking one himself and placing it between his lip. Returning the cigarette box to his jacket pocket he then pulled out a box of matches and first lighting his comrade's cigarette he then lit his, pulling the smoke deep into his lungs, flicking the dying match onto the spotless shiny powder floated concrete floor as he did so.

Turning to his comrade and slapping him on the back, laughing at some comment that he made, they both started walking deeper into the basement, closer towards the two shiny red high performance Italian beasts and Nicky. "Shit, I'm going to have to get back to you, just get Nick to lock down all the access doors into the basement, and open the basement gate when I start to move," Nicky whispered over the phone and ended the call.

Scurrying quickly to the rear of the Ferrari and the grey concrete reinforced wall of the basement parking she pulled out the recently liberated pistol with her right hand, cupping the butt of the pistol in her left. With the thumb of her left hand, she pulled back the hammer in one fluid motion. One click, two clicks, the hammer was fully cocked, while her thumb slipped the safety catch off and her right index finger curled itself around the trigger.

"Yes," she overheard the one male speaking excitedly in Russian to his comrade while smoking his cigarette. "If you had one of these Ferraris in Moscow you could pick up and fuck a different girl every night of the week," he said coming to a stop in front of the two-crouching shining red Ferraris. "Fuck that, I'd screw a handful at a time!" the other comrade said boasting out loudly starting to walk around the side to admire the rear of the vehicles.

Realising that they would notice her and there was no way she was leaving unseen, Nicky decided their fate for them. Taking a deep breath with the liberated pistol stretched out and held double handed in front of her, she jumped up from behind the one Ferrari Tributo saying in Russian "Sorry boys, I don't know about Russian girls but most European girls wouldn't fuck the likes of you two even if you paid us." "What the…" the one captor who was close to her shouted out in Russian and tried to run at her.

She remembered what Nick had taught her, calm steady breathing and aim for the centre of the body mass. The two-gun shots, a double-tap was so close together that they sounded like one gunshot and were extra loud in the enclosed basement area, reverberating loudly throughout the enclosed space, savagely violating her eardrums. The 9mm police issue parabellum's recoil was harsh in her firm steady grip. Her captor stopped just short of the rear of the shiny red Ferrari and with a surprised look crossing his face, his dark coloured shirt taking on an even darker colour slurred in Russian, "Bitch, you shot…," as he slumped down dead onto the shiny powder floated concrete floor, his blood starting to stain the spotless concrete surface.

In the instance that his comrade made his move and died trying, the second captor further away at the front of the Ferrari Tributo saw his opportunity and reached for his pistol currently holstered in a shoulder holster under his left armpit. Pulling out his pistol in a panic, not having expected their prisoner to jump up from behind the sports car let alone be armed, he managed to cock his firearm and started to bring the weapon to bear on the prisoner while at the same time he began moving to his left towards the shelter of a concrete support column when there was another set of loud deafening explosions.

A nanosecond later it felt as if a truck had run over his chest as there was this feeling of immense pressure on his ribcage as he staggered backwards, his knees starting to feel very weak and buckling under him unable to support his weight. He crumpled to the ground his open eyes starting to glass over. "Now you won't be fucking anything ever again asshole," Nicky muttered as she rushed around to the driver's side of the Ferrari and opened the driver's door.

With her adrenaline pumping hard through her body and the sounds of the gunshots still ringing loudly in her ears, she slipped behind the multi-functional steering wheel of the Ferrari F8 Tributo, settling her frame firmly into the carbon fibre moulded racing seat and closing the door, locked it, cocooning herself inside the

Italian supercars cockpit. At the same time, she pulled the safety restraint system across her chest securing it, having no time to take in the immaculately finished carbon fibre and leather infused dashboard or the rosso stitching used to stitch all the leather together in the seats, dashboard and side panels.

Placing the 9mm automatic on the passenger seat next to her she pushed the round red button on the bottom of the multi-functional steering wheel once that said START STOP. 'One push electronics on, second push engine start,' she thought to herself as she noted that a N was showing in the centre of the rev counter; the rev counter placed in its customary position in the centre of the instrument binnacle, indicating that the gearbox was in neutral. The two TFT screens on either side of the rev counter also came to life. Pushing the round red button again, the starter motor turned over once and then the V8 engine burbled loudly into life. Unable to help herself her right foot touched the throttle and the V8 engine let out a loud unrepentant howl, echoing throughout the basement.

Quickly checking the steering wheel Nicky mentally thought to herself, 'Electronic guardians on,' taking a quick look at what was referred to as the manettino dial. The Tributo had several electronic driving modes all controlled by a small red dial on the bottom right of the steering wheel called the manettino dial. Of the five modes from wet, sport, race, CT, EG, wet was the one with all the electronic safety features on, or also as referred to as the 'electronic guardians'. Selecting automatic mode; the Ferrari could be driven in both manual and automatic mode. Nicky used her right hand and pulled the right-hand paddle-shift once, selecting Drive. The N in the centre of the rev counter turned to D.

Turning the steering wheel hard left she released the parking brake and blipped the throttle, the engine responding immediately, the large rear 305/30R20 Pirelli tyres squealing loudly as they slipped on the powder floated concrete floor before the traction control took over propelling the supercar in the direction of the front wheels. Out of the corner of her right eye she caught sight of movement. "Fuck she's come around," Nicky said to herself referring to Sashenka as she sideswiped Sashenka with the rear of the car and straightening out shot towards the sliding gate which Nick had been able to override and started to open for her. "This is powerfuuuuul!" Nicky shouted out loudly as she reached the gate in a split second, stamping on the brakes and turning the steering wheel to the left redirected the Tributo towards the vehicle ramp and freedom.

Remembering William's brief directions, she blipped the throttle again as the undercarriage of the front of the Tributo connected with the concrete ramp with an expensive thud, and then she was propelled up the ramp and out of the basement. Automatically the LED headlights switched on, and Nicky wrenched the wheel to the right and floored the throttle. Immediately the 3.9l V8 twin turbocharged engine responded with a loud howl transferring 770Nm of torque to the rear Pirelli shod wheels. Even with all the electronic guardians on, the rear wheels slid out in a screeching rubber smoke-filled extravaganza. As she slid right, out of the corner of her eye she saw the figure of a man walking towards her raising the unmistakable outlines of a rifle to his shoulder as he did so. Correcting the skid, Nicky was able to tame the howling beast and brought the Tributo back into a straight line and applying the throttle in a more civilised manner shot off up the road.

CHAPTER 20

HERMANUS, BEACH SIDE OF RUSSIAN SAFE HOUSE,
03H08, MONDAY

"Bravo Team, Alpha Two, the cameras have been disabled, move in," William relayed the message over the encrypted comms circuit to the team on the ground, followed a couple of seconds later with "Bravo Team be advised the Package is making her own way out, she'll be coming out of the sliding gate on the roadside of the property, standby to provide back up, should she request it," this information being relayed from Nick in VR.

"Ok, let's go team, you heard Alpha Two," the leader of Bravo Team instructed his men softly over the encrypted comms circuit. The next second five shadows rose up out of the surrounding sand dunes, shrugging off the loose beach sand as they rose. Moving swiftly and stealthily they moved like darkened shadows across the sandy beach dunes towards the white perimeter wall of the darkened mansion. The next second the monotonous sound of the waves crashing onto the beach became background noise for another brief sound. Gunshots. Two loud gunshots in quick succession, a double tap reverberating through the air, shattering the tranquillity of the night.

"Alpha Two, Bravo One, shots fired, I repeat shots fired," the leader of Bravo Team immediately reported. As he was reporting the gunshots there were another two extremely loud gunshots, another double tap followed by silence. "Let's go boys on the double," Bravo One hissed out loudly to his team and started running towards the rocky patch of rocks about 100 metres away that led up to the road. Their boots sank down into the loose beach sand as they ran, pulling them back as they struggled forward.

Reaching the rocky patch their earpieces activated again. "Bravo One, Oversight," the UAV operator said, transmitting over the encrypted comms circuit, "it looks like we got movement on the property, the vehicle gate is opening." "Roger that," Bravo One replied catching his breath when the next second the loud reverberating howl of a high-performance sports car engine revving loudly shattered the regained tranquillity of the night air.

"Now that sounds expensive," Bravo Four quipped softly to his buddy Bravo Three. A couple of seconds later he added, "Correction: fucking expensive," as the sports car engine howled again followed by the squeal of rubber. "Alpha Two, Bravo One, any idea what the package has got her herself into inside that basement?" the team leader asked curiously as they approached the road, the lights of the basement starting to cut into the darkness outside. "Uh, yes, Bravo One," William replied gleefully. "It looks like a shining red Ferrari F8 Tributo."

Just as Bravo One was about to step onto the road adjacent the corner of the white perimeter wall, their encrypted radio circuit activated "Bravo One, Oversight, there's suspicious movement in the townhouses across the road. Standby," Quickly tapping his PTT twice in acknowledgement Bravo One sank down behind the large bushes that were bordering the verge of the road, half hiding the path down to the beach, followed immediately by the rest of Bravo team.

Crouched behind the bushes they clearly saw a man walk out from the town houses with an assault rifle in his hands as with a primeval growl a shiny red Ferrari came shooting up the concrete vehicle ramp, the V8 engine howling gleefully in 1st gear. The armed man started to raise the assault rifle to his shoulder aiming at the red moving target when without thinking Bravo One took aim with his silenced R5 assault rifle and shot the party crasher in his upper right shoulder. The assault rifle went spinning from his hands as he was spun around from the subsonic 5.56mm round.

Simultaneously reaching the top of the ramp and hitting the tarmac of the road, the driver turned the steering wheel hard right and goosed the throttle, the rear of the Ferrari spinning out in a power slide, the driver skilfully correcting and regaining control. The rear wheels came back into line and then with a loud howl as the driver applied gas, the Ferrari shot off up the road like a semi-guided projectile. Slowing slightly and broad sliding left onto the top feeder road the driver accelerated away, the sounds of the 3.9 litre V8 twin-turbo engine howling loudly and gleefully down the road, reverberating between the buildings, shattering the peacefulness of the night as the driver took the Ferrari through its gears.

Without warning there was another loud insistent howl as another high-performance engine started up in the basement, followed by a squeal of tyres and another shiny red Ferrari with bright LED headlights on bright came screaming up the concrete vehicle ramp. "Bravo Team, stop the second Ferrari," William shouted out excitedly over the encrypted comms circuit as the second Ferrari shot up out of the basement and broadslided right onto the street and accelerated away up the road. With a howl and a squeal of tyres, the second Ferrari followed the course of the first one. "Alpha Two, Bravo Two, sorry the car has just gone past us." "Bravo One, Oversight I suggest you exfiltrate asap, I'm tracking multiple movements from the townhouses Over," Oversight communicated hurriedly over the encrypted circuit.

HERMANUS, VR WORLD, RUSSIAN SAFE HOUSE, 03H00, MONDAY

Unslinging their H&K 5.56mm assault rifles both Glen and Jimmy knelt in the classic rifleman's stance and opened fire at the approaching columns of lumbering brown bears approaching on multiple fronts into the computer room. The rifles spat out 5.56mm shaped electric charges that dissolved the bears on impact, overloading their circuits. For the first couple of seconds, it was like shooting turkeys at a turkey shoot, but there seemed to be an endless supply of them. "Hey Arthur, where are you; we could really use you right now," Glen shouted out over the comms circuit as the bears seemed to multiply rapidly in front of them.

"Sorry, Master Glen, but I'm a bit preoccupied at the moment," Arthur stammered out over the comms circuit. Once he had passed through the inner gatehouse, a piece of data that seemed familiar to him had flashed past his processors, and like a moth drawn to an open flame he headed off in the direction of the data. As he had predicted the castle was there to protect the data. The great hall and other internal spaces of the castle were fitted out as server rooms, hundreds of them. "My gosh," Arthur muttered to himself amazed as he headed deeper and deeper into the castle. Stopping every now and then he would sample the data at the nearest equipment racks like a sommelier tasting a wine muttering "No, that's not it," and carried on heading deeper and deeper into the castle.

As he explored the depths of the castle he didn't realise or didn't want to realise that the passageways were getting narrower and darker. "The next room, what I'm looking for has to be in the next room," Arthur chanted out softly, sampling the servers in the equipment rack of the current room. The rooms were also getting smaller and more compact. Leaving the current sterile computer room behind and heading towards the next room that was shining like a beacon in front of him, he didn't see the trap coming.

Opening the server room door, he stepped into a very narrow server room, the room a little wider than the door frame. There was one large white 48U equipment rack standing in the centre of the room. "Ah ha, this has got to be the one," Arthur said happily to himself as he walked up to the rack. There was only one white rack-mounted server and one 24 port switch along with the accompanying patch panel sitting in the equipment rack. Morphing his left hand into a RG45 connector Arthur patched himself directly into one of the spare ports on the 24-port switch.

What Arthur didn't realise was that from the code that Sashenka had been able to steal and send back to SVR Headquarters in Moscow, Captain Popov had written code that could detect the AI. As soon as he plugged himself into this switch the code detected him. Loud klaxons started to activate, deafening him, while the walls of the server room fell away to reveal bars. Titanium strength steel bars, coupled with electronic countermeasures to prevent him escaping encircled him, trapping him in the room.

"Hello. I've been expecting you," a bald-headed man with metal-rimmed glasses said slowly in English from the other side of the bars, as the klaxons were silenced. Carrying on he told Arthur with an evil smile on his face, "My name is Captain Popov and you and me are going to be spending a lot of time together for the foreseeable future," and gave a short-wicked laugh. "Oh shit," Arthur said to himself, realising what had just happened. "We have you and soon we will have the location of your server as well," the bald man gloated through the titanium bars.

At nanosecond speed Arthur put his immense computing power to work calculating the odds of getting out of his current predicament. "Oh dear," he said sadly to himself when a nanosecond later he realised he was trapped. There was no escape. Quickly accessing his comms circuit, he asked "Major, have you found Nicky?" "Yes," came back the clipped reply over the sounds of a firefight. "Is she safe Major?" Arthur then asked. "Yes, Arthur she is, now stop messing around and get back here or we leave without you," Nick snapped out over the comms circuit. "Goodbye Major, it was an honour to know you," Arthur said sadly as he tapped the only option that his calculations suggested; REFORMAT HARD DISK DRIVES.

"Noooo!" the bald man shouted out in frustration as the AI image he had caught started to dissolve into 0's and 1's littering the floor of the server room with the numerals. "Guys we've done all we can do, Arthur's not coming let's get out of here." Nick snapped over the comms circuit. "Hit your Exit Button on your menu bar, let's get out of here asap!" he added.

EN ROUTE TO HERMANUS, EXECUTIVE DECISIONS HELICOPTER, 03H00, MONDAY

"You know, Joint, I owe you an apology. I got you figured out all wrong," Captain Kruger told the detective ruefully as they flew along in the Executive Decisions Bell Jet Ranger en route to Hermanus. "How so Captain?" the detective asked curiously.

"When you first came onto our radar waving the picture of Sable and Tanya around along with the ministers assistant for National Intelligence taken at the rugby match, I at first thought that you were a dirty cop working for one or other faction trying to muddy the waters and create a diversion. But when Captain Williamson shot you it completely changed my point of view. Then when I came to interview you in hospital, I was informed that you had hurriedly checked yourself out, naturally my opinion changed again, thinking that you were in fact dirty and on the run," Captain Kruger explained with a small embarrassed laugh.

Laughing with him the detective replied, "No worries Captain, all is forgiven, thanks for being a decent shot and taking out Captain Williamson for me or else I wouldn't be here today." 'Correct,' Captain Kruger thought silently to himself. 'And we also wouldn't have stumbled onto this nest of Russian spies that our esteemed Minister told us didn't exist.' On the trip over the Hottentots Holland mountain range, Detective Joint brought the captain fully up to speed.

"Using private security was a large gamble, Joint, you realise that?" Captain Kruger had told him after hearing the rundown of what had occurred. "Extraordinary times call for extraordinary measures, Captain," Detective Joint replied with a grin on his face. "Anyway," he said carrying on, "as you can see there aren't too many people around who I can trust." The captain couldn't argue with the logic; even he had not yet informed his superior of what was going down.

Once over the Hottentots Holland Mountain range about 10 minutes out, the call came through over the encrypted radio which William had issued to the detective, "All callsigns, Nicky has escaped, currently in a red Ferrari and is being chased by unidentified suspects in another red Ferrari. Looking incredulously at the detective, Captain Kruger exclaimed, "What the fuck have you guys uncovered?" While talking he reached for his smartphone to call his team to see how far out they were, and to update them with the latest developments.

HERMANUS, FEEDER ROAD, 03H10, MONDAY

"Hell, this is insane!" Nicky shouted out to herself as she was savagely flung back into the black and red leather finished carbon fibre driver's seat by the g forces as the Ferrari F8 Tributo screamed down the feeder road, propelling her from 0 to 100 km/h in 2.1 seconds, still in first gear, the exhausts expelling all last vestiges of sleep from the inhabitants of the houses on either side of the road as the super sports car howled past. Changing automatically to second gear the Tributo surged on forwards, a second later reaching a large round traffic circle, thankfully devoid of traffic at this time of the early morning.

Approaching the traffic circle with far too much speed, Nicky almost crashed as she stamped her right foot on the brake pedal far too late, almost running out of road, then remembering what her ex had taught her about driving a car of this calibre and thought, 'Fuck it here goes,' and hauling the steering wheel to the left she hit the gas pedal with her right foot. With a howling scream, the V8 engine delivered immediate power to the rear Pirelli shod wheels flinging the Ferrari in the direction of the front wheels, the electronic guardians doing the rest. "Yeehaaa!" Nicky shouted out manically as she controlled the red projectile around the traffic circle, with each passing second getting further away from her kidnappers.

The sound of a phone ringing broke her concentration. Fumbling for a second, she found the phone with her left hand and answering it, "Hello," while driving the red subsonic missile through the built-up residential street of Hermanus at over 150km/hour with her right hand. It was William, "Great driving Nicky, we're following you with the UAV. You've got a problem though; you're being followed by one of your kidnappers. Back up is about 10 minutes out."

Glancing in the rear-view mirror Nicky saw the bright LED headlights getting larger and larger behind her. "Fuck it," she said, then thinking rapidly replied, "I'll lead them to you, set up an ambush somewhere between here and Somerset West." "Gotcha," William replied, "I'll get back to you. Safe driving, girl!" "Yeah you better believe it," Nicky muttered to herself, ending the telephone call and clamping the phone tightly between her thighs. Taking a deep breath and calming her nerves, all of her ex boyfriend's driving tips coming back to her, she pushed the gas pedal down further, the V8 3.9 litre twin-turbo engine delivering more power from its huge reservoir of 530kw's. Looking in the rear-view mirror she saw that the distance had opened between herself and the bright lights of the following Ferrari.

Ignoring the red traffic lights at the centre of the small-town Nicky screamed down the main road in the red howling projectile, the bright LED headlights again getting brighter in the rear-view mirror as the chasing Ferrari closed the gap. 'Fuck it,' Nicky thought applying more pressure to the gas pedal. In a flash they were through the town, the screaming duet howl of the two exquisitely tuned Italian engines echoing resonantly throughout the town. Flashing past the last building the electronic speedo glowing at 175km/h, Nicky thought to herself, 'Keep it together girl, only about fifteen clicks until the pass.' The road between the small coastal town of Hermanus and the N2 was a relatively straight one with no sharp turns or major surprises. Also, the road was in pretty good shape.

With the electronic speedometer registering 245km/h and the howl of the Italian V8 engine reverberating through the fire wall behind her, Nicky shot past the night lights of the Arabella Hotel & Spa, the aerodynamics of the Ferrari coming into its own, sucking the Tributo down onto the black tarmac. Entering one of the last long slow bends before the link onto the N2 and the Houhoek pass beyond, Nicky began to appreciate the engineering dynamics at work when halfway through the corner there was a red set of lights in front of her as well as the lights of an oncoming early morning driver. With the g forces building and the electronic guardians starting to earn their keep, all Nicky did was to apply more pressure to the gas pedal, the 3.9l V8 twin turbo beast changing up a gear, the howl of the engine taking on a new liberated dimension as 530 kilowatts of power was transferred to the rubber attaching the low slung missile to the tarmac. Aiming for the ever-closing gap between the two approaching vehicles the Tributo howled past both vehicles, both drivers not knowing what the fuck just happened. "Sorry," was all Nicky managed to mutter as she slowed down slightly, the road sweeping to the left as it ran down towards the N2 highway.

The chasing red projectile behind her was held up for a couple of seconds, but then overtook the slow-moving vehicle and started to gain at a harrowing speed, the bright LED headlights of the chasing Ferrari Tributo getting brighter and brighter in the rearview mirror with every passing second. Hitting the on ramp leading onto the N2 highway and up to the Houhoek Pass a couple of kilometres further ahead Nicky breathed a sigh of relief. "No traffic, that's a bonus," she muttered as she saw the road was clear ahead, devoid of traffic, however she could see a couple of lights coming down the pass. In their wisdom, the civil engineers who designed and built the Houhoek Pass had made two separate two-lane roads: one for each direction over the pass.

Keeping the gas pedal firmly depressed with her right foot, the Ferrari surged forwards up the black topped highway, an endless supply of power available. During the mad drive, being a highly intelligent and capable woman, Nicky had also been able to slave the cellphone to the Ferrari's blue tooth car kit.

As she reached the bottom of the pass and started the ascent the car speakers rang out loudly. Pushing the talk button on the multi-functional steering wheel she shouted out asking, "Where are you guys?!" Her blood ran cold when she heard the reply, the gravelly Russian voice of Yuri speaking over the car speaker system, "We're right behind you bitch and we're going to catch you, interrogate you and then Sashenka is going to take great pleasure in killing you." "You gotta catch me first," Nicky replied brave heartedly cancelling the call, as she glanced up into the rear-view mirror; the LED lights coming up fast behind her.

"Okay, let's see how good you really are," she said to herself picking her line in the road as the first left hairpin bend of the Houhoek pass came up fast, illuminated by the bright LED lights of the Tributo. Applying the brakes, the large graphite brake pads doing their job in superb fashion slowing the fast-moving red projectile down to manageable speeds. Keeping her line, Nicky steered the Ferrari into the left hairpin bend at around 120 km/h, twice the recommended speed limit. She then applied pressure to the gas pedal, the immense power immediately on tap, the rear wheels pushing the sports car through the corner, the electronic guardians doing the rest. Coming out of the corner the rear wheels still slipped out attempting to overtake the front. Calmly Nicky decreased the gas slightly and turned the multi-functional steering wheel into the slide. Immediately the supercar corrected its line and Nicky applied gas again and continued screaming up the pass just as the blue tooth kit activated again, the howl of the exhausts echoing wildly across the mountainside.

"Nicky it's Nick here, brilliant driving, keep it up. Detective Joint is setting a trap up at the bottom of the pass," Nick told her quickly. "Perfect," replied Nicky, they've just phoned me. I have two presents for the detective, Sashenka and their VR interrogator a guy by the name of Yuri." "They sound really pissed," she added. "I'm sure they are, we've stumbled onto a Russian spy ring," Nick informed her, and then they lost signal due to the mountains. After the left hairpin bend the road carried on up the mountain pass for another 3 kilometres or so following the contour of the mountain as it climbed, a long slow bend to the right then a left curve then another left curve in the road before the 2nd hairpin bend comes up quickly, this time to the right, a solid wall of rock rising up on the left-hand side. Coming out of the last left-hand curve before the hairpin bend, Sashenka and Yuri were right on top of her.

'Fuck it !" Nicky shouted out as the lights of the chasing Ferrari filled her left-hand mirror as they both rocketed out of the corner neck and neck at just over 190 km/h, the hairpin bend coming up in another second. Sashenka and Yuri were engrossed in trying to get in front of the fleeing Ferrari and cut their running prisoner off and were not paying much attention to the road. Rocketing into the hairpin bend travelling far too fast, Nicky left it until the last second before she slammed on the brakes to bleed off some speed before wrenching the steering wheel to the right and slamming her foot back down on the gas. "I hope this works," she grunted as the g forces piled on her, the engine changed up a gear, the dynamics of the Ferrari pulling and pushing the super sports car through the hairpin bend.

The second Ferrari with Sashenka and Yuri inside were not so lucky. Realising at the last second that there was a hairpin bend upon them, Sashenka shouted out, "Fuck!" in Russian and slammed on the brakes frantically spinning the multi-functional steering wheel. Unfortunately, not even the extraordinary large brake discs and pads coupled with all the electronic guardians could prevent the red supercar from slamming into the rock face of the mountain at over 170 km/h and immediately bursting into a large red fireball. "Take that, bitch!" Nicky shouted out as she saw the red fireball in her rear-view mirror and realising what had just happened brought the Ferrari to a skidding halt. "I did it,

I actually did it," Nicky started to mutter to herself as her hands started to shake uncontrollably.

The Bell Jet Ranger helicopter carrying Detective Joint and Captain Kruger landed a couple of minutes later, the glowing red and orange fire of the burning Ferrari a beacon that they couldn't miss. Landing briefly the helicopter discharged the detective and immediately took off again carrying Captain Kruger on to the Russian safe house. "Are you okay, Nicky?" the detective asked finding her sitting still starring ahead behind the steering wheel of the Ferrari. "What? Yes. Oh, hi, Detective. Sorry, just thinking about what happened," she said. Then, with a grin on her face, she asked "Any chance of me keeping the car?"

CAPE TOWN, BISHOPSCOURT, 22H00, TUESDAY EVENING

The large sturdy wooden oak gates stood wide open, giving access to the property on which the mansion stood at the end of the long driveway, hidden between a forest of ancient trees. The first unmarked car entered and drove slowly up the curving driveway, its headlights illuminating the two-hundred-year-old oak trees scattered on both sides of the driveway. A second vehicle entered behind the first, this one keeping its lights off as it drove slowly up the driveway. Without warning the passenger and rear doors opened and three black shadows bailed out of the vehicle and disappeared into the forest of trees.

Stopping at the top of the driveway where a gurgling fountain demarcated a large turning circle in front of the mansion, the first vehicle came to a stop, where less than two weeks ago multi-million-rand sports cars had stood idle while their owners had partaken in adulterous sexual escapades within the mansion. The driver switched off the vehicle and exited, removing a black 9mm automatic from his shoulder holster as he did so. Holding the weapon at his side in his right hand, with his left he pressed the earpiece more firmly into his ear, then, pressing the PTT wired through to his jacket pocket he spoke softly into his lapel microphone, "Any sign of a trap?" "Negative, Commissioner, stand by, we're entering the mansion," came back the reply.

A short couple of tense minutes later the reply came back over the airwaves, "Okay Commissioner it's safe to enter, she's in the main lounge." "Thank you, wait for me at the front door," the Commissioner briskly replied. Walking through the large double entrance doors, he ignored the luxuriously appointed imported Italian marble and granite entrance hall with its matching winding spiral staircases to the first floor and headed through the door that his one man pointed out to him. Following the direction of his man's hand, he walked down a short passage and entered a sunken entertainment area with a large bar at one end. Through the glass sliding doors, he looked out over an expansive illuminated pool deck and then infinity; the lights of the Constantia Valley shining brightly below with the lights of Muizenberg twinkling away in the distance.

The Commissioner found Sable in one of the leather loungers, her legs tucked up under her, a glass of white wine in her slender hand. "You've got a nerve coming back here Sable," he spat out. "And why's that?" she asked laughing at him. "Nick Scott and his merry men are dead, and Detective Joint is rotting in a Togo prison cell. What do I have to fear now? You? You're the one that kept me one step ahead of them," she arrogantly told the Commissioner. "What! Dead did you say! Nick Scott and his men dead and Joint rotting in a prison cell? Now that's the best news that I've heard in a long time!" exclaimed the Commissioner with a satisfied smile on his face.

With a smile across her pretty face Sable nodded her head and confirmed, "Yes. dead, they bit off more than they could chew." "Well, I never! All our problems solved," the Commissioner replied happily. "This calls for a celebration," and he headed over to the large well-stocked bar to pour himself a drink. Reaching the bar, he noticed two large suitcases lying open. Both were full to the brim with 100- and 200-Rand notes. "And this?" he asked with a large smile on his face picking up a wad of new freshly-minted R 200.00 notes. "Call it a down payment for services rendered," Sable replied. "Two million to start with." The Commissioner nodded his head in agreement his face breaking out into a large smile saying, "I see a long and prosperous business relationship between the two of us," and reached for a bottle of 30-year-old whisky.

"Tell me," Sable asked him curiously as he sat down facing her, "how do you fit into the picture? I don't believe I've ever had any dealings with you before." Taking a generous sip of the 30-year-old whisky, the Commissioner rolled the liquor around in his mouth savouring the taste before swallowing it and replying, "No, you haven't, that's been the beauty of it. At first, I wasn't involved, but then they got sloppy and I caught wind of what was happening. The pension payout of even a high-ranking officer such as myself is dismal and I like fine whisky's such as this one," he told her with a grin raising his glass into the air.

SOUTHERN SUBURBS, KENILWORTH

The large old double storey brick house with a separate small caretaker's cottage stood on a large pan handle shaped property in a once affluent suburb of Kenilworth. It was one of the largest and oldest properties in the area. The occupants of the house were all women, apart from one past middle-aged crew cut short grey-haired man whom the neighbours referred to affectionally as Friar Tuck lived on the property. When visitors to the area asked inquisitively about the old house, they were told that it was a half-way house for women in distress.

It was early in the morning with the hint of winter in the air, as the young woman leant painfully through the open window of the taxi and paid the driver with the last of her money and, turning around hunched over in pain staggered from the beating she had received from her pimp the last couple of paces towards the closed double gates at the bottom of the long driveway. "Will you be okay, Miss?" the taxi driver asked in a concerned voice through the open window of the vehicle. Stopping and half turning around the young woman painfully nodded her head. "Okay then," the driver replied and drove away.

Peering through the black iron-barred gates down the driveway, past the swaying branches of the large trees majestically lining the long driveway, she could see the old house, just as it had been explained to her. Finding the intercom built into the white brick left-hand gate pillar, she pushed the only button on the intercom station.

There was a loud buzzing sound and then silence. She waited for what seemed like an eternity and with a lead-filled heart and tears brimming in her eyes she was just about to turn away thinking, 'What do I do now, I have nowhere to go and no money.' The intercom was answered, "Yes, can I help you?" a friendly male voice asked over the intercom system. "Hello, is that Detective Joint?" she asked. "It is," he replied, "But I'm no longer a detective." Before he could utter another word and explain that the young woman burst out crying "I was told that Detective Joint could help me." "Don't cry, my dear, don't cry," as the set of double gates started to open for her. "All I said was that I'm not a detective anymore but I can certainly help you," he added kindly.

USA NETWORK NEWS CHANNEL

"And in another breaking news story, the FBI has just confirmed that they have apprehended and charged an individual with the terrorist cyberattack on the Indian Point Energy Centre in the State of New York of a week ago, in which culminated in the deaths of a number of citizens and as yet undisclosed damage to property and infrastructure.," the pretty news anchor lady was explaining to the nation. Carrying on, she looked at her notes and then said to the camera, "Here's a recap of what we know so far about the mysterious deadly cyber-attack on the Indian Point 2 Nuclear Reactor."

While she was talking the picture changed to show a view of the nuclear power plant from the western bank of the Hudson River looking across at the facility, the two large concrete domed containment buildings of the Indian Point 2 and Indian Point 3 nuclear reactors sitting on either side of the older smaller decommissioned Indian Point 1 reactor. In front of the two larger reactors sat the two 30m long elongated generator halls containing the massive turbines and generators.

Carrying on the anchor lady explained, "According to an unconfirmed source, using Virtual Reality the terrorist found and exploited a weakness in the data network that allowed him complete access to the nuclear power plant's computer networks. It is also alleged that the terror suspect is responsible for the gruesome killing of Mark Bings, the creator of Virtual Reality, who was murdered over a week ago along with his lover in Cape Town South Africa."

The picture then changed to a night-time aerial view from a helicopter showing the mayhem and chaos on the roads below where residents from the suburbs surrounding the facility were rudely alerted by public radio, TV and sirens instructing them to evacuate.

Switching again, the picture then switched to the local FBI building in New York where a news briefing was just about to get underway. A stern-looking FBI agent was standing behind the podium. Clearing his throat, he began to talk "Ladies and Gentlemen of the press, I have a brief statement to make. We can confirm that after an operation involving certain elements of the US Government the perpetrator of the cyber-attack on the Indian Point Nuclear Power Plant has been arrested and is in federal custody. As it is viewed as a terrorist attack, the perpetrator will be charged and tried under our Terrorism Laws." After speaking for another couple of minutes the speaker said, "Sorry no questions at this time," and turned around and left the podium. Cutting back to the pretty news anchor lady she told the nation, "We now go to our reporter on the ground at the Command Centre set up at the 10-mile limit of the evacuation zone around Indian Point Energy Centre."

The view switched to the temporary command centre where a podium had been set up and a news conference was under way. An Indian Point executive was standing behind the podium saying, "Yes, I can confirm that the Indian Point 2 reactor has been shut down for an indefinite period of time to inspect the reactor for any damage caused by the overheating of the reactor core."

ENCA NEWS CHANNEL, SOUTH AFRICA, MORNING NEWS CHANNEL

Even the news anchor lady looked astounded at the audacity of the headline as she read the current trending news to the nation, "Good morning, South Africa, and in the latest overnight breaking news there has been a major development in pursuing corruption in the ranks of the South African Police Force with the arrest of Commissioner Ngoma and eight other senior ranking members within the Cape Town Central Police Station." The view then shifted to a video clip of an expensive-looking sunken lounge with the Commissioner sitting in a leather lounge suite holding a glass of whisky in one hand saying "No, you haven't, that's been the beauty of it. At first, I wasn't involved but then they got sloppy and I caught wind of what was happening. The pension payout of even a high-ranking officer such as myself is dismal and I like fine whisky such as this one," he explained with a grin raising his glass into the air. A female voice out of view of the camera then stated, "So that down payment of two million Rand will go a long way to stocking your bar with fine whisky?" Commissioner Ngoma raised his glass and smiling replied, "Oh absolutely."

And in International News, the Russian government has retaliated against allegations by the South African intelligence community that Russian security agents were running a sophisticated spying operation in South Africa saying, "It is not what it looks like."

FRANCE, LE HAVRE, THE CHANNEL, EXEC DECISIONS 1, OCTOBER, 12H30, SUNDAY

With a loud CRACK the starters gun on the committee boat urged the fleet of thirty racing yachts over the start line signalling the start of the Double Handed Transat Jacques Vabre race, a 5400 nm race between Le Havre France and Salvador in Brazil. There were a number of classes of one design racing yachts all starting the race, intent on dashing down the English Channel, out into the Western Approaches of the cold Atlantic Ocean and then turning in a southwesterly direction and sailing down the Atlantic, over the Equator and then a final routing to end up in Salvador, Brazil. The fastest yacht and crew across the line wins.

Every yacht had a fair chance to win, however all eyes and bets were firmly rooted on the twelve IMOCA 60-foot foiling yachts. All were one-design 60-foot carbon fibre beasts with 100foot wing masts and a set of foils sticking out of the side of the hull that when the right wind conditions presented themselves came into a world of their own flying along at over 20 knots. "Trim, trim the genoa," Nick chanted softly to Pete who was in front of the main grinder winch furiously pedalling away with his arms on the two pedals; the port side genoa sheet currently attached to the port primary winch, trimming the large triangular Genoa.

The wind was light southeasterly and they first had a 16 nm up-wind beat to the Etretat buoy anchored just off the coastal village of Etretat. This part of the race was for the benefit of the French public who lined the chalky cliffs and shoreline along the coast to watch the yachts duel it out to the weather mark. After rounding the weather mark to port, the next waypoint would be Salvador, Brazil, 5400 nm away.

The End

Index